Huntress Moon
A Thriller Award Nominee for Best E-Book
A Suspense Magazine *Pick for Best Thriller of 2012*
An Amazon Top Ten Bestseller

"This interstate manhunt has plenty of thrills . . . keeps the drama taut and the pages flying."
—*Kirkus Reviews*

"The intensity of her main characters is equally matched by the strength of the multi-layered plot . . . The next installment cannot release soon enough for me."
—*Suspense Magazine*

The Price
"Some of the most original and freshly unnerving work in the genre."
—*The New York Times Book Review*

"A heartbreakingly eerie page turner."
—*Library Journal*

"*The Price* is a gripping read full of questions about good, evil, and human nature . . . the devastating conclusion leaves the reader with an uncomfortable question to consider: 'If everyone has a price, what's yours?'"
—*Rue Morgue* magazine

The Unseen
"A creepy haunted house, reports of a 40-year-old poltergeist investigation, and a young researcher trying to rebuild her life take the "publish or perish" initiative for college professors to a terrifying new level in this spine-tingling story that has every indication of becoming a horror classic. Based on the famous Rhine ESP experiments at the Duke University parapsychology department that collapsed in the 1960s, this is a chillingly dark look into the unknown."
—*Romantic Times Book Reviews*

"Sokoloff keeps her story enticingly ambiguous, never clarifying until the climax whether the unfolding weirdness might be the result of the investigators' psychic sensitivities or the mischievous handiwork of a human villain."
—*Publisher's Weekly*

The Space Between

"Filled with vivid images, mystery, and a strong sense of danger . . . Sokoloff interlaces psychological elements, quantum physics, and the idea of multiple dimensions and parallel universes into her story; this definitely adds something different and original from other teen novels on the market today."
—*Seattle Post Intelligencer*

"Alexandra Sokoloff has created an intricate tapestry, a dark Young Adult novel with threads of horror and science fiction that make it a true original. Loaded with graphic, vivid images that place the reader in the midst of the mystery and danger, *The Space Between* takes psychological elements, quantum physics and multiple dimensions with parallel universes and creates a storyline that has no equal. A must-read."
—*Suspense Magazine*

blood moon

Books By Alexandra Sokoloff

The Huntress/FBI Thrillers
Huntress Moon: Book I
Blood Moon: Book II
Cold Moon: Book III

The Haunted Thrillers
The Harrowing
The Price
The Unseen
Book of Shadows
The Space Between

Paranormal
D-Girl on Doomsday (from *Apocalypse: Year Zero*)
The Shifters (from *The Keepers* trilogy)
Keeper of the Shadows (from *The Keepers: L.A.*)

Nonfiction
Screenwriting Tricks for Authors
Writing Love: Screenwriting Tricks for Authors II

Short Fiction
The Edge of Seventeen (in *Rage Against the Night*)
In Atlantis (in *Love is Murder*)

blood moon

Book II of the Huntress/FBI Thriller Series

by
alexandra sokoloff

. . . . .

THOMAS & MERCER

Published by Thomas & Mercer, Seattle

www.apub.com

Amazon, the Amazon logo, and Thomas & Mercer are trademarks of Amazon.com, Inc., or its affiliates.

ISBN-13: 9781477822050
ISBN-10: 1477822054

Cover design by Brandi Doane
Library of Congress Control Number: 2014951999

Printed in the United States of America

Blood Moon

Twenty-five years have passed since a savage killer terrorized California, massacring three ordinary families before disappearing without a trace.

The haunted child who was the only surviving victim of his rampage is now wanted by the FBI for brutal crimes of her own, and Special Agent Matthew Roarke is on an interstate manhunt for her, despite his conflicted sympathies for her history and motives.

But when his search for her unearths evidence of new family slayings, the dangerous woman Roarke seeks—and wants—may be his only hope of preventing another bloodbath.

Chapter 1

The dark concrete corridor stretched out before him, smelling of blood and semen and terror.

Roarke had been here before, these stinking hellholes, cellblock rooms barely big enough for a mattress and bed stand. Twenty-five girls to a block, locked in the rooms and drugged to the gills, servicing twenty-five to forty men a day, twelve hours a day, seven days a week. Not just ordinary johns tonight: it was a new shipment, private party for the traffickers themselves.

He could hear the shallow breathing of the agents surrounding him, feel the warmth of bodies: four men before him, three in back, encased in camouflage body armor and hoisting riot shields, brandishing an entire armory. Somewhere down the hall there was sobbing, a young girl's cries. "*Mátame. Por favor, mátame.*"

Kill me. Please kill me.

The number one man gestured the signal and the team shot forward in formation, then peeled off in a fluid dance, odd men to the right, even men to the left, kicking through doors, shouting: "FBI, drop your weapon! Face down on the floor!" Elsewhere in the corridor, shots blasting, more screaming, heavy thuds, and the jangle of cuffs as men were wrestled to the floor.

Roarke covered the agent ahead of him until the tiny room was secure, bad guy kissing concrete. Roarke looked once at the terrified teenage girl cowering naked on the filthy mattress, and said "*Es terminado.*" *It's over.* Then he moved out the door, leading with his Glock, down the corridor, past doorways open to similar scenes of hell.

He kicked open the next closed door and burst in—

A man with his pants half off turned, holding an enormous, ugly AK 47. Roarke shot twice, straight into his center mass. The man's chest opened, blooming red, and his body went down, jerking as if tasered.

Roarke stood, his heart booming crazily in his chest.

And then, though the trafficker was as dead as a person could get, Roarke followed procedure and turned the corpse over to cuff him.

As he straightened he saw the girl, tiny and frozen, huddled on the floor against the mattress, her back pressed into the wall, her eyes wide and glazed with fear. This one was twelve or thirteen years old at most, dressed in nothing but a cheap, stained camisole. Roarke felt a wave of primal anger he was able to suppress only by telling himself he must not frighten this child any further.

"*Estás seguro,*" he told her in the softest voice he could muster through the adrenaline raging through his bloodstream. *You are safe.* Although he wondered if any of the girls who walked out of this place, this night, would ever feel safe again.

There was movement behind him and he twisted around . . . to see Special Agent Damien Epps in the doorway. Tall, dark, lithe, and righteously pissed.

"All clear," Epps reported. His whole body was tense. "Thirteen of the fucks in custody, three—"

He paused as he glanced down at the dead man at Roarke's feet. "Four dead." And his face and body were suddenly tense in a different way. "Nice shooting," he added.

Roarke felt the jab. He had twelve years of Bureau service and before two weeks ago, he had never killed in the line of duty. The man at his feet was his third since then.

He gave Epps a warning look, nodding at the girl huddled against the wall. He wanted to help her up, give her the shirt under his vest, but he figured she wouldn't be wanting any man near her for a very, very long time. "Social Services?" he asked Epps quietly. They had social workers waiting in vans outside to take the rescued girls to hospitals and on to a shelter that specialized in support for trafficking victims.

"On their way in," Epps said.

Roarke spoke directly to the girl. "*Mujeres vienen. Usted se va a la casa.*" *Women are coming. You are going home.*

The girl didn't move, didn't acknowledge him. He stood for a moment, helpless, knowing he was not the one to help her. He moved to follow Epps out. And then he stopped, his eyes coming to rest on the bed stand.

Just above the gouged surface of the table there was a small drawing on the wall. Roarke stepped closer . . . to look down at a figure scratched in the concrete, a crude skeleton wearing a flowery crown. Scraps of food and torn bits of lace were laid carefully in front of it.

Epps was staring, too, stopped in the doorway. "What is it?"

"An altar," Roarke said. "To *Santa Muerte.*" Lady Death, Holy Death, protector of the lost.

He looked at the girl, still and silent on the floor, with her old and wary eyes, and wondered if somehow her prayer had been answered and the saint had intervened.

Social workers led the girls out of the former storage facility as dawn streaked the sky with orange over the desert. A good bust: thirteen traffickers arrested, twenty-five victims freed, hopefully before irreparable damage had been done.

They called these prisons residential brothels. Many of them were race-specific; this one was an LRB, Latino Residential Brothel. The location was a former storage facility, horrifically appropriate, since the girls were no more than objects to the men who stole and then sold them. Girls nineteen, sixteen, fourteen, thirteen, sometimes even younger, were kidnapped or tricked into leaving the poverty of their native towns and come to the U.S. expecting legitimate work. It was a $33 billion a year industry, a rising tide of evil that no agency under the sun had the resources to control, rivaling drugs and arms trafficking for the most profitable enterprise in the world, because after all, you could only sell a drug or a gun once, but you could sell a girl to the walking vermin known as johns twenty-five times a night.

As Roarke walked the empty corridors one last time, he felt more than emptiness surround him. It was more than the reeking, rancid smell. It felt like a darkness behind the doors, a concentration of malignance so outrageous it felt like a live thing.

How anything resembling a human being could do that to another human being, let alone a child . . .

He had to get out.

The sun was scorching the desert, searing his eyes, as he stepped out of the facility to see agents loading the last perps and victims into vehicles. The bust would be processed and prepared for prosecution by the Los Angeles Bureau. It was their jurisdiction, not San Francisco's. But since Roarke and Epps had made the initial bust leading into the trafficking ring, at a deserted concrete plant in the Mojave Desert, the two agents had come along for the takedown. Epps was coordinating with the Los Angeles Assistant SAC, meaning Roarke could leave now. It was out of his hands. He ran his hands through his thick, black hair, and rolled his neck to ease muscles still knotted with adrenaline. He felt relief, and emptiness.

He'd checked every inch of the facility, but his other quarry, the mass killer Cara Lindstrom, was nowhere on the premises. And yet he felt her presence.

Santa Muerte . . .

It had been Cara who'd led them to this trafficking ring.

She'd escaped from his custody at the concrete plant two weeks ago, and perhaps in some hidden part of his mind he had feared some trafficker had snatched her up. Her beauty would fetch any price in any number of countries. She would have killed others or herself before she'd let herself be taken, but she had been so badly wounded that night she may not have had the strength.

Roarke dreamed of her almost every night, and he always awoke feeling the curves of her body molded to his, as if she had seared into his own flesh that night that he had lifted her and carried her, wounded, across the sand past the bodies of men she had slain.

Cara Lindstrom was in his dreams.

Otherwise, he had no idea where she was, or if she was alive or dead.

But she had killed thirteen men that he knew of, probably many, many more, including one of his own team. It was his job to arrest her, and he was very good at his job.

He would find her, and he would bring her in.

Chapter 2

After not much sleep on his delayed plane, Roarke walked out of the Civic Center BART station into a gorgeous day. Fall in San Francisco was his favorite season, often warmer than summer. Views of the Golden Gate and Alcatraz Island and Berkeley and Sausalito were crystal clear and the brisk wind off the Bay was a tantalizing promise, but Roarke's only feeling was unease.

He strode on the bustling downtown streets, weaving through harried commuters and panhandling homeless and the pervasive smell of marijuana smoke on Market Street, up through the plaza between the Beaux-Arts facades of the Asian Art Museum and the main library. And he pretended he wasn't expecting to see Cara Lindstrom at every intersection, standing across the street from him as she had done the day he'd first seen her, the day his hunt for her had begun. The day she had looked at him for one endless moment before his undercover agent exploded in blood on the street between them, mowed down by a commercial truck . . .

He was spared further memory of that vision for the moment as the concrete and glass monolith of the Federal Building loomed up in front of him. Inside the lobby of blue-veined marble, he clipped on his plastic ID to bypass security and took the elevator. On the fifteenth floor he walked down gleaming halls with white walls decorated with framed sepia-toned newspaper accounts of famous busts and images of the history of the Bureau, toward the conference room the team had taken over for their manhunt. Manhunt being an ironic word for the investigation into Cara Lindstrom. There were no words for what she was, for what she had done, the Huntress.

His team was already assembled, waiting for him: Antara Singh, a stunning Indian tech goddess and researcher; Epps, *GQ* handsome, towering and dark as midnight; and Ryan Jones, a blond-haired, blue-eyed, California-born-and-bred jock, a new agent whom Roarke would have to put into undercover now that Greer was gone. But that was for later.

Roarke's eyes went immediately to the case board behind them, a seven-foot long white board on a standing metal frame taped with clusters of photos, documents, Post-its—everything they knew about Cara Lindstrom. The police sketch that was their only image of her looked down on him: blond and fine-featured, eyes concealed behind big dark sunglasses.

He forced his gaze away and looked around at his waiting team. "So where are we?"

He saw a flicker of anger on Epps' face, and Roarke knew why. He'd been uncharacteristically late, which for him meant he stepped into the briefing at their meeting time of nine on the dot, to avoid being cornered by Epps. It was the same reason he'd taken a different flight back from L.A. Roarke didn't want to talk to Epps alone, and Epps knowing that made him even more determined to talk to Roarke, and they had been doing this dance for days.

It would come to a head any moment now, Roarke knew. But he was not about to talk about that night, two weeks ago, the night he had helped Cara Lindstrom kill ten people. Ten men, to be specific, meth dealers, and human traffickers. Ten who needed killing, absolutely no doubt. But even there, that phrase: "Men who needed killing." In the last month since Roarke had been hunting Cara Lindstrom, thoughts like that were coming into his head with alarming frequency.

He didn't need Epps grilling him about it when he had no idea what it meant, himself.

But for the moment, Epps simply began his report. "All our paperwork on the cement plant bust is in to the L.A. Bureau. They're continuing the investigation into the trafficking stemming from the plant. At the cement plant, seven arrested, ten dead. At the storage facility, thirteen arrested, four dead."

Busts that never would have happened if Cara had not led them out to the desert.

"And victims released?" Roarke asked.

Epps' eyes flicked to meet his briefly. "Nineteen at the cement plant, twenty-five last night."

The numbers vibrated in the air between them. Forty-four women and children, victims of sex trafficking.

Roarke avoided Epps' eyes. "So we can put our focus on Lindstrom now. The question is, where is she?"

Ryan Jones was the first to speak. "I wasn't there, but from what you've laid out, she could be dead, right? A woman shot by the kind of military grade weapon we're talking about?"

Agent Singh leaned forward with the grace of a dancer, an earthy and enigmatic presence. She spoke in a musical Anglo-Indian accent. "The L.A. Division has been searching the desert outlying the plant. There have been bodies recovered in the gravel pits on the grounds, in the outlying alluvial area. None of them were Lindstrom's."

Roarke had also checked all nearby hospitals, asking about women admitted with gunshot wounds that night. There had been none.

"She's not dead," Epps said flatly.

Roarke looked at him.

"*You* don't think she is," Epps said.

In fact, Roarke didn't. The only thing he had to go on was an insane belief that he would simply know in his blood if she had died.

"I have no clue," he said without inflection. "But our job is to find her, if she's out there alive."

Only now did he let himself step to the case board. It was divided into three. First, the past. It started on the left hand side of the board with black-and-white photos of unspeakable carnage, the massacre of four members of an All-American, upper-middle class family, stabbed to death in their desert home by a faceless killer the media had christened the Reaper. The slaughter was the third in a series of similar family slayings that took place over a year's time exactly twenty-five years ago. It was the criminal case that had inspired Roarke's early obsession with law enforcement: a serial killer who had never been caught, who had disappeared into the realms of legend after the third family had been slaughtered. The Reaper's killing spree had left only one surviving victim: five-year-old Cara Lindstrom.

That angelic, blond-haired child came out of that bloody night with her throat slashed and her world view shattered into pieces that had reassembled themselves into a woman unlike anyone Roarke had ever encountered before, and had resulted in the carnage depicted in crime scene photos on the right-hand side of the board. A trail of five known male victims killed in three states in a two-year period, and ending with the mass slaughter of the traffickers at the concrete plant two weeks ago. Photos of the victims were pinned to a map of the Western United States: California, Oregon, Utah.

The middle of the board was blank. After a teenage history of foster homes, group homes, and juvenile prison, Cara Lindstrom had disappeared off the map at the age of twenty-one. She'd been invisible for eight years. The team had not found any hint of her location, her name, or any activities whatsoever until the day Roarke had seen her on the sidewalk behind Agent Greer just before his bloody demise. What Cara had done to Greer besides speak to him, naming his crime, was still unclear. What was clear was that Greer had turned, as undercovers sometimes do. He had been using the trafficked women he was sworn to protect, sexually abusing them rather than helping them to safety. Roarke had no idea how Cara could have known this about Greer, and he doubted they would ever be able to prove that murder, if murder was even what anyone could call it. That was the problem with Cara Lindstrom. She was forcing Roarke to come up with new definitions for everything he'd ever believed in.

But call it murder or call it—whatever—he had seen Cara kill eight men in one night and he had very little doubt that in the weeks to come they would find many, many more bodies to fill up that space in the middle of the board between Cara's childhood and the bloodshed of two weeks ago.

Singh was speaking and Roarke turned back into the room to listen. "She is on the Wanted list. Bulletins are out to the agencies throughout the states, as well as in Nevada, Oregon, and Utah. We have received the usual assortment of useless tips and a few confessions. Not one has checked out so far. The San Luis Obispo sheriff's department is putting together a package to take to the District Attorney, to see if there is enough there to charge her."

"If we can find her and deliver her," Epps muttered.

It was almost always preferable to have local police bring a case rather than federal prosecutors, not just faster: the sentences in non-federal courts were often more harsh. But in this case it was more complicated, being that the trucker whose throat Cara had slashed had a record of sexual assault, and had come after her in the women's bathroom.

Singh glanced at Roarke as if she'd heard his thoughts. "And it will be a difficult case to make, obviously. Any defense attorney will be able to introduce a strong motive of self-defense."

"We've got her for kidnapping," Jones said.

"Also not an easy case to make, under the circumstances," Singh replied. "My understanding is that Sebastian will never press charges. He and his son are more likely to appear for the defense."

Mark Sebastian was a newly divorced father who, along with his five-year-old son, had befriended Cara while they were on vacation in Pismo Beach; she had used the pair of them as both hideout and camouflage after Roarke had picked up her trail. Cara had ended up killing the drug dealer boyfriend of Sebastian's ex-wife. The dealer had been selling pictures of Jason to a pedophile ring. Another murder on her scorecard; another death not many people would ever lose sleep over.

Epps was speaking and Roarke forced himself back into the present to listen.

"We need to get her, and let the prosecutors worry about how to charge her," Epps said tightly.

Singh glanced at him without comment and then continued. "One more thing. So far our bulletins are confined to law enforcement agencies. Obviously, we could begin a more public appeal—"

"No," Roarke said, before she could finish the sentence.

His team looked at him.

"We don't want the media anywhere near this. A female serial killer?"

He didn't have to explain it. Female serial killers were exceedingly rare. There was even an argument to be made that no such thing existed that fit the textbook definition of sexual homicide, murder specifically for sexual gratification. Cara Lindstrom was a killer, the most unusual one Roarke had ever encountered. She hunted and killed, brutally and specifically. But psychologically she was more of a vigilante, her victims hand-picked for their crimes against women and especially children: child molesters, sex traffickers, and in one case, a homegrown terrorist who had been plotting to bomb a Portland street fair.

He spoke into the silence. "We let word leak out about what she's doing, we won't be able to take a step without cameras down our throats. It's too volatile, and a logistical nightmare. I say we do this quickly and quietly, and hope to God the press *doesn't* get wind of it."

He could see Epps struggling with himself, but finally he nodded reluctantly. "Agreed."

Roarke breathed an inner sigh of relief, then took control. "So. Her last known whereabouts are the cement plant. We know that she steals cars for transportation. She has a master key for Hondas at the very least." He turned to Singh.

"I have been monitoring reported car thefts in Southern California," she said in her precise lilt. "There were none that checked out in the Blythe area on the night she disappeared."

Roarke nodded. "The most likely scenario is that she took off in a car or a truck she stole from the plant site. Given how she was wounded, I can't see her getting out of there any other way." Privately he'd wondered if she might even have taken one of the criminal ring hostage, forced him to drive her out, and disposed of him on the way. He could see it happening in a heartbeat.

Epps chimed in. "None of the arrestees are admitting to a vehicle being stolen that night, but why would they? They're not cooperating on anything else, and it was probably stolen to begin with." He glanced to Roarke. "She's probably already ditched that vehicle, though."

Roarke looked toward Singh. "Keep on the stolen cars reports. It paid off for us before. As to where she would go from there . . . Singh, I'd like your take."

Singh looked grave. "I believe that Cara has several practically perfect IDs. She has demonstrated that she knows how to set them up. Unfortunately the name she gave the Sebastians was not attached to any existing identity papers or financial accounts; it appears to have been a name she invented on the spot. This woman knows how not to be found. And she has been hiding not for mischief, but for survival. If she is alive, she may well have gone somewhere that she has set up as a safe haven long ago, quite possibly years."

"And we know she's got plenty of money to get lost with," Jones added. Cara had come into over a million dollars of insurance money from the deaths of her family. The money, plus substantial interest, was hers the day she turned twenty-one, and she promptly disappeared from all public and financial records.

Epps' face was stony. "I say Mexico. No one's keeping track of anything down there. Anyone can set up a new life. That night at the cement plant we were two hours from Mexicali, tops. Why wouldn't she just cross the border?"

Roarke glanced toward the police sketch of Cara mounted on the corkboard: the delicate features behind sunglasses, the light and luxuriant hair. He willed himself to look away. "A blonde—that blonde—in Mexico? Trying to stay hidden?" He shook his head. "She knows the U.S. The Western U.S. That's her comfort zone. She's not going to be down there dodging *federales* and *narcos*."

"Why not? That seems right up her alley," Epps said tensely. "Take a bunch of the fuckers out. If she's after bad guys—" He stopped, remembering himself. "If she *thinks* she's after bad guys," he qualified, too late, "that would be a good place to start."

"No doubt," Roarke said. "But I don't see it."

Epps stared at him hard, and Roarke knew that he was revealing himself. "You don't see it," his man said softly. "So what do you see?"

Roarke locked his eyes for a beat. "If it were me? I'd go east." He did not know if he meant it at all. "Get out of her known hunting grounds."

"She doesn't know what we think her hunting grounds are," Epps pointed out. But Roarke suspected she did. In the little contact he'd had with her, she seemed to read him well enough to figure some things out.

"I only said it's what I would do. If I knew what she would do, I'd say that." Roarke was aware his voice was far too taut for the circumstances.

"We've got less than two weeks to another full moon," Epps said, glancing at the board, at the moon chart where Cara's killings were chronicled. Most had taken place on nights when the moon was full. It was a not-uncommon characteristic of serial killers; the Reaper, the killer of Cara's family, had also killed during full moons.

"I'm not so sure we have as much to worry about now," Roarke said aloud. From almost the beginning of Roarke's hunt for Cara Lindstrom, he had been consulting with his old mentor Chuck Snyder, a legendary profiler from the FBI's Behavioral Analysis Unit, and they had discussed this point in depth. "Snyder was very clear that the violent decompensation Cara was experiencing last month was triggered by the twenty-five year anniversary of her family's deaths." Anniversaries of traumatic events were known triggers for unstable and violent people. "After the bloodshed of that night, he thinks it's unlikely she would be feeling the same kind of compulsion to kill again so soon."

"Got it out of her system?" Jones suggested.

Roarke paused, and qualified, "For now." Most serial killers had a rhythm of killing that included a long build-up of fantasizing about a kill before the actual kill, and then a "cooling-off" period after the frenzy of the kill. Not that Cara, or any woman, could easily or even usefully be compared to male patterns of sexual homicide. The motive for women to kill was completely different, and there was simply not enough data available to develop a useful profile.

"But we don't know," Epps said.

"No. We don't know."

Singh spoke up, with that serene calm that always made Roarke's blood pressure lower a few notches just listening to her, no matter how gruesome the subject matter. "I am monitoring VICAP for all killings of adult men by slashed or slit throat. I also have a nationwide bulletin out asking for reports of such crimes from local law enforcement."

"But there have been no more incidences in the country in the last two weeks?" Roarke asked, feeling himself tensing as he waited for the response.

"Nothing in which the perpetrator was not immediately arrested," Singh answered. She reached for a stack of files, the gold armbands she always wore glinting on her wrists. "I am watching for all new cases. I also have a list from VICAP of all killings of adult men by slashed or slit throat from 2001 on. All states. And a nationwide bulletin out asking for reports from local law enforcement, previous cases that may not have made it into the VICAP database."

"How many cases on that list?"

"Just under two thousand." The temperature of the room dropped.

Singh acknowledged the reaction with a nod as she brushed her thick fall of dark hair back from her shoulders. "Most will be eliminated. I will start with the western states and work my way through it."

"See you next century," Jones muttered.

"You can start by working with just the kills that correspond to the full moons," Roarke said.

"Yes, the moon is the first sign," Singh agreed. "And I will ask local officers I speak with about the turtleneck or high collar." Cara wore high collars to conceal the old scar on her neck. "I am also narrowing the field by victim profile, looking only at sex offenders or men who have had sex offenses alleged against them."

"We don't know that's the only killing she's done," Epps said, with a dangerous edge.

"No, that's right, there was also the mad bomber planning on killing hundreds of people on a single day," Roarke said, and as he stared across the room at Epps, tension crackled between the two men.

"It is a tendency," Singh said calmly, and Roarke had the sensation she'd just stepped in between him and Epps, as distinctly as if she'd done it physically. "Using a victim profile merely narrows the field for my initial search."

Roarke was on his feet, walking the room. He never could stay in a chair for long. He focused on the board, that empty middle section.

"So Singh will be looking to fill in anything she can find on these years."

And then he looked at the middle chart, the teen years, the bleak list of Cara's residences: the foster homes, the group homes, the juvenile prison in Southern California. At the top was the photo he'd found of her in one of those case files, a slim blond waif of thirteen with enormous and watching eyes, too intense to be called beautiful, too mesmerizing to look away from.

"There," Roarke said, and put his hand on the list pinned to the board below the photo. "These are the people who knew her. The only places she ever stayed long enough for anyone to know her were the places she was confined. These are real people from those years who had prolonged interaction with her. During that time she may have dropped clues to what she did after she disappeared. Places she talked about, people she knew whom she may have sought out."

It was a slim thread, but it was something.

There was another thread he didn't mention: the real possibility that her first kill had been when she was only fourteen years old, the year she was released from nearly three years in juvenile detention. A former counselor at the group home where she'd been arrested for assault had been found with his throat cut. Roarke had not put that fact into the case file. He hadn't let himself consider why.

"It's someplace to start," he continued aloud. "Interview the family members"—he stepped to the board and read the names—"Patrick and Erin McNally, the cousins she lived with briefly after the deaths of her family. They would have been too young to remember her at the time of the massacre, but possibly she visited her aunt over the years. Families talk, especially about black sheep. And there's the aunt's second husband, Trent, the one who left the family after five-year-old Cara came to live with them."

His eyes skimmed the rest of the board. "Then teachers, counselors, whoever I can track down."

"You're thinking of going down to So Cal, then," Epps said.

Roarke answered evenly, "It's the most concrete trail to her habits, her thinking." He turned to Singh. "And while I'm on the road: Singh, you'll be tracking down any crimes in the last ten to twelve years that can be connected to Lindstrom."

"Yes, chief."

Just as Epps called him "boss," Singh called him "chief." He could not break either one of them of the habit; he'd long ago stopped trying.

"Epps will continue coordinating with the San Luis Obispo sheriffs and local agencies on the Salt Lake City and Portland cold cases. And Jones . . ."

He looked to the remaining member of the team, who had been holding the fort on the investigation into Ogromni, a transnational criminal organization that the team had been focused on until Greer had met his fate with that truck.

"I'm counting on you to move us forward on Ogromni. Check in with our CIs. Best case, we wrap up the investigation into Cara Lindstrom soonest and we can return our focus to Ogromni."

His words came out with a forced optimism, even to himself.

Singh spoke up. "One more thing. I ordered an age progression from the photographs we have of Lindstrom as a child. I thought it might be useful to have a photograph for the various agencies, since all we have of Lindstrom as an adult is the police sketch. But you will have to tell me if it is accurate." Her eyes rested briefly on Roarke.

He looked down at the manipulated photo. It was Cara, but not. The photo that had been progressed was of a child who had never experienced what Cara had. She was smiling, she was radiant, she was joyful. None of the things that Cara was now. The adult woman in the photograph was beautiful, calm, and entirely forgettable.

"Better stick with the police sketch," Epps finally said beside him.

"Yeah," Roarke said.

As Singh and Jones left the room, Roarke could see Epps lingering at the table, waiting to talk to him. This time there seemed no way to avoid it, and Roarke felt his stomach turn over in dread as Epps came toward him like a dark avenging angel. Then at the last minute Epps' trajectory was halted as Special Agent in Charge Reynolds stepped into the doorway and looked toward Roarke.

"Am I interrupting anything?"

Epps stopped mid-stride. Roarke gave an inner cheer, and just as instantly was seized with guilt.

"Not at all, we're just finished," he told Reynolds with relief, even though he knew this was most likely more of an "out of the frying pan into the fire" kind of rescue than a "saved by the bell" moment.

Epps' jaw tensed. His one veiled glance at Roarke all but shouted "*We're not done, here,*" but he left gracefully.

Reynolds remained standing in the doorway. "OPR is processing the investigation into the shooting last night. I don't anticipate a problem."

"There won't be," Roarke said.

The SAC walked into the room and stopped, taking a moment to study the case board.

"I'm not entirely comfortable with this case," he said, finally.

That makes at least three of us, Roarke thought. *I'm not at all comfortable with it. Epps sure as hell isn't comfortable with it, as he's never going to stop reminding me. There's nothing comfortable about it.* He said none of that as the SAC continued.

"Your unit is Criminal Organizations. The sooner you're back on that job, the more comfortable I'm going to be."

"I couldn't agree more," Roarke said.

Reynolds glanced at the board again. "We have to bring this one in. No doubt in my mind. Vigilante, serial killer, whatever she is, she can't be out there on the streets."

You forgot child abductor, Roarke thought silently. *Of course she saved the kid from an imminent fate of sexual exploitation and God only knows what else.* But he didn't say it.

Reynolds turned and looked at Roarke a moment as if he had heard anyway. And then he repeated himself. "She can't be out there on the streets. But I wish it wasn't this unit that had to deal with her."

"What can I do to make you feel better about it?" Roarke asked coolly.

Reynolds sighed. "Build your case. Arrest her. And turn it over to the prosecutors as soon as possible."

"We're on the same page," Roarke told him.

He moved out into the hall with a feeling that he'd dodged some kind of bullet.

Someone stepped up to him from behind and he twisted around. It was Epps, waiting for him in the hallway. Roarke realized he hadn't quite dodged that bullet after all.

"Haven't had much time to talk, boss," Epps said evenly. The cold in his voice was painful to hear. From the moment Roarke had hired him they had had an instinctive rhythm between them, working together as seamlessly as if they'd done it all their lives. The night at the cement plant had changed everything.

Roarke turned to face him. "I'm listening."

"Serious question. Did you even arrest her?"

He hadn't. The truth was, he hadn't even thought of it at the time. "You mean, arrest her for abducting Jason Sebastian when we know damn well she only did it to keep him out of that trafficking ring?"

Epps' face tightened. "There was a whole raft of other charges to choose from."

"None of which we have warrants for—"

Epps' voice was low, but explosive. "Bullshit. You are talking crazy talk."

Roarke was silent. Technically he was right about the warrants, there had been none. But morally, he knew he didn't have a leg to stand on.

Epps glanced down the corridor behind him, and stepped closer to Roarke. "What happened that night wasn't normal and it wasn't protocol."

Roarke looked him square in the eyes. "It wasn't. And it won't happen again."

Epps stared at him, trying to read him. "This girl is nothing to play with."

"No. She's not."

"All right, then. So long as we both know it." Epps turned and left him standing in the hall. And Roarke turned to the elevator in relief and release.

Chapter 3

The house lies on the outskirts of the desert community, lone and isolated. A strong wind blows over the surrounding land, swirling dust demons across the darkness of the fields. In the black of sky, a million stars tremble around the full moon. In the split rail fence encircling the large yard, the front gate stands open; as the wind moves it, the wood seems to be alive, shivering.

He passes through the opening and moves up the dirt road, through the small grove of eucalyptus and olive trees. The spicy scent surrounds him, the leaves whisper above, a dry rattle. The house comes into sight through the trees, and he sees the front door standing open as well.

The wind gusts around him and the feeling of doom closes in as he moves up the pavers toward the triangular arched front entrance and stops on the porch, listening . . .

Nothing but silence from the darkness within.

He steps through the open doorway, past the carved wooden door, into the entry hall with its white painted brick walls and tiled floor.

And then he sees the blood.

The horror comes rushing over him. He has been here a hundred times before. Every detail is as it always is, the tiled floor, the white stucco walls, cold moonlight through the tall arched windows. He can feel the presence of madness, hear the harsh breath of the unimaginable thing that is waiting for him at the end of the hallway.

He is no longer a man, but a boy, just a boy, no match for whatever lies behind that door. The terror has turned every cell in his body to ice; his feet can barely move him forward. On the floor around him is a pool of dark, he is up to his ankles in it, and it is not cold, like water, but warm, like . . .

Smells like . . .

Copper. Stink. Death.

And those crumpled shapes on the floor around him, the sleeping mounds . . . but not sleeping, no, the eyes are open, staring. An entire family, slashed, stabbed . . . slaughtered.

He turns to run.

In front of him a shadow looms . . . he can feel it reaching for him . . . feel the scream rising in his throat—

It is not a monster, but a woman who steps out of the shadows. Her face is beautiful, luminous in the pale moonlight.

The gash in her throat drips blood.

And when she reaches for him, he does not know if it is to embrace him—or kill him—

Roarke jarred awake, with the queasy feeling that he had spoken or shouted aloud. He lay in the motel bed, and forced himself to breathe, to slow his racing heart.

The dream was his past and his present, merged. An old nightmare from his childhood, that he'd had periodically since the Reaper had disappeared, never to be caught, never to be found. There was a new presence now: the adult Cara.

As he lay still in the motel bed, he listened to the unaccustomed silence, broken at last by the distant roar of a big rig, somewhere on the freeway. He reached for his phone on the bed stand to check the time. It was just past noon, and he was somewhere in the desert off Interstate 10, east of Los Angeles.

He'd gotten off the plane at LAX, picked up a car from a rental counter, then drove east. It was past midnight and the traffic was, while still astonishing for the hour, very light for Los Angeles, no impediment at all. Roarke was a night owl, so he'd pushed on past the vast sprawl of L.A., past the golden carpet of lights of the bedroom communities and the ever-increasing sprawl of Riverside into the desert, relaxing as the lights of towns grew farther apart and the black sky above him filled with stars.

He hadn't expect to make it all the way to Blythe that night, but he was wired from the flight and he wanted to wake up with views of mountains and palm trees rather than strip-mall suburbia. He'd achieved his goal. He was now somewhere past the turnoff to Palm Springs, close enough to the site of the Lindstrom massacre that the memories of the murders had invaded his dreams.

And more than just the memory of the murders. He could still feel the dream-touch of Cara's body against his.

He threw back the blankets to stand, and moved for the bathroom to shower and dress.

On the way back to the freeway he stopped for a burrito to go from a nearby stand, figuring the slight risk of botulism was a small price to pay for the ambrosial Mexican food to be had along any highway in Southern California. Then he drove on into the desert, into the sun, toward Blythe.

The town was a wide, flat stretch of sand, ringed by mountains in the far distance. Out the car windows he saw silky dunes and palm trees and barrel cactus. As he drove in, he couldn't help remembering the view from the air. In the desert outside Blythe, there were huge petroglyphs called *intaglios*, enormous drawings on the desert floor. The biggest and most famous one was called The Hunter, a primitive depiction of a giant with a spear. There was no way not to associate it with the killer who had massacred Cara's family. A monster had come out of this haunting setting to do his bloody work.

Roarke was going back to the very beginning: the first witness he intended to interview was Randall Timothy Trent. At the time of the massacre of Cara's family Trent had been married to Cara's aunt Joan, her father's sister. He was not any kind of blood relative: a second husband, not the natural father of Joan's two small children.

The aunt was made Cara's guardian by the court and the general hope had been that she and her then-husband would adopt the child, but Trent had left Joan and the children just a few months after Joan had taken five-year-old Cara in. Cara remained with the family for only six months before the aunt returned her to Family Services, claiming inability to deal with Cara's behavioral problems. Given that the child had witnessed the slaughter of her family by a psychopath, that she herself had nearly been killed by that same monster who left her for dead, Roarke would have hoped the aunt would have made more of an effort.

Now the aunt was dead of heart failure at fifty-four, and her two children had been just six months and eighteen months when she took Cara in, too young to remember their five-year-old cousin. Which meant Trent was one of the few people alive who had had prolonged contact with Cara Lindstrom right after the attack on her and her family.

And he was a captive audience, since he was currently incarcerated, in medium-security Ironwood Prison, just fifteen minutes outside the town where Cara's family had been butchered.

Whether Trent's present circumstances had anything to do with anything, Roarke didn't know. But in his short experience with Cara Lindstrom, he'd found that everything meant something.

The landscape was bleak: flat plains of sand and a dry red ridge of mountains behind the white expanse of prison, so stark in the desert setting the buildings seemed to have been dropped onto the middle of the desert by aliens.

Ironwood was a medium-security facility, not as dank as so many other California prisons, and the population taking exercise behind the fence in the outer grounds looked to be about fifty percent Latino. Roarke knew a whole building had been converted to house "sensitive needs" inmates, an unlikely mix of ex-gang members and sex offenders who were equally at risk for inmate-on-inmate violence.

Trent was neither a gang member nor a sex offender. He'd been convicted of assault on a prostitute, the last of a long line of assaults and altercations seeming to stem from anger impulse control, and undoubtedly alcoholism and other substance abuse issues. The assault on the prostitute crossed into a gray area that interested Roarke; it combined sex and rage, and that was more specifically the kind of offender that Cara Lindstrom was in the habit of dispatching.

Roarke didn't think that Trent had molested Cara, although he sure as hell had checked the Social Services records for any hint of it. Trent had had no priors for sexual assault or other similar charges. His criminal record had started a good five years after he'd moved out on Joan Lindstrom-Trent. There was no obvious evidence that he'd done anything at all untoward before then.

But a con didn't just become a con. It didn't just start at thirty-nine. Not in Roarke's experience.

Cara had been only five years old when she lived under the same roof as Trent just after her near-murder, and it was unlikely in the extreme that she had . . . Roarke had no idea how to even finish the thought. That she had seen the badness in Trent, that she had driven him out of the house . . .

At age five.

Epps' words in the corridor came back to him. *You are talking crazy talk.*

And yet the question hovered. *What happened?*

Inside the prison's main building Roarke surrendered his service weapon at the security gate and stripped off his belt, shoes, and personal belongings to send them through the X-ray machine. He redressed on the other end and was escorted by a guard through halls reeking of the biting faux-pine stench of some antiseptic cleaner. Steel gates clanged open before him and slammed locked behind him, and he felt himself flinching at the sounds. Prisons always made him tense, with their pervasive sense of desperation and madness, but today there was the added knowledge that he was looking at Cara Lindstrom's future, if she were alive and if he caught her. And he would catch her. It didn't mean he liked thinking about what that meant.

It wasn't a visiting day so he was the only one in the visitation room. It was bright from the long windows overlooking the desert and filled with rows of scarred rectangular folding tables and plastic bucket chairs. He remained standing at one of those windows, gazing out at an expansive view of the cloudless blue sky and the jagged red mountains.

A door opened behind him and Trent shambled in, escorted by a guard. He was a medium-tall and weathered man in his late fifties, with the hard bitterness of a convict, but there was enough tone left to his muscles and enough definition to his face that Roarke could see he had once been an attractive man. Not a good one, but an attractive one.

Trent stopped behind the chair right at the middle of the table and across from Roarke and eyed him. "Fed, huh," he said, half-bored, half-contemptuous.

Roarke moved toward the table. "Have a seat, Mr. Trent."

Trent shrugged, pulled the chair out and sat. "To what do I owe the honor?"

And some polish, too. Definitely a ladies' man in his time.

"I'm reinvestigating the Lindstrom murders," Roarke said, and while he watched the man's face he wondered why he'd said it that way.

Trent looked startled for a split-second, which he covered fairly skillfully. "You don't say. Can't help you. Wasn't even in the same town when it happened."

"Actually, I'm looking for Cara Lindstrom."

A different kind of look flashed across Trent's face, uninterpretable. "You have got to be kidding. Haven't seen the kid for a million years."

Roarke looked at him without expression. "That's right. You moved out—two months after Cara moved in with you?"

The convict shrugged again, disinterested. "I guess. Like I said. Long time ago."

Roarke flipped open a file, but he didn't need to check the report that Singh had compiled. He knew the date.

"Two months to the day." He looked back up at Trent. "Interesting timing."

"In what way?" Trent said, with a hint of a challenge.

"It looks almost like it might have had to do with the little girl."

The inmate smiled thinly. "We already had Joan's two. Three just broke the camel's back."

Roarke stared at him. "Kind of cold, isn't it?"

"Don't know what you mean."

"A child who'd been through all that—five years old. Seems like a person could give her a little time."

Trent's face and voice turned ugly. And more than ugly: furtive. "Yeah, well, you didn't have to live with the kid. She was not right."

"Not right," Roarke repeated colorlessly.

"Mental," Trent summed up.

"Like how?"

"Always watching. Always snooping around." The convict looked grimly angry.

Roarke kept his tone neutral, suppressing an urge to haul Trent up by his collar and slam him against the wall. "A five-year-old? Snooping?"

Trent assumed a look of righteous martyrdom. "The kid . . . you don't know what we had to deal with. Her waking up at night, screaming. Seeing things."

Hallucinations. That had been in the psychiatric reports, too.

"Seeing things like . . ."

"Monsters, she said. Always crying about *It.*"

There was an odd inflection he gave the word, an inflection Roarke had heard before. From Cara. He frowned, repeated it. "Always crying about monsters?"

"*It,*" Trent said again. "She was always talking about *It.*" He seemed agitated for the first time. "Spooked the kids. Creeped me out, too."

Roarke sat back and looked at him.

"No one could go near her sometimes. She'd just start screaming. In the end she needed more help than we could give her," Trent said piously.

Yeah, I believe that. Roarke gave himself a minute to breathe, and studied the man in front of him. *What went on? What are you hiding?*

"You're in for assault," he said aloud.

Trent's face turned sullen. "Self-defense," he said.

Sure, pal. Prostitutes are in the habit of attacking johns for no reason. "Not the first conviction, either," he said. "The rest of them self-defense, too?"

The convict moved explosively, a threatening gesture. "You got a point?"

"Just trying to see what she saw in you."

Trent looked truculent. "I was a good husband to Joanie."

The fact was, Roarke hadn't meant Joan Trent. He'd been thinking of Cara. *Just trying to see what she saw in you. At five years old.*

"Until Cara came along," Roarke said.

"The kid was damaged. Maybe always was, maybe got that way because of what happened. Either way, not a kid you wanted living in your house."

"So you split and left Joan with her and two other kids," Roarke said evenly.

Trent's eyes narrowed at Roarke speculatively. "Is this what the Feebs do these days? You're here to rag my ass about what a bad father I was to the poor little orphan? Telling you, I wasn't the one messed that kid up."

Roarke realized Trent was right in at least that one respect. And he'd strayed far from the topic. He refocused. "Did the Lindstroms have any vacation homes, favorite vacation spots, condos that you know of?" He knew that early imprints went deep, and if Cara had a safe house, as Singh had speculated, she may have unconsciously gravitated toward and established herself in a place that had warm memories from her earliest childhood.

Trent rolled his eyes. "I'm 'sposed to remember from what, twenty-five years ago? We didn't socialize much with Joan's family."

Maybe because her brother could see what a creep you are, Roarke thought wearily.

"And you never took the children anywhere, no family vacations?"

The convict barked a laugh. "It was enough of a time just getting the kid to sleep at night."

"Did you go to the funerals?" Roarke asked out of nowhere.

Trent looked startled. "Go to the . . . of course we did. What the hell?"

It was the most natural response Roarke had gotten from him yet, so he tried for more. "Killers often attend the funerals of their victims. I wondered if you might have noticed anyone out of place, anyone unusual."

Trent frowned, and his eyes clouded, as if he were seriously thinking about it. But he shook his head. "I was there when Joanie ID'd the bodies. Person who does that kind of thing . . . I don't think you can walk around hiding that."

"That's interesting," Roarke said. He meant it. He sat back in his chair and studied Trent. Trent stared back.

"You seriously opening all that up again?" The man shook his head. "Brother, good luck. No one ever had a clue."

Roarke had the feeling that Trent would sit talking to him all day if this were the topic. And what was surprising about that? A violent attack, an unsolved mystery, a brush with evil and legend. It's not something a person would get over. Cara hadn't. He himself hadn't.

"There's nothing at all you can remember, no hint that anyone got that this was going to happen?"

Trent laughed without humor. "Like why someone would want to kill them? Besides how damn perfect they were?" The ugly look was on his face again and Roarke thought, not for the first time, that as disordered as the killer seemed to have been, he was selective enough to consistently pick happy nuclear families, ones that could have aroused envy even in less overtly disturbed individuals.

"How about crank calls? Signs of an intruder, an attempted break-in, someone watching the house? Anything unusual. Anything at all."

"Just the rabbit," the convict said.

Roarke felt a sudden chill of significance. "What rabbit?"

"About a week before it all happened. Gillian—Joan's sister—found a jackrabbit all torn up on the porch. Out here . . ." Trent waved vaguely at the window, the desert outside. "Coyotes do that shit all the time. No one thought anything of it till afterward, but Joan said something about it later."

Roarke had read nothing of this in the police files.

"She said something 'later'? How much later?"

Trent shook his head. "She didn't even remember it for a while. A month or so, maybe."

"She told the cops?"

Trent frowned. " 'Course."

"You're sure," Roarke said intently. "She called in or went in to report finding the rabbit to the investigating officers a month or so later?"

He watched the thought process on Trent's face, the initial certainty turning to doubt. "Well . . . she had her hands full with the kids. Don't know for a fact."

That's it, Roarke thought, with a strange kind of elation. *Could it be? Something that everyone missed?*

Something that could finally, finally, bring the Reaper down?

Roarke left Trent to a guard, and processed himself out. Outside of the prison he squinted into the sun and breathed in dry desert air, and felt a rush of adrenaline and exhilaration. A clue. Slight as it was, it was something that might just have been overlooked in the frenzy that the investigation would have been by the time of a third family massacre. It could mean that the Reaper had watched the family, stalked them. He might have left the same kind of calling card at one of the other scenes. Someone else might have seen him. There might be a trail.

He ignored the fact that it was a trail to a twenty-five-year-old cold case and not his own, and reached for his phone to call Singh. When the dark velvet voice responded, he said without identifying himself, "In the police reports on the Reaper massacres, was there anything about animals? A dead rabbit left on the Lindstroms' porch, maybe a week before the murders?"

Roarke could hear Singh's fingernails clicking on computer keys, and felt his breath suspending as he waited. Her voice came back: "Nothing."

"How about in the other cases? Anything about animals? Pets killed, carcasses displayed, eviscerated . . ."

More clicking and an intense silence from Singh's end. Roarke watched the wind blow sand across the flat plains of desert.

"Nothing immediately comes up when I search. If you wish I will comb through the reports myself to be sure."

Roarke considered this. Was Trent just fucking with him? Throwing him a plausible clue to amuse himself? It happened all the time. But Roarke didn't feel the convict had been lying. It would have been a clever fabrication, diabolical, even.

"Do it," he told her. "Please."

She didn't ask him what this had to do with finding Cara Lindstrom. Which was fine with Roarke, since he didn't have any good answer to that at all.

He drove on the flat ribbon of highway past fields and horse properties and was halfway to the house before he realized where he was going. But it was inevitable. The Lindstrom house, site of the massacre twenty-five years ago, the place where Cara Lindstrom's life, and very probably her sanity, had been shattered for all time.

The house had been standing empty for years, a foreclosure, bank-owned. It had a history of high turnover, defaulted mortgages. Like a curse. Bad energy. A retired sheriff Roarke had interviewed about the Lindstrom case had suggested it would be best if the house burned to the ground.

It sat on a land lot of several acres, a house fanning out in four sections like an accordion, surrounded by thick patches of old-growth trees. The property was bordered by agricultural fields on three sides. The other side of the lot butted up against a road. There was no other house adjacent at all; the closest residence was across that highway. Isolated. A perfect setting for the gruesome work the Reaper had done.

There was a packed dirt road leading from the highway to the house, which was encircled by a split-rail fence. The lawn beyond was dry and brown, but the eucalyptus and olive trees were huge and healthy, cooling the air with their spicy sage green leaves. There was a large garage and also some kind of shed.

As he turned into the drive, Roarke stared out the windows with the same powerful feeling of déjà vu he always had, seeing it. As a child of nine he had watched the house on T.V. broadcasts countless times, riveted to news reports on the massacre. It was the case that had infected him with the desire to be an FBI agent, to solve crimes and lock up bad guys. He'd studied the case, dreamed it. And some force he did not understand had crossed his path with Cara Lindstrom's twenty-five years later.

He got out of the car and let the door shut with a hollow clunk before he moved up the pavers toward the front entrance. There was a dry breeze, a whispering in the trees around him that made the air seem alive.

The recessed porch had a high triangular arched entrance and a wide door with ornate carved wooden panels. He stepped up and looked down at the concrete slab of the porch, hearing Trent's voice in his head. *"She found a rabbit, all torn up. Out here coyotes do that kind of thing all the time . . ."*

But coyotes weren't in the habit of dragging animal carcasses up onto porches. If anything they shunned security lights.

He looked up toward the solid front door. There was a realtor's lock box on the door handle. Roarke remembered the combination from his previous visit, and mentally crossed his fingers that it had not been changed. He punched in the numbers, held his breath. The compartment slid open.

He removed the key and used it, and the door swung open into the silent house.

The entry hall was dark wood beams and white-painted brick walls, with Mexican tiled floors. The red light of sunset spilled through the windows but the house was cool. He stepped into the great room, huge and gorgeous, with two huge arched windows framing a double-size fireplace, cathedral ceilings of more beamed dark wood and antique ceiling fans.

He stood for a moment under the vaulted ceilings. Listening. Feeling. The whole house had an energy . . . it seemed to have been deserted for years. There was an eerie sense of arrested time.

He didn't know why he was there, except that he couldn't stay away, any more than Cara had been able to stay away. The place was imprinted with horror, and mystery. He felt the eternal pull of the cold case, the itch to know. *Who killed them? Where did he come from? Where did he go? What was his sickness?*

And there was the pull of something deeper. It was the great mystery of his childhood, the imprint that had decided the course of his life forever.

He moved toward the wing of the house that had housed the children's bedrooms. Room after room was completely empty; his footsteps echoed off the ubiquitous tiles. In his mind, the trail of blood the killer had left was still crimson on the floors, on the walls. Fifteen-year-old Joe. Thirteen-year-old Donny. Eight-year-old Amber. Pulled from their beds and stabbed dozens of times. Psychologists called it piquerism, a perverted substitute for the sexual act.

He moved to the end of the hall, inexorably drawn to the bedroom that had been Cara's.

The room vibrated with the things that she had said to Roarke in this very house, in this room, holding a gun on him as he told her he wanted to help her . . . and was not sure if that would be the death of him.

"It was a monster disguised as a man. It scratched me and now it plays with me."

In his mind he heard the heartbreaking voice of the five-year-old child caught on tape, the child Cara's absolute conviction that her family had been attacked not by a man, but by a monster.

"Monster. Beast. Monster."

The Reaper had broken her in this room, had left her with the dark visions which now appeared to lead her to the human monsters she killed.

The space suddenly seemed too small to breathe in. He stepped backward, through the door and out.

In the family room a sliding glass door led out to a tiled patio with the same high vaulted wood ceilings and ceiling fans, a brick barbeque, a dry pool with dry spa. The sky outside was deep blue twilight.

He pulled open the glass door and moved outside.

The desert wind was warm on his skin. It whispered in the eucalyptus grove, a lulling, beckoning sound.

He walked out further into the yard, feeling the absorbed heat of the day rising from the sand.

There were no outside lights on around the house, and so few neighboring houses that the sky above was already full of actual stars, stars the way they only appeared in the desert or out on the ocean. Blackness, infinity, and a hundred million diamond lights. The crescent moon was rising, but it was still low enough on the horizon that Roarke could pick out Orion and Cassiopeia, the Hunter and the Queen. Every star in the constellations was clear and brilliant.

As Roarke stared up, he felt his skin crawling, the icy feeling of being watched. He spun around, staring into the darkness. He knew it was nothing more than nerves; the Reaper had not struck for twenty-five years. Cara had been his last victim. But Roarke's skin still tingled.

A tumbleweed rolled across the sand, and off in the distance, a shadow, small and close to the ground, skittered between rocks.

He stood in the wind and the whisper of leaves and looked up again at the sky, wishing for a sign.

Chapter 4

I n the darkness, in the wind, under the starry sky, she watches.

She watches as Roarke walks in the dark and the desert wind, sometimes stopping to look out into the night as if he can see her.

She is not surprised to be seeing him again. She had not expected him, yet she is not surprised. Everything about Roarke is inevitable.

It is as the last moment she saw him. He is holding her, carrying her. She can feel his arms, the beating of his heart against her skin.

And there is pain, and his voice, telling her to breathe, to live.

He lays her down in the front seat of a truck, whispering that he will help her. Then he is gone, and there is only pain.

She lies on the seat floating in and out of consciousness. She is wounded, badly wounded, but death has circled her before without claiming her. Outside the truck men are fighting, Roarke and one of the flesh dealers. And then something outside herself jolts her to life. While Roarke fights hand-to-hand with another one of the monsters, she pulls herself up by the inside of the door.

It should not be possible to stand, to walk. But it is not entirely her, not her alone, that moves. She staggers out toward the vehicle she has seen earlier, the one she took keys from, for just this eventuality.

As the fire from the explosion in the meth lab roars and submachine guns blast, she escapes in that truck, driving out into the night, into the dark desert, driving until she has to stop or crash.

Some time before dawn she wakes and does not know where she is. Her ribs are screaming, an excruciating wound. The stabbing pulse of blood in the flesh of her side. Burning . . .

But not dead.

She is still alive enough to find an overnight convenience store, where the stoned clerk seems barely to notice her condition. She buys quantities of peroxide, antibiotic ointment, ibuprofen, a sewing kit, and uses them in the truck. The bullet has scraped her ribcage, ugly and bloody but not deep; no metal is lodged inside her.

Something has spared her, again, and this time whatever it is has used Roarke to do so.

She drives again, stops again, wakes again . . . and recognizes Joshua Tree, the national park in the desert just an hour away from her family's old home, a vaguely remembered wonderland from her childhood, the time before *the night*. An alien landscape of enormous wind-carved rocks and natural monuments, clean and vast, with no human life to soil it. On the outskirts of the park there are all kinds of rarely used vacation homes: cabins, lodges. Easy enough to break a back window in an isolated cabin, to settle there when she finds no signs of recent habitation. The object being to keep herself still enough to heal.

She spends her time dousing herself with bottles of hydrogen peroxide by the hour, slathering the bloody gash in her side with triple antibiotic ointment, sleeping. Infection sets in anyway, angry black and red lines crawling hotly from the wound, and she ventures out, breaking into one after another of the closed-up houses in the surrounding area, rifling through medicine cabinets until she finds an almost-full course of oral antibiotics, and some old codeine as well, for the pain.

And she heals.

She had not expected to survive the night at the concrete plant. In truth she had not wanted to. She had gone there with only one purpose: to kill as many of the monsters as she could before they took her down. When she asked Roarke to come, she had not expected him to, much less expected him to save her.

And yet it had happened.

She does not yet know what it means, but she lives by these signs.

She is longer in one spot than she can remember staying in a long, long time, resting, recovering . . . then venturing out, driving into the park and sitting for hours in the midst of house-sized boulders at Big Rock campground, where she can feel the desert sun and wind and the ancient peace restoring her.

It occurs to her that she can stay. Not in this cabin, but she has money, she could buy one for herself, stay clear of people as much as possible, and in that way maybe avoid the shadow that has pursued her for all of her life since *the night*. She lets herself wonder, for the first time, what it would be like: to be free, not to endlessly hunt and be hunted. Merely to live.

She remains in peace through the dark of the moon, and the whispers are quiet. But with the first sliver of new moon, the restlessness begins.

She ventures farther, almost always ending up at the house in Blythe, the house where it all started. Not going in, only watching, waiting for something that she has not known she is waiting for until just now, seeing Roarke. Roarke, alone this time, and looking for something, too. Looking up into the sky spiked with stars, the constellations standing out in brilliant dimensions. The wind stirs the air between them as he looks out into the night.

She feels the crescent moon behind her, hears it murmur.

The pain and pills have kept her deadened, have dulled the whispers of the moon. But the pain is receding and the next moon is growing, and it is talking to her.

At the beginning of her dark journey, an old Native American man had taught her that every moon has a name. This month is Blood Moon.

She will listen and wait for the signs.

Chapter 5

R oarke woke to white sunlight slanting through the windows of Cara's old bedroom. Of course he'd never made it to a motel, that had been a pleasant fantasy.

His back ached from sleeping on the floor, with his own coat for a pillow, but he hadn't dreamed, and no monster had come upon him while he slept. Though momentarily, as he stretched his way to his feet, he had an odd feeling of not-aloneness.

The feeling stayed with him as he walked through the silent house, which was somehow as familiar to him as if he'd lived there, all those years ago. A thought drifted through his mind: *I could buy it.* Compared to San Francisco real estate, the asking price was enticingly low. *All of this space. All of this privacy.*

And that was insane.

He shook his head, and headed for the door.

He locked the front door behind him and replaced the key in the lock box, and then stood on the porch, looking out over the eucalyptus, listening to the dry leaves stirring softly in the wind. Across a field, a horse cantered, a teenage girl on its back. Roarke watched them race in the field before he started for the car.

He had two choices for the day, which he considered as he sat behind the wheel studying the locations he'd programmed into the rental car's GPS. He could head to Palm Desert, where the former counselor from a group home Cara had lived in had been murdered sixteen years ago.

Had it been her first kill?

But investigating that long-ago murder was not going to get him closer to finding Cara.

He sat back against the seat and for a moment felt that same strange sensation of not being alone. He sat up and, knowing it was irrational, checked the back seat of the car. No one. Idiocy.

He looked at the GPS again, the addresses programmed into it. And he knew the most realistic choice was to go south, to San Diego, where Cara's cousin Erin McNally was in med school. The other cousin was working abroad and hadn't returned phone calls.

He started the car and drove, through the eucalyptus, and out onto the freedom of the road.

Outside of its major cities Southern California was an unrelenting desert, a whole world away from the coastal forest of the Bay Area and the port city Victoriana of San Francisco. On the I-10 Roarke skirted the borders of Joshua Tree National Park, a surrealist landscape of rounded rock formations and the bleak cactus-like trees that gave the park its name. He had always wanted to explore the park, and he felt a tug he couldn't interpret as he passed the entrance.

This isn't a vacation, he told himself, and drove on.

As he approached Indio on Interstate 10, he knew the highways split. He could go several different directions. He felt another urge to keep driving west, a slightly longer route that would take him through Temecula, the wine country town bordered by the Pechanga Reservation where Cara had briefly lived with her aunt, Randall Trent, and her two young cousins. But besides giving him more of a feel for Cara herself, chances were good there'd be nothing there that might yield as much information as Cara's cousin.

As he took the turnoff south toward San Diego, he remembered Epps' words that Mexicali was less than two hours from the cement plant, that Cara could have crossed the border and disappeared into that vast and ancient country, never to be found.

He recalled that Cara had spoken Spanish, too, during the shootout at the plant. Another skill that made her flexible, that made her options legion, that made finding her that much more challenging.

And suddenly he was seeing the crude altar in the brothel, the appeal to the shadowy saint.

Santa Muerte, he thought. *Where are you, Lady Death?*

Like every other city in California, San Diego had grown since Roarke had last visited it, and traffic had swelled to match. An hour outside the city the roads slowed to a crawl. He had plenty of time to marvel, with gritted teeth, at how the city had expanded for miles beyond the boundaries he remembered, densely packed housing with less and less land in between settlements.

The university was located on twelve hundred acres of coastal woodland near the Pacific Ocean in La Jolla. Any campus that close to the beach would normally be a party school, but S.D. had a staid reputation, probably because beyond the woods it was surrounded by a residential no-man's land. Students could walk down to the beach to surf between classes but were miles from the nightlife of the city center.

Cara Lindstrom's cousin Erin McNally was a med student, one would assume she had the attendant workload, but apparently she had immediately agreed to Roarke's request for a meeting. Singh had set up an appointment in front of the campus's Geisel Library. "She said you cannot miss it."

She was right—no one could have missed it. Roarke walked through the sunny, modern campus toward a concrete and glass structure looking for all the world like the Starship Enterprise: a spaceship-shaped oval perched on steep concrete ramps resembling loading docks.

Singh had sent through a photo of Erin, an olive-skinned girl with black hair and black horn-rimmed glasses, a studious type as far from Cara Lindstrom's edgy and feral beauty as a blood relative could get. The glasses made her easy to spot; she was poring over a thick textbook at a shaded table in the library plaza. She looked serious and much younger than her twenty-six years.

She squinted up at him as he stopped in front of her table. "Ms. McNally?" he asked.

"Agent Roarke," she said, and looked him over, not in a sexual way at all, but with a rather more scientific curiosity. He'd changed to a dress shirt and tie in the parking lot and shrugged on his suit coat on the way across campus, so he probably looked his part.

He motioned to the seat across from her and she nodded, old school manners for someone of her generation. "Agent Singh told you what I wanted to speak to you about?" he asked as he settled.

"My cousin," Erin said, and closed her textbook. *Pathologic Basis of Disease*, he noted. "What do you want with her?"

Her bluntness was startling. She might not look like Cara, but that sharp watchfulness apparently ran in the family.

"I'm trying to find her."

"I don't have a clue," Erin said, and looked at him so directly he knew it was true. Not that he'd really expected her to have an answer. It was going to take some digging, to see what she knew that she didn't know she knew.

"Why do you want to find her?" Erin asked. "Does it have to do with the murders?"

Roarke knew that she meant the murders of the Lindstrom family, not Cara's own killings. The APB that had been out for her when she'd kidnapped Jason Sebastian had gone out with the alias she was using at the time, Leila French, and Roarke doubted that Erin would have seen the FBI sketch that had briefly been released in central California. There was no reason Erin would know her cousin was wanted.

"Yes, something to do with them," he answered her.

"That's weird." She frowned. "After all this time." She looked disturbed.

"When was the last time you saw her?"

She hesitated. "I think when I was seventeen."

"You *think*?" he repeated. He doubted this precise young woman was in the habit of uncertainty.

She looked away from him, off into the distance. "No, I guess I know. I was a senior in high school. I was leaving school and I thought I saw her in a car parked across the street, looking at me. I can't be sure, because I hadn't seen her for years by then, not since I was . . . fourteen. But it looked like her, and she was looking at me, and this was just a week before she disappeared."

Roarke felt a little chill up his spine. "How do you mean, disappeared?"

"The day she turned twenty-one all the insurance money from the murders got signed over to her and no one ever heard from her again. My mother said that she fired the trustee and she asked for the whole lump of it to be wired somewhere and then her phone was turned off and her P.O. Box and her email were all shut down. The trustee was calling Mom every few days asking if she'd heard anything from her but she was just gone. We never heard anything about her after that."

"No calls, no postcards . . . ?" Roarke asked, though he knew the answer.

"She never wrote or called anyway."

"Not ever?"

Erin shook her head. "A couple of times my mother had her over, usually a holiday, Thanksgiving, Christmas. But that was a long time ago, when we were still kids."

"Can you remember the last time?"

There was a flicker on Erin's face. "I was ten. It was after she got out of juvie. I think Mom felt guilty, like she could've done more. It didn't work out so well. Patrick didn't like Cara, kind of ragged her, and she wouldn't talk around him. Not that she talked a lot anyway."

Patrick was Erin's slightly older brother. "Any reason for the friction between her and your brother?"

"Nothing that made sense." She gave him a thin smile. "You know, we grew up as the kids whose family got killed by the Reaper. Boogeyman kind of stuff: 'He's coming back to get you . . .' Like that. And the 'crazy cousin' thing didn't help."

"*Was* she crazy?" he asked without thinking, and immediately regretted it.

But she only looked at him steadily. "Well . . . who wouldn't be?"

He couldn't argue.

"When she did visit you, were there places you went, on a family vacation . . . or did your mother's family have some vacation spot?"

"Disneyland? Sea World?" Erin suggested. Roarke realized, startled, that she was making a dry joke.

"Can't see it," he told her.

"And you would be right." Erin looked away, down the long plaza. "She didn't like to be around people much. I think she liked it when we drove places, though. It felt like she relaxed more in a car, on the road. Especially out of the city."

It fit what Roarke knew of Cara himself. She was a traveler.

"Did you see her—" he stopped. Erin looked at him enquiringly. "Did you ever see her act out violently? Or talk"—he paused, searching for the words—"in an unbalanced way?"

Erin's face shadowed. "She wasn't violent around us. But she could look at you and stop your heart. I mean, she did it with Patrick, not with me, but she'd freeze me up when she did it to him. She watched *everyone*. All the time. There was so much going on inside her I thought she would burst. And once . . ."

Her eyes went distant in a way that made Roarke hold his breath, waiting for whatever she was going to say.

"I'm in med school. You don't have to guess. I was a shy kid. A brain. I got picked on. Maybe would have been even without the whole family ghost." She breathed in, a long breath. "Cara came over for one of the happy family meals one night when I was about ten, so she would have been fifteen. We went out to a restaurant, some stupid hamburger place, and Derek Sanders was there with his family. This guy from school. He'd made a special project out of me, the way kids like that do." She paused, and Roarke waited, feeling a sense of inevitability.

"He didn't say anything to me, and I didn't say anything to him, nobody said anything. I was just praying that nothing would happen. We ate our Happy Meals and Cara looked at me, and she looked at him, and she didn't say a word. And at the end of the night Cara went back to whatever home she was in at the time and I went back home to sleep . . . and the next morning Derek showed up to school with two black eyes and all hunched over. And when I passed him in the hall he *flinched* away from me. Flinched."

She stopped, and took another breath. "He never said another word to me." She looked at Roarke, with steady dark eyes. "Is that what you mean by violence?"

It's exactly what I meant, he thought. *It's Cara to a T.*

"You never told her anything about how he'd treated you."

She laughed shortly. "I didn't talk to Cara. Never anything beyond, 'Pass the bread.' My mom was afraid of her. I didn't know how to say that at the time, but I know it was true. She never spent the night at our house. I think Mom thought . . ."

Roarke felt his pulse start to race. "That she'd hurt you?"

Erin shook her head, and didn't look at him.

Her voice was hollow. "That he really would come back for her. The Reaper. And take the rest of us, too."

Roarke felt a heaviness in the air between them. He had heard that kind of superstitious talk before about the Reaper. An uncaught serial killer took on the aura of legend. He leaned forward to get her full attention. "Erin. I need to know. Did your mother ever talk about some sign, some indication that the massacre was going to happen? Anything unusual, any marker . . ."

Erin's head was down, black curls curtaining her face. She murmured something that set Roarke's hair on end, even as he was unsure what she had actually said. "I'm sorry, what—" he started, and this time he heard.

"The rabbit," she said, very softly.

"What about the rabbit?"

"Mom said that Aunt Gillian found a dead rabbit on the porch before it all happened."

So there. Trent hadn't been lying. It is a clue, something tangible from the past. Not to do with *his* case, of course, but Roarke felt the subterranean pull of the lead. It was a path to a killer, a marker of his personality, a trail.

What Roarke wanted with it was less clear. *Revenge? Just to know?* It was what he did. He hunted killers.

No. That had been before. Another life.

Erin was looking at him. "He's dead, isn't he?" she asked in a small voice. "He must be dead."

"Almost certainly," Roarke said. But he felt the hollowness of the words. "Or we would know by now. Men like that never stop." They sat in silence for a moment, and there was a chill in the sunny day.

"If you find Cara, would you tell her . . ." the young woman stopped, looked down at her books.

"What?" Roarke asked gently.

"I'd like to see her," she said, without raising her eyes. "I'd really like to see her."

Chapter 6

It was late afternoon, coming on sunset, and Roarke was far too close to the ocean not to find a beach. He had to think, and there was no better place.

He collected his car in the visitor lot and stopped to ask directions from a guard at a security kiosk, who turned and pointed. Torrey Pines State Reserve was just minutes from campus.

Roarke drove to the trailhead, where he stood by the open trunk of the car and exchanged his dress shirt and suit coat for a T-shirt and sweater, and his work shoes for the lightweight Hi-Tec hiking boots he always took on the road with him. Then he locked the car and set off along a sandy, post-fenced trail through the scattered long-needled pines, gnarled and twisted into surreal shapes by the wind. His feet crunched past low, soft coastal sage scrub and hard-leafed chaparral, and he felt his muscles loosening, his lungs filling with the pure spicy air as the natural setting worked its magic.

The trail opened out on a cliff and he stopped in his tracks to take in the spectacular overlook: a swoop of spotless beach under fantastically carved cliffs, the vast ocean with the sinking sun starting to glimmer orange across the water, outlining the streaks of cirrus clouds in light.

After a long moment of just drinking it in, he descended the steep trail with the wind blowing at his hair and seagulls sailing through the air beside him, down the bluff to a secluded beach. The temperature was dropping and fog was rolling in off the water, but there was a warmth from the golden sandstone cliff face. Roarke breathed in deeply, feeling clean, and a million miles away from civilization.

The beach curved along the wind-sculpted bluffs, and the long stretch of sand was nearly deserted, just a few lone walkers with dogs. A molten ball of sun poured orange light across the waves as it sank into the water.

Once at the shoreline, he slowed his pace, and then sat down in the still-warm sand amid patches of salt grass to think.

As far as his stated mission went, the trip so far had been a total bust. No one knew where Cara was. No one left on his list was likely to know where she was.

His biggest score of the journey had been on the Reaper: the fact that the killer had left a savaged animal as a calling card. In his mind he heard Erin's shaky voice.

"He's dead, isn't he? He must be dead."

He shook his head to dispel the feeling of unease.

Cara. Focus on Cara.

He could go back up through Palm Desert, look at the old files on the murder of the youth home counselor. But he knew that was only his own curiosity. Deep down he was sure that Cara had killed the man. At fourteen years old. He thought briefly of Erin's story, the bully who surely had had a private visit from Cara. At least whatever she'd done to the kid, he'd gotten away with his life.

But those old attacks had nothing to do with his hunt. As reluctant as he was to admit it, the best chance of finding her, barring a hospital report or getting lucky on a car she'd stolen, was to pick up her trail again at her next kill. Unless she was dead. And he knew in his bones she wasn't.

And whether she was in a cooling-off period or not, it was almost certain that she would kill again. Whatever drove her, she had been on her bloody mission for a long time.

He stared out at the rolling waves, the liquid gold of the melting sun, and felt the coarse sand under his fingers. Then he pushed himself up to his feet.

Somehow it would have to stop.

From the bluffs, she watches.

She follows along the narrow and sandy trail, keeping back from the cliff's edge, as far below her Roarke walks along the water.

She has followed him from Blythe.

Not literally; that would be far too risky. He is too astute not to pick up that he is being tailed on the road.

His rental car is a Camry; she has a master key for the make. So while Roarke had slept fitfully in her old house, her old room, she'd checked the GPS of the car, and found several destinations programmed into the device: Ironwood Prison—meaning he'd been to see that vermin Trent, her non-uncle. The police department in Palm Desert—meaning he must be thinking of asking questions about the group home counselor she'd taken care of so very many years ago now, after he and his sociopathic teen protégé had forced their way into her room one night, thinking that as the youngest female in the home she'd be easy prey.

She could tell Roarke all about it, how she'd fought back with everything in her, which turned out to be much more than she'd ever expected. The counselor had fled the premises for fear of discovery and then testified she'd attacked and tried to kill the older boy, whom she'd beaten into unconsciousness. For which she'd been sent up to Youth Authority, California's maximum-security juvenile facility, for three years.

By the time she'd got out, her fighting skills had improved immeasurably. The first thing she'd done upon release was make sure the counselor could never be a problem for anyone ever again.

The last address in Roarke's GPS was her cousin Erin. So this is where she has followed him, driving her own route down to San Diego and the campus, in the truck she took from the cement plant. The battered, dusty truck is naturally inconspicuous on the desert roads; she has passed many such trucks on her rare forays out of the Joshua Tree cabin. And there has been another point in its favor: she doubts the traffickers from the cement plant are cooperating with authorities in any way. They aren't about to report a stolen vehicle, if they even know or care it is gone.

She is still processing the oddity of seeing Roarke with Erin. Erin has grown into her looks, no longer the awkward and coltish, paralyzingly shy girl that Cara remembers from a far, far different life.

She is sure she knows what they were talking about. When had been the last time Erin had seen her, where she might be now . . .

Roarke is trying to find her, going first to that scum Trent, and then Erin. It is not an unreasonable plan. She has not contacted Erin over the years but she has always been aware of where she is, what she is doing. Erin is perhaps the only living being she feels any pull of connection to. Before, briefly, the boy Jason Sebastian.

She watches Roarke on the sand below her, and she listens to the whispers of the wind and tide and rising moon. They had led her to the boy, and the boy had led her to the nest of monsters, and Roarke had followed her path and had been there to save her that last bloody night. One clear step after another, a perfect trail.

Now Roarke is following the same sort of trail, and it will lead him to her.

The night at *the house* he had told her he'd gone into law enforcement because of her, because of *the night*, that it had set him on the track of hunting monsters. They are the same that way. Different, because he hunts and has never been hunted. But the same.

He is the only one who has ever seen her. The only one who understood from the start who she once was, what she does.

He saved her life, under the full moon. Now he is after her to arrest her.

And that, she will never let happen.

Never.

On the beach, Roarke sat up suddenly as he caught an arcing gleam against the water, backlit by the sun, and then a series of identical arcs, in perfect, fluid rhythm. His heart flipped as he realized he was looking at a pod of bottlenose dolphins, their sleek, streamlined bodies leaping and plunging through the swells of the surf, silver flashes against the dying sun.

And then, not knowing why, he looked back toward the cliffs. They loomed, silent . . . and empty.

He climbed the trail in rapidly encroaching darkness, knowing full well he had stayed too long past the setting of the sun. Not the smartest move on his part. One false step and he would tumble to his death on the rocks below. He had a small Maglite on his keychain but it would be next to useless in the deep blackness of the night. He brushed his hand along the rock wall beside him, and tried to tamp down a growing anxiety as he concentrated on finding his way up in the shadows.

He made the top of the cliff with his heart racing, not just from the climb. He turned back to look at the vast and slowly rolling carpet of ocean below him, thundering softly against the shore. Then he wound his way along the sandy trail through the silky whispers of the pines.

As he turned back toward the trail, a twig snapped and he spun, his weapon already in his hands.

His eyes searched the shadows . . . but he saw nothing.

He reached his car with no idea what could have had him so spooked. He stood and looked out at the spiky silhouettes of pines against the blue-black sky. The beach had put him in mind of the

Sebastians, the father and son with whom Cara had taken refuge in the middle of the killing spree leading up to the anniversary of the massacre of her family. They had found her on the beach, not knowing she'd cut the throat of a trucker in a rest stop bathroom just hours before.

His thoughts focused on Jason Sebastian, the five-year-old she had abducted. Or saved, depending on your point of view. He was the most recent witness to anything Cara had done or thought or planned.

Roarke had questioned the boy about Cara's possible whereabouts, but he had to be entirely honest with himself: he had no particular skills for extracting information from a five-year-old. Maybe the boy knew better than Roarke how to say what Roarke wanted to know.

He was restless, wired. It was barely 8:00 p.m., and the Sebastians lived in San Luis Obispo, en route to San Francisco. He could stay where he was and get a hotel and pace the room for the rest of the night. But from San Diego, now that it was after rush hour, the Sebastians were about a five-hour drive up the coast.

He looked out on the softly shifting moonlit pines, then pulled open the driver's door, dropped into the car, and drove.

Chapter 7

He woke in another motel, with a completely different landscape out the window: green rolling hills and twisted oak trees.

The Sebastians owned an olive ranch outside San Luis Obispo in central California, for Roarke's money about the most gorgeous stretch of California in existence. In a state where knockout scenery was the norm, that was saying a lot.

He'd driven five hours the night before, which put him into SLO about half-past midnight. Far too late for a casual drop-in, but he'd phoned Sebastian en route and asked to see Jason the next morning. Sebastian had agreed.

Roarke drove in from the motel as the sun was burning off the coastal mist. The olive ranch was just a few miles inland, a huge spread, rambling over the hills, with the sturdy little trees lined up in rows, not much taller than the grapevines that comprised the area's famous vineyards. Olives were an old crop in California but the gourmet and organic food craze had launched a whole new demand for artisanal olive oil. Roarke suspected that the Sebastians' "ranch" would more aptly be called a multimillion dollar agribusiness, and as he drove up the winding road toward the Sebastian home, he felt a tightness in his chest that he was aware was alpha male competitiveness. He stopped in front of the old Spanish-style ranch house beside a late-model Tundra parked in the drive, and took a deep breath to settle himself before he got out and moved toward the porch. Mark Sebastian stood waiting for him.

Sebastian was in his mid-thirties, dark blond and brown eyes, fit, tan and attractive in the casual way the wealthy and successful in California managed without seeming to spare a thought for it. But a genuine person, Roarke had to admit, a wounded recent divorcé who had succumbed to Cara Lindstrom's unusual charms.

He pushed the front door open for Roarke and Roarke instantly felt the underlying tension. Neither man would ever say it, but it was silently understood that Sebastian responded to Roarke's requests because it kept him connected to Cara, and because Roarke was probably the only human being on the planet who would understand that. She had been Sebastian's lover for three days at most, but her imprint on him would last a long time.

He had been no use in terms of evidence that would lead to her, though. The story she had given him had been completely false, and he had seen only what she wanted him to see.

His son Jason was a force, a quiet tornado of a boy who, like many children of addicts and alcoholics, observed and understood far more about the adult world around him than most boys his age. Young as he was, he seemed to have a better grasp on Cara Lindstrom than his father ever had.

"Special Agent Roarke!" he shouted as he ran into the room and stopped on a dime, two feet in front of Roarke, looking him over. "FBI Special Agent Roarke," he repeated.

"Hello, Jason," Roarke said, and felt a disquieting warmth in his chest at the boy's enthusiasm. Roarke was more than three years divorced himself and wasn't sure that children of his own were in his future, something he never thought anything about . . . except lately, in Jason Sebastian's compelling presence. He sat on a nearby ottoman to put himself at the boy's height.

"I wanted to talk to you some more, is that okay?"

"About Leila," Jason stated. It was the name Cara had given the Sesbastians, undoubtedly one of many aliases, but the only name Jason knew her by.

"Yes. I wondered if . . . " Roarke paused, and surprised himself with his next words. "If you had heard anything from her."

The boy looked at him, clear gray eyes. "Uh huh. She left me a dolphin last night."

Both Roarke and Mark Sebastian were electrified. "What?" "Jason, *what*?" The men overlapped each other. Roarke's throat was suddenly so dry he could barely swallow.

"Dolphin," Jason said impatiently. "She came and left a dolphin."

The men trouped after Jason into his bedroom, a huge room for a five-year-old, with a bed area, a TV and computer area, a play area, a low table for art. Jason stopped and pointed.

There was a stuffed dolphin on the bed, a big plush toy. Like the kind you could get at Sea World, or any number of souvenir shops—if you happened to be in San Diego.

For a moment Roarke was back on the beach, watching leaping flashes of silver against the setting sun.

"It's not his," Mark Sebastian said. "I've never seen it before."

Roarke crouched to the boy. "Did you see Leila?" The name was unfamiliar in his mouth. "Did she talk to you?"

Jason shook his head.

"How do you know the dolphin is from her?"

Jason shrugged. "It was outside," he said. "On the swing." Irrefutable logic.

"And how do you know it's from her?" Roarke repeated.

"Because it is," Jason said.

"Jesus Christ," Sebastian said under his breath. "She was here."

She's alive, Roarke thought. *She's alive.*

The two men strode out of the house, off the back porch. Roarke saw it immediately, a twisted tree that looked as if it had been there forever. A sturdy rope swing hung from a thick horizontal branch.

"Right there," Jason said, importantly, now caught up in the men's excitement. "It was there."

There was no fence around this part of the property. The house was set on the rolling hills and the wilderness came right up to the house. Roarke scanned the hills, searching between the gnarled olive trees, as if he would be able to see her.

"She's following me," he told Sebastian. "She must have followed me up from San Diego."

And while he'd been sleeping two miles away in a motel, she'd been right here.

Sebastian looked alarmed, and conflicted, parental protectiveness wrestling with something less definable in his face.

"You said she wouldn't come after Jason," he said.

No, you said that, Roarke thought, but didn't argue the point. "I don't think she's come after Jason. She left him a stuffed toy."

"Why?"

Roarke thought of the dolphins, the joyous arcs against the swells of waves. They had put him in mind of Jason, himself.

"Maybe she was just thinking of him."

And then something else occurred to him.

She wanted me to know she's out there. She followed me here last night and knew where I'd be going in the morning and she put the dolphin here so I would know she'd been here.

Was that really true? Or some wild speculation of his own?

But the dolphin couldn't be coincidence. And he had felt something on the bluffs. He'd felt—not alone.

Oh, yeah. That's scientific proof, all right.

He was jolted from his thoughts by Sebastian's agitated voice. The father was staring at him tensely. "Agent Roarke, I need to know if my son is safe. Any input you have on the subject would be appreciated."

Roarke stifled a flash of irritation, kept his voice even. "I don't think that she's after Jason. But I would take all precautions until . . ."

"Until you catch her?" Sebastian said, and Roarke's breath stilled. "Is that going to be soon?"

Roarke didn't know how to answer that.

He went through several variations of questions with Jason, but the boy was adamant that he had not received any other gifts or messages from Cara until the dolphin appeared.

"If you hear from her, or see her, you'll let your dad know right away, right, sport?"

"Uh huh," Jason said, but wasn't looking at Roarke. Roarke didn't know if that meant he was bored or upset or lying. He crouched again to look Jason in the eyes.

"Did Leila ever tell you about special places that she has? Places she likes to go? Or a place she said she would take you, sometime?"

"She likes the sky and the wind and the sand," Jason said. "And storms, she likes storms."

"She likes the outdoors," Roarke said.

"Uh huh."

"But was there any place she showed you on a map, or a place with a name?"

Jason frowned and shrugged. "She likes the beach. And the mountains. And butterflies."

That narrows it all down.

"Okay, Jason. You just keep talking to your dad, okay?" Roarke glanced at Sebastian, and the father nodded.

Then Roarke's eyes fell on the stuffed toy, and something tugged at his mind.

"Did you and Leila ever talk about dolphins?"

Jason considered this, shook his head. "No."

"Did you ever see a dolphin when you were with her? In the ocean, or in a store?"

"Uh uh."

"So . . . why do you think she left you a dolphin?"

Jason shrugged. "Dolphins are awesome."

Roarke stood, and felt a rush of certainty. *No, the dolphin isn't some special message to Jason. It's a message to me.*

Chapter 8

The team looked up simultaneously from the long table to see Roarke walk into the conference room. He hadn't called in from the road to tell them where he was, but after leaving the Sebastian ranch, he'd driven straight back up to the city.

"Boss. Weren't expecting you," Epps said. "Any luck?"

"In a weird way." The weirdest way possible. The trip he'd taken that seemed only to yield clues on a twenty-five-year-old case that wasn't his to investigate had resulted in not a trail to Cara, but to Cara herself.

Epps was staring at him. "You found Lindstrom?"

"She found me," Roarke said.

He filled them in about the dolphin toy. Even as he was recounting it he knew that it sounded absurd, no kind of proof at all. Jones was looking perplexed. "Because of a stuffed dolphin? I don't get why you think it was her."

"It was her," Epps said. "Of course it was her." He looked at Roarke. "She's alive. And she's after you."

"I wouldn't say she's *after* me," Roarke said.

"What would you say?" the other agent demanded.

Roarke found he didn't have any immediate answer, so he just shook his head. "I don't know. I honestly don't."

They all sat in silence. Roarke looked at the white board, at the police sketch he knew so well by now. Sunglasses, turtleneck, those fine, carved features.

"This is how we catch her," Epps said suddenly, with a tension Roarke recognized as excitement, and for a moment he had no idea what Epps was talking about. "We tail you and wait for her to show."

Roarke felt a sudden sinking in the pit of his stomach. "That's if she isn't three states away by now," he said.

Epps looked at him strangely. "She isn't."

He was right, of course. Roarke didn't know what Cara was doing following him, but he knew if that's what she was doing, she wasn't about to stop.

"What does she want?" Singh asked. Concern was grave in her voice. "Are you in danger?"

"I don't think so," Roarke said automatically. Cara could have killed him any number of times already. He said it aloud. "If she wanted to kill me, I'd be dead."

The fact was they had no evidence that she had ever killed anyone who wasn't dangerous or just plain evil. And she didn't seem to care much about self-defense, either, although he didn't want to think about what might happen in a law enforcement standoff, either to her or to law enforcement.

So what *did* she want? And how long had she been watching him? And then the obvious hit him.

"Blythe," he told them. "It had to be in Blythe. She followed me from there."

She must have picked up his trail when he'd gone back to her old home, the site of the massacre of her family. It made the most sense that she had been drawn back there, just as he had, but with a much stronger pull.

Epps was speaking. "So we stake out your place, we put a team on you everywhere you go. And you should be wearing a vest at all times."

"She's not going to shoot me," Roarke said, stiff with annoyance, and a tension that went deeper than that.

Epps looked at him stonily. "All due respect, you have no fucking clue what she's going to do. No one does."

He was right. Not that Roarke had any say in the matter, ultimately. Since he was suddenly the center of the investigation, it was on Epps to dictate the terms. Epps briefed Reynolds and pulled two other agents from another team in to rotate shifts with them. Roarke felt relegated to the sidelines as Epps conferred with the backup. He finally went for coffee to avoid looking useless.

When he came back to the conference room, Epps had the game plan. "So we start with you going home, in plain sight. No point in you staying in the building. She's not going to come after you here."

Roarke barely refrained from answering back about her "coming after him."

"We don't know she knows where I live," he said, but that was just contrariness, and Epps didn't even bother responding. No one in the room had any doubt that Cara Lindstrom could find out where he lived.

Epps continued as if he hadn't spoken. "We stake out the house today and tonight, see if we can just pick her up watching you. Let's remember that she uses wigs, sunglasses, to change her appearance."

And costumes, Roarke thought. He knew now she had gone with Mark and Jason Sebastian to a Halloween festival dressed in a Cat-woman costume. Under the circumstances, a perfect disguise.

Epps indicated the case board, the sketch of Cara. "But she's also distinctive, there's a focus about her that stands out. She won't be invisible. And she covers her neck, so always be on the lookout for a high collar, a turtleneck."

Yes, the turtleneck. Was she aware now of how that had given her away? Would she find some other way of covering her scar now? Or was it a moot point? It was fall, going on winter. Thousands, tens of thousands of women in San Francisco would be wearing scarves.

Epps had taken complete charge. "Singh, get word to the single room occupancies, and the sketch of her—"

Roarke spoke up automatically. "She won't use an SRO."

Everyone looked at him.

"She used an SRO last time she was in the city," he reminded them. "She won't do it again."

"How would she even know we knew that?" Epps asked, exasperated.

Roarke shook his head. "Doesn't matter if she knows it or not. She won't do the same thing again."

Epps' face was tight. "Maybe. Contact them anyway," he said to Singh.

When he was finally allowed to leave, Roarke exited the building in what felt like a painfully ostentatious way, walking with his carry-on suitcase on the sidewalk to the underground BART station, stopping in to a café to buy coffee, picking up a newspaper at a newsstand. Jones was tailing him and Epps was already headed over to Roarke's neighborhood to plant himself in a stakeout.

Roarke couldn't fault the plan, he knew it made sense. It still was a new and disturbing feeling that Cara was following him. He wondered if she knew that they'd be watching for her, if she'd anticipate that and take precautions not to be caught.

Despite himself, he spent the short train ride edgy and scanning the car and platforms for her, as if setting a trap for her would automatically manifest her. He exited the train at Twenty-Fourth Street/Mission and rode the escalator up to the plaza, where he walked through clouds of marijuana smoke strong enough to bring on a contact high. Twenty-Fourth Street was not quite the junkie central that

Sixteenth and Mission was, but the BART station plaza could sometimes give Sixteenth a run for its money. Pimps and dealers scattered like roaches as they saw Roarke coming. They could spot a lawman from two blocks away.

A block up from Mission the neighborhood abruptly changed, from taquerias and seedy bars to boutiques and specialty shops hawking overpriced artisanal food. Noe Valley had become so gentrified it had acquired the nickname "Stroller Valley," but being San Francisco, it was still light years more eccentric than most non-San Francisco neighborhoods, which suited Roarke just fine. He walked past flower stands and fresh-churned ice cream shops, and found himself fixating on every glimpse of blond hair he passed.

His own street was on one of Noe Valley's ubiquitous hills, lined with Victorian duplexes and triplexes. He let himself in through the porch gate and climbed the stairs to his top half of the building.

In the entry hall he dumped his roller bag in the closet and shrugged off his coat and suit coat, then turned to the side table in the entry hall to strip off his shoulder holster and service weapon, as much a nightly ritual for an agent as loosening and removing his tie.

He walked into the living room, and the emptiness of the apartment surrounded him. His life had been halved by his divorce, more than three years ago now, and that half-life was still reflected in the unfinished décor: minimal furniture, bare spots on the walls where framed prints had been.

Automatically he stepped to the window to survey the street below. Only mid-afternoon, but the sky was shading, the city lights intensifying on the hills. No sign of any agents out there, of course. Epps hadn't even told him where they were going to be holed up, and he didn't want to know. It would be too easy to give the game away by indicating the lookout points with his body language.

He turned back into the room and the emptiness of the apartment surrounded him, instantly oppressive. He wasn't used to being at home with nothing to do, and the idea set him on edge.

But he could work the case. The Reaper case.

He fished in a pocket and pulled out his phone to call Snyder, who had semi-retired to the wilderness outside Portland. Roarke had worked under Snyder during his years in the Bureau's Behavioral Analysis Unit, the division of the FBI responsible for profiling the most violent of killers. While his old mentor was not officially on the payroll, Roarke had been briefing him on Cara Lindstrom every step of the way. Luckily for Roarke's state of mind, Snyder was answering his phone.

"Did you have a successful trip?" Snyder asked without preamble, and there was no mistaking the quick interest in his voice. For a profiler, a female serial killer was too rare and fascinating a subject to ignore.

"She's alive. She's been following me," Roarke said into the phone, as he walked the softly gleaming hardwood floors of the living room.

There was electricity in the silence. He could picture Snyder: lean, craggy, ascetic, his eyes faraway, processing. "Of course," Snyder said softly.

"Of course?" Roarke said, his voice grating. "Really? Nice of you to let me know."

"I'll send you my bill for twenty-twenty hindsight," Snyder said dryly. "Did she approach you? Contact you?"

"Not exactly."

Roarke explained about the dolphins at Torrey Pines, the feeling of being watched, the stuffed dolphin that had been left for Jason Sebastian. He found himself vindicated when Snyder murmured:

"Undoubtedly from Cara. Undoubtedly a message to you."

"Maybe you can tell me what she wants, then."

Snyder took his time answering. "I can't, but I can observe that she brought you into her fantasy once, in that attack on the trafficking gang out in the desert. Arguably that was a success: you killed in tandem with her, a significant number of the men were eradicated, and she escaped, apparently without mortal injury."

Roarke had stopped pacing. He was completely fixated on Snyder's first sentence.

"She wants to bring me into her fantasy," he said.

There was a pause on the other end of the line. "You know repeat killers are driven by a very personalized fantasy."

"So she wants me to kill with her?" Roarke felt cold all over, a feeling of complete unreality.

"That I can't be sure of. And who knows how she sees it, inside her own delusion? I'm merely pointing out that she deliberately brought you into her planned massacre of that gang in the desert, and the practical result. And . . ." Roarke sensed a caution in Snyder's next words, "It was most likely a bonding moment."

You have no idea, Roarke thought grimly. Although there wasn't much that Snyder hadn't seen, and who knew what he might have speculated about that night at the cement plant? But Roarke volunteered nothing.

"She's a solitary," he said slowly. "As far as we know she's always been completely on her own."

He could hear the shrug in Snyder's voice. "But we know violent female killers far more often kill in tandem with a male partner than on their own. The impulse may be there. It's something to bear in mind." Roarke couldn't even begin to process it. After a moment, Snyder prodded, "In the meantime, what's the plan?"

"I'm bait," Roarke said. "There's a team watching me, seeing if she'll show herself."

"Yes," Snyder said, and Roarke could feel him nodding. "Sensible."

"I'm glad you feel good about it."

There was a slight pause. "I'm sure this must be very conflicting."

Oh, no, Roarke thought. *You're not getting anywhere near the inside of my head tonight.*

"More like annoying," he said aloud. "I'm stuck in for the night and I don't for a second expect her to show. But I'll be able to catch up on my paperwork tonight."

He felt a tension in the silence, and wondered if Snyder would probe him, but instead the older man said, "Nonetheless, be on your guard. There's really no way of predicting what she might do."

No, there isn't, Roarke thought. "I'll keep you posted."

As he hung up, he felt a little shaky, even though he suspected he'd been let off easy. He wondered how much Snyder had guessed. He wondered if he even knew himself what he felt.

He stood to dismiss the thought. Despite himself, he stepped to one of the bay windows in the front room and stood in the dark, looking out on the street as if he would see her. And as soon as he realized that was what he was looking for, he turned away.

He briefly considered ordering food, but didn't feel like coordinating a delivery with the watching agents, who would undoubtedly make it more of a production than Roarke was up for. There was always a stack of pizzas and Trader Joe's meals in his freezer, fine to get him through the evening. He wandered into the kitchen and chose a marsala to stick in the microwave.

As he stood waiting for it to heat, he realized he'd been so quick to get off the phone he'd forgotten to tell Snyder about the dead rabbit that had been left on the Lindstroms' porch.

But there was something he could occupy himself with that night. He felt a thrill of illicit excitement. The cold case was nothing like official business, but the Reaper case had been under his skin ever since he was nine years old. If this was his chance to lay that mystery to rest—

The microwave beeped shrilly, startling him. He pulled out the tray, dumped the steaming spicy chicken and rice on a plate and carried it out to the dining table he only ever used for work, to eat and think back over the case.

The Reaper had mysteriously vanished after the killing of the Lindstrom family, although the entire state of California and the bordering states had remained in a panic for more than a year after the killings. For years any violent incident involving a family had set the public into a tailspin. But the Reaper and his particular brand of madness had never been seen again.

Many law enforcement officials had speculated that the killer was dead. A suicide, possibly, or an accident. Nine-year-old Matt Roarke had even wondered, with a child's magical thinking, if perhaps Cara, the sole survivor, had vanquished the monster in some unfathomable way.

But Roarke the adult agent knew that serial killers rarely ended up suicides. They enjoyed what they did far too much. It was much more likely that the Reaper had been arrested for some less spectacular crime that had never been connected to the three family massacres, and had been quietly rotting away in prison ever since.

The thought made Roarke grab for a legal pad and scribble a list for Singh, starting with checking California prison records for 1987 arrests. He would have to brainstorm factors to narrow down the extreme list of arrestees that was likely to generate, but it was a start.

He could get Snyder to do a profile, unofficially, for characteristics to plug in: age range, likely crimes to have been committed . . .

And then a thought struck him so hard he felt himself vibrate with the insight.

Cara had *seen* him.

What she had seen, and described at the time, her five-year-old brain had interpreted as a monster. But she was an adult now, delusional maybe, but unquestionably intelligent. Her memories of the night might be accessed with the proper regression techniques.

With what she knew, they could come up with more than a profile: they could have an actual description.

If they could catch her, first. *And take her alive*, his mind added uneasily, something he didn't want to think too much about.

Even then, would she cooperate? He thought she would.

Snyder had talked about Cara's possible motivation to team up. *Pulling you into her fantasy*, he had said. The thought made Roarke queasy again. But what could be more likely to draw her than a hunt for the killer of her family, the monster that had haunted her for most of her conscious life?

Roarke stood abruptly from his chair, the cold and sinking feeling intruding again. If he himself wasn't the perfect lure to draw her out, a hunt for the Reaper surely would be. In fact, even without an actual trail to follow, if they put out the idea that they were on the hunt for the Reaper, it would pull Cara to them like a magnet.

He paced, feeling the tension of adrenaline in his jaw and nerves.

Leak word that another family has been killed in the same way.

How could she resist?

He could close both cases at once.

He stepped to the window again and stared out into the lengthening shadows. It was brilliant, the clear way to proceed.

And he hated himself for it.

Chapter 9

S he walks the meandering trails of the dreamy fantasy that is Golden Gate Park, with its towering eucalyptus trees and windblown cypress, past the rowboats and pedal boats drifting on the lakes and canals winding between botanical gardens and museums. She is drawn to it, this city, always; she feels more comfortable and anonymous in its wildly unconventional setting than she does in most towns.

She has dumped the trafficker's truck in a questionable area, leaving the doors unlocked and the keys in the ignition. It will be gone in no time, and there is no need for a vehicle in this place, with its excellent public transportation and draconian parking enforcement. She is better rid of it.

The bus she had boarded some blocks away took her through the city, and when the doors opened in front of the park, she disembarked, and now she wanders past the Victorian Conservatory of exotic flowers, the Temple of Music, the Japanese Tea Garden. The footpaths are sparsely traveled, but it is still an unaccustomed density of people to have around her, especially after her weeks alone in the desert.

As the afternoon shadows creep from between the trees, she knows she must consider accommodations.

SROs are good, single room occupancy flophouses—but she'd used one last time she was in the city and she never does the same thing twice. Unpredictability is her key to keeping invisible. She has been leaning instead toward a youth hostel. They are cheap, anonymous places with such a high turnover that she never has to be concerned about being remembered.

But something is pulling her toward the Haight, the legendary hippie mecca of Haight Ashbury, adjacent to the park.

She walks out of the park onto Haight Street, passing a mega record store and a free clinic with a sprawling street mural painted on its front wall, and cruises the proudly run-down streets past boutiques, used clothing stores, head shops, restaurants ranging from hole-in-the-wall dives to world cuisine, and the wall paintings of mythic and mystic symbols. Clouds of marijuana smoke drift from every other passerby.

The street is layered, era upon era, but the power of the sixties dominates all else. There are so many people, so many young people, drawn by the vortex, the power spot that it was and still is. Even though it is fading, she still feels the power.

She thinks about Roarke as she walks. He doesn't live far from his work at the Federal Building. She guesses that he wears a pretty familiar trail between his Victorian in the area San Franciscans call Noe Valley and the Civic Center, downtown.

He is being watched, staked out, by the other agent, the beautiful African one she now knows as Epps, and some other younger one. Undoubtedly because of her.

Roarke knows from the dolphin that she is alive and watching him. She had seen it in the way he stared out over the hills of the olive ranch as he stood with Mark and Jason Sebastian.

The father and the boy had been the path for a time. Now it is done. A new path has begun.

She stops in to one of the ubiquitous thrift stores to pick up some props. Hippie clothes are as much a uniform as ever in this hood. She can pass for far younger than she is, and for an extra level of concealment it isn't hard to look European: a battered backpack, an Aéropostale sweater, a little makeup to simulate world-traveler grime and jet lag circles under her eyes. There are so many young people here, and it is a good disguise for her; Roarke has only seen her in the edgy designer wear of a city professional. A teenager is not what he will be looking for.

She exits the store in her new persona, just another of the multitudes of waifs in this city, this neighborhood.

Ragged people sprawl on the sidewalks, panhandling and playing guitars and sometimes drawing elaborate murals on the concrete with rainbow chalks. Hippie ghosts flit at street corners, but meth has taken its toll; the homeless are rarely beatific, more usually ravaged and desperate.

The actual numbers of homeless have skyrocketed since the recession. She has seen it on her travels. It was getting better for a while; now it is far worse. And so many of them are kids. She looks at the ragged packs of young people and she knows it is not by accident that she has made her way here.

She stops on the corner of Haight and Ashbury, looking up at a stopped clock atop one of the buildings, forever fixed at 4:20.

She turns toward the next street . . . and sees a For Rent sign. The street address is 420.

She shoulders her bag and walks toward it.

The manager of 420 is a going-on-elderly Indian man with hazy eyes who has not the slightest interest in her; he is off on some distant plane of his own and will never be able to describe her even if he ever feels a desire to. He shows her the one-room plus kitchenette and bath in the crumbling Victorian, furnished with a bed, a bureau, a love seat, a folding table, and one chair. She can see the stopped clock on the corner of Haight and Ashbury from the recessed window.

Even better, in the hall just outside the room there is a side fire escape down to the street, in good working order, and another staircase up to the roof. Three accessible exits.

She hands the manager cash and he hands her a room key. Done.

Alone in the room, she puts her few items in the battered bureau, then stands in the middle of the floor, luxuriating in the sense of history in the room. There is a window seat in the rounded window, and she drifts to it and sits, looking out the curved glass of the windows at the perfect view of the street, so like a circus from this vantage.

Enormous sculpted plaster legs in fishnets and red high heels protrude from the upper windows of a sex toy shop. Outside a health food store bins of colorful organic fruits and vegetables line the sidewalk. Musicians play on street corners. Skate punks cruise past shopping hipsters.

She sits and rests and watches, like a cat in the windowsill. And when it is dark, she curls up there and sleeps.

Chapter 10

As so often lately, Roarke woke and had to lie still a moment until he could remember where he was. The fog drifting in the pre-dawn outside his window was the clue. His own bed this time . . . alone, as he has been for too long now. And no messages, which meant Cara still walked free.

He checked in with his surveillance, then after he'd showered and dressed, the back-up shift of agents who had replaced Epps and Jones at 1:00 a.m. tailed him to work along his usual route: walking the deserted sidewalks to the BART stop, riding the train to Civic Center, striding through the plaza, past sleeping homeless and pigeons to the Federal Building. There were no blitz attacks by crazed female serial killers and Roarke felt a little ridiculous. It seemed glaringly evident what they were doing, the most clumsy and predictable of stings.

Then again, no one was seriously expecting Cara to attack him. All they had to do was catch her following, or watching.

But privately Roarke was sure she wasn't going to come near . . . unless there was something more to draw her. It was time for a new plan.

• • • • •

Dawn is a curious shade of gray; the fog drifting outside the windows above her is so thick it is nearly impossible to tell the time of day.

She re-dresses in faded jeans and a thick pullover with a high neck, and goes downstairs, silent steps on the worn carpet of the stairs, out into the mist. The shops are closed, metal gates pulled over windows, and there are huddled bundles of people sleeping in every third door-way, some alone, some in clusters; some sheltered by cardboard struc-tures, some cocooned in sleeping bags, amorphous, sexless lumps. She passes a group of three outside a record store, one curled in fetal posi-tion around a skateboard, another with one shoeless foot sticking out of a blanket, an empty bag of chips between them. Further down the street someone has chained his bicycle to a parking meter and draped a tarp over it to make himself a tent. Pigeons strut at the curb beside him, feeding on what is left of his meal. The sheer number of camping homeless is startling, as is the apparent tolerance for their makeshift accommodations: a patrol car cruises by without even slowing to take notice.

She stops and watches the taillights disappear into the mist, and knows that something will happen today. She is not done after all.

In the division offices, Roarke's team assembled in the conference room over scones and coffee in black cups emblazoned with the FBI seal, and Roarke listened to reports of—nothing. There had been no sign of Cara the night before. In a rebellious part of his mind he exulted in the idea that she would not fall for such an obvious set-up.

At the end of Jones' report, Roarke stood. "I'm not going to sit around in my apartment day after day waiting for her to *maybe* show up. Nights, okay, stake me out." He looked around the table at his agents. "My bet, though? She's not going to show."

There was an edge in Epps' voice. "Got something else in mind?"

Roarke looked back across the table. "Yeah, I do. I'm going to look into the original Reaper case. I have some new potential information to start with—"

"What does that have to do with catching Cara Lindstrom?" Epps was saying, before Roarke had even finished.

Roarke kept his voice even. "You don't think that would draw her? An investigation into the man who killed her family?"

Epps was silent.

"I see," Singh said, and Roarke was encouraged by the thoughtful tone of her voice.

"What's this new information?" Epps demanded.

"When I talked to Randall Trent and Erin McNally, they both mentioned the same thing."

"The rabbit," Singh said, and the men turned to her. "It wasn't in the police reports."

Roarke nodded to her. Epps looked from Singh to Roarke. Roarke let Singh tell it.

"According to Trent and Erin, Cara's mother found a disemboweled jackrabbit on the porch of the house about a week before the massacre."

Roarke continued. "Gillian Lindstrom told her sister-in-law Joan Trent about the rabbit, but Trent and Erin aren't sure that Joan ever told the cops."

"They are correct," Singh affirmed. "I've searched through every police report. There is not one mention of the rabbit."

Roarke felt that rush again. *It is a new clue, then. After all these years.* He was already on his feet. "It stands to reason Joan could have forgotten the detail in the aftermath of the massacres. And that's part of a signature that might get us closer to a potential suspect."

He could feel the quickening interest of his team. They were alert, leaning forward at the table. He felt the same excitement building himself.

"The Reaper completely disappeared after the Lindstrom murders. No similar murders ever turned up. There was never a trail. So either he's dead, or he got himself arrested for something else entirely. What I propose is that we take the original BSU profile of the Reaper, get Snyder to look at it and add or subtract details, and start combing the prison databases for someone of that description who was arrested and sent up in 1987 or 1988."

Jones looked skeptical. "But chances are this guy is dead, right? Realistically."

"But *she* doesn't know that," Epps said. "If it looks like we're looking for him, she'll follow." He looked at Roarke. "Right?"

Roarke had to breathe through a spike of adrenaline. "I think."

"Two birds with one stone," Epps said. Roarke's exact thought.

Jones frowned. "How do we make her think that's what we're doing?"

It was a good question, one that had kept Roarke up most of the night. "Tactically we have to get this investigation out into the open. She's not going to infiltrate the building. I need to be out and about, doing things that she can observe and put together what we're doing. What we *want* her to think we're doing."

"Or just do a press release that we're reopening this investigation," Jones said.

"No," Roarke and Epps said simultaneously, and looked at each other.

"We can't," Roarke explained to Jones. "It would cause a panic. We don't need the public thinking that the Reaper is out there and active again." Jones was too young to have any idea what it had been like to live under that shadowy threat.

The agents sat back in their chairs and thought it over.

"Get Snyder to come and meet with you somewhere in public to hand off the profile," Epps mused aloud.

Roarke considered it. It made sense. Cara had researched Roarke from their one encounter; he knew she was perfectly capable of figuring out who Snyder was. "But why would she think we were meeting about the Reaper? The logical assumption would be it's about *her*. We need to do something Reaper-specific."

All the agents were silent again, thinking.

Roarke spoke first. "Arcata. That's the site of the first family massacre." A trip there, to the police department and the house where the Granger family was slain, might convince Cara they were re-investigating the Reaper. "She followed me to San Diego—probably from Blythe, and I never saw her. We know she's comfortable on the road. How long a drive is it to Arcata? Or Bishop, the site of the second massacre?"

Singh's fingers were already flying on the keyboard of her tablet, searching. "Five hours to Arcata, six and a half to Bishop."

Roarke moved, impatiently. It was easy to forget how big California was. Cara might well follow them, but that was a long trip for their purposes, one that might lead nowhere. He spoke reluctantly. "It's a possibility, but a long trip for a long shot. There might be a better way. I'm going to get Snyder's input."

Epps stood as well. "Go out of the building to do it, then. Go have breakfast, let Jones tail you. We stick to the first plan until we figure this the hell out."

Though he felt foolish and conspicuous doing it, Roarke left the building and walked through the fog, over to a taqueria on McAllister that had a wicked breakfast burrito. He was uncomfortably aware of Jones on his tail.

Inside the warm, mural-painted hole in the wall he ordered his *comida* to go, and then walked back out toward the plaza, through denizens of Market Street doing their business: spare-changing, hugging each other to slip various substances into pockets. The green smell of pot wafted through the air.

On the plaza he found a bench in between the rows of bare mulberry trees and unwrapped his burrito. Homeless drifted in front of him like dream figures in the fog, some lost and silent, some talking very actively to themselves and whoever else would listen. There were multitudes of them on San Francisco's streets, drawn by the excellent services the city provided its most downtrodden: soup kitchens, shelters, free clinics. Since the recession, the population seemed to have doubled.

Roarke fixed on one ragged man who had stopped still on the pavement and was gently rocking on his heels, apparently listening to some inner voice.

As the Reaper might be doing right now.

Roarke found himself thinking back to a question that had plagued him ever since a psych residency after college: What made some of those voices turn people self-destructive, while others made the afflicted one torture and kill?

He pulled out his phone to call Snyder.

Snyder picked up his phone immediately, and Roarke didn't bother with pleasantries.

"I need a profile. Unofficially and yesterday." There were advantages to having a killer so unique that he could make that request to one of the best profilers in the field and know he'd comply.

"For Cara Lindstrom?" Snyder didn't sound angry, but puzzled. He'd already profiled Cara, or rather forced Roarke to do his own profile and then agreed with it. Once a teacher, always a teacher.

"For the Reaper," Roarke told him.

"Ah," Snyder said. "Interesting."

"And don't tell me to do it myself, this time."

Snyder laughed, a rare sound. "Matthew, I know your relationship to this case. I know you've had a profile in your head for years, decades, probably."

It was true. At nine years old, Roarke had dreamed a monster killing those families. As a Behavioral Analysis trainee, one of the first things he'd done was to profile the Reaper.

"Haven't you?" Snyder prodded.

"Of course," Roarke admitted grudgingly.

"So?"

"All right." Roarke glanced around him at the oddly populated square and hunched on the bench, lowering his voice. "The frenzied-ness of the attacks indicates a highly disorganized killer, almost certainly psychotic." He paused for a moment, studying the examples right in front of him in the plaza. One of the transients was now crouched on the pavement, tracing an intricate invisible pattern on the asphalt with his finger.

"I would say a likely paranoid schizophrenic: he has a fantasy of violent murder based on a delusion. The closest prototype I know of is Richard Trenton Chase." Chase had shot and killed six people in the Sacramento area within the span of a month in late 1977 and 1978. Despite the relatively low body count he was one of the most notorious of serial killers, dubbed "The Vampire Killer," "The Vampire of Sacramento," and "The Dracula Killer," for his gruesome signature behavior of drinking his victims' blood and cannibalizing their remains.

Roarke could feel Snyder nodding agreement at the end of the line. "Chase is the most likely model, I agree. What specifics of Chase's background and signature are you thinking of?"

Roarke had spent several hours last night refreshing his memory on the details. "Most obviously, in childhood he exhibited signs of the Macdonald triad." In law enforcement this syndrome was also known as the "sociopathy triad": pyromania, bedwetting, and cruelty to animals. Almost a given with a serial killer. "As a teenager he was already a chronic alcoholic and substance abuser, primarily marijuana and LSD. He began to demonstrate paranoid and psychotic symptoms in his early twenties that had a very specific theme: a threat to his heart or his blood. He often complained that his heart had stopped beating, or that someone had stolen his pulmonary artery. He was involuntarily committed to a mental institution at the age of twenty-five after being caught injecting rabbit's blood into his veins. He believed he needed the blood to prevent his heart from shrinking."

"In the institution he continued to kill birds and drink their blood, and confessed to fantasies of killing animals, but his condition improved with a treatment of antipsychotics, and in 1976 he was released to the custody of his mother, who according to him had abused him as a child. She decided he didn't need the medication and 'weaned' him off it. He was caught the next year in a field, naked and covered with what was determined to be cow's blood, but was never charged with any crime. His killing spree began shortly afterward."

Roarke paused for breath and Snyder prompted him. "So extrapolating from Chase to the Reaper?"

Roarke looked out over the plaza and the ragged denizens of the street.

"Our killer would have been young—early to late twenties, with an unkempt appearance and most likely living with a parent or other relative or recently out of such a situation. He would have demonstrated psychotic symptoms, a history of substance abuse, and antisocial behavior. He's sexually dysfunctional; the piquerism is his substitute for the sex act."

Roarke concentrated harder as he got down to the finer details. "He has a delusion that is satisfied or quieted by the violent slaying of families, specifically. These weren't random crimes, he chose these families, and a certain kind of family: Middle- to upper-middle-class, educated parents, several children of pre-teen to teen age, and living in smallish communities rather than cities."

He didn't even attempt to guess at what that delusion might be. He knew at the heart of it there was nothing poetic or metaphorical about it. The core motivation for all serial killers was the same: they got sexual release from rape, torture, pain, and murder. There was no other "why." Trying to wrap it up in some elaborate psychological package was less than useless.

Aloud he continued, "Also it's notable that the massacres all occurred in California towns quite some distance from each other, four or five hundred miles away."

"And fairly equidistant," Snyder pointed out.

"That's true. That could get us somewhere." Roarke considered it. It was called geographical profiling, an investigative methodology that analyzed the locations of a series of crimes to determine where the perpetrator was most likely to reside. While geographical analysis had always figured into criminal investigation to some extent, the formalized method known as geographical profiling had not been developed until two years after the Lindstrom massacre and would not have been used in compiling a profile. Roarke felt a warm rush of significance as he realized that.

Snyder was thinking aloud. "A key principle in the geographical profiling model is that offenders will generally travel only limited distances to commit crimes. Put this together with the Reaper's very disordered mind and it's a conundrum, these distances. To have a hunting zone of the entire state of California, the Reaper must have traveled quite a lot, regularly, for some reason."

Roarke picked up the thought, with building excitement. "So we should concentrate on professions like truck driving that would take him to these particular locations, give him a familiarity with them. A truck route with regular stops in all three towns."

"And that would have allowed his path to cross with all three of the families."

A possibility . . . though as he thought it through, Roarke wasn't sure he believed that someone as disordered as the Reaper would be to hold down even a truck-driving job.

As if hearing his thoughts, Snyder spoke. "Remember that the Reaper had a significant cooling off period. These weren't sprees. He went for six months at least between killings. That speaks to some level of control."

It made sense, although Roarke didn't like to think it. A psychotic killer with that degree of control . . . a nightmare combination.

"And usually you don't see a killer traveling this kind of distance until he's built up a history of successful kills. As confidence increases, the hunting zone will expand."

Roarke spoke aloud. "On the other hand, if the killer is psychotic, or thinks he has some special power or protection, that could also instill confidence, yes?"

"Quite right," Snyder agreed. "Another thing interests me here. This specific M.O., the massacres of entire families, is very unusual. Generally a family massacre involves an adult, most often the father, killing his own family and then himself."

Roarke considered this, and sensed the glimmering of an idea. "We were thinking in our group meeting that we could road trip to Arcata, hoping she would follow us and extrapolate from our stops that we were re-opening the Reaper case. But what if we found something closer to home?"

"*Found* something?" Snyder asked with a hint of wariness.

Roarke felt a superstitious chill even speaking it aloud. "Another massacre to investigate. Something recent. A family murder–suicide like you're talking about."

From the silence on Snyder's end, he knew his old mentor was feeling the same unease.

"I see," Snyder said slowly. "A family massacre that you would investigate as a new Reaper killing. Yes, I think so. I think that might exactly do the trick."

Chapter 11

The Haight Street eateries begin to open about the same time that she realizes she is hungry. She finds herself drawn to an Asian fusion restaurant, painted olive green with an enormous pink lotus flower design, and a whole wall of glass looking out on the street.

Inside the scents are delicate and layered, but the food she cares nothing about. It is the window that draws her.

She lets the tiny Asian hostess lead her to a perfect table beside the wall, and she sits and loses herself for some time, watching the parade of humanity through the glass, waiting for whatever the window has to offer.

It is not long. Striding up the street, wobbling on too-high heels, comes a girl with blazing eyes, a feral intensity, a brash sexual confidence. Wild blond hair, huge gray eyes like rain. A beauty, despite the meth sores on her face and neck. And no more than sixteen, she is sure of it.

Despite the November chill, the girl is dressed in a miniskirt and boots, and an open-collar sweater that falls off her thin and shapely shoulders, exposing an elaborate fairy tale of a tattoo on her back: a girl dancing in flames, trees and vines blooming with fiery flowers, a whole mythology inked into her flesh. The art scrolls up onto her neck, disappearing under her hair, a dangerous and illegal process requiring weeks, months, of pain.

She is high, horribly high, moving back and forth across the street and talking loudly to every man and boy who passes, bumming cigarettes, spare-changing.

Behind the window, Cara can see the mixed lust and revulsion on their faces.

She is jostled from her thoughts as the birdlike Asian woman serves her, and she uses chopsticks on a delicate concoction of glazed sugar peas and shrimp and watches the girl outside the window, waiting.

It doesn't take long, either, until the pimp shows up, pale flesh over bone, with pirate boots and long shaggy black hair, a steampunk panderer. He puts an arm around the girl, pulls her out of the street and levers her down to sit on the curb with him, speaking into her hair and stroking her back. The drugs burn through his eyes and skin and Cara sees the entire scenario: the seduction and the beatings, the promises of a house together after "just a few more months" of tricks, the five other girls he is telling the same thing to while making hundreds of thousands a year off their bodies, turning them out, these girls, to be used by pedophiles night after night.

The pimp stands and takes the burning girl by the hand, tugging, coaxing her up; then ordering, slapping her, pointing a finger. No more words. She will comply.

He swaggers off down the street, leaving her.

As Cara watches, the girl suddenly looks straight at her through the window, sees her gaze, her attention, as if the glass isn't there at all. And in a manic flurry, she strides toward the restaurant, straight in through the door.

The tiny manager at the counter is already running toward the girl to ward her away, but the girl strides straight to Cara's table and snatches a shrimp off her plate with her fingers.

"Do you mind?" she says, locking eyes with Cara with ultimate defiance and pops the shrimp into her mouth, sucking the sauce from it then swallowing, as if she is giving head.

The manager is now shouting into a cell phone, certainly to the police, and the other patrons recoil, horrified, but Cara says quietly, "It's all right," and looks only at the girl.

The blazing girl turns on her heel and strides out as abruptly as she entered.

Cara watches from behind the wide plate glass window as the girl goes back out on the street, and collapses bonelessly onto the curb, her head between her knees.

As the hostess hovers, apologizing, Cara asks for the check and a takeout box.

Outside on the street, she walks up behind the girl, who is motionless, slumped over on the curb, passed out, asleep, or possibly dead. But as Cara steps behind her, the girl jerks her head up and looks at her.

Cara looks down at her, then stoops and sets the box of food on the curb beside her.

They lock eyes, and Cara sees herself as if in a mirror.

Then she turns and walks down the street.

It does not take her long to find him again; those boots and that long black dreadlocked hair stand out even among the denizens of this strip. The pimp walks slowly ahead of her on the sidewalk, intent in conversation with a man of forty or so in jeans and denim jacket and cowboy boots, whose personal hygiene leaves much to be desired. She can feel the stench of him from six yards behind. The man nods greedily and reaches into his pocket as he walks, then slips something into the pimp's pocket beside him. The pimp puts a friendly arm over his shoulder, steers him into an alleyway.

She moves closer, sees their shadows darting obscenely on the bricks of the building.

The pimp comes out of the alley on his own a few moments later, strolling loose hipped down the street.

She watches him get halfway down the block, then moves quickly into the alley. The narrow passageway is empty, but there are Dumpsters near the end.

She walks deliberately toward the trash bins.

On the other side of a bin, the man in cowboy boots stands against the wall. A young girl, dark and plump, is on her knees in front of him, unbuckling the enormous buckle on his leather belt.

The girl freezes as she hears the step behind her. The man looks up, startled.

"I've got this," Cara says aloud to the girl, and when the girl hesitates, she jerks her head to the side, dismissing her.

The girl scrambles to her feet and scurries obediently away, down the alley toward the street.

The john is staring at her open-mouthed, trying to process what has just gone on. "The fuck is this—" he starts, but she is stepping forward, her hands reaching for his belt, skillful fingers pulling the tongue loose from the buckle, unzipping his pants. Already his face has gone mindless and slack in anticipation. She works his pants down, encasing his knees . . .

He never sees it coming as she brings her hands up and slams both her fists against the sides of his neck. He staggers in pain, hobbled by his own trousers. She catches him by the hair and smashes his face into the brick wall, once, twice . . . She feels the warm blood on her hands, hears the crunch as his nose breaks and his mouth crushes to pulp. There is one muffled gag of pain, but the third slam knocks him out.

She lets him drop and steps back, her breath coming ragged as she stares down at him, crumpled and bare-assed, blood streaming from his face.

Her hand reaches for the razor in her pocket. But she cannot, must not. It is too much of a risk.

She stares down at him, and takes a deep, centering breath.

Not dead, not this time.

But not likely to follow any teenage girls down alleys in the foreseeable future.

She turns and walks, past the Dumpsters, toward the street. The work has just begun.

Chapter 12

Returning to the office, Roarke nearly collided with Jones while walking in through the door of the conference room. He absently snapped, "Taking that tail too literally, Jones." Then he felt a surge of curiosity and turned back on the agent. "Did you—"

"No sign of her," said the younger agent.

Roarke felt disappointment, and also inevitability. So she'd followed him on the road, but not in the city?

Knowing what he did about Cara, he thought it entirely possible that the city was intolerable to her. On the other hand, it would be child's play to lose yourself in this densely packed city, especially for someone so expert in disappearing. So she was here, but staying back?

And doing what in the meantime?

It was an uneasy thought.

He took the seat at the head of the table, then instantly stood up again, as usual too edgy to sit. "We can't expect Lindstrom to come to us without a reason. So we're going to give her a reason. We're going to find a case that we can use to make it look like we're investigating another Reaper killing. A case that will make it seem as if the killer of her family has reemerged."

There was a stunned silence in the room. Then Jones and Epps overlapped each other. "How the hell are we going to do that?" "*Fake* a case, you mean?"

"We look for a family massacre," Roarke told them, and again felt a superstitious chill just saying it. He ignored it and pressed on. "A murder-suicide. Preferably in California, but any bordering state would work. If we mobilize to investigate, she's going to think it's because we think it's the Reaper."

Jones wasn't buying it at all. "That seems like a hell of a stretch."

"It's not," Roarke said flatly. "We know she's watching. She'll interpret it exactly as we want her to." He turned to their researcher, and as always when looking at her directly was briefly startled by her exotic beauty. Then he spoke. "Singh, you need to find us a crime. A home invasion where the family is killed, or a murder-suicide—a parent killing a whole family."

Singh looked momentarily startled herself . . . and then Roarke could see her begin to process the why of it. He continued.

"The bloodier the better, or if you can't find something that fits, something close to it, with few details released to the public. We'll let her imagine what exactly happened." He felt like a prick saying it, but it was the plan, it was the way. He looked over the room. Epps was no longer protesting. His eyes were distant, imagining the scenario. And Roarke knew he was not wrong.

He focused back on Singh. "How long do you need to hunt this down?"

"It should not take long to find a recent incident of this nature, if there is one to be found," she answered in her musical voice. "Perhaps a half-hour break, and reconvene?"

"Go. See what you can come up with."

"Yes, chief." She rose instantly and moved for the door.

Roarke looked at Epps and Jones. "Once Singh finds us a case, we'll put on a show so Lindstrom knows where we're going. And she'll follow."

As he turned to leave, he couldn't help seeing his agents' faces, their looks of unease. He didn't blame them. They were in the Twilight Zone now, no question.

He retreated to his office to think, and stood at the window, staring down through the glass at the hills of the city. She was there, somewhere. Waiting.

He sensed a presence behind him, knew from the height and bulk and sheer power of that presence that it was Epps. Roarke turned, speaking before he even saw Epps in the door. "Am I crazy? You think she'll buy this?"

Epps stepped into the room, not too far. There was still a distance between them, and Roarke was sorry for that. "Buy it or not, she'll follow. It's about you. Whatever you do, she'll follow you."

"Sure," Roarke laughed shortly.

"Positive," Epps said. The two men looked at each other.

"It's about you," Epps repeated, and suddenly the air between them was thick. "You sure you're up for this, boss?" he said softly.

Roarke wanted to answer, he owed Epps an answer. The man had been waiting long enough.

And then he felt a cold, vast place open inside him. He had the urge to say no, no, not only was he not up for it, he had no idea what they were getting themselves into. He wanted to abandon the whole thing, before something horrific and inevitable came down on them.

But at that moment Jones stuck his head in through the open door.

"Singh's got something," he said.

Roarke was used to thinking of Singh as a lake of depthless calm, but as the men joined her in the conference room she was practically bubbly.

"This is clearly a perfect plan, as I have found a perfect case as our stalking horse," she enthused. "I started with California. I am astonished by how many there are to choose from," she said, suddenly transitioning to gravity. "This family massacre, or mass murder–suicide, or familicide, is a very prevalent occurrence in the U.S. Approximately ninety-five cases per year take place in the state of California alone: nearly two per week, almost always the father killing first his family, then himself. In my country of origin only the wife will be killed."

Roarke felt a twinge at her words, the matter-of-fact, grotesque reality of them. He suddenly wondered what Cara and Singh might have to say to each other, if ever they should meet. He saw Epps glance at him as if he might be thinking something similar.

Singh continued. "The latest such crime in this state was a mere sixteen hours ago, in Fresno County. The father shot and killed his wife and three children, then turned the gun on himself. There was another three days ago in Antelope Valley: the bodies of an entire family, father, mother, three children, found burned in a car on the highway. Cause of death, gunshot wounds; the father's was self-inflicted. And therein is the problem. The vast majority, ninety-two percent of these family slayings, are by gun, which is not useful for our purposes."

Roarke realized she was right. The Reaper's signature, his particular turn-on, was the invasion of flesh, slashing and stabbing.

Singh opened a file folder and removed a set of faxed photos, which she passed across the table to Roarke. "However, there was an instance two weeks ago in Nevada which could have been designed for us. A father stabbed his wife and three children to death and then cut his own throat. The crime was bloody, it was violent, it occurred in the family home, and it occurred just a few miles over the border, on the outskirts of Reno, practically in California."

Roarke looked down . . . at shots of hell. A woman lying prone on a bed in blood-soaked sheets, a man slumped in a desk chair with dark blood splashed on the walls behind him, and the unbearable images of children, half in, half off their beds, slain in their bedrooms.

He passed the photos to Epps, suppressing a shudder of revulsion even as he thought, *She's right on. It's perfect.* And the thought was a wave of cold.

It was even within the geographical range of the Reaper's massacres: two hundred fifty miles from Bishop, three hundred thirty miles from Arcata.

And a four-hour drive from San Francisco.

"So it's a road trip," Epps said. His face was taut as he passed the photos to Jones.

The younger agent also flinched as he shuffled through the images of carnage. But when he looked up, his face was composed—and skeptical. "How are we going to be sure she picks up on the trail? Send an email? Take out an ad?"

Roarke knew where Jones was coming from. It did seem completely implausible. And yet he knew it wasn't. "I'm going to have to put on a show," he said. "I'll park my car on the street outside the house and take a couple of trips down to pack up."

"Pop the hood, check the oil and water," Epps suggested. "Eyeball the tires."

"Leave a map of Reno on the passenger seat," Roarke added.

He was highly aware of the flaws in the plan. It assumed that Cara would be there watching him every moment, which was unlikely, and if she were watching like that it also suggested they should simply continue to stake out his apartment and catch her that way.

But then, nothing about Cara was simple.

He looked at Epps. "She knows you, and you're easy to spot. You come over, we pack the car. Transfer your things into my car, or vice-versa. We give her all the chances we can to get a look at what we're doing."

"I don't know," Jones said.

Roarke didn't know how to explain it. "She figured out how to track me to San Diego. I never once saw her tailing me. If she's around, she'll follow."

"And if she doesn't?"

"If she doesn't follow, it means she's not tailing me, and we can drop this stakeout charade," Roarke snapped. "It's just an overnight trip. No huge loss."

"All right, when?" Epps asked.

"Right now. This afternoon. Before traffic." If they waited until rush hour, traffic would add three hours to the trip, easily. "We have a few hours to put on a show to get her interested, and then we get on the road."

He turned to Singh. "We need to set up an interview with the local detectives and get all case files. Schedule a walk-through of the house, preferably this evening. We should be able to get there by seven. We play it as if we're really investigating and we need to take a look at the case files and the crime scene."

Then he addressed the men. "We take separate cars. Two separate cars. Epps and me in one, and Jones, you need to be shadowing us in some tourist car. If we get lucky, we might catch her out on the road."

Roarke was back at his building by one-thirty, where he illegally parked the black Crown Vic from the office fleet right in front of the house by using his Official FBI Business placard. From there the agents followed the script. Upstairs in his flat he put on a light for extra visibility and stayed near his front windows as he packed and pretended to speak on the phone. Then he took his roller bag down to stow it in the car trunk.

He went back upstairs, waited a bit longer, and went down to the car again, this time with a duffel bag that he'd stuffed with a coat. He stayed at the car, made another fake phone call, checked the oil and fluids, did a slow walk around looking at the tires, feeling like a bit of an ass.

Is this just ridiculous? he wondered. *Is there any chance in hell she's watching?*

And yet he could not shake the feeling that Reno was the next right move.

He was prowling his flat looking for anything to load into the car to keep up the whole charade, when his phone buzzed. He punched on to talk to Epps, who told him, "I'm pulling up right now. You can come down and meet me and be visible."

Roarke grabbed a small cooler from the kitchen, and as an afterthought threw in some bottled cappuccinos and ice, then went downstairs.

Epps had parked half a block down. He carried a large duffel and a binder. He stopped on the sidewalk in front of the car while Roarke opened the trunk for him to put his bag in. He added the cooler to the back seat as well, saying under his breath, "I was running out of ways to hang out at the car."

Epps closed the trunk lid and extended the notebook to Roarke. "Take a look at this. We can stand here and talk about that for a minute."

Roarke took it with a frown and opened the binder, resting it on the roof of the car. It was full of scans and copies of case reports. "A little light reading for the road," Epps said. "Singh put it together. She's been on the horn to Reno PD, talking them out of everything they have on the murder–suicide. Looks all official, don't it?"

Roarke flipped through a few pages. Singh had done her usual stellar work; it looked like everything he would ever want to know about the Leland family massacre.

"What exactly are we telling Reno PD, anyway?" Epps was asking. "This is an open-and-shut case of murder–suicide. We don't want them freaking out that they got it wrong."

Roarke had been thinking it through himself. "Singh told them we're doing a Bureau study on family massacres. Warning signs, that kind of thing. Maybe once we're there we'll give them the truth. We'll have to play it by ear."

He glanced up the street. "I think we've put on all the stage play we can afford to. She's either watching or she isn't. Come on upstairs to give it one more shot and then we'll hit the road."

• • • • •

Leaving San Francisco was always laced with a touch of the mystic: crossing under the soaring arches of the Bay Bridge, speeding past the silver-gleaming bay with its central island of Alcatraz, dominated by the brooding, fortresslike former prison.

Off the bridge the route was two hundred twenty straight miles on I-80 to the California/Nevada border. Through the flats of Sacramento, the tourist town of Auburn, and up into the Tahoe National Forest, passing to the north of Lake Tahoe itself, and then Reno was just across the state border. Roarke had driven the route a million times on ski trips with his family, fighting with his older brother in the back seat.

Roarke loved his adopted city. But as always he felt a huge release of tension once they were out and on the open road. At the same time, he was realizing he had overlooked the huge flaw in his plan. He would be in a car alone with Epps for four hours, and that meant they would have to talk. To stave off the inevitable, he instantly buried himself in the case file.

The case was already closed, as Epps had said, an open-and-shut case. It was completely apparent to Reno PD and the coroner's office what had transpired. Professor Leland had stabbed his way through his family members, and when everyone else was dead he sat at the desk in his study and cut his own throat.

It had been shortly after two-thirty in the morning and the family had been asleep. Leland had first slain his wife in their bed using a kitchen knife, then walked out into the hall to the children's rooms and fatally slashed all the boys in order of their bedrooms. There was blood on his bedroom slippers from where he'd walked through, and his footprints in the blood.

The similarities to the Reaper case were startling from the first moment, almost unnerving. Roarke spoke aloud to Epps as he read, and the flatlands sped by outside the window.

"It's the exact family type the Reaper chose. Middle-class, educated parents, several young children, none older than mid-teens." It was one of the reasons that at age nine Roarke had been so grimly riveted to the TV reports of the case: the families had been so very much like his own family. One of those fathers had been a college professor, too, like Roarke's father, with two boys, like Roarke and his brother. It had all seemed so disturbingly close.

And now in this unrelated massacre, the father, Leland, was an engineering professor at the University of Nevada, Reno. His wife had worked in the campus housing department. Their children were three boys: thirteen, eleven, and seven.

Epps spoke beside him at the wheel. "And of course, no one saw it coming. He was such a good guy," he said with an ironic tinge.

"Of course."

They heard it all the time. No one ever saw anything coming.

Roarke flipped through the file, reading background. "No history of psychological problems, no extraordinary financial stresses, stable employment, bills up to date, some savings in the bank." He frowned. "Doesn't make a lot of sense, actually."

Epps glanced at him. "We don't have to investigate it."

"Right." Roarke had forgotten for a moment that the case was just a cover, a ruse to draw Cara.

He looked out the window, brooding on it as he watched the road. When he was a kid the drive from San Francisco to Sacramento had been almost all fields. Now it was an occasional field in between a seemingly endless stretch of strip malls, car dealerships, fast food stops, and office park developments. In another ten years it would probably be all strip malls. It was very, very flat. If Cara wanted to follow them, it wouldn't be hard to do it on this stretch. He wondered again if the plan was just crazy. But somehow he didn't think it was.

He laid the notebook Singh had made up for him open on his lap and removed the inner file of photocopied crime scene photos. He immediately felt an electric buzz at the back of his neck.

Singh had added to the initial photographs the team had looked over. What he was looking at now was more than a simple stabbing. The family had been butchered. Not merely killed, but slashed in a frenzy.

There was blood everywhere: soaking the clothing and skin of Mrs. Leland and the three children, soaking the carpet, sprayed on the wall.

And there were neck cuts.

"Jesus," he said, and didn't realize he'd spoken until Epps looked at him. Roarke tore his eyes away from the photos. "This looks just like them. The family massacres. The Reaper's."

Epps glanced at him, puzzled. "That's good, right? It backs up our story."

I didn't expect something this close, Roarke thought. *Not anywhere near this close.*

He stared out the windshield. The approach in to Sacramento (*Sack o' Tomatoes*, Roarke and his brother had called it as kids) took them over miles of wetlands. There had been some unaccustomed rain, several straight days of it the week before, and the water was so high on the flatland it looked as if they were driving on a freeway over a lake.

He picked up the file again. He had only intended to get familiar with basic details of the case. Now he started from the beginning, page one, and read every word.

When he finally looked up, they were into the Sierra Nevada foot-hills, and there was much more to look at, with increasing forested areas and granite outcroppings. Cold but clear. He'd been careful to check the weather before they left; it was still just mid-November but the Sierras were nothing to fool around with even in a light snowstorm.

Signs beside the road informed them they were passing through Auburn, a historic Gold Rush town with meticulously preserved original buildings. After Auburn the territory became increasingly rural.

"80 is a major truck route," Roarke mused aloud as he stared out the window.

Epps glanced at him. "Yeah."

"And a major ski vacation roadway," Roarke continued.

"Right . . ." Epps said, a question in his voice.

"I'm just thinking. This geographic element. Between four and six hours driving distance between kills. This is someone who's on the road a lot. He has a comfort level with it. Bishop is a major ski resort gateway, with hiking and boating in the summer. Blythe is en route to major desert resorts, including Palm Springs. And Reno: another ski resort, summer resort highway . . ."

Epps glanced at him from the wheel. "Only Reno has nothing to do with the others."

Roarke had forgotten again. "Right."

And he had to admit that Arcata, the site of the first massacre in 1987, didn't exactly qualify as a resort town.

He stared down at the file with the nagging feeling he was missing something incredibly significant about the massacre, something right there in front of him . . .

But just then Epps turned off the road, pulling in to a rest stop. As he cruised past the trees to park in front of the restroom area, Roarke was uncomfortably reminded of one of Cara's most recent slayings: a trucker with a history of sexual assault who appeared to have been on the verge of attacking her in the women's restroom of a rest stop. She had sliced his throat with two deep, irrevocable cuts and left the bathroom looking like an abattoir.

Roarke was certain that Epps had chosen the rest stop rather than a convenience store to make a silent but deliberate point.

Or he was being ridiculously paranoid. *I know she's dangerous*, he thought. *I don't need my nose rubbed in it.*

He got out of the car and used the men's room, avoiding looking at his ghost reflection in the cloudy metal mirror, then went back outside to buy a candy bar and Cheetos at the vending machines. *What's a road trip without junk food?*

He walked over to a picnic table, surveying the landscaped grounds. There was no sign of Jones at the stop, but Roarke knew that he'd be nearby.

Epps joined him at the table. Roarke offered him the bag of orangey cheese twists and Epps recoiled. "That's not food."

"I never said it was." Roarke dipped into the bag with fingers already coated in orange dust.

"Sick," Epps muttered.

They both looked out at the foothills leading up to steep mountains. And then Epps looked back at the rest stop, the restrooms, the women's restroom. Roarke could feel it coming, the question he'd been dreading; it was vibrating in the air between them.

"You didn't cuff her," Epps said softly.

Roarke felt his blood rising. "I thought she was *dying*. She couldn't walk. She could barely breathe. I thought she was dying."

"But you would have cuffed a man. Not two days ago I saw you cuff a *dead* man." Epps looked at him, and his dark eyes looked old.

"She's not a man," Roarke answered tightly.

"I'm sayin. You have a blind spot. You do."

Roarke looked at him full on. "Not anymore."

"Okay," Epps said. His dark and regal face was set, troubled. But Roarke thought he was safe for now.

Chapter 13

Roarke took the wheel for the next part of the drive. The agents got a call from Jones once they were back on the road. "Any sign of her?" Epps asked the younger agent on speaker.

"Nothing."

Roarke was silent. He'd known it, but it was a new wave of unease. "Okay. On to Reno, then," Epps said into the phone, and clicked off.

The Sierras were, of course, spectacular. Streams rushed over the granite cliffs that ran along the freeway. Roarke felt himself breathing deeper as the stunning, crystalline views worked their magic on his frayed nerves. He was also glad there was still some daylight left. It was an unforgiving road at night.

The descent on the east side of the mountain range into the Reno area was steep, and the geography changed radically again. Reno sat in a high desert valley, the Great Basin Desert, at the foot of the Sierra Nevada mountain range. The plants were smaller and there was far less color; vibrant evergreens gave way to muted greenish-grays and browns.

The glitzy, neon-lit arch over Virginia Street, complete with rotating star, proclaimed Reno "The biggest little city in the world." Roarke drove the strip through the much smaller, retro version of Vegas, famous for its casinos and its history as a mecca for quick divorces before the advent of the "no-fault" divorce. The campus of the University of Nevada, Reno, was located north of the city, overlooking Truckee Meadows to one side and the downtown casinos on the other. Mountain ranges rimmed the valley, already dusted with white from the first snowstorm of the year. The temperature was a crisp mid-forties.

The Lelands had lived on the southwest side of campus, an older and established residential neighborhood called Juniper Hills, a collection of 1950's ranchers and older two-stories on spacious half-acre lots near the Truckee River. Roarke got a distinctly rural feel as they motored past horse properties, which gave him a frisson of déjà vu. *So much like the Lindstrom house. So many parallels, here.*

The house was a big older two-story with a wide front porch. There were a total of nine Robbery-Homicide detectives on Reno's two hundred eighty-eight officer force, and the two who had closed the case were waiting outside. Detective Lundgren was a long-boned, hawk-faced man with pale hair and eyes who looked like the product of Scandinavian ancestors who'd been in the valley forever. Beside him was Detective Samson, whose longish, shining black hair and ruddy skin clued Roarke in to some Native American blood. Lundgren was instantly on the defensive; Samson was silent, impossible to read.

Reno averaged nine homicides a year, and almost all of those were homicides committed during the course of a robbery. The Leland family had constituted more than half that total in a single night, and robbery had had nothing to do with anything.

As the four men met on the sidewalk, Epps began, "We appreciate you gentlemen coming out—"

Detective Lundgren interrupted, going straight to the key question. "How exactly is this case supposed to be connected to one of yours?"

In the moment, Roarke decided to go with the "We're doing a Federal study on familicide" story. "Triggers, indicators," he elaborated. "Economic factors."

"It was trouble in the marriage," Lundgren said immediately. "They separated back in the summer."

The silent detective, Samson, finally spoke. "But they were back together. The sister said they were working it out."

"*Leland's* sister said they were working it out," Lundgren said, and shot a baleful look at his partner that was not lost on Roarke. "There was money stuff, too. Wife lost her job in the recession. They were struggling like everyone else."

That's not the story in their bank accounts, Roarke thought, but didn't say. "But Leland had no previous history of violence?" he asked.

"None," the Native American said implacably.

"That we know of," Lundgren shot back.

Roarke and Epps exchanged a glance. The tension between the two detectives was palpable. The agents weren't actually there to investigate the Leland massacre, but it was looking more and more as if there was something to investigate.

"Would you take us through?" Roarke asked.

Of course there was nothing like blood on the walls; the crime-scene cleaners had done their work. The house was still furnished; no relative had yet cleared away the personal belongings. But the space had the hollow feeling of a tragedy.

Somewhere outside there was the monotonous thud of a basketball on concrete, some lone player practicing free throws. A suburban sound carrying a ghostly resonance.

Roarke stood for a moment, recalling the floor plan: living room, dining room, kitchen, utility room, and study downstairs; master bedroom and two bedrooms upstairs for the three boys: thirteen, eleven, and seven. The details of the household were familiar to him: stuffed bookcases and masculine, well-used furniture. Another wall of books was visible through the study door, and the corner of a heavy desk. An academic house, much like his own childhood home.

He moved first toward the stairs, wanting it in order. He felt less and less comfortable with every step into the rustic, fifties-style house, as he pictured the brutal scene from the crime scene photos.

The whole feel of the place was familiar. *Like the Lindstroms' house. So like the Lindstroms.*

The family had been asleep, except for Leland. He had been dressed for bed in pajama bottoms and a T-shirt but his side of the bed in the master bedroom had not been slept in and a neighbor had reported a light on in his study late into the night. Some time around two-thirty in the morning he had walked upstairs carrying a carving knife, and stabbed his wife to death while she lay sleeping.

"So this all took place starting at about two-thirty in the morning," Roarke said aloud to the detectives as they climbed the staircase.

This time Samson answered first. "A neighbor thought she heard something that may have been a cry at just before three. She was barely awake. It was windy, and she didn't hear anything further, so she fell back asleep."

"And he killed his wife, first," Roarke said, not a question. He stepped into the master bedroom.

Like Cara's mother, Gillian Lindstrom, Trish Leland had never made it out of bed. The blankets and mattress had been soaked with her blood.

Roarke stared at the bed frame, imagining the dark spreading stains. Then he backed his way out of the room and walked down the hall to the kids' rooms. Pieces of carpet had been cut up from various areas, taken as evidence.

"And then he started on the kids."

Lundgren answered tensely. "S'right."

Roarke stopped in the doorway of the younger boys' room to look in. The carpet was gone but the bedclothes and personal belongings remained: comforters printed with sports insignia, shelves lined with video game boxes and models of cars and space aliens, a desk with a computer, hockey sticks and face masks piled in a box.

At some point during the initial attack the two younger boys must have been awakened, very likely by their mother's cries. Evidence showed the two boys had taken refuge in their closet. The killer had dragged them out and killed first eleven-year-old Paul and then seven-year-old Baxter. Both were slashed and stabbed but apparently dispatched quickly. Thirteen-year-old Seth was last. Leland had stabbed him over two dozen times.

Roarke moved down the hall to the last room. Here the bed was stripped; Leland had sat on Seth's bed for perhaps some time and the photos had shown smears of blood on the bedspread. Roarke stood in the room, pondering this detail, which felt like it needed attention.

And then Leland had walked downstairs, back down to the study, where he sat in his chair and cut his own throat. A neighbor boy had found him there the next morning in a pool of his own blood, when the boy had come over to walk with Seth to school. The weapon was on the floor beside the father's body, his fingerprints on it. There had been no note.

And it all bothered Roarke in a way he couldn't even begin to express.

That kind of frenzy? The man's whole family? Then he goes downstairs and opens his own throat?

He could feel the Reno detectives hovering in the hall outside the door. "The knife was from the kitchen?" he asked aloud.

"From the knife block," Lundgren answered.

"Did Leland own a gun?"

"Excuse me?"

Roarke turned and looked Lundgren in the face. "A gun. Did Professor Leland own a gun?"

"I don't know, Agent Roarke." The detective's tone was murderous.

Epps gave Roarke a mild look that for Epps was the equivalent of a four-alarm fire. Roarke pressed on. "You found the blood of every family member on him, correct? On his bedroom slippers, his pajama bottoms, T-shirt, knife, hands? Was all the blood typed and identified?"

Lundgren seemed to relax somewhat at the question. He answered with confidence. "The crime lab found two types of blood on him: O positive and A negative. The oldest and the middle boy had the same blood type as Leland. Mrs. Leland was A neg."

"And the youngest boy?

"O neg."

"So there was no evidence of the youngest boy's blood on him?"

"The crime lab didn't find any, no—"

"You didn't do DNA testing?"

The detective bristled. "We have a full-service forensic science division in Washoe County. But we don't get instant results, Agent Roarke. There's a long wait list."

"Of course," Epps said. "Cutbacks all over the country." He did not actually shoot a warning glance at Roarke but he might just as well have. Roarke felt a twinge of guilt. He knew budget cuts had been devastating for local law enforcement agencies. Labs were closing all over the country and the backlog on lab results, especially more complex ones like DNA analysis, was appalling.

Epps' attempt to smooth Lundgren's feathers had failed. The detective stepped back and looked from one agent to another.

"The man had a history of stressors and his prints were on the knife. What are you getting at, Agent Roarke? Are you trying to suggest something else happened here?"

Roarke kept his voice even. "Not trying to suggest anything. Just trying to understand your crime scene."

"What's not to understand?" Lundgren challenged him.

That is the question, isn't it?

The wife dying in bed in her sleep, the killer walking from master bedroom to the kids' rooms. The kids slain in their beds. *Like the Lindstroms. And the Grangers. And the Merrills.*

And there was something else about it, the thing that had been nagging him in the car. His mind was racing over what he'd read of the case in the notebook Singh had prepared. He couldn't quite get to it, but remembered something else.

"The neighbor kid who found them. He walked right in?"

"That's right."

"So the door was open."

"It was unlocked, he said."

"Strange, isn't it?"

Lundgren gave him a thin smile. "This isn't San Francisco, Agent Roarke."

Fair enough, Roarke thought. *But something is wildly off here. Something critical.*

Suddenly the thought that had been eluding him ever since the drive up crashed into him like a freight train. "Full moon," he said.

The two detectives and Epps looked at him.

"That night. Here. Was it a full moon?" He was already pulling out his phone to check a calendar . . . and then it hit him. He didn't have to check. He knew it was a full moon. Because he'd been out under it that very night. Out in the desert. At the concrete plant. With Cara Lindstrom.

"October twenty-ninth," Roarke said, looking at Epps. Epps had been about to speak, no doubt to shut Roarke down. Now he froze, instantly grasping the significance.

Not just a full moon, a blue moon. The Leland family had been killed on the twenty-five-year anniversary of the Lindstrom massacre.

Roarke knew he could not talk about it in front of the Reno detectives. Not until he and Epps had had some time to process it themselves. "We appreciate your time, detectives," he said casually, nodding to the two men, then looked at Epps. "I think we've seen enough."

Epps followed him downstairs, already muttering under his breath. "Boss, this is crazy."

Roarke matched his tone. "I know." His face felt numb, frozen.

"No, I mean, batshit crazy."

"Right. On a scale of one to ten, an eleven this side of crazy. We need to get out of here and talk."

Chapter 14

Outside the house there was a chill in the air and the sky was turning to dusk. As the lawmen walked through the yard toward their respective cars, Roarke saw the basketball player, a gangly, stooped kid of twelve or thirteen in the driveway two doors down. He continued to shoot hoops, but Roarke had the strong sense the game was a ruse. The boy was watching the men.

Epps thanked the detectives effusively but the damage had been done. Lundgren was downright glacial as they said goodbye on the sidewalk.

Roarke and Epps got into the Crown Vic and Epps reached to start the engine.

"What is it we're thinking, here, boss?" he asked tightly, as they sat in the warming car, shadows reaching around them.

"You heard what Singh said about the statistics for familicide." Roarke said in a low voice, though they could not be overheard. "Ninety-two percent are by gun. Ninety-two percent. The Lelands get slashed and stabbed to death in the exact same way the Reaper's victims were killed—and on the twenty-fifth anniversary of the

Lindstrom massacre. Full moon—no, *blue* moon . . . twenty-fifth anniversary."

"You think Leland was the Reaper?" Epps said incredulously.

Roarke hadn't even considered that and he had to summon his swirling thoughts. "No. Not that."

The two Reno detectives were still standing on the sidewalk, looking at the agents in the car. "Drive," Roarke said softly. "They're waiting for us to leave."

He tipped a salute through the window as they passed the detectives' Cavalier. "Drive out a few blocks out then circle back," Roarke said under his breath.

"O-kay," Epps said, and put the car in gear.

"I think that kid shooting hoops is the one who found them," Roarke continued as the car motored down the street. "Neighbor boy, same age as the oldest Leland kid. I want to talk to him."

Roarke could feel the tension seething in Epps, but the agent was silent as he drove the rectangle of the block. Roarke opened Singh's notebook and looked up the witness report. The name of the discovering witness was Stephen Marsden and his address matched the basketball player's.

Epps turned another corner and circled back around to the Lelands' block. The detectives' Cavalier was gone from the curb. The kid was now sitting on the steps of the front porch with the ball. His hair was dirty blond; his cheekbones had the same Scandinavian farm look as Lundgren. He was pale and hollow-eyed, drained of the usual bouncing-off-the-walls energy of the age. But his spine straightened as he saw Roarke and Epps get out of the car again.

Roarke walked up the sidewalk and stopped outside the waist-high gate of the fenced-in yard. "Stephen Marsden?"

"Yeah . . ." the kid said warily, looking from one agent to the other.

"We're with the FBI. I'm Special Agent Roarke and this is Special Agent Epps."

He saw the quick interest in Stephen's eyes. *Kids don't change,* he thought. There was an eternal allure to law enforcement for boys that age.

"Are your parents home, Stephen?" he asked aloud.

"My mom," Stephen said, in a tone that made it sound as if the mother was all there was.

"Will you go in and get her? I'd like to ask her if we can talk to you for a few minutes."

"About the Lelands?" the boy asked, with an ambiguous look.

"That's right," Roarke said, and felt an ache in his throat. "I'm very sorry for your loss."

Stephen shrugged and stood. He went into the house, the custom-carved wooden screen door banging sharply against the frame, like the report of a gun.

Roarke reached over the fence to unlatch the gate. As he and Epps walked up the path toward the porch, a woman in her early thirties with her son's blond hair and cheekbones stepped out onto the porch, dusting flour from her hands onto the apron tied around her waist.

Lundgren was right about one thing. It's not San Francisco.

Stephen trailed after her, pretending not to look at the men.

"We're Federal agents, Ms. Marsden," Roarke said. He climbed the porch stairs and showed his credentials wallet. "We'd like to speak with Stephen for a few minutes."

The woman looked down at the wallet, and then up. "He's just thirteen, you know," she said, but without fight.

"I'm sorry, Ms. Marsden," Roarke said gently. "Believe me, we know what you've been through. We'll be as brief as we can."

She nodded, and made a small gesture to Stephen. "I'll be right inside."

Roarke took a seat on the porch glider and Epps perched his long frame on the sturdy porch railing. Stephen glanced around him and sat awkwardly in a rocking chair.

Porch and footpath lights were going on all over the neighborhood. Roarke looked toward the Leland house, silent and dark.

"I'm sorry you had to find them," he told the boy.

Stephen shrugged again. Roarke couldn't even imagine what it would do to a kid's world view to be thinking his best friend's father flipped out and suddenly killed the entire family. *How do you ever get your sense of safety back?*

He felt a flare of anger for Stephen's lost innocence, but stifled it to keep calm for the boy.

"We need you to tell us a few things. That morning . . . you walked right into the house, right? The door was unlocked?"

Stephen stiffened. "I rang first," he said with a slightly raised voice. "We were gonna be late for school."

"Nothing wrong with that, son," Epps assured him. "You rang, and no one came to the door?"

The boy shook his head. "So I tried the door and it opened and I went in."

"Did you say anything? Call inside first, maybe?" Roarke suggested.

Stephen frowned. "Maybe. Yeah, I think so."

Roarke had read the report. The boy had moved through the house in search of his friend and had found the father dead in the study. Bad enough, but at least he'd been spared the sight of his own friend's savaged corpse.

"Did the Lelands usually leave their front door unlocked?"

"I guess, during the day."

"Had you ever found the door unlocked in the morning before?"

Stephen thought for a minute. "Don't think so."

"Did you hear anything strange the night before?"

"Huh uh."

No surprise there. Teenage boys tended to sleep like the dead.

Roarke took a breath. Now came the question he was afraid to ask. Afraid, of what the answer might be—and of what it would mean for all sense of reality.

"Did Seth talk about anything weird that had happened the week that—they died?"

Epps looked at Roarke sharply and he lifted a hand slightly, begging silence.

"Weird like what?" the boy asked warily.

"Strange phone calls, anyone watching, anything disturbing . . . something maybe left somewhere . . ."

"The cat," Stephen said, and Roarke felt a chill at the back of his neck.

"What cat?" he said, very softly.

"Someone dumped a cat on their porch. With its guts ripped out."

Epps was frozen in his place on the porch rail. Roarke willed himself to stay calm.

"When was this, Stephen?"

The boy frowned, concentrating. "Monday. We had band practice that day. Seth showed it to me in the trashcan. It was all tore up."

There had been nothing in the police report, but there was no reason for the detectives to have known to ask, and the boy wouldn't necessarily have volunteered it.

"Did you tell the police?"

Stephen looked confused. "No. I mean, why?"

"No reason you should have."

"Nobody asked," the boy insisted, and Roarke could hear tears behind his voice.

"You did just fine, Stephen. Nobody knew to ask. I'm glad you knew about it and could tell us now."

His thoughts were racing. Monday was almost a full week before the murders. Same time frame as the eviscerated rabbit deposited on the Lindstroms' porch. It would be gold if they could lock down a day, to have a better idea how long the killer might have been there watching.

Because that's what happened, wasn't it? A killer was there watching.

He suppressed his urgency, kept his voice casual.

"Did you recognize the cat? Did it belong to one of the neighbors?"

The boy thought. "Don't think so."

"Did it have a collar?"

"Huh uh."

"What color was it?"

"Black."

"Black and white, or just black?"

"All I could see was black. And blood."

"Long hair or short hair?"

"Long."

The boy was starting to glaze over, sinking into himself. A dead cat and a dead friend, it was too much. Roarke backed off.

"You've been a huge help. I'm going to give your mom my card. You have her call us if you think of anything, anything at all that seems weird, all right?"

The boy nodded, shyly proud at the responsibility.

"You go back inside now, right?" Roarke told him. Stephen stood obediently, and looked back at the men before he slipped back in through the door.

"Holy motherfucking shit," Epps breathed, as they walked out the front gate, toward the car. "You're really thinking . . ."

"I think we need Lam and Stotlemyre up here. I think the father died first. I think someone killed them all."

Neither said it, but the name resonated in the silence. *The Reaper.*

They drove back toward downtown to find a motel to set up camp. Roarke had been expecting casino kitsch, but the downtown had been developed and revitalized, with a Riverwalk and all kinds of modern glass and concrete structures.

Epps drove, shaking his head as he stared out the windshield. "Not downtown," he said. "She's not going to walk into a big hotel. We need a motel, someplace she would take the chance and come up close to."

It took Roarke a beat to understand what Epps was saying. He'd again forgotten the initial purpose of this trip: to draw Cara out. His head was too filled with the disturbing parallels between the Reaper's massacres and this new case that couldn't possibly be connected to it.

Not possibly.

And yet . . .

His phone vibrated, startling him. He glanced at the screen to see Jones' name. Roarke knew he'd been watching the Leland house from down the block but they hadn't called in to let the agent know what was happening.

"You want to tell me what the hell is going on, there?" Jones demanded.

Roarke shook his head as if Jones could see. "I wish to God I knew. We need to find a motel. Follow us."

On the outskirts of town there was a rustic Old West-style motor lodge with connected cabins, arrangements of farm implements lining the walkways, corral-style fence posts, saddles, a pioneer wagon, even a giant concrete steer.

The sleeping quarters consisted of two rows of connected cabin-like rooms.

Epps checked them in, two cabins next door to each other. Jones could check into one across the way and have a perfect vantage for surveillance.

Roarke was talking, words spilling over before his door was even closed, before Epps could speak.

"Just listen. It's a small town. They almost never see a case like this. The background of trouble in the marriage fits the outside visual of the scene, which is that the father goes crazy, kills the family. Lundgren isn't the sharpest tool in the shed, doesn't bother to look at the statistics for murder–suicide to see that a stabbing M.O. for this kind of assault is almost unheard of. He sees it as a slam-dunk and clears the case. A rush to the obvious conclusion that the killer wants everyone to draw. But statistically, the likelihood of the father flipping out and slashing up his children like this? It isn't how it happens."

He paced. "What really happens is our guy gets into the house, maybe through a window, maybe the front door's actually open like Lundgren said. Maybe there's a hide-a-key, he could have figured that out if he's been watching the place for a week." He made a mental note to check about a hide-a-key. "The whole family's asleep. The killer takes the father out first, then goes upstairs after the mother and the kids. Goes back down to the study, puts Leland's slippers back on him, puts the knife in Leland's hands to get the prints, and lets it fall."

Epps was on his feet, too. "I don't buy it. I don't. Let's get real. What are the chances the Reaper just picks up and starts killing all over again exactly twenty-five years later?"

Roarke was so deep in thought it took him a long time to pull himself back to the present to respond.

"I'm thinking Shawcross. Arthur Shawcross killed twelve prostitutes from 1988 to 1989 in the Rochester area, upstate New York. He was first arrested for rape and murder in 1972 and served fourteen and a half years in prison, after which he was paroled and went straight back to killing. The profilers on the case figured him for fifteen years younger because he was still showing all the emotional characteristics of the age at which he'd been incarcerated, but really he'd just picked up right where he left off."

Epps actually took a few beats to think about it, but shook his head. "Uh uh. Here's what I don't like. What are the chances we start investigating all this just when it starts happening again?"

Roarke had been thinking that, too. Or rather, trying not to think about it. It was worse than coincidence . . . more dangerous, somehow. "I can't explain it. But the anniversary of the Lindstrom massacre is a trigger for Cara Lindstrom. Why wouldn't it be a trigger for the killer?"

Epps held his hands up in protest. "The Reaper massacres were straight-up killings. They weren't staged. No father suicide. It's a huge anomaly."

"But the Reaper would be twenty-five years older now. That's long enough to learn some control. He still needs the frenzy, the release. He needs it to be a knife, needs the cutting, the slashing, the blood. But what if he learned a couple of tricks in prison? He's had a long, long time to plot how to cover his tracks when he finally got out."

Epps looked away. "If anyone had arrested the Reaper they'd have thrown away the key."

Roarke pointed at him. "Exactly. So he had to have been arrested for something else. Something big, twenty-five years worth of big, but nowhere near what he really deserved. Nobody knew they had the Reaper. He was never connected to the massacres."

Now Epps was the one to pace, pressing his big hands against his temples. "Man. And I thought this shit couldn't get any crazier. You are entirely tripping me out right now."

"I know." It was like being dropped through the rabbit hole, all semblance of reality wavering.

Epps finally stopped still and they looked at each other.

"Only one way to find out," Roarke said. "We get Lam and Stotle-myre up here to go over the evidence with the coroner."

Chapter 15

W e've got a problem," Roarke told Singh on the phone.

As he filled her in, her silence was epic, and he thought again that they had slipped into some territory that he wasn't sure he wanted any part of.

He told her to get Lam and Stotlemyre, the division's best crime scene techs, up to Reno, and instruct them to take a cab to the Leland house upon arrival. She would be sending him photos of the Reaper massacres for comparison to the Leland killings.

"And we need to find out who owned that cat," he told her, and gave her Stephen Marsden's description of the animal. "Whoever it was may have seen someone watching *their* house. If we can find out when the cat went missing, we'll know when the killer was here."

"I will start with the animal shelters and lost pet sites," Singh assured him.

Next Roarke pulled Bureau rank with the Reno Chief of Detectives to get access to the Leland house, this time without Detectives Lundgren and Samson.

He had time for a short nap, as they waited for the techs to arrive. Not anywhere near enough before his phone was ringing him awake at quarter past midnight.

The half moon was high as he joined Epps at the car. Jones was nowhere in sight, but Roarke knew he'd be shadowing them, still on the lookout for Cara.

Epps drove through a fast-food franchise for coffees, then they headed to the Leland house to meet Lam and Stotlemyre. They were Roarke's favorite techs of the San Francisco Division's six Evidence Response Teams to work with, one an enormous blond German, the other a reed-thin Vietnamese, joined at the hip. They'd been working together for eons and Roarke suspected they were joined at the hip personally, too, though no one ever asked. It might be the San Francisco FBI, but it was still the FBI.

The four men greeted each other in the Lelands' front hall. No handshaking. No one ever shook hands at a crime scene.

"So tell me—am I crazy?" Roarke asked, not joking.

"Not necessarily," Lam said cheerfully. They all moved into the living room as he explained. "It's not exactly sloppy detective work but it's clear the lead detective had a bias. There's been a rash of family murder-suicides in the last two years and the media has been hitting it hard, domestic violence linked to the recession, that kind of thing."

Stotlemyre nodded assent. "It's an easy enough conclusion to come to. When these cases keep showing up in the news . . ."

"It's infectious," Lam finished beside him. Roarke and Epps exchanged a glance. The extensive news coverage of some high profile crimes like school shootings and workplace massacres almost always seemed to trigger similar crimes across the nation, the intense media attention pushing other potential killers over the edge. Mass murder going viral.

"Except for the statistical improbability of a knife as the murder and suicide weapon," Roarke said.

"Exactly," Lam pointed toward him.

Stotlemyre concurred. "In fact I can only think of two: one in Arizona in 2002, where the father burned down the house after stabbing the family to death, and one back in the Dark Ages, 1970, the Jeffrey Macdonald killings. That turned out to be a staged home invasion, the father trying to make it look like his family had been killed by a Manson family copycat." As he spoke, Lam used the dining room table to spread out crime scene photos, the two techs working together seamlessly as they always did. Now Stotlemyre stepped to the table to look down at the photos. "The Reno forensics techs did a good job with blood location. And the location of blood in each room throughout the house was consistent with the scenario the detectives settled on."

Lam took over. "The crime lab typed the blood, and the murder weapon looks exactly like it should in a murder-suicide scenario. The oldest and the second boy had the same blood type as the father, the youngest and mother had different types, and all three blood types were found on the knife. And the father's prints were on the knife, of course. All very damning, fine, no problem. But given the level of violence, the multiple stabbings, the struggle of the victims, the father realistically should have had all three types of blood somewhere on his clothing and/or skin. The lab found only two types mixed on the father's clothing. The oldest boy's, no surprise: the kid fought him and was really slashed up." Lam put out a photo of the carnage in Seth Leland's bedroom.

Roarke felt a twinge at the tech's words that was not just the sheer horror of the scenario, but an additional prickle of significance. There was something here, something crucial he had to pay attention to. But before he could follow the thought, Lam added, "But we find it odd that nowhere on Leland's person or clothes was there any blood from the youngest child."

Stotlemyre continued. "Since the oldest and middle child's blood type was the same, we were wondering if just possibly there was blood from only one of those two on Leland's clothes. If there was no blood from the youngest or the middle boy on Leland, it would give more weight to your theory of an outside killer," he nodded to Roarke. "So that's the first thing to check. DNA testing can separate various DNA profiles from a mixed blood sample."

The techs exchanged a glance, then Lam spoke for both of them. "We're getting the mixed blood samples from the crime lab and sending them to Quantico to rush the DNA."

"Sounds like a long shot," Epps said.

And a longer wait than we can afford, Roarke thought uneasily. *We're racing the moon, here.*

Stotlemyre shrugged philosophically. "It wouldn't get you a conviction, but if you're trying to establish that the father didn't kill the family, it's a place to start. Meanwhile we'll comb through the rest of the evidence."

"You need to handle everyone on the case with kid gloves," Roarke told them, too aware that he himself hadn't. "Assure them that there's no way they could have seen these things unless they knew to look. We need to get them to cooperate and turn over all potential evidence to us."

As Epps took Lam and Stotlemyre upstairs for a walk-through, Roarke drifted back to the study to picture the scene.

He didn't turn on the light, but stepped to the window to open the slatted wood blind, and then just let his eyes adjust to the ambient light from the streetlights outside.

Leland had been drinking alone in his study, another reason for the Reno detectives to assume marital problems. According to the tox screens his blood alcohol level had been fairly high; it could well be that he'd fallen asleep at the desk. The window blinds had been up that night, an across-the-street neighbor had glimpsed him at the desk as she turned off her own lights on the way to bed. So someone else could have seen him there as well. Someone not so benign.

The Reaper had watched his victims for days; the time frame was more nearly a week, judging by the dead animals left on the porches.

Perhaps in the Reaper's head the animals were a warning, a clue to the families that might have saved them had they been attuned to the signs. Or it was some ritual only known to him.

Roarke stepped to the desk. The office chair of course had been removed; there had been too much blood to clean it. He pulled up a chair that sat against the opposite wall and sat down in front of the desk in Professor Leland's place, looking out the window, staring through the trees and shrubbery in the front yard. He could see the street, and two of the neighbor's houses across it, dark now, with just porch lights on.

Between the two houses there was a gap . . . not a driveway, but what looked like a kind of alley, an unpaved back road winding behind the houses, providing easy access to garages and trash collection.

A perfect observation point for a killer.

He stood and headed for the door.

The hallway connected to the utility room that led to the outside through the side door. He stepped outside quietly without turning on any lights. The chill of the November night hit him and he could see his breath clouding in the air as he looped around the side of the house. There was a side gate as well, opening on to the gravel alley beside the Leland house. Roarke eased it open without knowing exactly why he was being so careful; the stillness of the night seemed to require it.

He couldn't help but be aware of the half moon climbing in the sky above him. *Half moon, half a month . . . no, on the moon cycle, less than that. Just a week now.*

The "road" was packed dirt and lined with wooden shelters that housed the large city trash and recycling containers. The collection truck could run up and down the side roads and pick up the trash on collection day without owners having to trundle the bins out to the street. The back route also provided extra parking for pickup trucks, trailers, and some boats.

He looked across the dark main street to where the access road continued across the street, and started walking that way.

Across the street he stopped on the side road to look back at the Leland house.

He had a perfect view of the open window of Leland's study. Sitting at the desk, Leland would have been completely visible to someone standing where Roarke was standing now.

Wind shivered through the trees above him. He turned back and stared through the night at the trash shelters. Any one of them would be a good hiding place for a watcher; the killer might have left evidence as he stood watching. It had been two weeks, and there had been rain. The chances of evidence remaining were slim, but the alley would have to be processed.

Above the shadows of trees, the half moon glowed. Roarke looked up toward the pale disc . . . and had a sudden, prickly feeling he was being watched. He twisted toward the shadows, and his body froze even as his eyes focused more keenly, searching the darkness . . .

His breath stopped, and he stepped forward . . . a name on his lips. "Cara?"

A scrabbling sound came from behind the fence. Roarke twisted, his pulse skyrocketing as a dog erupted into wild barking in the yard beside him. And then a hand came down on his shoulder, and he jerked around, grabbing for his weapon—

Epps shoved him backward and stared into his face, his anger livid in the darkness. "What the hell are you doing out here on your own? You somehow forget you're *bait*?"

Jones was there a moment later, pounding into the alley at a dead run. "Sorry . . . sorry . . ." he gasped to Epps. "I was on the other side of the house. I didn't expect—"

Epps walked in a circle, glaring at Roarke. "Not your fault, it's his. *Fool.*"

Roarke shook his head, willing his pulse to slow. "I don't think she's here," he said. "I do think the Reaper was."

"What the fuck? Just now?" Epps' voice spiked in incredulity.

"No," Roarke said. But even as he thought it, he heard an engine roar to life, a car taking off somewhere on another street. He took a few automatic steps toward the sound, but halted as the car gunned away in the distance. *No way.* Too late to see who.

But what if . . .

He suppressed the urge to run after it, and turned back to his agents. "I meant that night. And maybe for days before. Get Lam and Stotlemyre. They need to process this alley."

Then despite himself, he strode several paces into the alley, staring out into the dark.

Chapter 16

The trees are tall, towering above her in the quiet grove, as she crouches by the shining pool of water and washes the blood from her hands.

The growing moon is reflected in the water, through the shadows of the pines and cypress, and the soft scents and stillness of the grove surround her. Her heart is still racing, but the chill of the water and the air is reviving, and the hush of this isolated place deeply soothing.

It is done.

On a street perpendicular to Roarke's there is a sandwich shop, two levels: a downstairs, and an upstairs with a perfect view of Roarke's Victorian. Earlier in the day, she had sat upstairs in one of the round, windowed turrets and watched in absorbed detachment as Roarke and Epps drove off to wherever they were going.

She feels no particular pull to follow them. Whatever they are doing is clearly staged, possibly for her benefit, but it impacts her not in the least, and she is still tired, so tired, not fully recovered from the wounds from the desert, the third near-death experience of her life.

So she watches the show they put on in the street, and when their car has gone she drifts back uptown toward her little room in the battered Victorian in the Haight, where she falls into a black and dreamless sleep.

It is the sounds that wake her . . . as the street below her windows starts to come alive with music and hilarity, instruments tuning up, sound checks, guitar riffs and the thump of bass.

She stands and moves to the curved glass of the alcove. Looking down on the street she can see platforms that have appeared as if by magic, constructed at the ends of each block like bookends: band shells and stages. Live indie bands are beginning to play on every block, food carts and craft tables line the sidewalks, the shop doors are open wide. A street fair.

She finds a thick sweater, scarf and hat, and moves downstairs.

As she opens the side door of her building into the alley, the fair hits her like a tidal wave. The music overlaps, reggae, nouveau punk, a Grateful Dead tribute band. The sidewalks pulse with it. Stoned buskers hand out flyers for shows, food carts hawk fragrant dishes from all nations, craft merchants preside over tables of jewelry and art and batik T-shirts and blown glass drug paraphernalia on the sidewalks. The host of sensations is both overwhelming and welcome; it is a happy kind of overload, and she is as anonymous as she can ever hope to be.

She wades into the experience, and when she sees the girl with the flaming, flowering tattoos, she knows. This is inevitable, what is going to happen. It is why she is here.

The girl dances by herself in the crowded street, the tattoos on her back coming alive: a girl writhing in a ring of fire, a tree dropping blossoms of flame.

She watches as the girl twirls in a circle, laughing, shrieking . . . and suddenly she catches sight of Cara and stops her spinning. She smiles, a strange, high smile in the midst of that pounding street music . . . and then she is dancing backward, slipping into the crowd.

When the girl disappears, Cara moves on through the dancers and the vendors. Within a block she sees him, that rock star fall of dark hair, the snakelike sinuousness. The pirate pimp. He is high already; perhaps he is never not, a being on the brink of self-immolation.

He has an entirely different girl in his grasp and is roughly steering her down the sidewalk. This girl has neither the intelligence nor the experience of the girl in flames; this is no more than a child. The baby fat is obvious in her limbs and in her face, in the soft roundness of her stomach, bared to midriff even in the November cold. She is no more than thirteen, fourteen at most.

The pimp has her by the elbow and wrestles her through the crowd. She stumbles along shakily, staggering on her platform heels. She has been used recently.

Cara follows in the crowd, sees him make a sharp turn at a corner.

In the semi-privacy of an alley the pimp wrests cash from the girl, reaching his hand up her skirt and pulling the roll of bills out of her underwear, giving her a hard squeeze that makes her gasp before he withdraws his hand.

He counts the money while still holding her, then sticks it in his pocket and shoves the girl away, pointing her back toward the street. An order for more.

All this Cara watches from the shadows, and begins a slow burn, thinking of the night the girl will have. Thirteen years old, if that.

She turns after the pimp, and walks.

There is nothing easier than following this one through the crowd. He is too stoned to be vigilant and there are so many others on the street; he feels safe, in his element. He strides on the side-walk through the fair, and others on the street move out of his way automatically, not even consciously, with some sixth sense for self-preservation.

She trails him through the carnival-like psychedelia, past the open shops and food stands and revelers. At the bottom of the street they pass the mural on the free clinic, a sprawling painted street scene that mirrors the live scene in front of it.

The pimp crosses the street toward the tall dark shadows of the park. As he turns off the sidewalk onto a footpath, she follows him into the corridors between the trees.

He walks under the towering eucalyptus and cypress of the Panhandle, a narrow strip of park jutting out from the main mass of the park, notorious for drug deals and robberies. She follows silently, her pulse and senses heightened in the night. The path winds deeper into the trees, and there are other figures lurking now, in the shadows, in the bushes, smoking, shooting up, or just making camp for the night. A few of the men look up with quickened interest at the sight of a lone woman, but something they sense in her makes them freeze and turn away. She sees the shadows moving in them, and her spine stiffens, an instant, atavistic reaction, but she will not let herself be distracted.

The pimp walks on past the huddled street people. He is on some mission. The moon makes him easy to follow at a great distance; every time the path splits the moonlight illuminates him, showing her the way. The trail winds through more eucalyptus, with their spicy, healing fragrance, and magnolias with their luminous waxy blossoms, even redwoods: ancient towering trees with the peace of primeval forest.

At the bottom of the hill the vegetation changes, from coastal undergrowth to an unexpected profusion of flowers lining the path: hydrangeas with globes of flowers shining pale in the moonlight; trumpet vine blossoms hanging like bells; feathery Mexican sage.

As she steps out of the undergrowth, a palace rises up in the moonlight: the Victorian hallucination that is the Conservatory of Flowers. It glows like a whitewashed temple, with its painted glass domes and pillars, the palm trees adding to the Taj Mahal illusion.

She must give the pimp scum credit for the romanticism of the setting. If she were setting out to trip this is where she would want to be.

It is a section of park she knows, and she understands exactly where he is going, and why. She has seen it in the daytime, a short tunnel across the wide landscaped lawn from the conservatory, a walkway underneath the road, an arch of granite framed by pampas grass with its feathery plumes. By day it attracts street musicians because of the tourist traffic and the acoustics. At night it is fetid and ominous, used for a far less lofty purpose. Deliveries can be made in seconds; a car stopping on the road, above, a runner sprinting down the path to the tunnel to make an exchange, then the runner heading back up the stairs to the car. Done and done.

The pimp heads straight for it.

She holds back, and when she moves, she circles the periphery of the lawns, moving silently through the taller flowerbeds on the sloped grounds to reach the archway.

The tunnel is short, dark, and cold. It reeks of body fluids and a smell like burning plastic, and any number of other things. The truth is, this procurer will not last long at his current rate of addiction. The question is, how many children will he take down with him?

No more.

She can't see him in the dark, but she can feel him, and hear his breathing. She knows he does not sense her, so intent is he on the task at hand.

Then there is the flare of a lighter, held to a cloudy glass pipe, and he freezes, seeing her illuminated in the arch of the tunnel.

He can't believe that a woman is approaching him like this. For a moment he's amused, intrigued. High, to be sure, but amused and intrigued. His smile is slow, dangerous.

"Want something, bitch?"

She lets her eyes go to the pipe in his hand, so that what he sees in the moment is a junkie, someone not so much older than the girls in his stable, and his addled brain is calculating the possibilities even as she makes her move.

The long hair makes it easy and the drug, even easier. She strides forward and takes him by those locks, exposing his throat. She knows the key veins and arteries by heart; the blade goes exactly where it needs to go.

A flash of gleaming metal and his blood arcs in the tunnel, just another body fluid splashing on the stones. It gushes hot and hard over her hands as he makes astonished, inarticulate noises, desperate and panicked.

One fist twined in his hair, she holds his body against hers as he struggles, but the blood is geysering, pumped by his heart, and it takes mere seconds for him to bleed out.

She releases her grip, lets the body slip heavily to the floor of the tunnel.

Her heart is pounding in her chest, echoing in her ears. She stands in the darkness above the body, feet planted to hold herself up.

Suddenly there is a sound she does not recognize, some small object dropping and rolling. And then she hears harsh, rapid breathing that is not her own.

She turns slowly and in the dim blue light of the moon outside the tunnel, she sees the silhouette. The flaming girl.

The girl doesn't say anything, just stares at her.

Cara starts forward and the girl flinches back.

Cara crouches beside the body, reaches into the pimp's pocket, takes out a roll of cash—what he had stolen from the child earlier, and a lot more, rubber-banded together. She tosses it at the girl, who unfreezes to catch it.

"Get out," she says to the girl, softly.

They look at each other, a long, held look, then the girl scrambles away, out of the darkness of the tunnel, into the light of the moon.

She stands for a frozen second in the tunnel, catching her breath . . . then walks a wide circle around the body, avoiding the blood she has spilled, and slips out into the night.

The forest grove where she takes off her outer layer of clothes and washes herself clean is deep in a ravine of the park, a memorial grove. There is a round stone circle surrounded by a bench into which the names of dead men are carved in a spiral, and a circle of bench set into the earth wall surrounding it. Fading flowers are heaped in the center of the names.

A stream leads to a pool surrounded by rocks also carved with memorials to mourned lovers, and it is in this pool that she washes off the blood, kneeling on a carpet of fragrant pine fronds, with the fattening moon glistening above the redwoods.

The loamy scents calm the nausea, which rises and falls like a roller-coaster. The flaming girl has seen. It is wrong, dangerous . . . there will be a reckoning. But there is nothing to be done for it now. She must leave this peaceful place and get away, get to shelter.

The water is freezing on her skin and clothes as she stands. She sways on her feet, catches herself. Then she breathes in moonlight, and forces herself to move, out through the trees, out of the grove.

It seems miles through the forest, the flowered undergrowth, the homeless encampments, but finally she is out on the street, walking on shaky legs back into the fair that is finally winding down, vendors packing their goods and tables and tents, musicians casing their instruments, wildly drunken revelers stumbling in the street, looking for some continuance to the party.

The packs of children are out again, huddling in doorways, in alleys, their voices high and shrill, mostly high. On every corner, it seems. Abandoned, abused, dancing on the edge.

Too much, too much . . .

She stops, holds herself up on the wall of a closed shop, swallowing back bile. And then there is a hard voice behind her asking, "Miss? Are you all right?"

She twists around to see a beat cop standing on the sidewalk, looking at her suspiciously. Blood has soaked through to the remaining layer of her clothes, and though everything she wears is dark, it will not take long for him to spot it.

She uses all her strength to straighten, keep her voice steady. "Thank you, Officer, it's the baby. I shouldn't be out. I'm going home."

She sees mixed suspicion and discomfort on the cop's face, and with one hand she reaches for the razor in her pocket . . . only to realize it is missing, left in the tunnel or somewhere along the path. Her legs tense as she prepares to flee or fight . . .

Then he nods, dismissing her. "You do that."

She exhales long and slow, and moves down the street toward rest.

Chapter 17

The sound of a basketball thudding on concrete echoes on the quiet suburban street. In the curve of a driveway, a boy is running, dodging, bounding and rebounding, playing a fierce game against himself. He crouches, stills his breath and throws . . . the ball sails through the air to drop perfectly into the hoop, and the boy catches the bounce.

The afternoon shadows lengthen, creeping across the driveway, as he runs and shoots, gangly teenage body focused with effort, dribbling the ball across the concrete, popping the ball up. The shadows broaden, blending in to each other . . .

Then a darkness falls that has nothing to do with the lowering sun, a vast, cold emptiness . . .

That reaches for him—

Roarke jerked awake as if he'd fallen, and lay in the dark in the motel room bed. In his half-sleep, he still heard the faint, monotonous thud of a basketball, and Stephen Marsden's face was in his mind, the hollow-eyed, shell-shocked boy.

The boy.

Thirteen years old. His best friend on the bedroom floor above him, stabbed so many times . . .

The Reaper had watched. Staring at the house, obsessing, fantasizing. But it was not the father he fantasized about. The father was only an impediment, a gatekeeper, to be disposed of as quickly as possible so the real fantasy could begin. And what was that fantasy? Not the mother. An attractive adult woman, Roarke had noted from the photos Singh had collected. But Trish Leland had been dispatched quickly and nearly effortlessly. There had been no lingering over her. She was not the Reaper's target.

Roarke closed his eyes and heard the thudding of a basketball.

He and his brother had played in their own driveway, Matt nine years old, Marty thirteen, the only year he'd ever shown the slightest interest in sports.

And Stephen Marsden and Seth Leland had played together, in full sight of the alley, hadn't they? Lanky, joyous thirteen-year-olds.

Seth's bedroom was at the front of the house, just above the father's study, in plain view of the alley.

And Seth was the one most grievously attacked. Oh, without question, compared to the rest of the family, the assault on Seth had been inconceivable, a frenzied attack like . . .

Roarke thought back, seeing quick, violent flashes of horrible crime scene photos.

Like the one on Cara's brother. Who was also thirteen.

But not just Cara's brother. The Merrill family had also had a thirteen-year-old boy.

Or was that the Grangers?

Or . . .

Roarke vaulted to his feet and switched on a light, grabbed for the case files he'd dumped on the bureau.

Ten minutes later, he looked up from the files and his case notes, with a sickening certainty.

Every single family had had a thirteen-year-old boy.

He had been so focused on five-year-old Cara he hadn't looked at her brother, at the common denominator between the three original Reaper murders. The boys. All three families had thirteen-year-old boys.

It is such a clear common factor he was amazed, angry, that no one had seen it before.

The Reaper was after the boys.

The realization brought a new, immediate terror.

He flipped on the headboard light and paged through a file for a number, then dialed the Lelands' neighbor. A sleepy woman's voice answered and he spoke as calmly as he could manage.

"Mrs. Marsden, it's Agent Roarke. I'm sorry to wake you."

The woman murmured something incomprehensible in his ear.

"Is everything all right, there?" he asked.

Her voice was instantly alert. "What do you mean?"

"I don't want to alarm you, but would you please go check on Stephen?"

She didn't even answer him. He could hear quick movement, then silence, and after a long, long moment, she was back.

"He's in bed, he's sleeping. What's wrong?"

"Mrs. Marsden, do you have other children?"

"Just Stephen."

Roarke's thoughts were racing. The Reaper had always struck families with several children; it was a clear pattern. The Marsdens were probably okay. But probably wasn't good enough.

Mrs. Marsden's voice crept up in pitch. "Agent Roarke, please tell me what this is about."

He took a breath. "I don't want to scare you, but the deaths of the Lelands may be more than they appear to be on the surface. I'm going to send a patrol car over there to watch the house. But is there any chance of you taking Stephen and going out of town somewhere for a few days?"

A long silence on the phone.

"Mrs. Marsden—"

"Yes," she said. "Yes, I'll do it."

Even as he spoke again, making arrangements, he knew.

I can't protect all the boys he's going to come in contact with. Except by catching him. We have to get him.

Chapter 18

When Roarke finally slept, it was on the plane. Exactly forty minutes, but better than nothing.

It was barely seven in the morning when they walked into the office, but Singh was there to meet them in the conference room with steaming fresh coffee and a full breakfast: samosas and mango chutney, pakora, and an assortment of pastries.

The men fell on the food while Singh started a new whiteboard and laid all four cases out: the Grangers, the Merrills, the Lindstroms, the Lelands. At some point Roarke looked up from the feasting and stepped to the board, staring at the clusters of photos of the dead families. He shuffled through the case files and pinned up photos of his own: school photos of the smiling thirteen-year-old boys. Two with real smiles, two with shyly pained grimaces. All four were slim, one wore Harry Potter–style glasses. All just at the brink of life, far too young to die.

He found a marker and circled the photos of the boys in red. "This is what he's after."

Singh had been watching him in silence as he pinned up the photos. Now she spoke. "This is really this—Reaper?" She looked from Roarke to Epps. Epps' jaw tightened; he looked away.

Roarke answered her. "The M.O. is exactly the same. We have to move forward with the possibility that this could be the Reaper."

Singh murmured something that was not English. Roarke didn't have to ask her what she meant. It was unreal.

"What about a copycat?" Epps asked.

It was a fair question, mostly because film and television portrayals had muddied the water on the subject. "There's really no such thing in sexual homicide," Roarke responded. "Men who commit this kind of murder have a very specific fantasy in mind, excruciatingly personal. But I'll have Snyder compare the Leland case with the others." He paused. "And while it's unlikely that the Reaper would kill again so soon, we also have to be aware that the moon will be full again in just over a week: the twenty-sixth."

He could feel the focused stillness of his agents across from him, the collective suspended breath. He gave them a moment to take it in, then hardened his voice.

"Here's what we need to hone in on. The Reaper was killing in California in 1986 and 1987. So almost certainly he lived in state. If he was arrested and imprisoned for something else, some lesser crime that never tied him to the family massacres, chances are he served time in California. And what we're postulating now is that he gets released and goes right back to where he was before, a full-on family massacre. Only he's picked up a few tricks, gained some self-control with age. He's figured out how to adjust a few things at the crime scene and make it look like murder–suicide. He's also gone outside California for the first time. Just barely over the border, but enough to confuse the jurisdictions, cover his tracks a bit. But, and this is important—he's not going outside of what we've seen is his geographical comfort zone."

Singh was nodding, thinking on it.

"Also, I'm betting he wouldn't have waited long to kill again, so chances are good he was released very recently, unless somehow we now find other family massacres out there. Singh, that's the first thing you should be checking."

"Understood," she murmured, and glanced toward the board, her face troubled.

"It's not likely this kind of crime would have gone undetected for long. You need to be checking every familicide on the West Coast, in the last two years especially . . . but let's say in the last ten years before. Any with the same M.O. Stabbing and slashing. With or without a parental suicide. And particularly familicides that have an eleven- to fourteen-year-old boy in the family . . ."

He paused as he became aware of another presence in the room. Reynolds had stepped into the doorway. He looked across the room at the new whiteboard, then at Roarke.

"My office."

Reporting to Reynolds was vastly uncomfortable. Roarke wasn't sure he'd ever seen his ranking officer so still, and after Roarke had finished his summary the SAC was silent for far longer than he would have liked. Finally he spoke. "You set up a sting by faking a Reaper case and now you're telling me you think it was the actual Reaper."

Roarke kept his face as neutral as he could manage. "We were looking for a case that matched. We found it."

After another long moment, Reynolds said, "Where are you on Lindstrom?"

"If she followed us, she never showed herself." Roarke thought briefly of the moment in the alley that he had felt watched. *Cara? Not Cara?* He had no idea. He wondered what she would say about the new massacre. If he were able to talk to her about it, would she recognize this killing as the Reaper? Would she see things that they couldn't see? How would she react to the idea that the Reaper was alive and killing again? The very thought of it gave him a chill.

Reynolds still hadn't moved. Roarke didn't like the look on his face.

"This is not your case," the SAC said, finally. "Cara Lindstrom is a ticking time bomb."

Roarke fought for calm. "It's not the same thing. The people she kills—"

Reynolds turned on him. "Yes?"

There was a warning note in his voice but Roarke went ahead anyway. "The people she kills are not what anyone could call as high-priority victims as the families that may be at risk from the Reaper, or whoever this killer is. And we may not have much time—"

"Cara Lindstrom is your case," Reynolds said sharply. "You need to focus on your own case."

"I believe it's the same case," Roarke said.

"You *believe*. You took a team of evidence techs out of state to investigate a closed case that has nothing to do with this office's jurisdiction. Do you have one single piece of evidence that this is not a murder–suicide?"

"Not yet."

"You can't afford to lose focus—"

"I'm not losing focus." Roarke kept his tone even, but let a warning note creep in, just enough to let Reynolds know he meant business. "Cara Lindstrom is a priority. But we have less than a week now until the next full moon. The Reaper—if that's who this is—kills families. Whole families. He kills on the full moon. I'm not going to rest easy unless we nail this guy before then."

Reynolds leaned back in his chair. "You are not hearing me. I am ordering you off this track."

Roarke looked at his superior officer in total shock.

"I've taken Lam and Stotlemyre off. You're to drop it. Cara Lindstrom is your case. Work your case. Bring her in. Period."

Roarke walked out of the office, hearing nothing but the rush of blood in his ears. He was shaking with anger. Reynolds had never directly interfered with one of his cases before; he couldn't believe it was happening now.

Fuck that, he thought. *Fuck it.*

Epps was waiting for him in the hall. Tall, dark, imposing as always, but there was just something about him that made Roarke stop.

"Looking pretty intense, there," Roarke said. His skin prickled with anticipation, and not the good kind.

"There's been another killing," Epps said.

Roarke felt his breath catch, and suddenly the ground didn't seem so incredibly stable. "A family?" he managed.

"No. One of hers," Epps said.

Chapter 19

As they drove into Golden Gate Park, Roarke sat like a concrete statue in the passenger seat. He felt as if he would explode at any second. Epps kept glancing at him from the driver's seat. Finally he spoke. "Maybe Reynolds is right. It's a hell of a long shot."

"It's the Reaper," Roarke said.

"So, we work the Lindstrom case while we wait for the DNA analysis and go in with more—"

Roarke interrupted. "How did we find out about this homicide so fast?"

Epps stared out the windshield. "I've been monitoring all male homicides in the city and surrounding areas since you got back from San Diego."

For one second Roarke felt a blinding rage. He breathed in and used all the self-control he had to tamp it down, and he stared out the window until he felt sanity returning. Furious as he was, he had to wonder just a little if he had started to lose all objectivity. He had not in any way been anticipating another killing from Cara. He was still reeling that one had occurred under their noses, or what would have been under their noses if they had been in the city at the time.

In reality another killing from Cara was the most obvious thing that was going to happen.

Epps, on the other hand, had not only anticipated it, he'd apparently been watching out for exactly this. Casting a net, as it were.

Roarke was jarred from his thoughts as they turned onto the curve of Conservatory Drive. The white palace of the Conservatory of Flowers loomed up into view and he knew he had to focus.

He knew the park and this area of it well. The tunnel where the body had been found was across the road from the Victorian extravagance of the conservatory. A romantic setting by day; musicians hoping to score spare change from the tourists used the short, arched, ivy-covered tunnel to play in because of its acoustics. At night it was a favorite rendezvous for addicts and dealers. The victim, Danny Ramirez, had apparently been accosted while dosing in the tunnel.

Epps parked on the road above the tunnel, and they walked downhill on the path under towering eucalyptus and cypress. Yellow crime scene tape kept the usual bedraggled onlookers from approaching, but they watched the cops working the scene with interest. Epps spoke low.

"It was around midnight. He probably met a dealer here. It's an easy drop off."

A loud and familiar voice spoke behind them. "Aww, don't tell me the Feebles are on this." Epps and Roarke turned to see a figure shambling from the tunnel, a large bald man dressed in khaki pants and a Hawaiian shirt, Birkenstocks flopping on his feet. He had the rubbery, horsey face of a comedian: thick lips and bulbous eyes, and a jock's body gone to seed.

Epps harassed him back. "Oh my Lord, who let Mills out of the asylum?"

SFPD homicide inspector Clifton Mills was one of San Francisco's myriad eccentrics. He'd read everything Kerouac and Kesey ever put to paper and had probably lost half of his not inconsiderable brain cells to acid at Dead concerts while Jerry was still alive. Other cops tended to think he was one burger short of a Happy Meal.

Mills stopped in front of the agents in a truculent stance and looked them up and down.

"Why oh why would the Most Illustrious be interested in my poor little homicide? For that matter, why would anyone? Guy was pond scum. Has a sheet as long as my dick."

"For what?" Epps asked tensely. Roarke was equally tense beside him.

"The milieu doesn't give you a hint?" Mills opened his arms expansively. "Where do I start? Pimping, pandering, sodomy, forced oral intercourse, trafficking of minors . . ."

Epps gave Roarke a significant look. Exactly the kind of criminal Cara was prone to target. They both knew it.

"So why wasn't he locked up?" Roarke asked.

Mills looked injured. "I have to spell this out? You got to get the girls to testify and they just won't. This one was a Romeo." He meant a pimp who alternately romanced and terrorized his stable, a master at emotional manipulation.

A CSI shouted for Mills and he bellowed back, "Hold your shit!" But he headed back toward the tunnel, leaving Epps and Roarke alone.

Epps was looking at Roarke.

Roarke began. "We don't know—"

"Bullshit we don't," Epps said, a soft explosion. "You know. M.O., victim profile. She is what she is. She does what she does."

Mills hustled back from the dark mouth of the tunnel, Birkenstocks slapping on the asphalt. He was singing his own version of a Rodgers and Hammerstein tune Roarke recognized only because *Oklahoma!* had been a favorite show of his musically inclined mother. "Th' lawmen and th' Feebles should be friends . . ."

Mills broke off the song and grinned at the agents. "It's my lucky day. Someone saw it." He beckoned them toward the tunnel.

As they stepped into the arch of the tunnel the cold hit Roarke, a good fifteen degrees cooler inside the passageway. Then came the coppery stink.

Stark halogen lights lit up the garish scene. Arterial spray was splashed on the rounded walls. The coroner crouched beside a crumpled body in a massive pool of congealing blood.

Mills gestured. "Meet the corpse formerly known as Danny Ramirez. And behold . . . our evidence." He shined his Maglite toward an edge of the lake of red. Roarke caught the glint of metal: a gold band around a small tube.

"Lipstick case," Mills informed them. He angled the flashlight again to reveal a smear of a footprint in the pimp's blood.

"Angle of the spatter means my bad guy killed him from here." Mills directed the flashlight to the opposite side of the corpse and the blood pool. "Held him, slashed him. Don't know why that lipstick and print would be way over there unless someone else was standing there. Dropped the case, stepped in the blood to get away. Probably one of Ramirez's girls."

"We need to talk to this wit," Epps said.

"Nuh uh," Mills said cheerfully. "Not until you tell me what this is all about, friend."

"We're looking for the doer," Epps told him.

Mills snorted. "City gonna give him a medal?"

Epps shook his head. "Not him. Her."

"*Her?*" The detective glanced toward the corpse in its bloody pool. Roarke knew what he was thinking. This was not something they saw every day. Mills turned back, looking from one agent to the other. "Wait a minute. You know my perp?"

"We might," Roarke acknowledged.

Mills drawled. "Boys, we need to talk. Preferably someplace my reputation won't be compromised by me being seen fraternizing with Feebs."

"We'll meet you," Roarke said. "Text when you're finished."

• • • • •

They met downtown at Bourbon and Branch, a former 1920's speak-easy that had been converted into a millennial speakeasy. The luxuri-ous dark space boasted velvet-papered walls and gleaming dark wood beams under a spiky Art Deco chandelier, a cigar shop and smoking parlor, and five secret tunnels built in the Prohibition days. In the eve-nings reservations were mandatory, but Epps, with his horror of the ordinary, had cultivated the management. The agents didn't even have to use the password to be shown directly into "The Library," with its classic pressed tin ceiling and floor-to-ceiling bookshelves filled with leather-bound volumes. Bartenders in Roaring Twenties attire were busily mixing specialty cocktails at the two bars.

"Overpriced tourist trap," Mills grumbled as he joined them at a high-backed booth.

"Beats hell out of your North Beach cop dives," Epps retorted.

In truth you'd have to be comatose not to appreciate the period elegance of the place. Roarke could feel the dark and resonant ambi-ance working to slow his racing thoughts. He wondered briefly if he'd ever experience as much of the real San Francisco if Epps weren't so insistent about doing it right.

A waitress set down their drinks and when she was out of earshot, Mills leaned forward. "I fully expect the good dirt. Word is you got yourselves some kind of exotic, a triple serial or something."

At least, Roarke thought, and saw the same thought reflected in Epps' face. Mills looked from one to the other.

"So? Did I hear y'all say my doer is a woman?"

Epps slid the police sketch of Cara across the table.

Mills whistled softly. "Mamacita. She a working girl?"

"No," Roarke said tightly. Epps gave him a brief and ambiguous look.

Mills slapped his hands on his knees. "Someone needs to set me up with this babe. She killed Danny Boy she's all right by me."

Epps exploded. "So that's okay now? Seriously? Killing people?"

Mills was taken aback for a moment. "I miss something here?"

The tension between Epps and Roarke was so thick either one of them could have walked across it. Again, this was not lost on Mills. "What is she, Most Wanted or somethin'?"

"She's dangerous," Epps said softly. "You watch yourself, this case."

"Aw, now you're scarin' me," Mills said cheerfully, but then his eyes turned shrewd. "You want her so bad, why isn't she on the news?"

Epps glanced at Roarke and said nothing.

"She knows we know she's in town, she's gone," Roarke said. "She's been under the radar for years."

Mills swished his frothy cocktail. "Okay. So why? Why is she doing it? And what'd she do to get you Feds after her?"

Roarke found himself unable to speak. After a moment, Epps said, "Some kind of vigilante thing, we think. She killed one of ours, and five, six other men interstate. That we know of. Cuts their throats, mostly, but not always."

Mills could only stare for a moment. "You shitting me?" Neither agent said a word. The detective whistled under his breath. "Busy girl."

"Probably not even close to half of it," Epps said, without looking at Roarke. Roarke didn't say anything. He *knew* they didn't know even half of it.

Now Mills laughed, but the sound was hollow. "'Kay, now you guys really *are* freaking me out a little bit."

"Freakish is what it is," Epps said.

"So you taking this case away from me or what?" the big man asked.

"It's not like that," Roarke said. *It's just complicated*, he thought.

"You know we love you, Mills," Epps said. "Enough here to go around."

"Good. Cause I wouldn't want you guys to have all the fun. And this one is giving me a hard-on just thinking about it."

"We'll deal you in," Epps assured him. "But we need to find the girl. The wit." Despite Cara's trail of murders, they had no material witnesses to any of the homicides . . . except Roarke himself.

"Right," Mills said, staring into the archaic dimness of the bar. "Right. So there's that halfway house on Belvedere. Intake for minors they try to get off the street." Roarke nodded, vaguely familiar with it. "You want to talk to Rachel Elliott. If anyone knows Danny's girls, she would."

Chapter 20

Belvedere Avenue was in the heart of the Haight. Roarke and Epps drove past old buildings painted in rainbow colors, bottom floors largely taken up with cafés and grunge boutiques, top floors occupied by tenants who still strung beads from the windows as curtains, clinging to the Summer of Love dream.

Roarke looked out through the passenger window at the stopped clock on the corner of Haight and Ashbury. For him it was the most obvious symbol of the neighborhood. San Francisco, especially this district of San Francisco, was a time capsule. While other cities kept their history alive through carefully calculated tourism campaigns, San Francisco held to its mythos with an almost violent longing, and people still came from all over the world for a taste of the psychedelic experience.

A clutch of ragged teenagers was seated cross-legged on the sidewalk below the clock. *More of them on the streets than ever*, he thought bleakly.

Two blocks up from Haight Street, the shelter was an old Victorian of an unlikely shade of pink, or some kind of purple, maybe, he wasn't sure.

"Mauve," Epps said under his breath as they walked up the steep front stairs. The porch was gated and they were buzzed in after announcing themselves into a speaker on the wall.

The heavy door clicked open automatically as well, and a rope of Nepalese bells jangled on the doorknob. Inside, the tall bay windows were filled with crystal light catchers. The agents walked into a hall-way full of rainbows. The room to their left was filled with battered and overstuffed furniture, some tables, a massive old television. The lounge. The room to the right was an office. A set of stairs in the hall led up, and another set led down. Roarke could hear feminine voices on the lower floor, and the bass-heavy thump of street music. In the hall there was a wall of pictures. They were all of teenage girls: snapshots, printed-out candids from camera phones. Not just dozens but hundreds, rows of them, so many he felt an uneasy twinge, looking at them.

A woman stepped out of the office as the door jingled closed behind them. For a moment her hair was haloed in the bright sunlight, then she stepped forward and Roarke could see her clearly.

Rachel Elliott was in her mid-thirties and tired, but pretty in an earthy, classically San Francisco way. Her hair was red-brown and curly, past her shoulders, and her body was toned, no doubt by all the endless walking on the nearly vertical San Francisco streets. Her eyes were gray and wary. Cop's eyes. The rest of her was softer. She looked the two men over and Roarke could see in that one take that she had a long history of dealing with law enforcement, some of it good, some bad.

He flipped his credentials wallet. "Agents Roarke and Epps, San Francisco Bureau. Inspector Mills said you might be able to help us."

"Mills," she said, in the amused, exasperated voice so many people seemed to take on whenever Mills was mentioned.

"Yeah," Roarke said. "Mills."

She pushed open the door behind her and they followed her into a round office with a huge battered desk, built-in bookcases, a worn loveseat. There was an inner door and Roarke got a glimpse of a small side room with a single bed that hinted at frequent night shifts.

Elliott sat behind the desk, and Roarke got to the point. "We're looking for a prostitute."

Her eyes and voice turned to ice. "They're not prostitutes," she said. "They're sexually abused and commercially exploited youth."

Roarke had to bite back an angry reply. The endless political correctness of the Bay Area could work anyone's last nerve, even though she was right, and he knew she was right. It was a Bay Area epidemic. Since the crackdown on the street drug trade, gangs and dealers had shifted their focus from crack to the much safer and more lucrative business of selling children for sex.

"Of course they are," he said. But he could hear the grating irritation in his own voice and naturally Rachel Elliott mistook his sleeplessness for mockery. She didn't waste a second jumping all over him.

"You people should know that Federal law recognizes recruiting minors for prostitution as human trafficking—"

"We're all on the same side here," Epps interjected, the classic conciliator, but Elliott turned on him, clearly unmoved and ready to tell him exactly why. Roarke spoke quickly to deflect another outburst.

"Are you familiar with a Danny Ramirez?"

A look of sheer loathing crossed Elliott's face. "Jesus. Ramirez. What now?"

"Someone killed him last night."

She looked startled, but quickly covered it. "And what, I'm supposed to be sorry? He was the worst kind of scum."

And how often have I heard someone say that about one of Cara's . . . projects?

"You're not supposed to be anything," he said evenly. "We're looking for one of his girls."

Now her eyes were wary. "You think one of them killed him?"

"We think one of them saw who did."

She half-laughed. "And you think any one of them is going to talk—no—*testify* against a dealer or pimp? Good luck with that."

Roarke suppressed a sigh. "We'd be grateful if you could just steer us in the right direction."

She stared at him for a long moment and he braced himself for a political diatribe. Instead she surprised him.

"He's got six that I know of. That's a full stable for one of these guys. Five or six teenagers and they can make six hundred grand a year, the bastards. Danny is—was—a real Romeo, had a whole Russell Brand look going on."

"You know his girls, then? We really need to talk to them."

She gave Roarke a quick, assessing glance.

"They'll run if they see you two coming," she said automatically, and then hesitated. "I'll go out tonight and try to talk them into coming to the house. If Ramirez is dead this is my best shot to move them off the street before some other slimebag gets hold of them. If it's not too late." She flicked another glance at Roarke. "If I can get them here, I'll ask them to talk to you."

Surprise and sleeplessness caught him off-guard and he could only stare at her for a moment. Epps jumped in quickly. "We would seriously appreciate that, Ms. Elliott."

Roarke muttered agreement.

Now Rachel Elliott seemed to be avoiding Roarke's eyes. "If you can lock another one of the bastards away, I'm too happy to help." He realized she'd jumped to the logical conclusion that Ramirez had been killed by another pimp. No way was he going to complicate the issue by correcting that impression.

Epps was already handing her a card. "If there's anything you need from us, don't hesitate to call. We'll be waiting."

She took the card without enthusiasm. "I can't promise anything."

"We know that," Epps assured her. "Anything at all would help."

Roarke fished out one of his own cards. As he handed it to her, he said, "Be safe," surprising himself.

She looked up at him quickly, and Roarke saw her cheeks flush, an involuntary reaction which was instantly uncomfortable for him. She half-laughed. "On the street, you mean? It's my job, Agent Roarke," she said, her voice taut again.

But their eyes held for a beat before Roarke turned away.

As the door shut behind them and the agents walked down the stairs to the street, Roarke caught Epps giving him a sideways glance.

"What?" Roarke snapped.

"Nothing," Epps said. "Nothin' at all, no." And continued under his breath, something that sounded suspiciously like, "Your picker is broken."

Roarke felt a wave of anger all out of proportion to the circumstance. Yes, Rachel Elliott was attractive. In the normal world, normal people met other normal people and followed up on normal human connections, didn't they? Wasn't that what it was supposed to be like?

He was too tired to think. So he pretended he hadn't heard.

The whole last twenty-four hours suddenly hit like a tidal wave crashing over him. The massacre. The whole surreal question of the Reaper. Reynolds' ultimatum. The sight of the pimp's body in the tunnel. There was no sense to any of it.

"I've got to go home," he told Epps. "Sleep."

"I'm with you on that," Epps said, and to Roarke's annoyance he added, "I'll drop you there."

Still worried Cara would hurt him. *A killer of pimps, child abusers, bombers, and you think she'd kill me? Dream on, pal o' mine. Dream on.*

Roarke had just stepped through the doorway of his flat when his phone buzzed. He shoved his hand in his pocket to fish out the phone, and his pulse quickened to see Snyder's name on the screen. Roarke had left a message and forwarded Singh's scanned files on the Leland killings the night before.

He punched "on."

"Are you in Reno?" Snyder's voice asked him.

"Back home. I take it you got the files."

"I did."

Roarke sat on the couch and ran a hand through his hair. "Is it the Reaper?" An unanswerable question, but he knew Snyder would know what he meant.

The profiler answered slowly. "The use of a knife as a murder weapon, the violent stabbing and slashing, the nuclear family unit . . . these are unique crimes. There are zero instances of copycats in sexual homicide; the gratification in these crimes is specific to the perpetrator." Snyder paused, and Roarke could picture him shaking his head. "Statistically it's almost impossible it could be someone else."

"And the coincidence?"

"The coincidence is extreme. And worrisome."

Roarke sat quietly, feeling the buzzing in his head. Then Snyder spoke again. "Let's put that aside and look at the history for a moment. Familicide is almost *always* perpetrated by a parent, almost always the father, killing the family unit. It is extremely rare for a family to be killed by an outside perpetrator, and such cases are almost always home invasions. A serial killer who targets whole families is almost unheard of. Dennis Rader, the BTK killer, killed two families; Richard Trenton Chase, the Vampire Killer, killed a family. But the consistency of this particular killer, the Reaper, striking nuclear families, the M.O.—was very precise, and it was unprecedented."

Roarke followed his words with a sick feeling, though he knew it, had known it in his gut as well as in his head.

"But with the Reno killings, you've found no clear evidence it was an outside perpetrator rather than a murder–suicide by the father?"

"Not yet," Roarke said tightly. "I've been instructed to drop this line of inquiry."

"I see." There was a long pause. "I'm not entirely sorry."

Roarke was startled, and then angry. "I don't follow. What am I supposed to do, wait until he kills again? Because if this is the Reaper, he damn well is going to kill again."

"Yes," Snyder said, and there was a heaviness in his voice. "No doubt."

Roarke half-laughed. "Oh yes, and Cara Lindstrom killed a pimp in Golden Gate Park last night. Her usual M.O."

"I see. You do have your hands full."

"I'll send you the files."

Again, a pause. "Thank you. And what are you going to do?"

Roarke dropped his head back on the back of the couch. "I'm going to get some sleep before I pass out. I'll call you in the morning."

Chapter 21

He is in the tunnel, with cold, mossy stones around him. The dark is paralyzing, he can't see, can't move . . . but he can smell rancid copper, the pimp's blood, even feel it in the air.

Behind him Epps' voice speaks in his ear. *"This is who she is. This is what she does."*

A shadow looms on the wall at the end of the tunnel, waiting . . .

And a buzzing starts, loud, alarming . . .

He was not in the tunnel. He was in bed, and his phone was vibrating on the bed stand. He reached for it groggily, saw an unfamiliar local number. "Roarke," he muttered into the phone through a dry mouth.

"Agent Roarke."

It was a woman's voice and for a split second he was flooded with adrenaline, but almost as instantly he knew it was not Cara. It was a voice he should have recognized, husky and feminine, but he couldn't quite get to it.

"This is Rachel Elliott"—and after a pause, she added—"from the Belvedere House."

He sat up, his brain connecting. "Hello," he started, and grabbed for the travel clock on his bed stand. 7:30 a.m. He'd slept fourteen hours. "Sorry, I must have—"

She was speaking, barreling over him. "I know it's early, I probably shouldn't have—"

They both stopped and it was an awkward and loaded silence, and then she started again.

"Mills was just here. He showed me a police sketch of a woman . . ."

Roarke went still.

"I saw her. In the Haight. She was with one of Danny Ramirez's girls."

Rachel Elliott was waiting inside the People's Café, a Haight Ashbury institution. She was seated at a table behind the big plate-glass window, and gave Roarke a direct look through the glass, a look he felt in his groin. He stifled a wave of something like irritation as he pulled open the door. The overwhelming fragrance of coffee and buttery pastry hit him. The café had the look of a tavern: a high counter that was clearly once a bar, ceiling fans, a pressed tin ceiling. Summer of Love posters adorned the walls: Jefferson Airplane, Wavy Gravy.

He joined Elliott at the table. She looked fresh and clean, light years better than he felt, and she had two giant mugs of coffee in front of her. As he sat across from her she pushed one toward him. "It's black," she said, and blushed faintly, giving herself away.

Rachel Elliott, your picker is broken, he thought, and drank from the mug.

As if to avoid his unspoken thought, she busied herself with her own coffee. "So I think I know the girl you're looking for. I should have known from the start, probably. She calls herself Jade. She's a new one, not completely destroyed yet. It doesn't take long, though."

She shook her head, shaking it off, and looked at him directly. "The thing is, I saw this woman you're looking for with her, two days ago."

Roarke slid the police sketch of Cara out of his leather binder and put it down on the table between them. "You're sure."

Rachel glanced down at the image. "Positive. I'm not sure why I noticed them, honestly, there was just something—odd."

"Where was this? What happened?" he asked, trying to keep the tension out of his voice.

"There." She nodded to the sidewalk outside. "Across the street, in front of the Lotus Flower." He turned to the window beside him to look; there was an Asian restaurant across the street, painted sage green with red trim and a huge pink blossom over its large plate glass window. "I walk down here for lunch most days, or just to get out. I was sitting just about here, and I could see Jade sitting on the curb—she looked as if she'd collapsed there. I was thinking I would go out to see if she was all right, try to talk to her, and just then that woman in your sketch came out of the restaurant and put a to-go box down beside her."

Unmistakably Cara, he thought. He looked down at the sketch. Underneath the glass top of the table was a shallow box frame filled with coffee beans. It made him feel more caffeinated.

"Did she say anything to her?" he asked aloud. "Did they speak?"

"They didn't, but . . ." she hesitated.

"What?" he said, too sharply.

She spoke slowly. "They *looked* at each other. I mean, like they knew each other." She shook her head slightly. "I thought, anyway."

"And then what?"

She nodded down toward the sketch of Cara. "She turned and walked away."

Roarke tried to keep the urgency out of his voice. "Did you see where she went, a car, a house . . ."

Rachel shook her head. "Just walked on down the street. I don't know where she was headed."

"How was she was dressed?"

The counselor frowned. "Well . . . young, I thought. Jeans and a hoodie, high tops. You could have taken her for a teenager, if you weren't really looking. But the way she approached Jade—so focused—she didn't move like a kid."

No. Not a kid.

She was studying him. "Does this woman have something to do with Ramirez?"

Roarke didn't answer her. Cara stared up from the sketch on the table between them, eyes hidden behind shades. He wanted to put the sketch away, but the action would call attention to itself, so he left her there.

"You have any idea where to find this Jade?" he asked brusquely.

Rachel looked flustered. "I would have said Danny's crash pad, one of them, anyway, but . . . not if she saw him killed."

Exactly what Roarke had been thinking. At the counter behind them the cappuccino steamer hissed.

Rachel continued. "I've been looking for her, but no luck so far, I'm afraid. Not last night, not today. She's probably hiding out, but I have no idea where."

Or she's someplace far away. Hopefully not picked up by some other asswipe, to sell in another city, Roarke thought. It happened all the time.

"What do you know about her?" he asked.

She frowned. "She showed up on the street two, three months ago. I've tried talking with her half a dozen times, not much luck. They're skittish as deer, these girls. They're all under orders not to talk to anyone but the johns. They get the shit beaten out of them if they even make eye contact with anyone else. The Romeos," she said, and there was loathing in her voice. "They run five or six girls at a time, keep up a relationship with all of them. They know how to pick the damaged ones, and they know how to work them. Promise a house, kids." She mimicked a man's seductive street drawl. 'Just a few more months, baby, do it for me a few more months, we can make it happen.'" She pushed her coffee away from her.

"This girl Jade is smarter than that, really. She has fire. I didn't think he quite had her yet, but the meth is rotting her brain. I hadn't seen her for a few days and I was thinking . . ." She glanced out the window. "Stupid, but I thought she might have broken away."

"Can you describe her for me?"

Rachel looked wry. "She's hard to miss, actually. She has body art, this whole scene on her back and arms. A dancer in fire, trees with these flaming flowers. Must have hurt like hell, I can't even imagine. And she's a beauty, too, at least you can see she was before the meth." She paused, and then added, "There's something different about her. She's a fighter."

Roarke felt a buzzing in his brain that he knew meant this was the right track. And if Cara had taken an interest in this girl, Jade, she wouldn't have thought twice about eliminating the pimp.

It's who she is. It's what she does.

"Ramirez's other girls. Did you find any of them?"

She gave him a cynical look. "Did you want to talk to them?"

"I meant, were you able to get them into the house?"

Now she looked startled, and dropped her eyes. "Two of them."

"That's good."

"One of them is thirteen. You know what they say, the pimps? 'The best kids to have are the ones who've been had by their daddies.' "

He heard the anger in her voice, could see it in her eyes. There was her anger, and there was Cara's anger. There was her way, and there was Cara's way. Not so different in theory, but miles apart in practice.

She saw him evaluating her, and sighed, pushed back her hair. "It's a long road."

"But it's a start," he said.

"It is."

Their eyes met across the table . . . and he had the impression of a door opening between them, of an unspoken invitation. He knew what to do next: ask her how she'd gotten into this business, where she was from originally, all those things that people say and do, the dance.

And he said none of it.

The silence continued, became thick and awkward. She broke it, finally. "So this woman, in the sketch. You think she killed Danny?"

Roarke looked away. "Probably."

"Why?" She found his gaze again, held it, probing. "Just because he needed killing?"

"That's about the size of it."

She raised her eyebrows. "That's . . . something to think about. Is Jade in danger?"

He didn't know what she meant at first. "From the suspect?" he asked. He'd almost said, "From Cara?"

"Jade is a witness," Rachel pointed out. "I want to know if you think the killer will come after her."

"That's not at all likely." In fact, it struck him that Cara was in more danger from Jade, if the girl could identify her as Ramirez's killer. She might well end up being the key to Cara's eventual prosecution. *If we can take her alive*, a voice in his mind said. The café suddenly felt hot, stifling. The smell of coffee was starting to make him sick.

He saw that Rachel was waiting for him to explain, to say more. "Her only victims so far are adult males." He knew he should add, as far as we know, but he felt a reluctance to discuss Cara with Rachel that he couldn't have explained to himself, or didn't want to look at.

"So this is some kind of vigilante thing?"

"We think so, yes."

"She kills pimps?"

"Child molesters. Rapists. Sex traffickers."

Rachel stared at him. "Seriously?" She shook her head, looked out the window at the street. "My God . . ."

"What?" he said suddenly. "What are you thinking? I'd like to know."

She was silent for a moment, thinking. "Well, I'm not sorry," she said, finally. "How do you feel about it?"

For some reason he told her the truth. "I don't know. I know how I'm supposed to feel."

She glanced at him. "Maybe you should order breakfast."

"Sorry, what?" he said.

"Or lunch. I find everything tends to go better when a man's blood sugar is stable." She looked at him, with clear gray eyes, flushed cheeks. For a suspended second Roarke found himself considering the invitation . . . both of them—

And then his phone buzzed.

He checked the number. Singh. He made an apologetic gesture toward Rachel. She shook her head slightly: no apology necessary.

Roarke turned away from her toward the window, put the phone to his ear. "I'm here."

"We have a possible hit, chief."

"A hit?"

There was a pause on the phone. "I took the liberty of searching the prison databases last night for parolees who fit our criteria for the Reaper."

Roarke felt a jolt of exhilaration. They were moving into dangerous territory. But the fact that Singh had pursued it herself was its own kind of validation.

"Tell me," he said, through a dry mouth.

"Jeffrey Martin Santos, paroled from San Quentin on seventeen October. He matches our time frame for arrest, and our time frame for release. DOB twelve-twelve sixty-six, arrested January 1988 at the age of twenty-two and charged with aggravated assault—"

"On a child?" Roarke asked before she could even finish the sentence.

"No, on an adult male. The interesting factor, though, is that the man's twelve-year-old son was there with him."

Roarke felt his adrenaline spike again. *He's forty-six now, the age range fits, and so does the crime.*

"So he may have been going after the kid."

"That is what I am thinking. And before his arrest, Santos had been institutionalized and diagnosed as paranoid schizophrenic. He claimed, among other things, that the government had illegally implanted a monitoring device in his brain."

"Where was he paroled to?"

"San Jose."

It was just an hour away.

"I am sending his mug shot right now," Singh said. Roarke's phone pinged. He clicked over to the message, stared down at an image of a gaunt and hollow-cheeked man, stringy dark hair, bad skin set off by the classic toxic orange jumpsuit.

"I have a call in to his parole officer," Singh continued. "He did not pick up the call, no surprise there." Roarke knew what she meant. Considering the caseload the officers carried these days, it was a miracle any phone calls got returned within a year.

"Is there a current address?" He held his breath, praying Santos wasn't homeless, a common condition of parolees which made them incredibly hard to track.

"It is a halfway house his P.O. set him up in."

Roarke felt another adrenaline spike. *Get on the freeway to San Jose . . . chances are we could be there before we ever get a call back.*

"I also thought you should know that SAC Reynolds has already departed. For the holiday weekend."

Roarke had completely forgotten it was Thanksgiving tomorrow. *But with Reynolds gone . . .*

He spoke into the phone. "I'm at the People's Café on Haight. Get Epps to come pick me up. We're going down there to talk to him." He glanced at Rachel. She was looking out the window at the street, but he was fairly certain she wasn't missing a thing. He lowered his voice. "You need to pull Santos' DNA profile and check it in CODIS against any unidentified DNA at any of the—cold cases." He'd almost said "massacres."

"Already in progress, chief," Singh assured him. "And I will clock you and Agent Epps out. For the holiday."

"Appreciate it. Good work." He punched off the phone and turned back to the table. Rachel was sitting very still; from her face it was obvious she'd heard much of the conversation. Or at least enough.

"Whatever this is, it's much bigger than Danny Ramirez, isn't it?" she asked softly.

He opened his mouth to give a bullshit reply, and instead found himself saying, "It is. And I'm going to have to go."

Rachel glanced down at the sketch of Cara, and back up at Roarke.

"Be careful," she said.

Chapter 22

Wasn't sure you'd be up for this," Roarke said as he dropped into the passenger seat of the fleet car beside Epps.

Epps stared ahead through the windshield, his hands tight on the steering wheel. "Not like I could stop you. And our best shot at catching Lindstrom is surveilling you. You go, I go."

Roarke didn't think he wanted to press the issue.

They hit the freeway just after morning traffic and made it to San Jose in under an hour. The halfway house where Santos had been paroled was in a depressed area of the city where neighbors were less likely to ask questions about the criminal history of the residents. Roarke stared out the window beside him as Epps drove by a string of seedy apartment complexes and boarded-up buildings with the occasional vacant lot and Christian ministry and auto repair yard.

The building did not announce itself as a transitional living accommodation by any signs in the yard or above the door, but it was unmistakable nonetheless. It looked like a free-standing prison cellblock: a concrete rectangle painted white with dull blue trim and blue-painted bars on the windows. The lawn was tiny and dead. A tired white bulldog was tied up to a sprinkler pipe, panting in the shadows. One side of the building had no windows at all. The other side had a caged staircase and another cage around a side door, the manager's place.

As the agents got out of the car, Roarke looked up the street. Why he would think of Cara at a moment like this was beyond him . . . maybe just the knowing that she had spent almost all of her childhood in buildings as bleak as this one. Epps caught his look. He turned to give the street a glance of his own, a deliberate and faintly ironic once-over. Before they started toward the building they both did a weapons check: shoulder holster, the belted waist pouch to be sure the plastic cuffs were available in one smooth move.

The agents buzzed at the cage. A wary-looking white man with some hard years of alcohol etched on his face opened the door to look out through the cage at them.

"Federal agents," Roarke told him, and displayed his credentials wallet, though a man like the one standing inside this doorway wouldn't need to see it to know the Fed. "We're here to talk to Jeffrey Santos."

"Gone," the manager said.

Roarke felt a cold twist of dread. "Gone as in—?"

"Gone as in he missed curfew two weeks ago and no one's seen him since. Nobody gets no curfew violations here. One strike you're out."

Both agents were vibrating with tension.

Two weeks ago. Just before the Leland murders.

"Does his parole officer know?" Roarke demanded.

"I phoned it in," the manager said truculently. "Got no call back."

Epps was already turned away, diving into the file Singh had prepared on Santos, punching numbers into his phone.

Roarke turned back to the manager. "Did Santos have any means of transportation?"

The man snorted. "You're kidding, right? Miracle the guy could walk on his own. Thought for a few days he just wandered off, got lost, you know?"

"Schizophrenic?"

"At least. He was on meds, but he still had the whole word salad thing going on." The unique speech pattern of schizophrenics, he meant.

Epps looked over at Roarke from the phone. "He's scheduled to check in every two weeks. He missed his appointment two days ago."

Roarke reached out for the phone and Epps handed it to him. "This is Assistant Special Agent in Charge Roarke. What are you doing to find Santos?"

The voice on the other end was rough and male. "He's a PAL. I reported him to DAPO. Their job now."

The parole officer meant Santos had been classified as a Parolee at Large, and he'd reported him to the Division of Adult Parole Operations.

On the surface this was good news. DAPO had established four California Parole Apprehension Teams, one of which was based in San Jose. The CPAT teams were trained in fugitive apprehension, database searches, field tactics, and firearms. All fine, but the immediate issue was that DAPO didn't know what they had with Santos. *Potentially* had.

"But he's not on record as a sex offender," Roarke said aloud. A sex offender would have been under the maximum level of supervision, the highest risk classification—in fact, he would have been required to wear a GPS ankle bracelet, and his disappearance would have triggered a concerted effort to find him, immediately transferred to the intelligence and field units. But Santos had only been convicted of assault on an adult.

"Hell, no," the P.O. said on the other end, and Roarke could hear the surprise in his voice. "First I've heard of it."

"Who's your DAPO contact?" Roarke asked. He fished his own phone out of his suit coat pocket to hand to Epps. He repeated the name and number aloud as the P.O. spoke it. Epps instantly punched in the numbers.

While Epps stepped away and spoke quickly into the phone, Roarke told the P.O., "Thanks. We'll be calling you back," and disconnected. He turned and looked at the manager head on. The man looked wary.

"We need to see Santos' place."

The manager spread his hands. "There's someone else in it already. Got a wait list ten yards long. Place's been cleaned out."

Roarke's heart sank. Unless by some chance . . .

"What did you do with his stuff?"

The manager brightened, if anyone could use that word for someone so washed out. "Wasn't enough room in the trash for all of it last week. There's a garbage bag in the laundry room."

Roarke tensed. "I'd like to see that bag."

He nodded to Epps, still on the phone, and followed the manager into the main building, trying and failing to contain the rush of hope he was feeling. Trash was fair game for law enforcement. They could take the whole bag and comb through it for incriminating evidence that Santos was planning the killing, or even blood or other DNA evidence if by any slim chance Santos had returned to the place after killing the Lelands. *Possibly killing the Lelands*, Roarke added in his head as he walked with the manager through a dank, hopeless hallway with dirty walls, rank with the smell of unwashed men. There were hundreds of these places in the state, thousands, housing the overflow from California's bursting prison system. Men who had been too broken by the things they had done or that had been done to them ever to rejoin society. Insanity compounded by years confined in insane conditions. *Like the creature that was the Reaper*, Roarke thought, *a sick mind becoming sicker, slow cooking to a more potent state of madness . . .*

He forced himself away from the train of thought and spoke aloud to the manager as they walked. "Did you get a sense of sexual interest in children? Twelve-, thirteen-year-old boys?"

The manager looked taken aback. "No. Not like I hung out with him but . . . shit, no." He frowned. "Some of these guys, though . . . it's like there's no *there* there, you know?"

Roarke knew.

They stepped through a back doorway into the sunlight again. There was a second door in the back wall of the building. As they approached that door, an obnoxious ring tone jangled, with buzzing for good measure. The manager shoved his hand into his pocket, scooping out a phone.

He shrugged an apology to Roarke as he moved aside. Roarke ignored him and opened the door into a dark space, with a short set of stairs leading down into a laundry room.

A tiny window at ground level provided a minimum of feeble light. He felt along the inside wall for a light switch and found nothing, so he stood, letting his eyes adjust to the darkness. Below he made out the shapes of a standard washer and dryer gleaming whitely beside rows of trash bins.

He started down the stairs. As he neared the bottom, he felt along the wall again for a light switch, and then stopped . . . sensing presence. He twisted around—

Suddenly wild eyes shone from the dark, and a hulking form barreled toward him.

Roarke reached out instinctively to grab his attacker's wrist and used the momentum to slam him against the concrete wall. The man howled in rage and thrust his body backward. Roarke grabbed him in a headlock and wrestled him down to the ground, holding him down. He got a whiff of stale clothes and the faint burned-plastic stench of meth as he pinned his struggling captive to the floor and breathed through the adrenaline rush in his head.

He knew what he was dealing with from the smell, even before the overhead light sizzled on, as somewhere at the top of the stairs the manager flipped the switch . . . revealing a large and dirty man writhing on the floor beneath Roarke.

Roarke held the man down on the concrete with a fist in his hair and a knee in his back, and cuffed him with plastic cuffs.

The manager rushed down the stairs. "Jesus, Bronson. How many fucking times—"

"You know this guy?" Roarke demanded over the pounding of his own heart. He kept his knee firmly in the center of his captive's body mass.

"Former resident," the manager said. "He knows he's not supposed to be here, but he keeps coming back."

"Call the local cops," Roarke ordered. He rolled the dirty man onto his side. "I'm going to help you up on three," he said, and counted off. No stranger to handcuffs, obviously, the man opted for cooperation rather than pain. He heaved up to his knees and let Roarke haul him to his feet.

Roarke manhandled the guy up the stairs, using pressure on his cuffed arms to lever him forward. The manager followed at a safe distance, carrying the trash bag. At the top of the stairs, Roarke pushed his prisoner through the door, squinting against the sudden daylight.

Epps was rushing up the drive, looking over the man in cuffs. "Jesus. You okay?" he asked Roarke.

"Fine," Roarke told him.

"Is it Santos?"

Roarke shook his head, catching his breath through the buzz of adrenaline in his blood. "Some former resident, off his meds and on meth. Local cops are on their way. Can you take him?"

"Got it." Epps hooked the guy's arm and spoke in a voice that brooked no argument. "We're going to the curb to wait for your ride, sir."

Roarke took a deep, steadying breath, then turned to the manager and took the trash bag. He opened it and without removing anything, did a quick visual scan.

Some ratty clothes, a chaos of papers, clipped newspaper articles that probably made sense to Santos and Santos alone, something that looked like a dead mouse. There was a smell of sickness to the clothes that put Roarke right back into his year of psych internship.

He looked over at the manager. "Anything else you noticed? Anything else you could tell us that he had in the apartment? Anything you might have kept?"

The manager was suddenly evasive. Roarke could feel the change in his posture instantly. And there was a particular quality to the evasion that Roarke recognized.

"What was it, porn?" he said. "What kind?" In his experience, porn was a better indicator of a person than a lie detector test.

The manager tried not very successfully to compose his face and Roarke made his voice hard. "Don't make me get a search warrant for *your* place."

The manager gave him a hostile look, but nodded toward his own front door and started for it.

Inside the seedy little apartment Roarke looked over a spread that the manager had hauled out from a drawer, including *Hustler*, *Juggs*, *Spicy Latinas* . . . women with ballooning breasts, gaping genitals.

"This all of it?" he asked, feeling tired.

The manager fidgeted behind him. "I swear."

"Nothing with kids?" Roarke demanded.

The manager looked injured. "Hell no. Think I'd take that?"

"*Nothing*? Teenagers, boys?"

"Swear ta Christ." Now the man was indignant. "Totally mainstream."

As Roarke and the manager emerged from the apartment into the afternoon sunlight, Epps was coming up on them, without the prisoner, and talking into his phone. "Here's Assistant Special Agent in Charge Roarke," he said, and extended the phone to Roarke. Roarke took it, exchanging it for the black plastic bag of Santos' belongings.

The man at the other end introduced himself as Lieutenant Montez, with DAPO. "Your man's been saying we might have a sex offender on our hands."

Roarke had the queasy thought that "sex offender" might be the least of their problems. "Possible sex offender and possible mass murderer," he said.

There was a beat of silence on the other end, then the lieutenant said tersely, "I just kicked this PAL up to the highest risk classification level. Our San Jose intelligence and field units will be putting out an immediate and concerted effort to find him. We're already on the line with Reno PD, see if we can pick up a trail there."

It was lucky for them there was a local force already in place to handle fugitive apprehension. It cut through all the bureaucracy and got the proper authorities instantly on the case.

"Appreciate it," Roarke said. "Anything our office can do, we'll be all over it, just let us know."

He punched off and was about to hand the phone back to Epps when he realized they'd switched phones in the process. He pocketed his phone and handed Epps' phone back to him.

Then he turned to the manager and extended a card. "Any sign of Santos, any word on where he might be, we want to know immediately."

"Course," the manager said. Roarke could hear the dislike in his voice.

Feeling's mutual, pal.

The agents walked away, back down the cracked concrete drive toward the car.

Epps finally spoke. "I sure enough don't want to explain to Reynolds what we were doing here."

Roarke looked back toward the door of the laundry room. He was having an uneasy feeling that had nothing to do with the adrenaline crash or the thought of what the SAC would have to say.

"All right, what?" Epps said. "What are you thinking?"

Roarke spoke reluctantly. "Santos left a stash of porn when he lit out. Not kids. Adult women. Bondage." In his mind he kept going back to the plain fact that men are excruciatingly specific about their particular sexual fantasies.

Epps knew it, thought on it. "Doesn't fit. But it could be a blind. Covering his tracks in case the P.O. does a drop-in."

Roarke found himself shaking his head. "The guy sounds too disordered to pull that kind of planning off. In fact, I'm wondering if someone that disordered could have enough control to kill the Leland

170

father like that. So pro that a professional law enforcement team would have seen it as a suicide."

"Timing fits," Epps said. "He could have blown town right after his last check-in and done the Lelands. Two weeks until he shows up as officially missing."

"The timing fits," Roarke agreed. He didn't like the feeling in his gut. "I hope we're on to him, but . . ." he trailed off. "Damn it. I don't like it."

Epps frowned. "Well, DAPO's on that case. Leaves us free to . . ." He left the sentence hanging.

Free to what was the question. *Pursue Cara? Let her pursue me?*

"I don't know," Roarke said. He pulled himself together. "I appreciate you being on board with it, though."

"I wouldn't say 'on board,' " Epps said stiffly. "But . . ." He stopped, stared out into the darkening sky. "If there's any chance you're right . . . we can't let it go."

Chapter 23

The drive back was nightmarish. Thick fog had rolled in from the ocean, waves of it, and the traffic up the 101 had slowed to a crawl.

"Thanksgiving," Epps muttered, and Roarke looked at him, startled again at the mention of the holiday.

"Damn," he said.

"Yeah," Epps said.

Offices would be closed all over for the next two days. It would slow down any information they were after, when they had no time to lose. On the other hand, he would be on his own, without Reynolds looking over his shoulder . . . or suspending him outright.

Back at the office, Roarke left Epps to check back in with Singh while he took the bags of Santos' belongings to the lab for Lam and Stotlemyre, who providentially were still in.

"This is a favor," he told them, and explained he needed them to comb through for hair and other DNA evidence that might be matched to the Leland murders and the Reaper scenes. "It's asking a lot . . ."

Lam and Stotlemyre exchanged a glance. "Since you mention it . . ." Lam started.

"Look, we know Reynolds shut the Reno inquiry down . . ." Stotlemyre continued.

"But you know how he is." Lam rolled his eyes toward Stotlemyre. "Once he gets the bit between his teeth."

"So we've been doing a little work on this, and we think you should see this."

Lam grabbed for a file. "It's all about the voids."

Roarke knew he meant the empty places in spilled or spattered blood that indicated that an object or a person had caught the projected blood rather than the surrounding area.

Lam put down a series of photos, which coldly captured the father slumped in his office chair in a pool of his own blood. "You can see in theses photos: these curtain-like patterns of blood on the wall from the arterial spray, caused by the last contractions of the father's heart."

Roarke's face tensed as he looked at the images. It was always unnerving to see how much blood geysered from the human body when a major artery was cut. The sight also made him wonder again how much Cara's predilection for cutting throats came from experiencing this very crime herself, from seeing her sister murdered in front of her, from feeling the knife in her own throat, all those many years ago.

He had to force himself to focus back on the present.

"But here's the thing that contradicts the other visual evidence. You see this void here in the projected blood?" Stotlemyre was pointing to a close-up, indicating a blank space at the edge of the spray. "It's subtle, the guy was actually quite careful under the circumstances, but if Leland were sitting here . . ." The tech took a chair and placed it in front of a lab table, sat down in it. "When you calculate the angle of the spray, it's hard to explain the void in the spatter."

Lam stepped up behind the chair. "Unless someone was standing behind him," he finished.

Roarke felt his heart constrict. Behind him Epps said softly, "Someone else killed them." Roarke turned to see the agent standing in the doorway. He hadn't even heard him come in.

Roarke looked back to the techs. "How sure are you about this?"

The techs exchanged a glance, then Lam spoke for both of them. "Not sure enough. It would help a lot to get confirmation about the blood on the father. We sent the mixed blood samples to Quantico to rush the DNA—did that before Reynolds lowered the boom. But we're confident about the void."

Stotlemyre nodded agreement.

Roarke took the elevator back down a floor and went straight in to see Singh. Her face was lit by the desk lamp in her cubicle, her raven hair shimmering around her shoulders. Working late, even on a holiday eve. It occurred to him, not for the first time, that unmarried agents were an anomaly in the Bureau, but he led a team of entirely single people. He supposed that had something to do with him.

She looked up as he stepped forward. "Chief."

"Any more Reaper potentials on that list of yours?" he asked.

Singh looked surprised, and then thoughtful. "Santos is not the one, then?"

Roarke looked toward the row of windows behind her, the thick view of fog and muted city lights. "I don't know. And I don't want to focus on him exclusively until we know more. We don't have much time. We can't afford a wild goose chase."

Singh reached for her desk organizer and withdrew a purple file. From her first day on the job she had ignored the standard-issue manila folders and brought her own rainbow of colors into the office, an intricate coded system intelligible only to her.

"In California this year there were 127, 314 adult men released from prison to parole."

Roarke was familiar with the stats, but even so, the number seemed out of some dystopian fantasy. He thought of the dank, sour halls of the halfway house. Thousands of those all over the state, not to mention the country. They were looking for a needle in a haystack. He felt a prickle of dread, but forced himself back to what Singh was saying.

"I have screened all inmates arrested and released within our parameters and winnowed it by the other profile characteristics."

Roarke felt himself tensing as he waited for the number . . .

"I am afraid there are five hundred and fourteen men on that list."

Worse even than he had imagined.

"Fortunately there are not so many who have spent an entire twenty-five years in prison. I have been checking up on them all afternoon and eliminated some by checking with P.O.s and halfway houses, checking curfews and check-ins to establish unofficial alibis. It is past close of business, and there is the holiday tomorrow, but I will leave messages for all contacts before I leave tonight, and I will check in regularly for responses."

"Brilliant, Singh. Thank you." She looked down modestly, then looked up, and her eyes were troubled. "I have read the profile that you and Agent Snyder have outlined. It seems to me that such a delusion must manifest in demonstrably odd behavior. Someone will have noticed him. We will find him."

There was a sudden intensity in her voice that made him pay attention. "Whenever possible I will talk to these parole officers in person. Such evil cannot walk about unnoticed. There will be a sense, I think, of something beyond the norm. I am sure of it—that if one asks the right questions, the sense of the madness will have left an impression."

She was looking at him expectantly, waiting for some kind of answer, and he met her eyes. "I have to think you're right." And then he added, "And Singh . . ."

She frowned at his tone.

"We proceed quietly."

"Of course," she said serenely.

"Have a good . . ." He didn't know if Singh even celebrated Thanksgiving, or whom she might celebrate with. "Holiday," he ended.

"And you as well," she told him. And then as he headed for the door, she spoke behind him. "Chief . . ."

He turned back to look at her.

"By profile, Santos is still by far the most likely of any of the men on the list."

He stood still in the doorway, and nodded. *But it doesn't feel right,* he thought bleakly. *I'm not feeling it at all.*

Chapter 24

The ocean of fog was even thicker as Epps drove out of the underground parking, the lights atop skyscrapers hovering like UFOs in the mist.

Both agents stared out the windshield into the fog. The shadows of cars emerged and disappeared on the street before them. Epps shook his head. "We need proof. So far this is nothing but a suspicion. It may be a suspicion we all have, but we need something real, damn it."

Roarke didn't have to say anything. There was nothing to do but agree.

Instead of turning on Market toward Noe Valley, Epps made a right turn onto Seventh. Roarke looked at him.

"We're checking in with Mills," Epps told him. He added ironically, "Need to account for what we did today on our own case."

Roarke was silent, chagrined.

The homicide division was housed in the Hall of Justice, more popularly known as The Hall, or The Hall of Whispers, in reference to San Francisco's paranoia-inducing city politics. It was a massive granite structure on Bryant Street, just a mile from the Federal Building, connected via underground and above-ground passageways to the

County Jail, a modernistic curve of metal and glass with an inexplicable mechanistic sculpture on the lawn outside.

Across the street was a row of bail bonds offices, with a couple of cafés and a bar interspersed. Epps parked at the end of the row of police vehicles packed two deep at the curb, and the agents walked up a wide set of steps past a motley assortment of loitering characters: cops, criminals, some even scruffier defense attorneys.

The lobby was salmon pink marble, lit by three huge and vaguely ominous Art Deco globes, and still bustling on the holiday eve.

"Crime never sleeps," Epps said under his breath as the agents bypassed the line at the security gates by showing their credentials to a guard at a podium.

Upstairs in the detectives' bullpen, the agents walked through the usual chaos of desks and detectives and ringing phones. Mills sat behind a desk as frightfully sloppy as the man himself. He looked up and cowered in mock terror as the agents approached.

"Oh Lordy, the Apocalypse is surely here. An Assistant Special Agent in Charge and company in my lowly office."

Roarke rolled his eyes and took a seat. Epps leaned against a cubicle wall as he spoke. "We're following up on Jade. Rachel Elliott said she ID'd her for you. Any luck finding her?"

Mills waggled his hand in a "so-so" gesture. "Good news is we pulled a usable print off the lipstick case. Bad news is she's not in the system. She's got no record. Nothing with that name, anyhoo. She was a new fish, no one had caught her yet."

Roarke heard Rachel's voice: *There's something different about her.*

The detective continued. "I've got word out to Oakland and Richmond Vice and the Alameda trafficking unit. You boys know how this works. If some other slime got hold of her, chances are she's already been shipped out to Vegas or San Diego. Portland, maybe."

The cities were part of the West Coast prostitution track. The pimps moved the girls regularly to keep them from making friends and allies, and to keep the johns supplied with fresh meat.

"Because God forbid anyone should have to fuck the same fifteen-year-old twice in a week," Epps said, and Roarke could hear the anger taut in his voice.

Mills nodded assent. "But I got Elliott to draw the kid's tats for me and I'm getting the sketch out to the parlors. She spent one hell of a long time with some artist. If I can find the guy or gal, they might know where she's keeping herself."

Roarke and Epps looked at each other. It was a good plan.

"Any other witnesses?" Epps asked.

Mills snorted. "Who were conscious in that place, at that time? Good luck with that."

"Any other pimps turn up dead?" Roarke queried. He'd meant it only as a morbid joke, but then the reality of it hit him. He couldn't believe he hadn't considered it before.

Mills looked at him with a sudden sharp interest. "You think they will?"

"Could be," Roarke said, his mouth dry.

Mills scratched his chin. "M'I supposed to worry about this?"

Roarke didn't answer. Epps looked as though he had a lot to say, but remained silent. Mills looked from one agent to the other. "Alrighty, let me rephrase. No actual *humans* are in danger?"

Roarke let himself say what he thought. "Not so far." Epps shifted on his feet, angrily or unhappily, Roarke couldn't tell. Mills scrubbed a hand over his shiny head.

"Well, hell, I'll keep an eye peeled, but I'm not about to go out and warn the fuckers. Fuck 'em. Happy Thanksgiving."

The agents stood silently in the metallically gleaming elevator as they rode down to street level. Suddenly Roarke spoke. "Rachel Elliott asked me if Jade is in danger from Cara."

Epps looked at him sharply.

"What do you think?" Roarke asked, and braced himself for the response.

Epps shook his head. "Man. Doesn't fit, but . . . there's always a first time. It never crossed my mind."

"Mine either," Roarke admitted, and felt relief.

Epps stood still as the elevator door opened. "I don't know. I just don't know."

Full dark as Epps dropped Roarke off at his place. Upstairs, Roarke turned the key and opened the door into his flat. As he closed the door behind him in the hall and stepped into the open frame of the living room, he looked automatically toward his two arched front bay windows with their view of the city, hazy pinpricks of light in the fog.

He stood for a moment, taking it in.

Then he shrugged out of his suit coat and stripped off his shoulder holster and service weapon, to set them on the end table. His service belt was light, and he stepped to the hall closet and found another set of cuffs to replace the ones he'd put on his attacker that afternoon.

He took a second to turn up the thermostat, then walked through the living room into the in-name-only dining room and tossed his briefcase on the table. Then he upended it, spilling out the files: the Reaper, the Lelands, Santos, Cara . . . and stood looking down on them.

He flipped open the file they'd gotten from the parole officer on Santos and spread the contents out: photos, arrest record. He walked around the table, staring down at the paperwork.

His gut feeling was that Santos was a dead end.

And we can't waste time on this.

The next thought was dangerous.

There's a shortcut to all of it.

He was absolutely sure that Cara could take one look at a photo of Santos and tell him yes or no.

He turned toward the front windows. He knew Jones—or a backup agent—was out there watching the flat, and he felt a sudden surge of anger about it, like a teenager sentenced to detention. And the thought wouldn't go away:

Cara will know. If this guy is the Reaper, she'll know.

He stood for a long while. But long before he moved to do it, he knew what he was going to do.

He picked up Santos' file from the table, turned on his heel and crossed to the wall to kill the lights in the living room, then headed toward the bedroom, where he flicked the lights on and dimmed them. He stepped to the windows and stood for a moment looking out in mock contemplation, before he reached up and drew the drapes. But not quite all the way. Instead he left the panels just very slightly parted, enough to give anyone watching from outside a glimpse of movement, but nothing in the least substantial.

He turned on the T.V. to create the impression of motion, the illusion of himself hunkered down for the night, as clearly evidenced by the flickering light of the screen that would be visible through the crack in the curtains.

He stripped off his clothes and changed into dark track pants, a dark sweatshirt, and dark windbreaker. Standing in the doorway of his closet, he glanced at his bullet-resistant vest, hanging on its hook just inside the door. But it wouldn't cover his throat, which was the only thing he really had to worry about, so he left it.

Besides, he didn't think that Cara would come after him. He never had thought it.

There remained only his weapon.

He walked out into the front hall and looked at the equipment on the end table. He pulled out the drawer of the table and removed a conceal-carry belt designed for running, a Thunderwear holster that strapped around his hips and had pockets for his Glock, cuffs, ID, extra mags—and a lock-picking set. He holstered the weapon and strapped the belt around his waist.

Then, sending a silent apology toward Jones, he left through the front door and headed out down the back stairs.

The back stairwell of his building opened into a small enclosed courtyard shared with the building behind. The night was cold, but the misty air on his face felt calming. He moved quietly out into the courtyard, through drifting fog.

There was a tree with a few stunted apples, a grill, some mismatched tables and chairs, a plot with someone's attempt at an urban garden, a door to a laundry room. Behind a tall gate was the trash cubicle of the building behind. At the back of the cubicle another gate opened to an alley for trash pickup. Roarke stepped through the first gate, past the trash bins, and tried the inner back door. Locked, of course.

He pulled tools out of his belt and started on the lock.

There was a footfall in the courtyard behind him and the gate to the trash enclosure squealed open. He twisted around to see the young father from the building opposite, hefting a sack of trash. He stopped in his tracks, as startled to see Roarke as Roarke was to see him.

"Agent Roarke," the man said uneasily.

Roarke knew how the situation looked. "Threw something away that I need," he explained, lamely.

"Oh," the man said. "Have a good Thanksgiving, then." He dropped his trash hastily in a bin and backed up into the courtyard.

Roarke breathed in to slow his heart as he listened for the sound of the side door closing . . . then finished with the lock, and was out into the dark alley a second later. He checked both ways and saw no one, but he waited a good five minutes in the dark to make sure before he headed for the street.

He kept to the darker streets, watching every shadow, matching his pace to the night as he moved silently through the fog toward Dolores Park.

By day the park was overrun by Noe Valley's families and high school kids from the adjacent school. At night it was ominous, lit by antique iron street lamps shining through the drifting fog. The grounds sprawled on the slope of a hill, and there was a spectacular view of city lights, now hazy and pointillistic in the mist. Across the street was the big brass dome of Dolores Park Church, perfectly round. The top of the park was bordered by Muni tracks; in the center of the park was a sunken island of concrete with a children's playground: stations of the usual swing sets, slides, sandpits, a climbing pyramid. A walking track circled around it, curving through concrete planters of drought-resistant foliage, spiky pink tea tree and white fronds of pampas grass interspersed with whimsical public art. A larger packed dirt path made a bigger circle for running, this one curving past tennis courts and a small clubhouse.

Roarke stood for a moment taking it all in, then walked the outer paths, passing sleeping clumps of homeless camped out under the trees, thinking, but really just letting himself be seen by . . . whoever might be watching.

He found a bench in a cluster of bushy palm trees and sat for a while contemplating the city lights through the soup of fog. Then he stood.

Leaving the case file on the bench.

His heart was beating faster already. He would arrest her if he had the chance. He was crystal clear on that point. But as far as he was concerned, they could arrest her later. If a few more pimps, child molesters, or rapists died in the next week, so be it, if Cara knew anything that could help him catch the Reaper.

He did some stretching as he moved out of the grove of trees, more than usually aware of the Glock hanging heavy at his waist, and then moved forward, easing into a slow run up the steep incline. Close as the park was to his house, he rarely used the track for running. It was too crowded with nannies and kids and dogs by day. But at night and deserted like this it would do, and pass the time. He hadn't had a chance to run in weeks and it was irritating to feel himself losing muscle tone. His thighs and hamstrings warmed and loosened and he picked up speed on his second lap, running full out for his third and fourth, recapturing the sense of power in his own body. He slowed for one last round, riding the buzz of endorphins, feeling the knotted parts of his soul unraveling, knowing he was an idiot for not making time for this every single day.

And that was when he saw her.

He saw *something*.

A figure, ghost pale and slim, standing in the palms.

He stopped dead in his tracks. Just as quickly the shape was gone, slipping into the trees.

After one suspended second he bolted forward, legs pumping, barreling across the grass toward the grove.

His heart was pounding out of his chest when he hit the palm grove. He stopped in the midst of fallen fronds, looking around him.

The trees were not so densely packed that someone could hide. It was only the thick mist that had been concealing. There was no sign of anyone.

He ran through the trees, dodging the thick trunks, looking around him frantically . . . but aside from the sleeping lumps of the homeless, there was no one else stirring.

His heart had slowed, but it started to race again as he moved back through the palm sanctuary, approaching the bench . . .

He stared ahead in the dark, and his heart spasmed.

The contents of the file were scattered, on the bench, on the ground, pages everywhere. Pieces of a photograph were torn and flung like confetti. He stooped and gathered a few of the ragged squares. It was the wild-eyed mug shot of Santos that had been destroyed.

He stood, moved slowly to the bench, where the file folder itself lay, intact. The word NO was scrawled on the face of it with the pen he had left inside the file. Huge, angry slashes.

The word paralyzed him. What did she mean? No as in Santos was not the Reaper? Or just a no of protest against old horrors?

He turned and stared into the drifting mist.

She was here. Where? To where could she have disappeared?

He focused on the one building inside the park: a tiny clubhouse with restrooms underneath. Too small to make much of a hiding place, but he ran toward the structure and circled the building, trying all the doors, alert to any sound. The doors were all closed, locked.

He stepped away and turned toward the hill, scanned the park through the mist. There was only one other place she could have vanished so quickly. In the shallow ravine that housed the Muni tracks, there was a bridge and trestle.

He sprinted up the slope toward the tracks, and stopped at the top, panting, staring down toward the bridge.

Across the tracks was a slope with trees and thick undergrowth, with any number of places for anyone to crouch in and hide. He scanned the shrubbery, looking for a flash of blond . . .

From the bridge came the hollow thud of rock on rock.

He sidestepped down the slope, heading for the trestle even as it crossed his mind that she had killed in spots like this more than once, not just Ramirez but also the Preacherman, a home-grown anarchist who had been making a bomb to set off at a Portland street fair—before Cara had sliced his neck open in a culvert.

As Roarke reached the bridge he pressed himself against the wall of the arch and drew his weapon automatically. The place felt resonant as he tried to sense a presence.

He leaned against the wall, his thoughts racing.

He highly doubted she was armed with more than a razor. But he had no idea what she might do if she felt cornered. It was like approaching a tigress: if threatened, he had no doubt she would attack instinctively and completely.

"Cara," he spoke aloud, and his voice echoed in the arch of the bridge. His eyes searched the darknesses beyond. His whole body was humming but he had no idea if she was there.

"I think the Reaper is out there. I don't know how, but . . . it's him. If it's not Santos, it's someone." He listened, focusing every nerve he had to hear. "We don't have much time. If you can help—" He stopped mid-sentence, remembering that Cara's idea of help was different from the rest of the world.

He held his breath, listening to the silence. There was a tautness in his stomach and thighs that he knew was more than adrenaline.

Almost desperate now, he took one more shot. "If there's anything you can tell me, I need to know. You're the only one who does know." Again he strained all of his senses into the night, listening . . . hoping for some sign. And then he spoke words he didn't know he was going to say until they were in his mouth. "I'm going to get him. I swear to you, I'll get him."

He stared into the darkness, willing her to step out, dreading her stepping out . . . not for what she would do, but for what he would have to do.

He waited for what started to seem like forever. But there was no one.

Chapter 25

The crime scene photos were gone.

The images of the Lelands killed in their beds, the slaughtered children. Cara had taken them.

Roarke stood at the bench looking down at the open folder with a sick feeling in the pit of his stomach. He'd searched all around the hill, the nearby palm groves, thinking she might just have scattered the photos in her frenzy. But they were gone.

What she would do with them, he had no idea. But he realized he'd completely crossed a line.

Images raced through his mind. *The pimp in a lake of blood. The carnage at the cement plant; ten men lying dead in the sand.*

There was no telling what Cara would do with the knowledge that the Reaper was out there. Whether or not it was true, letting her think it was like unleashing a search-and-destroy missile, if such a thing had existed.

She had been here, and he had lost her, and whatever blood came next, it was on his hands.

• • • • •

There is another park that divides the upper Haight from the lower, Buena Vista Park, a hill that has been host to more hippies and homeless than almost any other in the city.

It is there she comes to rest, in the hours before dawn. The cold is numbing, but though her room is just three blocks away, she is too jittery to be confined inside, and she needs to listen now, listen to the night and to the moon.

From the hill she can see the fog-shrouded bay, and Alcatraz, the dark fortress-like former prison on the island in the middle of the bay, with its even darker history: men going slowly or not so slowly insane under unimaginable conditions. Men who deserved to be there . . . and perhaps some who didn't.

The crime scene photos are spread out on the grass in front of her, like screenshots taken of a nightmare, her own nightmare. The echo of screams is in the shadows of the shots.

She feels panic rising, panic and darkness and fury.

There are paths converging. The present: the flaming girl who now knows her like no one has ever known her, and the danger that means. And the past, the monster showing its face again.

The pimp in the tunnel, the family slaughtered in their beds.

Two tracks, two poles. She feels her head splitting apart.

And as she huddles into herself, her hair falling over her face, she can still hear Roarke's voice, calling to her in the dark. She can see him, a shadow under the bridge, his body tense, his weapon drawn. She has no idea what will happen if she steps out.

But she knows this, all of this, for what it is.

A trap. A trap. A trap.

She beats her hands on the cold ground and feels the screams rising, rising into the night, rising to the moon, and she does not know if the screams are the earth's or her own.

Chapter 26

Roarke nearly jumped out of his skin as his phone buzzed in his trouser pocket. He looked around him, orienting himself. Home. The night was still dark outside his living room. He'd gotten himself upstairs, back through the back gate and up to his flat, where he'd sat for what he'd intended to be only a moment. Instead he'd fallen asleep in the armchair.

He dug for the phone, lifted it to his face.

A familiar voice said into his ear, "We got her."

Roarke's pulse spiked with adrenaline and disorientation. *Got her? Cara? Here? Did she follow me?* He had no idea who he was talking to or what was being said to him. After a split second he identified the caller.

"Mills?"

"No, your mother," the homicide inspector snorted on the other end. "The fuck did you think?"

"You got . . ."

Mills said impatiently. "Hello? Is this *Special* Agent Roarke I'm talkin' to? I got the *girl*."

Roarke finally realized Mills meant the young street hustler. Jade. "You arrested her?"

Mills made a scornful sound. "Yah, and have Rachel Elliott riding my ass from here to eternity?" A lustful note crept into his voice. "Although come to think, that's not the worst scenario I can envision. However, no, the girl is not arrested. She's sort of being held for possession."

"*Sort* of?" Roarke repeated.

"I've got her for possession but I gave her the choice: talk to us or get busted."

"Is she talking?" *Did she see it?* was what he meant. *Is she a real witness?*

"So far, baby, she ain't said shit. No, that's wrong, she did say 'shit.' Also 'motherfucker,' 'cunting bastard,' some other things about my anatomy and what I could do with it, all very creative. But nothing useful, if you see my point."

"Mills, I never see your point."

"My point is, I don't know how long I can hold her, this being the People's Republic of San Francisco and some people thinkin' that other people have rights and all. And I gotta say, this kid is jumpy as hell. She's going to rabbit as soon as I cut her loose. No one's ever gwan see her again. So if you want at her, you need to tell me now."

"Yeah. I want to talk to her."

Mills was holding Jade at San Francisco's Juvenile Hall, on Woodside Avenue.

Roarke jumped into the shower to wake himself up, and leaned back against the tiled wall as the water ran over him.

Maybe Jade is the key. Maybe we can arrest Cara before she does something . . . inevitable.

His thoughts turned to the trestle.

Had she been there? Had he felt her?

He stood in the steaming water, water teasing over his skin . . . and felt again the unbearable tension from the tunnel, his thighs and abdomen tightening with desire, his body straining toward a presence in the dark . . .

Abruptly he reached for the faucet handles and shut the water off.

He came out of the bathroom, towel wrapped around him, and sat on the bed. Then he reached for his phone on the nightstand and dialed Rachel Elliott.

When she picked up, he said, "It's Matt Roarke," not realizing he had used his first name until it was out. He instantly regretted it.

"Hello," she said, and waited, but he could feel the suspended breath in the pause.

"I'm sorry to call you so late. It's about Jade."

A silence, and then a voice braced with dread. "What happened?"

"She's all right," Roarke assured her quickly. "Mills arrested her but he's not going to hold her. But I need to question her and I was hoping you'd come down and sit in." In California, law enforcement officials were able to question minors without the supervision of a parent or guardian, but he thought Rachel's presence might help. Or not. Or maybe there was some other reason he needed her there that he wasn't letting himself acknowledge.

He could feel her thinking on the other end of the line, a live, crackling energy.

"You'll release her to me when you're done?" she finally asked.

"Of course."

"Not that she'll stay," Rachel said. "All right, I'll be there."

The building was modernistic, geometrical shapes of raw concrete with curved walls leading up to it. The halls were shining and clean, the grand entryway was three stories of almost all glass, with big bright green and yellow circles patterned on the floor. But it was still jail. Roarke signed in, took off shoes and belt and emptied his pockets, passed his belongings through the X-ray machine as he went through security, and headed back into the holding area. He was feeling an anxiety that only increased as he passed by bars and gates, various holding cells, and an interview room just as bleak as any in an adult jail.

Mills was on a bench, scrolling through email on his phone. He rose when he saw Roarke and his eyes ran over Roarke's suit. "Aw, you didn't have to dress up for me." He gestured down the hall and Roarke fell into step with him.

"How did you find her?"

Mills shrugged. "Tattoo parlors panned out. I found the guy who did hers and staked out the shop, and what do you know? She cruised by."

Roarke raised an eyebrow, impressed. But then, he'd never thought Mills was a fool.

"I called Elliott," he told the detective. "I thought having her here might help."

Mills considered. "Could. Kid's not talking to me. You, maybe, pretty as you are."

Roarke ignored that. "Any more info on her from the system?"

"Nada. Not listed as a missing person. We don't even have a real name on her. She's going by Jade Lauren, but there's no such somebody on record, of course. She's not carrying an ID. She won't say where she's from. Her prints don't match any in AFIS. At least we've got them now. They match the lipstick from the scene, by the way."

So they had her at the scene of the murder. She'd be able to identify Cara. Roarke felt the realization in the pit of his stomach as an acid rush of dread.

It's what you need, isn't it?

Mills was talking on. "It's weird, 'cause most parents print their children these days. This one—not a thing."

"That says something, doesn't it?" a female voice said behind them.

Mills looked over Roarke's shoulder, said under his breath, "Watch out."

Roarke turned to see Rachel Elliott striding down the hall toward them, dressed in jeans and a red cashmere sweater under a dark pea coat and scarf. She was flushed and her hair was a heavy swirling cloud around her face.

She stopped in front of them, righteously pissed. "Mills, you asshole. You have no right."

Mills held up his hands. "Hey, she was holding."

"Like you're not," Rachel shot back at him, and Roarke almost laughed. She was probably right.

"Want to search me?" Mills said, unperturbed. "Roarke needs to get his girl, don't he?"

"Let's just do it," Rachel said tightly.

Roarke and Rachel walked down the hall together, following Mills. Roarke's sleeplessness was catching up with him and it made him clumsy, swaying into her personal space. They were close enough that he could feel her anger radiating from her like heat.

He tried to keep his voice neutral. "Have you had any luck finding out where she came from?"

"Nothing," Rachel said. "No one's put out anything on the missing child hotlines or websites trying to find her. I thought I might find something through foster care—more than half the teens in the life are runaways from foster homes. But she's not in the California system, anyway."

Before they entered the interview room, Roarke stepped into the adjacent viewing room to take a look at her through the observation mirror.

The girl who called herself Jade was seated at the table, leaning far back in the plastic chair, long legs stretched in front of her to rest on the edge of the table with an exaggerated sensuality. She was raccoon-eyed with heavy makeup and looked supremely bored with her surroundings. At the same time that he could see she was hypervigilant, she wasn't missing a thing. She looked up at the camera at regular intervals, staring at it insolently.

Her hoodie was fashionably distressed and only partly zipped so it was slipping off her shoulders, baring her collarbone and part of her back. The tattoos there were instantly arresting; intricate patterns that he could only see the top of but which clearly covered most of her back.

And she was very young, her druggie thinness softened by skin round and smooth with baby fat.

Rachel stood at the door, watching him watch the girl. "Any tips?" he asked.

"She's sixteen," she said dryly. "Good luck."

He opened the door for Rachel but made sure that he was positioned where he could see Jade as soon as the door cracked.

She looked up instantly as the door opened. Rachel, then Roarke stepped through, followed by Mills.

Rachel didn't touch the girl, but the social worker radiated a gentleness that Roarke hadn't seen in her before as she sat and leaned forward across the table.

"Hello, Jade," she said. "This is Special Agent Roarke, of the FBI. He has some questions for you, along with Inspector Mills, and I'm here to supervise. Are you comfortable? Do you need anything?"

"I'd blow all of you for a cigarette," Jade drawled.

Rachel didn't even blink; Roarke had to admire it. "Anything to drink? Eat?" she asked, as if she hadn't heard.

Jade waved a languid hand at the soda can in front of her. "I'm all set."

Roarke pulled a chair out for Rachel across the table from Jade, and sat in the one beside her. Mills remained standing, leaned a shoulder against the wall.

The girl watched Roarke's every move, her eyes slipping over him like hands, a blatantly sexual appraisal. He kept his face neutral, but he was startled by the blazing energy coming off her. Maybe she was still high. Whatever it was, she burned.

Christ, he thought. *Sixteen.*

Rachel shifted beside him, cleared her throat. He spoke to the girl. "We're not holding you for the dope, Jade. Rachel can take you home in the morning."

Jade's eyes flicked toward Rachel, with no readable expression. "Happy days."

"But we need to ask you some questions about Danny Ramirez."

She shrugged lazily. "I have a choice?"

"Would you like a lawyer?"

She stared at him with blank eyes, then smiled thinly. "Crowded enough in here already, doncha think? All these people for little ol' me." She shifted in the chair, and leaned back again. "Just do it."

While she had been talking Roarke had been studying her: speech patterns, mannerisms, the way she dressed. *West Coast*, he thought. *Southwest, Pacific Northwest, or California.* Or at least she'd been in California long enough to assimilate the style. Despite a street defensiveness, her body language was open, her speech a casual drawl with no Eastern or Southern affect. She was intelligent, too, she had the arrogance of a naturally high IQ and she wasn't intimidated by adults.

He decided his best course of action would be to get right to it, not coddle her, but treat her as an adult.

"You witnessed the death of Danny Ramirez."

"No clue what you're talking about," she said stonily.

"We have your prints on a lipstick that was dropped at the scene."

"I didn't kill Danny."

"We know you didn't kill Danny. But you saw it, didn't you?"

There was a lot on her face now, but she was silent.

"All I'm asking is what you saw."

Her eyes flicked to the side. "It was dark."

"Let's start with the basics. Even in the dark I think you can tell a man from a woman."

She gave him a smile so hard it made him cold, and said nothing. Roarke put the police sketch of Cara down on the table.

"Was this the person you saw?" He watched Jade's face.

She took her time before she looked down, and then she looked at the sketch a long time. "Who is she?"

"Is this the person you saw?"

"Probably. Without the sunglasses. It being night, and all."

"Can you talk us through what happened? How did you get to the tunnel?"

She shrugged, yawned. "Danny texted me to meet him."

"Why was that?" Mills asked dryly.

"Guess," she said, looking straight at him.

Beside Roarke, Rachel suddenly leaned forward. Her voice was soft, and compelling. "I know it must have been hard to see. No matter what else you felt about him. It must have been hard."

Jade looked back at her. "It was a lot of blood," the girl said. "A lot of blood."

"I know," Rachel said. "Tell us."

Roarke held his breath, feeling the connection between the two of them resonate in the room. The moment seemed to last forever, then Jade looked away from Rachel again. But miraculously, she spoke.

"He said to meet in the tunnel so I walked down from the fair, on Haight? So I get into the tunnel and I see that he's with someone and I don't know what's going on so I wait. Back a little. It's really dark so I can't see much, but it's someone thin, pants and a jacket. I figure it's someone making a buy. But when Danny lights up I see her in the flame."

Roarke had a sudden, very clear picture of the scene, Cara appearing in the dark, as pale and blond as she was. The last thing Ramirez would have expected in that dank tunnel.

"Did they say anything to each other?" Rachel asked, exactly right, a total pro.

Jade shrugged. "Danny talked some shit. 'Whatchu want, bitch,' his usual charm. Wrong thing to say, turns out." But her voice shook when she said it, and she reached for the soda can to drink.

Roarke made sure his own voice was steady, neutral, when he asked the next. "Did she say anything?"

Jade put the can down. "Nope. She just stepped up and grabbed his hair and . . . sliced him."

She wrapped her arms around her thin torso. Her hoodie slipped down off her shoulders, exposing more of the tattoo, a female figure inside a cone of flames.

"There was so much blood . . ." she said in a hollow voice.

Roarke's head was buzzing. *She saw it. She saw the whole thing. A direct, material witness.*

But he sensed there was more that she wasn't saying.

"Did she see you?"

The girl's eyes flicked to his face. "It was so dark. I couldn't move. I just stood there hoping she wouldn't see."

"You were afraid of her?" he asked, and heard the sharpness in his voice. Rachel looked at him, startled.

"She's standing there with a razor, Danny's there bleeding out at her feet? Are you kidding?" Jade sounded insulted . . . but not afraid, exactly. He couldn't read her.

"She didn't say anything to you," he said, and again Rachel glanced at his face, a questioning look.

"No," Jade said defiantly. "She didn't see me."

Lying, Roarke thought, suddenly sure. *Why?*

"What happened then?" he said neutrally.

Jade looked away. "She leaned over, took his roll."

"Money, you mean?"

"Yeah."

"And?"

"Pocketed it. And then she was gone." She finally met his eyes. "I waited until I was sure. And I ran."

She was leaving something out, he knew it. "She said *nothing* to you."

Rachel shifted in her chair. Jade's eyes blazed across at him. "She *didn't see me*." She spat the words at him.

He sat for a moment, and then asked, "Why do you think she killed him?"

Rachel shifted again beside him.

Jade stared hard at him, then her mouth quirked, not quite a smile. "I guess she thought he needed killing."

Roarke stared back at her for a long moment. "Could you identify her if you saw her again?"

There was a quick, furtive look on her face, instantly gone. "Like I'm gonna forget?" she retorted.

Roarke sat, chair pushed back from the table, just looking at her. She looked right back. "So who is she?" Jade said.

"Our suspect."

"And what else?"

Roarke looked at her. She stared steadily back at him. "Agent Roarke, right? Special Agent Roarke? So why are you here? Why isn't Beavis over there handling this?"

"Hey," Mills grumbled.

"What do *you* want her for?" Jade continued, never looking away from him.

"Murder," Roarke said flatly. And he stood, ending the interview.

As they stepped out into the hall, a guard was waiting to take Jade back to a room.

"I'll be by first thing in the morning," Rachel told the girl. It would take that long to get her processed out.

"Whatever," Jade said, and her eyes slid toward Roarke, a watching look.

In a moment, he decided, used it, leaned forward and closed his fingers around her wrist. She looked up at him, startled. "If you think of anything else, you'll call, won't you."

"You bet," she drawled, but he felt her pulse quicken under the pressure of his hand.

He released her slowly. "Thanks for all your help."

He turned and walked down the hall, Rachel and Mills following after a moment in his wake.

• • • • •

At this hour the glare of the fluorescents in the corridor was a dream-like haze. Rachel was silent, but Roarke could feel her thoughts ticking. Beside her, Mills was brooding. "I'm not so sure she'll rabbit after all. I think she might play this for whatever she can get."

Roarke thought he might be right.

They walked across the lobby and a guard tripped the doors so they could exit. The fog was so thick for a moment Roarke couldn't make out the parking lot in front of them. Rachel shivered beside him.

As they wound their way down the curved entry and the front steps into the dark of the parking lot, Mills suddenly said, "She was lying, but I can't figure out about what."

"Yeah. Not sure either," Roarke said. He shot a glance toward Rachel. "We need to work on finding out where she's from so we can have half a snowball's chance to find her again."

"And to start to help her work through everything she's been through," Rachel said dryly.

"Right," Roarke said. "And that."

"I'll do what I can," she said.

Mills turned to her. "So you'll let me know when she vamooses?"

"I'll call you," she said, shaking her head.

"Nice seein' you," the detective said to Roarke. "Happy Turkey Day." And he ambled off into the fog.

Roarke turned to Rachel. "Where's your car?"

"I'm all right—"

"Don't be stupid," he said, and she fell silent. She nodded down a row and they walked together in the drifting fog between cars. His mind was a chaos of thoughts. They finally had a witness. For the first time someone had seen Cara do murder that wasn't self-defense. Jade could put Cara away. And all this could be over.

Rachel glanced at him, as if she could feel the intensity of his inner monologue. But she was silent. She turned in to the next row of cars and stopped—at a Prius, of course. As she pulled keys from her coat pocket, he stepped close to her.

"Rachel."

She turned and looked up at him in the dark.

"I need anything that can open Jade up, pinpoint where she's from."

For a long moment he didn't know if she was going to say anything.

"I keep a log of my encounters with any of the girls I talk to."

Roarke felt a tightening in his stomach that he realized had nothing to do with the case. "I would love to see that."

She looked away from him. "I'm not going home anyway, not now. You might as well come by the shelter."

At night the Belvedere place looked like the grand house it had been, a bit of a Victorian time warp, all the windows dark except for the porch light, and the fog. No available parking spot of course, despite the hour. Roarke pulled his car up onto the sidewalk.

As he climbed the steps the door opened, and Rachel stood, half-in, half-out of the light. Roarke felt electricity as he stepped past her.

So that is what this is, he thought, and felt a soft darkness open inside him.

She closed and locked the door and moved down the dark hall toward her office.

In the hall there was the wall of pictures, the rows of teenage girls: snapshots, printed-out candids from camera phones. Some brash, some sullen, some haunted . . . all shadowed in some way.

Rachel slowed in front of it, looking up at the faces. When she spoke, her voice was low, but harsh with anger. "I don't understand people. How does anyone resembling a human being use a child like that?"

Roarke heard his own words, felt a rush of longing, then an old emptiness. "I don't know. I've never known."

"This world," she said. "It never ends." She turned abruptly away toward the office.

There was a low light on inside, the desk lamp casting a pool of light, and as Roarke stepped past her he could smell her perfume, something rich and autumnal. He remembered the glimpse through the inner door he'd gotten when they'd been in here before, the bed in the back room.

What are you doing? he asked himself, and had no answer. He forced himself to speak.

"I'm keeping you up all night, I'm sorry."

She didn't answer, but went to a file cabinet and unlocked it, leaned in to pull out a drugstore composition book with a mottled cover. "This is the last three months. You'll have to look through it but there are names, places—where I saw her, what she said when I tried to talk to her."

She opened it on the desk and he stepped beside her, feeling heat surge through his body. He looked down at the book. Her writing was small and feminine.

"The names are easy to find. I box them." She touched her finger to the page, and he saw she had drawn thick rectangles around dates and names.

"Your woman is in there," she said, and he glanced at her sharply. "The one you're looking for. I told you I saw her with Jade."

He remembered. She gave the girl takeout and then she killed her pimp. That was Cara.

"Who is she?" Rachel asked.

He felt boxed in, like the names on the page.

"What Jade was asking in there, I saw how you reacted." She didn't look at him. "What's happening?"

His mouth was dry. "I wish I knew."

"Did she really kill Ramirez just because . . . he deserved it? To help Jade? Is that what it is?"

"Something like that."

She looked at him so intensely he couldn't look away. "But you're out to arrest her? Or is it something else?"

He felt a tidal wave of emotion rising, threatening to overwhelm him. "I don't know what it is. I have no idea." He turned away from her, pressed his hand onto the desk. "Everything's all twisted. I can't see . . ."

She reached to touch him. "It's all right . . ."

He turned his head, and she looked up into his face, and he felt the sizzle of attraction. He pulled abruptly back. He could see the jolted look on her face.

"I'm sorry, I was wrong . . ."

"No, you weren't. It's my fault," he said. "I'll go." He didn't move. She stepped forward and put her hand against his cheek. He reached up and took her wrist, and time was suspended between them. And then he pulled her hard into him, thigh to thigh, hip to hip, and he laced his hand in her hair and he kissed her, felt her mouth open to his, felt her hunger and her longing, felt her softness against his hardness . . .

He tried one last time to pull back, but she sighed against his neck . . . and he was lost.

Chapter 27

He lay in the narrow bed with Rachel's warm soft curves wrapped around him. Her breathing was slow and even and he hoped she was asleep.

He still throbbed from the force of his climax, and with a new dark dread: the feeling that all this would have to be paid for.

He sat up too quickly, and froze, afraid she would move, wake. But she lay still, and he eased out of the bed, stooped to the floor for his clothes.

In the bed, Rachel opened her eyes, listening to the door close as he left.

Outside he eased the front door shut to avoid the jangling of bells, and walked down the steps into the dark, lit only by streetlights in the fog.

He stopped on the sidewalk, aware that something was wrong and not sure what it was. And then he realized his car was gone, towed by San Francisco's hypervigilant traffic division. He shook his head, thought of instant karma . . . and then turned south toward home to walk.

The pre-dawn was thick and still around him, and the guilt increased with every step; the fog that rolled around him seemed to be coming from somewhere inside him.

What were you thinking?

But he knew what he'd been thinking, however much thinking had to do with it. *Relief, release, something normal, something sane.* To grab on to some human connection before he crossed some irrevocable line, fell off the edge into an abyss.

He'd left Rachel a note on her desk pleading work, he'd call, she was lovely. None of which was likely to fool her.

There were the first anemic streaks of light in the sky as a cathedral loomed up in the dark in the block ahead.

He slowed and stopped on the sidewalk. He hadn't properly been in a church since he was ten, but he was seized with the desire to confess.

As he stood there in the shadows outside the building, he felt the darkness around him deepen. He was seized with the feeling that he was not alone. And in a heart-stopping moment he knew it was Cara, knew that she had followed him, that she had watched him with Rachel, that he'd finally crossed the line that would be his undoing.

And in the moment, he didn't care.

He turned to face the darkness . . .

And the air was shattered by the sound of a car roaring around a corner.

He spun, reaching automatically for his weapon—until he saw it was a fleet car, a Crown Vic.

The car skidded to a stop by the curb. The driver's door opened, and Epps unfolded himself to standing.

Roarke stared at him from across the hood of the car. "How did you know I was—"

Epps shook his head. "Jones has been following you all night. The plan, remember?"

Before Roarke could fully process what "all night" meant, Epps told him, "I hate it when you're right."

And Roarke's stomach plummeted.

"Tell me."

Chapter 28

t was a family in Lake Arrowhead, in the San Bernardino Mountains, a couple hours east of Los Angeles. Arrowhead was an upscale resort town of about eleven thousand locals that had been popular with Hollywood celebrities back in the heyday of film noir, and still drew a brisk tourist trade for skiing in the winter and for boating, hiking, and fishing in the summer.

"Slaughtered," Singh said gently, her velvet voice somber with regret. "The whole family."

The team was gathered around the table in the conference room, pulled away from their beds. There was a dreary light outside the windows now. Everyone was standing; they were all too wired to sit.

Singh continued. "They died some time last night; the bodies weren't discovered until this morning. The housekeeper came over early to drop off groceries for Thanksgiving before she left town, and found them."

There were faxed photos of the crime scene on the table in front of them. Heartbreaking photos.

"The same as the others," Singh explained as the agents looked down at the carnage. "Upper middle-class family, the Cavanaughs. Father a real estate agent in town. Mother owned an arts and crafts shop. Three children: two girls, fourteen and ten, and a thirteen-year-old boy. All stabbed, and the father apparently dead of a self-inflicted gunshot wound." She put an ironic emphasis on the word *apparently*. "A hunting rifle—"

She fell silent as Reynolds stepped into the doorway. Everyone on the team froze. Reynolds locked eyes with Roarke, then he looked at Singh. "Go on," he said.

After a moment, she did. "The central heating in the house was turned off and the temperature has been in the twenties overnight and below forty today, which means the scene is fairly pristine."

Roarke felt a jolt of adrenaline. Before he could even say a word, Singh continued. "I have been monitoring all police reports in the state and have had an urgent bulletin out asking that all familicides be reported immediately. Providentially, a local deputy had seen the bulletin and reported the crime directly to us. Nothing has been released to the media yet. The initial thought was murder–suicide. But there is some question."

Roarke was almost lightheaded with their luck. FBI bulletins were far too often filed in the circular file or immediately buried by a dozen other notices on police station corkboards.

"The full moon is still four days away," Epps said.

"Yes," Roarke said. "We won't know until we see."

But they all understood it was too similar to discount. Too close to the full moon to discount. And Roarke knew. It was the Reaper. He felt another paralyzing stab of guilt, unreasonable as it was, and had to force himself to focus on the present.

Singh continued carefully. "Now, the scene is already in process. I am getting some pushback from the sheriff about how much access we will be allowed. However, I have persuaded him to allow us to view the scene."

Roarke didn't even have to ask how she'd managed. Singh's magic calm had worked wonders on him often enough.

She permitted herself a small smile. "They are particularly interested in the lab resources we can offer. I promised . . . in essence, anything they need."

Beside Roarke, Epps breathed out. "Amazing, woman." Roarke's thoughts exactly. She was a goddess.

Singh spoke as if she hadn't heard. "My suggestion is that you leave immediately for the airport before they can change their minds. I will book you on the next flight down to Ontario and arrange for a car; it is just over an hour drive up into the mountains. I thought you would want Lam and Stotlemyre, so I have put in calls to them as well. I have informed them of the need to . . ."

"Bend over," Jones muttered.

"Cooperate," Singh said with a straight face.

Reynolds waited until the team cleared out of the room to approach Roarke. He looked both pissed and guilty. Roarke willed himself into a state of calm. "I-told-you-so's" were never in any way useful.

The SAC spoke gruffly. "Take whoever you need. Find out what the hell this is. If it's the guy, take him down."

"Thanks," Roarke said, without rancor. "We will." And as he turned away, the first thought in his head was that the person he most needed was the one person he couldn't take.

As they waited at the San Francisco airport for their flight, he called Snyder and quickly filled him in. "It's a fresh crime scene. Can you come down?"

There was a silence on the other end that seemed like more than an ordinary hesitation.

"You can do this, Matthew," the profiler said. "You always could."

"It's not about that." Roarke didn't know if he was telling the truth about that or not. But he knew he was telling the truth about what he said next. "If we're right, it's another whole family massacred. No one person is enough against that. If this is the Reaper, we have to make sure this doesn't happen again."

There was a longer silence on the phone than Roarke would have liked, but finally Snyder spoke. "All right, Matthew. Go. Have Singh call me with the details and I'll be down."

Roarke felt a surge of excitement, of purpose—and of sheer relief that he would not be alone.

Chapter 29

Ontario International was a mid-sized airport servicing the densely populated bedroom communities in the inland valleys east of Los Angeles.

Jones remained behind in the terminal to wait for Snyder, while Roarke, Epps, Lam, and Stotlemyre picked up the cases that contained the crime techs' portable laboratory and piled into the Jeep Singh had reserved for them for the hour drive up to the resort town. Epps drove, Roarke riding shotgun, Lam and Stotlemyre in the back seat, immediately spreading faxed photos of the crime scene out on the seat between them and commencing to argue like an old married couple.

They passed through the valley cities of Rancho Cucamonga and Fontana, with stunning mountains and foothills looming beside the freeway. The valleys were notorious for trapping smog in the summer, but fall winds had cleaned out the skies. Spectacular banks of clouds layered the sky in white, gray, and black, but the valleys were clear, and Roarke could see for miles, long vistas of palm trees and even orange groves.

Epps turned off the freeway at the former base town of San Bernardino, onto a street that was a straight shot toward the mountains, a steeply climbing road of hairpin curves that provided breathtaking views of the valley and the unique desert/mountain mix of Southern California: bleak granite outcroppings and drought-stressed Western and Jeffrey pines, red-barked manzanita scrub tucked into the folds and curves of the earth. Hawks circled above and the valley was softly indistinct below, an industrial grid with patches of trees.

"Hope no one gets carsick," Epps muttered as he twisted the wheel in another stomach-lurching spin.

Roarke's thoughts kept drifting back to Rachel, unbidden sexual flashbacks.

She knew what she was doing, a cold voice said in his mind, but he knew it instantly for the lie it was. *She has no idea what this is. How can she, when I don't know myself?*

He had to stop his thoughts, force his mind back to the car, to the present. *You're going to have to self-flagellate later. You've got a killer to catch.*

The scrub brush gave way to tall pines and the view opened up onto the most encompassing view yet, ridge after ridge of jagged blue mountains framing the valley.

"Daaaamn," Epps said admiringly.

Roarke had to agree. He knew people who lived in these mountains often commuted hours to work, even as far as L.A., and he'd always thought it insane. Now he wasn't so sure.

At the sweep of town that called itself Rim of the World they passed the high school that the Cavanaugh children now would never attend, and road signs to ski resorts.

"Resort towns," Roarke muttered in the front seat.

Epps glanced his way.

"Bishop, Reno, Blythe, Arrowhead . . . all the kill sites, they're resort towns, tourist towns. Or near to them." *Except Arcata*, he reminded himself. *But maybe there's something I'm overlooking there.* "Mountains, desert. Skiing, spas . . . What kind of business would service them?"

Epps' hands were tight on the steering wheel as he thought on it. "I get you. Some kind of traveling . . . service person. A low-level delivery kind of job. Something that would take the Reaper all over the state."

"Yeah. Like that."

"Ski supplies?"

"Wouldn't work for the desert."

"Skiing and boating?"

Roarke considered. *Boating . . . maybe, but . . .* "Sports equipment salespeople tend to be jocks. Snyder's profile of the Reaper is weirder than that, unkempt. The guy isn't going to have people skills."

Epps frowned. "Not sales, then. Just straight delivery."

"Maybe."

They sunk into silence, staring out at granite cliffs, thinking.

Past Rim of the World the ascent became more vertical; the agents all swallowed to equalize the pressure in their eardrums. Outside the car a cold mist set in. The drop-offs from the road were steeper and the pines thicker. Fog drifted across the highway. There were even a few patches of ice left over from an early snow, and one stretch of charred trees from a summer wildfire, a black and dead moonscape.

The town of Lake Arrowhead was a definite cut above the scattered cabins they'd been passing so far, instantly and obviously more affluent. The car motored past art galleries, and shops of upscale home furnishings. Every other storefront had a realtor shingle. The fire station was startlingly massive, but it made sense. Fire season was brutal in these parched mountains.

As they drove through, Roarke skimmed the demographics and details Singh had collected in a packet for him.

Epps spoke beside him. "Nice . . ."

Roarke looked up to see a stretch of blue between the trees. The lake was relatively small, about two miles by two miles, but strikingly scenic, azure and clear with a clean curve of shore, and private, for use by town property owners only. It was ringed by hotels, motels, bed-and-breakfasts, private cabins for rent, and lodges popular for business conferences. The town's economy was almost entirely supported by tourism.

Serious money had gone into the development of the town center beside the lake; the Village was a series of interconnected gazebos, boutiques, plazas, bandstands, bars and restaurants, and several huge parking lots around a central pavilion, all with a quaint alpine/deco style to the architecture: steepled roofs, whitewashed buildings with brown trim. Roarke saw there was even a small amusement park for the kids. It all looked vaguely familiar, probably due to the number of films that had been shot in the town and surrounding area over the years.

There was no police department in the town itself. As an unincorporated community, it was serviced by the county sheriff's department in Twin Peaks, about three miles out of town, a station of twenty sworn officers, three detectives, and five ranking officers, charged with patrolling an area of over 340 square miles of territory, including numerous mountain resort towns and the National Forest.

Epps parked the Jeep in the drive of the tiny, angular concrete building set next to a log-cabin style Masonic lodge. Lam and Stotlemyre remained in the car as Roarke and Epps got out. "Kid gloves," Roarke muttered, as they walked up to the glass doors. He knew he was the one who needed the reminder.

Inside they were met by Lieutenant Tyson.

"Appreciate your willingness to work with us," Roarke told the lieutenant as they shook hands and followed him into his office, where all the men seated themselves stiffly. Tension was thick in the room. Tyson didn't waste any time getting down to brass tacks.

"Your Agent Singh said you believe this is not a murder–suicide. That you've seen this guy before," he stated.

Epps was as ever the perfect mediator—strong, serious, yet deferential. "We strongly suspect this is a multiple murder staged by a perp we've been pursuing."

"We understand you have some doubt about the murder–suicide angle," Roarke added.

Tyson looked at him, finally answered warily. "We have questions."

Epps jumped in. "We're here to provide all the support and resources you can use, including our crime lab. We've got our best crime scene techs with us."

"Appreciate the offer," Tyson said coolly. "But living in these mountains, it's like being on an island. We know the locals, the players. You don't. If there's an outside perp, we can get this guy faster than you can."

Pushback, as Singh had warned. Roarke fought to keep impatience out of his voice. "If it is our guy, he's long gone. He doesn't stick around after his kills. His latest was just over two weeks ago. Another whole family. In Nevada."

Tyson's eyes darkened at that last. Roarke knew exactly what he was thinking: it was a slow enough process to get files from other agencies in-state, never mind a different state altogether. He jumped to emphasize the point. "We can put you together with the key people in the Reno departments, expedite your investigation in whatever ways you need."

And then he played his best card. He stood and lay photos of the Reno crime scene down on the desk, the very worst shots. Tyson stood and moved reluctantly to look down at the images. His face didn't change, but Roarke felt the temperature of the room drop.

He sees it. It looks the same, he thought, with a rush of dread . . . and hope.

He lowered his voice. "It's your case, your collar, your trial. We'll get DNA, any tests you need moved to the top of the list. But this guy likes killing on the full moon, and there's one four days away now. We just want to see what you've got."

The agents and the lieutenant looked at each other across the photos. Roarke held his breath, feeling lives in the balance.

Finally Tyson nodded curtly. "We'll take you over for a look."

The agents followed the lieutenant's vehicle to the scene.

The Cavanaughs had lived a few miles from the central village, down another twisting mountain road, in a neighborhood with views of the desert rather than the lake. It was a startling contrast to the green forest and blue water inside of the town, a stark and lonely landscape that Roarke found strangely preferable to the trees as he stared out through the car window over layers of hills slanting down to a vast desert valley. *It is an island*, he thought.

The Cavanaugh house was three stories of river rock and pine, set back from the road, almost invisible to any casual passerby. Lieutenant Tyson had said the neighboring houses were vacant; the town generally emptied out for the Thanksgiving weekend. So far that fact had allowed the department to keep the news of the murders under wraps.

Deputies were stationed around the perimeter of the house, guarding the scene.

"It's an army," Lam said from the back seat, resignation in his voice. Roarke knew what he meant. The more first responders, the more chance of crucial evidence being destroyed.

Stotlemyre leaned up in the seat to speak to Epps and Roarke as Epps parked the Jeep. "Here's the plan. I'll stay with the techs and work on them to let us assist."

"And I'll tour the house with you," Lam said, as if the two techs had talked it over between them, which Roarke knew that they hadn't.

Stotlemyre added, "The front threshold's probably shot but hopefully the perp went in the side and we can get something off that porch. Don't let anyone go near the side entry."

As the agents got out of the Jeep, one of the deputies stepped up to have all the men sign a security log. So far everything by the book.

Lieutenant Tyson introduced the agents to Detective Aceves, the lead, and his partner Detective Lambert, then took his leave while the agents suited up in white coveralls, and pulled on latex gloves and paper booties in the driveway outside. Roarke slid his hands into the jumper's pockets to further ensure he would touch nothing, and the other men followed suit.

As they approached the house Roarke saw Lam looking over the uniformed deputies patrolling the perimeter and heard him mutter to Stotlemyre, "We need to get their *shoes.*"

All of the men paused on the doorstep before they stepped through the door, a beat of silence. They all knew the moment for what it was: they were entering a tomb.

Through the front door there was an entry hall with a flagstone floor. Inside, the living room featured a towering stone chimney and tall slanting windows showcasing the views. A gorgeous house, Roarke had to admit, superbly designed to capture all of the wild and haunting beauty of the wilderness setting. He could feel Epps, the taste master, nodding unconscious approval as the agents followed the detectives through the entry and took in the living room.

There was no blood in this elegant living space or open cook's kitchen; all the killing had been done in the bedrooms. And yet there was a darkness in the house. The rooms were refrigerator-cold but the smell of death was there in the chill, a coppery butcher shop stench under the holiday scent of spicy apple-cinnamon pot-pourri.

Roarke turned to Detective Aceves. "He killed the mother first, then the girls, saved the boy for last?"

The detective gave him a sharp look. "Looks like it."

Singh had compiled a whole file, including floor plans, so Roarke knew the house had three levels: a basement game room that opened out on the back patio and yard, the main level of two-story living room, plus a master suite and guest room/library, and three bedrooms upstairs. A mountain chalet that spoke of long ski weekends in winter and boating trips in summer. *Skiing and boating,* he thought again. *Delivery. A regular route. Something . . .*

As they moved through the house he noted that there was a sameness to the look of all the three houses he had visited on the Reaper's path of destruction. It was something in the slanted ceilings, the wood beams. He frowned, wondering.

The detectives led the agents down a short hall toward the master suite. The men hugged the wall, moving past the bathroom toward the open bedroom door.

Roarke braced himself as he stepped into the doorway.

It was bad. The peach-painted walls behind the bed were darkly curtained in Eileen Cavanaugh's blood. She lay in bed half-in and half-out of the covers, her throat gaping open to severed cartilage, the bedclothes stiff with more congealed blood. She'd died alone with the monster . . . but mercifully quickly; she may even have been sliced open in her sleep. No more than a few moments of disorientation and terror, Roarke silently hoped.

The body was stiff and ghostly white, seeming frozen and inhuman in the chill of the house.

He did not move into the room. He wanted to get a look at the whole picture and let the detectives warm to him, then hopefully they'd let Lam and Stotlemyre do their work.

"The knife was from the kitchen?" he asked aloud.

"From a set in a butcher block on the kitchen island," Aceves said. "But . . ." He stopped.

Roarke looked at him. "But?"

Aceves seemed to be debating with himself, then he finished, "Why use a knife on the family if he had a gun?"

Roarke nodded slowly. "Exactly." He held Aceves' gaze, and felt the beginnings of a bond.

Aceves turned from the door and indicated the upstairs with a jerk of his head. The team eased out of the hallway and toward the stairs. Aceves led, and Roarke started up behind him, staying against the chest-high wall of the staircase as they trod a careful trail upwards.

All the men were tense as they gathered on the upper landing, steeling themselves to go into the children's rooms. Of course there was no way ever to prepare for what they were about to see.

The first room was the teenage girl's: Shannon. Heartbreakingly typical, on the cusp of girl and woman: rock stars and actors Roarke didn't recognize on the walls, the posters now spattered with Shannon's blood. Her body was rigid as a mannequin's, the pink comforter and the flannel pajama bottoms and tank top she wore were stiff with dark red from multiple stab wounds.

"Christ," Epps said, in a voice that could have cut steel.

Roarke could see the girl still had ear buds in her ears. She'd fallen asleep with them or was still half-awake listening to music when she died. Like her mother, she probably—hopefully—never knew what hit her.

They all turned from the door and their queasiness was palpable.

The second bedroom door was the ten-year-old, Megan. It was clear at first look that Megan had not died as quietly as her mother and sister. She had heard something, *known* something. Her body was halfway under her desk. She had tried to crawl under it, or had been hiding under it. The killer had dragged her out to cut her; there were wide smears of blood underneath her body in the beige carpet. Roarke felt knots of anger and sorrow in his stomach, in his throat.

But the worst was yet to come.

In Robbie Cavanaugh's room, there was blood everywhere, splashed on the wall, staining the carpet, spattering the shelves of video games and models. The boy's body was on the bed, but there were signs of his struggle smeared into the rug. His arms were flung above his head and there were stab wounds in his neck and chest, too; he had been pierced so many times Roarke could see bits of his intestines, even from the doorway. His pajama pants were nearly black with it.

It was an outrage, this kind of carnage in a room so full of life. And while the other rooms had been like cold dark holes, there was a *feeling* in this room. Roarke had no idea really what he meant by that, but he could sense something live, like the echo of screams.

He said aloud, "Escalating."

Beside him, Epps said, in a barely audible voice. "Yeah."

"Holy Christ." It was Lam speaking, from far away. "We have got to get this guy."

Roarke closed his eyes, briefly, and had to steady his voice. "And the father?"

"Basement," Detective Aceves said. "The game room."

Stotlemyre rejoined them as they headed down the carpeted stairs to the game room. Roarke's legs felt shaky as they descended.

There was a billiard table and a Ping-Pong table and a foosball table and a jukebox and a dartboard on the wall. And of course, a large flat screen T.V. A comfortable and well-stocked family room, including a wet bar with a locked liquor cabinet and a closet with door standing open, shelves packed with tennis rackets and snowshoes and ice skates. All the accoutrements of a well-off, athletic family in a room now tainted with the overwhelming presence of death.

The father was slumped in a club chair in front of the television with a rifle at his feet and a bloody cavern where his head had been. Blood and brains sprayed the carpet beneath him.

At first glimpse just about anyone would see it as a suicide.

"Basement is concrete block," Epps said. "Family probably never heard the shot."

"The gun his?" Roarke asked, and heard the edge in his voice.

"From the cabinet upstairs. Guy is a sportsman," Aceves answered.

"The gun cabinet wasn't locked?"

"No—" Aceves said, and stopped, his eyes narrowing.

"Three kids," Roarke said. The number of people who left guns around unlocked where any kid could find one any time was always staggering to him. Though that was never going to be a problem for the Cavanaugh children now. But the liquor cabinet had been locked, despite the fact that Cavanaugh had been drinking. Habitual behavior was strong; if Cavanaugh had taken the gun out, he would likely have locked the gun cabinet. The Reaper might not have.

Roarke was betting he'd seen where the keys were hidden. After all, he'd been watching them. It was what he did.

Roarke turned back into the room and let himself imagine how it had gone this time. The father having a beer and watching the build-up to today's games, the killer coming silently down the carpeted stairs . . .

Only something was wrong.

"The T.V. was on or off?" he demanded tersely of the detective.

"Off," Aceves answered, surprised.

"That's not right," Roarke said. "It was on."

"Sports fan," Epps said. "Watching the pre-game chatter."

"Exactly," Roarke nodded. "The killer must have turned if off after. The father didn't hear him coming."

Detective Aceves shot a glance at the body. The chair wasn't facing the big screen.

"Force of the blast spun the chair," Lam said. "It's on a swivel base."

Lam and Stotlemyre approached the ruined body, one on either side, crouching in tandem on opposite sides of the chair. Both of them looked up at the same time, and Roarke and Epps automatically followed their gaze to the ceiling. Bits of blood and gray matter were crusted on the ceiling.

"Rifle was angled from below. The shot came up through his jaw," Stotlemyre said.

"How the hell did the guy manage that?" Detective Lambert asked.

"Crawled," Lam said. He waddled backward on his haunches, astonishingly limber, straightened, looked around him, and picked up a billiard cue to simulate the weapon. He held the stick like a rifle, crouched with it, and then dropped silently to his knees, balancing on one palm and edging his way forward in a crawl while holding the "gun." It was like watching the rehearsal of a stealth jungle attack in a war movie. He didn't make a sound in the thick carpet. In no time he was beside the chair and angling the gun up toward the slumped corpse. He held the pose for a moment, staring up the line of the pool cue.

"Yep. Perfect angle. He was here, on the floor."

Stotlemyre nodded thoughtfully, staring at the human tissue on the ceiling. "Smart fucker. He thought it through."

"That's a lot of control," Epps said.

A lot, Roarke thought. *The Reaper's improved his game with age. Unless . . .* He didn't want to think it. *Unless it's not the Reaper.*

He stared around the basement room, focused on the sliding glass doors leading out to the patio. The drapes weren't drawn.

He said aloud, "The killer was watching the family in Reno. He knew when the father was isolated, T.V. was on, masking sound—that's when he struck." He turned to Aceves and Lambert. "The Reaper had a view of this room, and if the gun is Cavanaugh's the guy also must have had a view of wherever the gun was locked up, knew how to get to it—"

Aceves said sharply behind him, "Hold up."

Roarke's heart sank. He'd blown it, overstepped. He turned back. Aceves was staring at him.

"You said 'the Reaper.' Are you shitting me? You think this guy is the *Reaper*?" He stared around at the agents.

So Aceves knew the case. Roarke said a quick and silent prayer that it would count in their favor. "We have evidence to suggest it. That's what we're trying to find out."

"Holy Christ," Aceves muttered, and looked at Lambert. "We need to find where he was watching from outside, process those areas. *Now*."

Lambert nodded, and headed up the stairs.

Roarke turned to Aceves. "Did the family report a dead animal?"

The detective frowned. "How do you mean?"

"A pet killed, or the corpse of a wild animal left on the doorstep. Any time in the last week or so. This perp watches the house, leaves the animal, maybe as a message."

"Definitely no reports like that that we've received," Aceves said.

"Neighbors or friends of the family may have heard about it. It would help to nail down how long he was watching them."

"You're pretty sure about this," Aceves said.

"It's what he does."

The detective nodded curtly. "Most people on this block were out of town for the holiday. I'll start the deputies re-interviewing anyone in the neighborhood who was here, and branch out some. And we can put the query about missing pets on the Village website."

Roarke was relieved; his team seemed to have passed some test, the detective not just accepting their presence but amenable to input. He seized the moment and stepped to the doorway to get the widest vantage of the room. "If it's like the Reno massacre here's how it went down. Family's sleeping. The killer's watching all this from outside, can see the father go downstairs to watch the sports channel. If he came at the father from the stairwell, then the point of entry was upstairs, unless he was hiding in the house. He does his commando thing, shoots the father, leaves the rifle. Then he goes upstairs and takes out the mother, then the two girls. Every one of them dispatched as quickly as possible. Then he takes his time with the boy."

"Jesus," Aceves said.

Roarke was on a roll. "Even so, he's not here long. He doesn't stay. He's able to keep hold of himself up front, enough to make the father's death look like a suicide. But then it all rollercoasters. He kills in an increasing frenzy, and saves the best for last."

The detective was looking at him in a way that didn't quite cover his revulsion, and Roarke remembered how it used to be, working BAU, the things that would come out of his mouth that would get him that exact look from anyone in the vicinity.

"More control up front and less at the end," Epps said, and Roarke realized he was right.

"Yeah."

"Not good," Epps muttered, and he was right about that, too.

Aceves spoke. "We'll get this house processed." And then he glanced at Lam and Stotlemyre, and back to Roarke. "We'd appreciate your guys' help."

Roarke walked outside into the crisp cold of the forest air, a welcome relief after the heavy smell and *feel* of death in the house.

A major battle won; they had access to the scene now. It was up to Lam and Stotlemyre to bring him the evidence he needed.

He breathed in and looked out over the desert. Then while his team worked inside, he circled the house. It was a beautiful piece of property, desert and forest and a glimmer of the lake in the distance. The air was so clear and thin you could get drunk on it, and the vast surprise of the desert view really did make the mountain seem like some kind of faraway island. He was shocked to find himself thinking that he could live there. He felt a relief and an excitement in the idea of finding a refuge completely off the grid, somewhere he would not have to answer to anyone. Where he could get lost and . . .

And what? he asked himself sharply.

Get lost for what?

Not answer to anyone for what?

The forest seemed darker, suddenly, and he remembered the grisly business he was there for. He turned his attention back to finding the killer's vantage point.

He had no sense whatsoever that he was being watched.

Chapter 30

Snyder arrived in the late afternoon, driven by Jones. He emerged from the car and stood still—tall, lean, craggy, looking up at the house like an arctic explorer contemplating the vastness of the tundra.

The coroner had done his work and two ambulances were just pulling up to take the bodies of the Cavanaugh family down the mountain to the coroner's office, but Roarke begged an extra ten minutes for Snyder to see the scene.

He showed the profiler into the frigid house, now dusted in Black Dragon fingerprint powder. Number markers dotted the carpet and floors, placed at key points in the layout.

The local forensics, now plus Lam and Stotlemyre, were vacuuming and plucking and dusting and photographing, lifting footprints from dust residue, cutting carpets and bedspreads to pieces to take with them to the county lab. Everyone seemed to have warmed to the idea of expert extra hands.

Back at the Bureau's lab all the hair and fiber and particle evidence they picked up at the Reno crime scene would be crosschecked with the Arrowhead scene. Any trace evidence that was found at both scenes would likely be from the Reaper. That would be something they could work with, a hair, a print, a bit of sand or fiber to narrow down a location.

Roarke followed behind as Snyder moved through the rooms, taking the same path that Roarke and the team had taken. Roarke could see the profiler's eyes processing, years of ingrained police procedure crossed with an uncanny sense for the worst brutality that human beings could inflict on each other. Snyder absorbed details while taking in the totality of the scene. There was nothing good about what Roarke was reading on the older man's face.

In the boy's room, Snyder crouched beside the savaged body like a priest administering benediction.

In the basement game room, he took in the staged suicide with all the agitation that Roarke himself had felt, seeing it.

Finally they moved out through the glass doors into the yard. The sky was darkening and the wind slipped softly through the pine trees above them. When Snyder turned to Roarke his face was grave.

"I don't have to tell you. This is very alarming. The level of staging indicates both a level of pre-planning and a control during the attack that is rare and disturbing."

Roarke asked the question that had been nagging at him all afternoon. "Is it *too* controlled for the Reaper? And there's also the anomaly that this was not a full moon, when every other kill of the Reaper's has been on the exact night of it."

Before Snyder could speak, Roarke voiced the objection he knew would be coming. "And I know, I know. Sexual homicide is a very personal crime. There are no copycats on the books. Even so. *Could* we be looking at a copycat?"

Snyder took his time answering. "The question is who? And why?" His eyes were troubled. "These crimes are significant to you, because you are pursuing crimes directly related to the Reaper's only known surviving victim. But what copycat would suddenly start to duplicate the Reaper's crimes, coinciding with your investigation of Cara

Lindstrom's murders? It makes no logical sense. Who would even know to do it?"

That's the question, Roarke thought. *That's exactly the question.*

"How much sense does it make that the Reaper would start killing again just as we started investigating him?" he asked tensely.

Snyder shook his head. "You don't know when he started killing again. It could have been years ago, and you merely found the latest ones because you were looking for recent crimes."

"But two in one month . . ."

"Yes. It looks like decompensation. There's another explanation. We are fairly certain the Reaper was/is a schizophrenic. And there's no question that as a schizophrenic, the Reaper would have been receiving mandatory drug therapy while incarcerated, and almost no doubt that he would have discontinued the medication once he jumped parole. You are going to find more anomalies showing up as his illness takes over again."

Roarke stared at him. "But if he was recently released, that brings it back to the coincidence of us starting on the investigation of the Reaper just as he began killing again."

"I know," Snyder said. "I don't have any explanation. That doesn't mean there isn't one." He looked back at the house. "There's something else, and it's not good. As you said, this killing did not take place on the full moon. But it did take place on Thanksgiving, a significant holiday with a particular emphasis on family."

Roarke felt a chill as he absorbed the words. Snyder continued.

"For all we know Thanksgiving, or the holiday season in general, is a trigger—associated with some family trauma in the Reaper's early life, that compels him to attack families. Between that and the possibility of decompensation, we can't rule out another killing on the full moon."

"I'm going to find him before then," Roarke said. His voice was hard.

Snyder didn't object, exactly, but his next words were slow and measured. "Your biggest problem now is that his hunting radius is very wide. That plus the likely return and escalation of his psychotic symptoms makes his next move very difficult to predict." He glanced at Roarke. "Agent Jones said that you had a lead, a recent parolee, diagnosed schizophrenic, who fits the time range and profile."

Roarke paused. "I've eliminated him."

"How did you eliminate him?"

Roarke was pulled up short by the question, and then decided not to lie. "Cara. Cara eliminated him."

Snyder gave him a brief, ambiguous look. "You've been in contact with her," he said neutrally.

Roarke felt his hackles rising. "I don't have time not to use every option at my disposal. I needed to eliminate a suspect and I did."

For whatever reason, Snyder didn't pursue it. The wind picked up, and Roarke turned as if someone had touched him, looking out over the hills. "Do you think he could still be in the area? Does he stick around to watch?"

Snyder shook his head. "Of that, I have no idea. But of course you have to proceed as if he has."

The men both turned at the sound of footsteps. A deputy hustled up the path toward them. "Agent Roarke, there's a woman on the tip line you should talk to."

Chapter 31

The woman who'd called, Lynn Fairchild, lived on the other side of the lake from the Cavanaughs. It was an equally affluent area, and her house was a similar, well-kept two-story, with a swing set and other plastic children's toys in the yard. The sun was going down over the water as Roarke and Epps drove the Jeep up into the drive. Snyder had remained at the Cavanaugh scene. The wind was icy and biting as they walked up to the door.

A woman in her thirties answered the doorbell but kept the chain on the door and looked out at the agents without making a move to unlock it.

"Ms. Fairchild?" Epps asked.

"Yes . . ."

Roarke showed his credentials wallet. "Agents Roarke and Epps. You called us?"

She studied his ID a beat longer than he would have expected, then closed the door to remove the chain and opened it, stepping aside. "Sorry about that. Please come in."

She was probably thirty-seven or thirty-eight, casually but expensively dressed, and trim, with an athletic energy and youthful prettiness. As Roarke stepped past her, he could see she had a small girl in tow, who hid behind her, peering around her mother's hip at the agents. Five or six and blond, like her mother. *Like Cara.*

The mother ushered the agents through the entryway into a big double-tiered living room with a tall rock fireplace, a wall of glass looking out on a rock slab patio, with forest beyond. A carpeted staircase led up to a second level of bedrooms. It was all eerily similar to the Cavanaugh house.

The presence of children was evident inside as well: stuffed animals and dolls were scattered throughout the living room, and through the kitchen door Roarke could see photos stuck to the refrigerator with magnets, kindergarten-style art work, including Thanksgiving turkeys made by cutting around the shape of small hands. He could hear a television somewhere upstairs. Outside the sliding glass doors the sky was purple twilight.

Lynn Fairchild picked up one of the dolls and crouched to hand her over to her daughter. "Take Madeline and go play upstairs, sweetie. I'll be up in a minute, okay?"

The little girl gazed up at Roarke, clear blue eyes. He thought of Cara.

The mother waited until her daughter was upstairs, out of sight, and then turned to the agents. "Please sit. Can I get you coffee?"

"Thanks, we're fine," Roarke said, and took a seat only in the hope that it would calm her. She was hiding it fairly well, but he could see she was incredibly jumpy. She sat, hovering on the edge of her armchair like a butterfly about to take flight, and laughed nervously.

"This is probably crazy. But I saw online that you were asking about missing pets . . ."

Roarke's antenna went up on alert. "That's right. Are you missing one?"

She shook her head. "Not missing. Killed."

The feeling became a full-on chill. Beside him, Epps shot him a surreptitious glance.

"It's my fault," she said. "She's an indoor cat of course, you can only have indoor cats up here, there are hawks, coyotes, bear, you name it. She got out somehow and something got to her . . ."

"Wait," Roarke said. He was confused, and also feeling a growing sense of dread. "You found your *own* cat? Where?"

Now Lynn Fairchild was the one who looked confused. "On our patio." She glanced toward the wall of glass doors, the darkness outside. "My husband says that she must have been attacked and dragged herself up, trying to get to the house." Roarke saw a glimmer of tears in her eyes. "Breaks my heart. But I think he's wrong. I have this weird feeling about it. It's probably nothing . . ."

"What feels weird to you?" he asked intently.

"For one thing, she was right in the middle of the patio. Right exactly in the middle." She looked toward the doors again. "You can't see now. My husband washed down the blood. But . . . right in the middle?"

"When was this?"

"Saturday."

Five days ago. Roarke felt so close to something . . . something just out of reach. "But there's something else, isn't there?" he asked.

She colored. "It's just that . . . I've just been so creeped out since then. I've been watching the kids like . . ." she trailed off, as if unwilling to complete the thought.

"How old are your children, Mrs. Fairchild?" Epps asked. Roarke could hear the tension he was hiding in his voice.

She waved a hand distractedly. "Please, I'm Lynn. Well, you met Sherry, she's six. Michael is ten, and Tanner just turned thirteen."

Roarke and Epps looked at each other. The exchange was subtle, nothing like a double take, but Lynn Fairchild stiffened. "What? What is it?"

"You've been here, though?" Roarke asked. "And nothing else has happened?"

She stared at him. "Nothing else like what?"

Like your whole family being murdered, he thought. *Just that.*

"Were you here at the house all day yesterday?" he asked. "Your family?"

"No, we weren't. My husband has been out of town on business, and he got delayed in that big snowstorm in the Midwest. All the Chicago flights were cancelled and he didn't make it back yesterday and . . ."

"And what?"

"And I didn't want to be here without him. I took the kids and we went down the mountain and stayed with my sister in Riverside. I know it sounds stupid but I just . . . didn't want to be here."

Not only not stupid—you probably saved your family's lives, Roarke thought, and looked at Epps. *They went out of town and the Reaper took the Cavanaughs instead.*

But he didn't want to freak her out too much. Yet. "When did you get back?" he asked calmly.

"This afternoon. Paul was supposed to get in around seven, but the flight's already been delayed again—"

"Do you know the Cavanaugh family?" Epps asked, before she had quite finished.

Lynn Fairchild stared at him. "Do I . . . not really. To say hello to. Robbie Cavanaugh is at Tanner's school. Why?"

"Are Tanner and Robbie friends?" Roarke asked, careful to keep the question in the present tense.

"Not to speak of," Lynn Fairchild said, looking from one agent to the other.

"They don't play together, hang together?"

She frowned. "It's harder to keep track now that he's in middle school, but he's not a close friend, definitely."

"He's never been to the house?"

"No," she answered, and opened her mouth to say something. Before she could, Roarke jumped in again.

"You said you've been creeped out. Have you seen anyone watching the house? Following you on the road?"

She had gone very still, and was looking from one agent to the other. "Agent Roarke, you're really scaring me."

"You're all right," Epps said instantly. "You all are going to be fine. We're going to make sure of that."

Roarke sat for a moment, thinking. "Is Tanner home? Do you mind if we ask him a few questions?"

"Tanner?" she repeated, immediately on the defensive.

"About Robbie Cavanaugh."

She flinched. "Has something happened to Robbie?"

Again, that perception. "Lynn, if you could get Tanner, we'd appreciate it."

She stood and left the room reluctantly, glancing back at them from the stairs. As soon as she disappeared into the upstairs hall, Epps was talking in a low whisper.

"Jesus. He was watching them, too?"

Roarke was already on his feet. "He was watching them *first*. The cat was killed five days before Thanksgiving. Then they went away and thwarted him."

"You're thinking he snapped, killed the Cavanaughs on impulse." Epps finished. The two men looked at each other in consternation. Roarke circled the room.

"Either that, or he was planning to kill on Thanksgiving, so he did the Cavanaughs when the Fairchilds went away . . ." He stopped in front of the fireplace, looking over framed photos of the family: active shots, skiing, boating, horseback riding. He focused in on one studio portrait: Lynn Fairchild, her husband, the little girl they'd seen before, a towheaded younger boy and a cocky, fair-haired thirteen-year-old. He took the portrait from the mantle and handed it to Epps, who looked down on the family.

"But if he did kill the Cavanaughs impulsively, we've got a big problem—"

Epps finished for him. "The full moon is this weekend."

They were interrupted by fast steps on the balcony, and then Lynn Fairchild's terrified face appeared over the balcony wall.

"I can't find him. I can't find Tanner."

The agents were already heading for the stairs. "When did you last see him?" Epps demanded.

She stopped at the top of the stairs, holding on to the railing. "Before you came . . . maybe a half hour . . . he's been here all day. He didn't say he was going anywhere. Oh my God, what's happening?"

"Stay here," Roarke ordered her.

The agents ran for the sliding glass door. Epps jerked it open and they burst out onto the patio. The chill of the night hit them, white mist blanketing the dark.

Past the concrete circle the woods were all around them. Epps was already on the phone, shouting the address. "Possible child abduction. Request immediate backup."

Roarke circled the periphery of the patio, staring out into the trees, looking for a path, any opening, some hint of where to begin looking.

He spotted a footpath and ran for it, into the pines. The light from the porch receded and the night was suddenly so dark he had to stop on the path to let his eyes adjust.

Lynn Fairchild had completely ignored his order. He could hear her behind him, between the trees, calling frantically for her son.

He looked up through a gap in the crowns of firs, to where the moon was shining through the mist, so near full now, and his heart was pounding.

No, you bastard. You are not taking this boy.

He turned on his heel and ran back on the path, over crunching pine needles and crackling leaves, in the direction of Lynn Fairchild's voice. She twisted around as he burst through the underbrush, and the beam from her flashlight nearly blinded him. He strode forward and took the light from her, grasped her arm. "Is there a place in the woods he would have gone?" She stared up at him, as pale as snow in the night.

And then there was a crashing sound from the trees, somehow familiar. Roarke and Lynn spun toward the sound.

A shadow shot out from between the trees, so fast Roarke jumped back. It was a rider on a bike, who halted, frozen, as the light of the flashlight hit him. The boy from the photo.

"Mom?" he said, and looked at Roarke, confused.

Lynn Fairchild burst into tears and ran for her son. She shook him and hugged him at once, an awkward tangle of limbs and bicycle. "What were you *doing*? What were you thinking?"

Then before Roarke knew what was happening, Lynn Fairchild was standing, bearing down on him, sobbing. "You tell me *now*. You tell me what's happening."

Floodlights now blazed in the yard as sheriffs and deputies and forensics techs prowled the perimeter of the house. Tanner Fairchild was upstairs in his room. Ironically, he'd gone out on the trails behind the house looking for the cat; Lynn Fairchild had not had the heart to tell the children their pet was dead.

Inside the living room, she sat on the couch as if carved out of ice as the agents told her about the Cavanaughs.

"The whole family," she said, staring at her hands in her lap. "If we'd stayed . . ." She shuddered convulsively.

"You can't think like that," Epps said firmly.

She looked up. "Are there others? Besides the Cavanaughs?"

Both agents paused, and she seized on the silence. "Oh God. How many?"

Roarke took a breath before answering. "We're not sure yet. But we think this might be connected to an old case—"

She stood up. "The Reaper," she said. She crossed her arms around her waist as she stared at Roarke. Her face had gone pale.

"Yes," he said, and found his mouth was dry. "You know the case." He told himself it wasn't unusual, not unusual at all. Anyone his age who'd grown up in California would know the case . . .

"I was ten," Lynn Fairchild said. "I lived in Arcata."

He stared at her, thinking he must have heard wrong. *Must* have.

"You knew the Grangers?" he said. His own voice sounded far away, and he wasn't entirely sure he could move.

She nodded. "I rode at the same stables as Terry Granger." He stared at her in silence and she looked back at him in disbelief. "You don't think I . . . that the Reaper . . ."

"I'm sure there's no connection," he said firmly, and hoped he sounded sure enough for her to believe him. "Now go upstairs. Pack enough clothes and essentials for a few days and we're going to take you and the children out of here, someplace safe. We'll pick up your husband at the airport and bring him to you. Go."

Lynn moved toward the stairs in what looked like a trance, but when she hit the bottom of the stairs she climbed them with resolve.

"What the *hell* is going on?" Epps asked, as soon as she was out of sight. There was a tinge of outrage in his voice.

"It's not that strong a connection," Roarke said, hoping to make himself believe it.

"Jesus," Epps said. And Roarke felt that familiar vertigo; the sickness of reality shifting, like quicksand under his feet.

After a consultation with Lieutenant Tyson it was decided to take the Fairchilds to the town of Crestline, lower down the mountain, where there was a cabin the sheriff's department sometimes used as a safe house. They could be safely guarded, but would also be close enough for questioning. Roarke intended to take Snyder with him and go over Lynn Fairchild's Arcata memories with a fine-tooth comb.

Detectives Aceves and Lambert conferred with Roarke and Epps. "We've got deputies out waking up school officials and the boys' teachers," Aceves said. "The killer could have been watching Tanner

Fairchild at school. He could have seen Robbie Cavanaugh there, too."
Roarke agreed it was a place to start, and Lieutenant Tyson had been
right, local law enforcement were much more useful than the agents at
that task. They could more quickly sort out locals from strangers.

Lam and Stotlemyre arrived, with Snyder, and Epps took the techs
out to the patio. Roarke could see him through the glass doors, pointing out the spot on the patio where the cat had been found. Unfortunately the husband had thrown away the animal's mutilated corpse
rather than burying it. There was no way to examine it for clues.

Other deputies started to search the perimeter of the house for any
signs of the watcher. Forensics would have to process the outside to see
if there were any signs of the Reaper there. But given a recent snow, the
possibility of trace evidence turning up was not good.

"We've got more chance of evidence surfacing at the Cavanaugh
house." Roarke paced in the living room while Snyder looked over the
photographs of the Fairchild family. "What we need is a forensic hit.
Something to ID this guy."

Snyder turned and regarded him silently. Roarke continued to rail.
"He's angry that he missed the Fairchilds. What if that caused a snap
and he goes from stalking to a spree?" It had happened with Ted Bundy
and Richard Speck.

"Let's just focus on the facts," Snyder said with maddening calm.

Roarke moved explosively. "All right, here's a *fact*. Lynn Fairchild is
from Arcata. She rode at the same stables as the Granger boy."

Snyder was still for a moment, processing this. Roarke couldn't
wait for an answer. "He came after her specifically. He had to."

The profiler finally turned to him. "Did he?"

The question inflamed Roarke. "What else could it be? What are
the chances?" he demanded.

Snyder lifted his hands. "What are the chances of Cara Lindstrom
killing your agent, Greer? Not just killing your agent: killing your agent
in front of you?"

Roarke stopped his frenetic pacing and stared at him. "What are you saying?"

"There may be a tangible connection based in Arcata, yes. Did the killer recognize Lynn Fairchild? Did he pursue her?" There was a strange calm to the profiler's voice. "Or was he drawn to her in some way, in the same way that you were drawn to Cara, or she to you?"

"What the hell . . ."

"There does seem to be some vortex to this case. The Reaper was drawn to Mrs. Fairchild. Was it conscious? Or was it perhaps in some way we may never understand?"

Roarke felt his whole body tensing in instinctive resistance. "I don't get what you're saying at all."

Snyder gave him a brief glance that said he was a liar, but he didn't say it aloud. "I think we need to focus on what we can solidly pursue in this case, but not ignore signposts that we may not immediately understand."

He looked out through the glass wall into the forest, the tops of trees moving in the night wind, under stars. "We're going to be here for some time, I think. Do you have hotel rooms yet?" he asked.

They didn't.

"Then I'd suggest we set up camp."

Chapter 32

The Arrowhead Lodge was a Triple-A accommodation right at the gateway to the central village, a five-minute walk from the lake down a hushed, meandering path through the forest. Across the parking lot was a shopping complex with a 7-Eleven and a large neon sign advertising psychic readings.

"Just what we need," Epps muttered from the seat beside him, but Roarke felt a wild secret urge to walk over and ask for a consultation.

The main lodge was a historic building. "Built in nineteen seventeen," the desk clerk told the agents as they checked in and stood in the firelit lobby looking around the two stories of rock walls and staggered dormer windows, molded ceilings, modern lighting wired into the original gaslight fixtures, an octagonal bar in the lounge.

Epps nodded at the period detail with satisfaction. "That's what I'm talking about."

"As long as you're happy," Roarke said dryly.

Outside the main lodge the complex also had several dozen standalone cottages with mini-kitchens. There was a warren of them between the tall pines, all connected by wooden bridges over dry creek beds.

Weddings, Roarke thought. *Just perfect for weddings and tracking serial killers.*

The swollen moon was high above the trees as Epps parked their vehicle in the space assigned to their cabins. Roarke got out of the Jeep. A hulking shadow loomed beside him and he startled back . . . then realized he was facing an enormous chainsaw-carved sculpture of a standing bear.

He shook his head at his own jumpiness and followed Epps down stepping stones laid between cabins.

He and Epps had two cabins, one above the other on the walkway, with secluded porches; Jones was across the way. Lam and Stotlemyre had remained at the Fairchilds, but Epps had booked them a two-story unit in the next row, and Snyder a fourth cabin below them. Another walkway led out to a gazebo lit by strings of white lights.

Roarke turned to face Epps, Jones, and Snyder. "Let's try to get an hour's rest and meet back here in an hour-fifteen."

He walked in through the door of his cabin and found a much bigger space than he'd expected from the outside. A bathroom connected the living room with a bedroom. A kitchenette on the other side of the living room led out to a second entrance.

The bedroom had wood paneling halfway up the walls and fleur-de-lis-patterned wallpaper above that. The slanted ceiling was probably cozy in below-freezing temperatures, but also claustrophobic; he felt too enclosed. On the bright side there was a spa tub in the tiled bathroom. He stood looking down on it, but knew his mind would never let him rest if he didn't settle something first.

He stripped off his coat and suit coat and found his phone, then, not trusting himself to lie on the bed, he took a seat in one of the armchairs in the dim sitting area, facing the window and the light of the moon, and dialed Rachel. She had called twice during the day without leaving a message, and he dreaded speaking with her, but he owed her much more than that for his behavior.

The phone rang and rang and he thought he might have been reprieved . . . just before she picked up.

"Hello," she said, and despite everything, her voice was a sexual charge.

"I wasn't sure I was going to get you," he said. "How are you?"

"Doing okay," she said, but he could hear the wariness in the words.

"I'm glad. I'm sorry I haven't called before now—"

"I understand," she said, cutting him off.

"I don't think you—"

"I understand about work," she said.

Silence crackled through the line between them. She finally spoke. "I called for a reason. You know I have two of Danny's girls with us at the house now, besides Jade. I showed them the police sketch of that woman."

Roarke felt a sudden twist in the pit of his stomach. "Yes," he said.

"Shauna, one of the other girls, saw her too. She says she saw her beat up a john, smash his head against a brick wall in an alley. Hurt him pretty badly, it sounds like. I thought you would want to know."

"When was this?" he asked, too sharply.

"Three days ago, she said."

Before the pimp was killed.

"In the Haight?"

"Yes, just a few blocks away from here."

Which means that Cara probably is staying somewhere in the Haight. Which means . . .

"Look, I want you to be careful," he said abruptly. "Don't go out alone at night. Report anything that seems suspicious."

There was a beat of silence before Rachel answered. "What do you mean? Why?"

He found he had no answer. *Because Cara might feel possessive of me and slash you to pieces on a whim?* It wasn't what she did. Unless it was.

"Just be careful. Please." He felt emotions spiraling dangerously out of control. "How is Jade?" he asked, to steady himself.

"Still here," Rachel said. "Terrorizing the others." She was joking, but Roarke imagined there was truth in it, too. "I don't know for how long, but she seems to have settled in for the time being. Sometimes they get tired of running. Maybe she has."

"That's good," he said. *So we have a witness after all.*

"I'll try to find out where she's from," Rachel said, before he could ask.

"I appreciate that." He was suddenly rabid to get off the phone. She seemed to sense it, because after a few beats of silence she spoke before he could.

"I don't want to keep you."

"I should get some sleep, really," he admitted. "I just wanted to see how you were."

"I'll be all right," she said, and he thought there was an ambiguous tone in her voice, but he was too suddenly drowsy to tell.

"Be careful," she said again, quickly, and disconnected.

He punched off the phone and sat in the moonlight. So Cara had been busy, following a track of her own. He found it ironic, and humbling, that they'd been fishing for her with the wrong bait. She had her own unpredictable yet unrelenting agenda, and he had no doubt there was more to be revealed about what she'd been up to.

And despite his to-the-bone fatigue, he sat for a long time.

In his own cabin, Snyder shut the door behind him and locked it, breathing in as he tried to release the images from the Cavanaugh house.

The profiler had long had his own means of coping with horrors, the investigation of which was his life's work. Detachment was key. Detachment was not the same as peace, the spiritual goal cultivated by Buddhists. Snyder was too much a product of his Protestant background, even long abandoned, to find that kind of comfort. His own detachment was merely a hard-won ability to look at acts that other cultures had no qualms about calling demonic, and reduce them to quantifiable statistics, characteristics, probabilities. *This* has happened in seventy percent of cases with variable X and factor Y, so there is a seventy percent probability that it will happen here.

But lately, as he felt his own death draw inexorably closer, he had become more interested in those cultures' more layered views of life and death, good and evil, and he sometimes found himself wondering what truths he may have been overlooking in his rational approach to his work.

The carnage at the Cavanaugh house was enough to give the most hardened rationalist pause.

He stepped to the window and drew back the heavy drape to look out. It was going to be an icy night; the wind was whispering through the trees, swirling leaves on the ground. He shivered, turning away.

As he moved around in the excessively quaint cabin, lighting the gas logs in the fireplace, hanging up his coat, he felt an agitation, a sickness somewhat like fear. *Revulsion*, he thought. There was a revulsion triggered by the sight of human evil, or its aftermath. The smell of death was still on him; even the frigidity of the Cavanaugh's unheated house had not been able to cut that stench, and he was thinking that a shower would wash away the anxiety aroused by the lingering smell, a nearly palpable presence in the room.

He turned toward the bathroom . . .

A blond woman stepped out through the door.

And he realized the anxiety he felt had not been a reaction to the smell of death. Not at all.

He looked into Cara Lindstrom's fine, pale face, as she stood very still in the half-light, looking at him.

"Hello," he said softly, and tried to breathe through the jolt of adrenaline to his heart. He had no idea what this visit might be about, but he knew he was not the one who had control over it.

In his cabin, Roarke finally stood and moved for the bedroom, but stopped in the bathroom, looking down at the Jacuzzi tub.

"Fuck it," he mumbled, and reached to turn on the jets.

Snyder could not keep his eyes off her. She was quite beautiful, though not in any conventional way: the sharp curves of her bone structure, and the intensity, almost hyper-focus, her body still, yet seeming to vibrate with tension. She was present.

"I'm Chuck Snyder," he said, through a mouth gone perfectly dry. "But I imagine you know that."

"I know," she said. Hearing words from her was a relief, perhaps false relief, but in the moment, any kind of normalcy was welcome. Behind him, the gas logs sizzled.

"Do you know about the Reaper, too?" he asked, speaking slowly and calmly.

She looked at him without answering. Snyder realized he was pouring sweat from every pore in his body. He swallowed.

"Is there anything you can tell us . . . anything at all that would help us catch him?"

"Roarke is wrong," she said, and despite his fear, he felt a sharp spur of curiosity.

"What is he wrong about?"

Her eyes were looking past him, toward the moon, he thought. "The Reaper," she said.

"What about the Reaper?"

"I know," she said, and the sudden agitation in her voice froze his blood.

"What do you know?"

She turned back to him, and in the shadows, her eyes were dark, almost black. "It's a trap."

Chapter 33

Now clean and changed and shaven, Roarke stepped out of his cabin into the icy wind. The bath had been lifesaving, but all the heat of that delicious soak had leached out of him by the time he crossed the low-lit path to Snyder's cabin.

He knocked on the door, and stood in the dark and the wind, shivering. Wind whistled through the treetops, shaking the long pine needles.

After a few seconds he knocked again, harder.

There was no answer, and he noticed, no light on inside, either.

"Chuck?" he called.

He reached for the doorknob automatically, and to his surprise, it turned. Unlocked.

Adrenaline flooded his system. He pushed the door open and pressed his body against the frame as he looked cautiously inside.

"Chuck?" he said sharply.

He pulled away from the door and drew his weapon. He reached into the room and snapped on the light, then barged in, swiveling in a firing stance, scanning the room.

Empty.

He spun at the sound of a muffled thud from the bedroom. He shoved through the connecting bathroom door, checked the space, pushed open the bedroom door, scanned that room. The bedroom was empty, moonlight filtering through the shuttered window. Across the room a chair was shoved under the doorknob of the closet door.

He strode forward and kicked the chair out of position, twisted open the door with one hand.

Snyder looked up at him from the dark of the closet floor. His hands were tied behind his back, his mouth gagged with a shirt tied around his head. Roarke crouched to untie the gag.

"Well, I've met Cara," Snyder said ruefully.

When Roarke barreled out the cabin door onto the deck, Jones and Epps were already there, weapons drawn. All three agents raised their weapons, showing their hands.

Jones spoke tautly. "I was watching from across the way. I saw you go in. Then no lights went on . . ."

"Cara was here," Roarke told them.

"*Shit*," Epps exploded. He spun to look around them. The pines towered above and the night was as black as tar.

"Snyder says it was at least twenty minutes ago," Roarke told them. "He's okay. But she's long gone." On the inside he was ballistic, though who or what he was angry with was unclear, even to him.

Back in Snyder's room, Epps paced on the phone to the sheriff's office, coordinating an immediate search of the area and a BOLO for Cara to all local authorities.

Roarke turned to Snyder with a combination of fury and filial worry.

"I'm perfectly fine." Snyder said mildly, massaging his wrists. "She only wanted to deliver a message."

"To you." Roarke could hear the outrage in his own voice.

"Every man on your team is watching you like hawks, as they should be," Snyder said. "How could she get near you?"

"What message?" Roarke couldn't contain himself. "What the hell did she say?

Snyder glanced at Epps, who was looking over from the phone, listening. He took his time answering.

"Your plan worked. She has been drawn out by the hunt for her family's killer. Not surprisingly, she feels personally involved in this case. I think perhaps she wanted my take."

Roarke felt he'd been punched in the gut. She was ahead of him, behind him, all around him . . .

How close she must have been to know where he was going.

It was the first thing Epps seized on, too, as soon as he signed off his phone and turned to the other men. "She's in your email," he told Roarke. "How else would she know to come here?" He stabbed his finger toward the ground.

Roarke shook his head. "I can't see it." He had no proof, no idea, really, but it didn't seem to him that technology was her style. It was far too easy to track someone online now, and she was a physical person, a traveler, too restless even to sit. Definitely not a hacker type.

He remembered his walk out of the shelter on Belvedere, after being with Rachel . . . the feeling of darkness closing in, of not being alone. "It must have been when you picked me up. On the street. In the Haight. She overheard us talking about Arrowhead."

Had she seen him leave the shelter? Or arrive at it? His stomach dropped as he thought of Cara watching him with Rachel Elliott. *What had she thought?*

And then there was the even more ominous thought, arising again out of some dark and ambiguous place in him:

Is Rachel in danger?

"Jesus," Epps muttered. "She was right there with you?"

Roarke scrubbed his face with a hand. "All right, we knew this. *I* knew it." Taking the blame was peremptory; Epps would be down his throat once he'd recovered from the initial shock. After all, it had been Roarke who had slipped his tail, his bodyguard, deliberately and consciously. He was trying to have it both ways, play both sides of the board, however anyone would want to call it.

He finished aloud. "The fact is, she's here."

"So we can catch her," Epps said, with a rush of energy. "We know she's right on top of you, we can nail her. Finally."

Roarke felt a flash of rage that he channeled into low, precise words. "Or we concentrate everything we've got on going after the Reaper before that fuck kills another family full of kids."

Epps swore softly. "That's no choice at all."

"Exactly," Roarke said. "It's no choice at all. She's not going to hurt me—"

"You don't *know* that—"

"I'm not worried about it," Roarke overrode him. "Not for one second. But I do know that some monster who has butchered five families now, twenty-four people, fourteen *kids*, is out there looking to do it again, sooner rather than later. You were in that house. You saw it. What's the priority here?"

For a moment Roarke thought he had pushed his man too far, as he saw a glimpse of the deadly force Epps would have been if he hadn't made it out of the street life.

Then the face of the agent, the lawman, returned. He circled the small room. "I don't like it. I don't like it. You, her, it, any of it."

"We don't have to like it. We just have to get this piece of shit."

Epps halted, and they stared each other down.

Roarke broke the standoff. "Go. Put out an APB. And then let's focus on the Reaper."

"Right," Epps said. He moved for the door to the deck and pulled it open. But at the threshold, he suddenly stepped close to Roarke, so that only he could hear him. "Here's my problem, boss man. You like it. You like it this way." His eyes bored into Roarke's, then he shook his head, and stepped back, out the door, off the deck, down the path, heading back toward his cabin.

Roarke turned back inside the room and closed the door. Snyder had seated himself in an armchair beside the fireplace, blue flames now blazing through the gas logs. He looked up at Roarke, waiting for what he had to say next.

Roarke shook his head. "You could never have been in a room with anyone for more than two seconds and have gotten so little from it."

Snyder spread his hands in acknowledgment.

"So what did she want?"

"She wanted to talk about you," Snyder said quietly. There was something in his tone that gave Roarke pause.

"What about me?" he asked warily.

"Anything about you, I think," Snyder said, and Roarke felt a vortex inside him, swirling feelings, swirling thoughts, nothing clear.

So he moved away from it. "What did she say *exactly*?"

"She said '*It's* a trap.'"

Roarke felt cold. "She knows we're trying to trap her." But he was not surprised. He'd known she would know.

"No. She said *It* is a trap."

Roarke felt hollow, through and through. "It. Some monster, you mean." Some abstraction of evil he didn't fully understand.

Snyder had explained elements of Cara's psychological state before: her almost-death as a child had fixed her in the age of the trauma, five years old, before the age of reason. She existed in a state of magical thinking, ruled by fantasy, metaphor that appeared real to her, and driven by synchronicities. She'd seen the Reaper as a monster; now she saw the men she killed as monsters.

"Something larger than human, yes," Snyder said. "She does not see the world in the same way that we do."

Roarke stood still with that.

Then Snyder spoke again. "There was one more thing she said." Roarke looked at him, and Snyder spoke softly, obviously quoting. "'It's me *It* wants. Tell him.'"

Roarke stared at him, in complete turmoil. "Tell me . . . to use her as bait?"

"I believe that's what she meant, yes."

Bait, again, traps and trapping, but this time the hunted was offering herself up to bait the trap. It was all twisting in on itself.

"That's insane," he said aloud, and paced the room. "Why would she want to do that? Why would she even . . ." He fell silent, then anger rose in him. "It's impossible anyway. I'm supposed to arrest her, not—"

He stopped. There had been a slight, startled reaction on Snyder's face, so uncharacteristic for him that Roarke caught his own slip instantly. He'd said, "I'm supposed to arrest her." *Supposed to.*

"Use her as bait." He slammed his hand against the wall. "What do I do with that?"

"I don't know," Snyder said. "I don't know."

Chapter 34

When Roarke finally left Snyder's cabin, he was too agitated to go back to his own. He needed a game plan. He needed to process everything that had happened in the day if he had any chance of his next move making any sense at all, let alone being the right one.

So instead of going up the porch stairs to his cabin, he kept walking up the stepping stones to the road beyond. The asphalt ended at a dirt path and he kept going, into the towering shadows of trees. The air was freezing and the moonlight was a brilliant white, glistening on crunchy patches of leftover snow. Orion and Cassiopeia were up, the fog had lifted and the night was so clear that the constellations were still visible in the sky despite the brightness of the almost-full moon.

It was not until he could no longer see the shapes of cabins behind him that he was finally able to let himself consider Cara's words.

"It's me It wants."

To use her as bait was impossible. *Isn't it?* He couldn't begin to think how she might have meant it.

And why would she want to? To kill the Reaper? Kill *It*? Or was there something more?

Something that had to do with him?

In his mind, he heard Snyder's words:

"She wanted to talk about you."

"What about me?"

"Anything about you, I think."

It was then he realized that he was out in the night not to clear his mind, not to walk off tension. He was looking for her.

The underbrush rustled on the path beside him, freezing his heart, and then some large presence crashed forward in the brush and loomed up in the dark above him with huge, alien, glistening eyes . . .

Roarke jolted back, and realized he was staring up at a horse. It stopped still in the moonlight, towering above him, and seeming just as mesmerized by Roarke as he was by it. And then it turned and bolted back into the trees.

It took Roarke a heart-pounding moment to realize there was a split-rail fence in front of him, almost completely concealed by the bushes. As he moved closer to it he could see the field enclosed by the fence, and long low buildings in the dark. A sign above the double stable doors read Arrowhead Riding Academy.

Stables.

He stared, his mind whirling.

Lynn Fairchild rode at the same stables as Terry Granger.

And then he strode toward the fence and grasped the rough railing, eyes searching the darkness, finding the curve of parking lot: pickup trucks, buggies . . .

And a row of silver horse trailers.

He took the path back to the cabins at a run, and was panting by the time he sprinted around the corner of his cabin. He nearly jumped out of his skin as Epps turned on the porch with Glock in hands; he had Roarke dead to rights. Roarke raised his hands and told him, "Horses."

Epps stared down at him in the dark.

"We were thinking the Fairchild and Cavanaugh kids might have been watched at their school. But what if Tanner Fairchild rides horses, like his mother? There's a riding academy right down the road. What if the Reaper spotted the boys at the stables?"

"Horse trailers," Epps said slowly, and Roarke could hear the excitement in his voice. "The Reaper drives horse trailers."

Epps was reaching for the phone to call Singh when they were interrupted by the slash of headlights through the trees, followed by the sound of an engine and tires on gravel. They moved toward the parking lot, and stepped into the lights of a sheriff's SUV. It stopped in one of the parking spaces near the cabins and Lam piled out of the back seat, followed by Stotlemyre from the passenger side.

"We've got something," Stotlemyre announced.

"Horse hair," Lam reported simultaneously, with something like glee. "We found horse hair."

"From both crime scenes," Stotlemyre added.

Roarke went to rouse Snyder. He came to the door fully dressed, wide-awake. Jones joined them and the agents gathered in the small living room of Roarke's cabin, while Stotlemyre started the narrative.

"There were a few equine hairs identified in the Leland evidence but it wasn't a red flag, it's a horse neighborhood. But—the horse hair at both scenes was only collected from the rooms of the two thirteen-year-old boys, Seth Leland and Robbie Cavanaugh."

The rooms where the Reaper spent the most time.

Lam added, "And the hairs we found are consistent in color and length. We have to get them under the microscope to compare . . ."

"And it's a long shot," Stotlemyre warned. He glanced from Roarke to Epps. "But on the drive up you two were talking about resort activities and sports, a delivery route that would bring a driver or salesman into all of the towns where the massacres have occurred . . ."

Roarke hadn't even known that the techs had been listening, and he felt a rush of adrenaline. This was what he thought of the sweet spot of a case, when everything started to converge. *If only we have enough time.*

"We're already on that. What do you need?" he demanded.

Stotlemyre looked at Lam. "We need to get all the trace evidence back to a lab and compare the hairs under a polarized light scope for microscopic consistencies. But the real clincher—"

"Would be DNA," Lam said. "The Jockey Club registers thoroughbreds. Owners have to provide DNA to prove the horse's parentage. So if it's the same horse, and it's registered with the Jockey Club, then we'll know the owner, and we can get a schedule of drivers who have worked with the specific horse, and we can nail this fucker."

The work suddenly had a trail, a focus. The techs had already sent the horse hair via a deputy to the nearest airport to rush to Quantico for expedited DNA testing. Lam and Stotlemyre divided themselves up: Stotlemyre would stay with the scene, Lam would go down the mountain to the sheriff's lab in San Bernardino to start the comparison of the horse hair and other trace evidence, and also to be close at hand as the county coroner performed the autopsies on the Cavanaugh family.

Epps got on the phone with Singh to get her checking horse transport companies and driving routes that included Reno and Arrowhead, and asking about employees who might fit the age range and Snyder's profile of the Reaper.

From the corner by the fire, Snyder said to Epps, "Tell Singh to focus on employees at horse transport companies in or near Arcata."

"Arcata?" Roarke stared at him, knowing it was right, but a beat behind. "Why?"

"Because as you said yourself, it's the anomaly. Not a resort town. And it was the site of the first massacre. That makes it likely to be the killer's home base."

"You really think Arcata . . ." Roarke started.

"I think the signs are pointing that way. There's no obvious link but . . . I don't think we should ignore it."

"You're going mystical on me," Roarke said. Snyder didn't answer him, which he didn't want to think too much about. But the Arcata connection decided his next move.

"I'm going down to Crestline," he announced. "To interview Lynn and Tanner Fairchild."

"I'm on the riding academy," Epps told him. "Anyone who set foot on that place in the last month I'm going to know it."

"Good. We're close now." And then as Roarke headed for the door, he stopped, turned, and looked at his team. "Watch yourselves. Be safe."

As he stepped outside the cabin into the night, it started to snow.

Chapter 35

Snow fell thickly on the curves of highway as a deputy drove Roarke down the hill to the nearby mountain town where the sheriff's department was keeping the Fairchilds under guard.

Crestline was a less upscale version of Arrowhead, with more sprawling, less elegant family homes and cabins set back from the road that circled a small dark lake.

The deputy turned off the main road at a collection of mailboxes and rumbled down a dirt road toward the water. The house was set even further back from the dirt access road, near the shoreline. The deputy parked at the end of the road and escorted Roarke down a packed-earth path, speaking into a cell phone to inform the on-duty guards they were approaching.

The yard, such as it was, was simply a clearing. No lawn or landscaping, just empty spaces beneath trees. There was a wooden trash enclosure by the side of the house, dormant roses in a few simple flowerbeds, a swing set off to the other side, and a concrete birdbath near the entrance. The downstairs lights were on inside the house, and bright security lights outside it. Roarke saw a uniformed man in the elongated shadows between trees, nodding to them as they approached the porch. He felt a knot in his chest loosen slightly. Everything looked well under control.

Another deputy came to the door, and Roarke followed him into a wood-paneled den where Lynn Fairchild sat on a sofa by the fire. No gas logs here; Roarke could smell pinesap. Despite the hour Lynn was fully dressed, an expensive sweater and slacks. Her face was pale, devoid of makeup.

"I appreciate your seeing me," he told her.

"It's not like I was sleeping," she said. Irony was heavy in her voice.

"Your husband isn't back yet?"

She shook her head. "Chicago's still snowed in." She stood. "Would you like coffee?"

"Coffee would be great, but . . . it's really Tanner I need to speak with."

She looked back at him in betrayal, and Roarke understood, but there was nothing to be done about it. "I'm sorry, but I thought you would be more likely to let me talk to him if I was already here." He added softly, before she could deny him. "The Reaper kills on the full moon. We have three days to get him before he does this again."

She took an abrupt step toward him and her hand trembled at her side as if she wanted to slap him, but then she shook her head. "I know I have to let you. I don't have to like it."

He nodded to her. "Thank you. I need to know first—does Tanner ride horses? At the Arrowhead Academy, maybe?"

"Not anymore. Definitely not at the Academy."

"Not ever?"

"He did when he was younger, but you know, boys . . ." She sounded resigned.

"I don't know. What do you mean?"

"Horses are a 'girl thing.' " She shrugged. "Around eleven, he just lost all interest."

Roarke actually did understand. He wouldn't have been caught dead on a horse at that age either.

She turned away toward the stairs, and then paused and glanced back, her face shadowed. "You can get your own coffee."

The kitchen was more knotty pine. Roarke found a pot of hot coffee already made in the brewer on the counter. When he emerged from the kitchen with a cup, Tanner Fairchild was thumping down the stairs, a kid with every bit of his mother's blond good looks, dressed in sweatpants, a thick sweatshirt, and oversized socks. He stood beside Lynn as she introduced Roarke, then he slumped in a chair while she walked back upstairs without looking at Roarke.

The boy was sleepy and irritable from the start, a hostility Roarke figured he was entitled to. He sat down on the edge of the armchair opposite Tanner. "I'm sorry to have to wake you like this," he began.

"Yeah," Tanner said.

"But it's very important that we know what you were doing in the last week. Have you noticed anyone watching you? Any men?"

"Any pervs, you mean," the boy said harshly. "They already asked this, you know."

Roarke did know. "And you said you didn't see anyone at school or in town. But what about at the stables?"

The boy looked away from him. "Why would I be at the stables?"

Roarke looked at him. Tanner was bouncing his foot on the floor, a sign of agitation. Something here.

"You know what I mean, though. The riding academy."

"I don't ride horses. It's gay."

There was no time for a lecture on tolerance. "I don't think gay has much to do with horses," Roarke said mildly. "And horses are pretty magnificent, if you ask me."

The boy fidgeted, looking at him warily.

"Maybe you went over to look at them," Roarke suggested.

The boy was sullenly silent.

"This is important, Tanner. Were you and Robbie Cavanaugh ever at the stables together?"

The boy looked away from him. "Robbie doesn't ride."

"Okay, Robbie doesn't ride. But were you at the stables together some time this week? Even just outside, to look?"

The boy looked flustered, defensive . . . caught. Roarke knew he was close to something. "You're not in any trouble," he said softly. "But I need to know."

Beside them, the fire snapped, and Tanner flinched, then burst out: "We were just looking. We weren't hurting anything."

"Of course you weren't. What day was that?"

The boy swallowed, thought. "Last week. Thursday, I think. We were watching the jumps."

That was good. Roarke could get the exact schedule from the stables, and a list of anyone who might have been there. He spoke again.

"I only want to know if you saw anyone hanging out, or"—he phrased the next question carefully—"if anyone saw you?"

"No one saw us."

Not that boys would have noticed. Roarke tried a different tack. "Could you see the horse trailers from where you were?"

"Yeah . . ."

"Was there anyone around there, standing nearby?"

"No. Yeah. There was a guy," Tanner said, and looked surprised that he'd said it.

"Good," Roarke said, and could barely breathe. "What guy?"

Tanner frowned. "Some skinny guy with greasy hair."

"And why did you notice him?"

"Kinda creepy," Tanner admitted. And then he shuddered, an involuntary spasm of dread, and Roarke felt a shiver of his own. *He saw him. The Reaper was there.*

"White or black or Latino?" he asked aloud, his voice firm and authoritative, in command.

"White."

"Dark hair or blond?"

"Dark. Black."

Now they were on a roll, Tanner answering automatically. Roarke kept the questions short and simple, to keep the boy in a rhythm.

"Long hair or short?"

"Kinda long."

"How he was dressed?"

"Dirty. Jeans, some old ratty coat."

"Shoes or boots?"

"Shoes. Kinda beat up and muddy."

Ten minutes later Roarke was thrilled to have a decent description of a man who sounded like a recent convict: gaunt, pasty-faced, stringy black hair, something intense in his eyes. *Finally, a break*, he thought, with exhaustion bordering on desperation. He pushed that all down to focus on Tanner.

"Tanner, you're being a huge help with this investigation. I'm going to ask you one more thing. I'm going to send a sketch artist for you to say these same things to, and help us come up with a picture."

During the questioning Tanner had been caught up in the back-and-forth rhythm, just as Roarke had intended. But now that the questioning was over, he seemed agitated.

"What did he do?" Tanner asked him. His eyes were too big, too dark.

Roarke didn't want to lie to the boy but he also didn't want to get into the details of what the Reaper had actually done.

"I don't know yet," he answered.

"He killed our cat?" There was outrage in the boy's voice.

Much worse than that, Roarke thought. "I don't know yet," he repeated. "But he's a bad guy. And you've just made it a lot easier for us to catch him."

Roarke called in to the sheriff's office to request a sketch artist. As he disconnected, he turned to see Lynn Fairchild in the doorway, watching him. She had a glass in her hand, what looked to him like Scotch.

"Did you get what you wanted?" she asked, and the bitterness was plain in her voice.

"I'm sorry it had to be this way," Roarke said. "But what Tanner knows may save lives."

Her face crumpled. "I know I'm being a bitch. I do."

"Not at all," he said swiftly.

"It's just that . . . I thought I could protect him from all this."

"Life?" he asked.

"No," she said savagely. "Not *life*." She threw her glass at the fireplace, shattering it against the hearth. Liquid hissed in the fire. "He's ruined. He doesn't even know that Robbie's dead, yet."

But he does, Roarke thought. *Oh yes, he does.*

Lynn was crying now, harsh, ugly tears. "I tried to keep them away from all this. Damn him. Damn him. Oh God . . ."

Roarke moved toward her, took her shoulders, then just put his arms around her. She was shuddering.

"I know. I know. It's a terrible shock—"

She pulled away from him violently. "But it's *not* a shock. That's what's so terrible about it. All these years . . . I was always waiting for him to come after me. I *knew*." Around them, the shadows of the fire moved on the walls.

And despite himself, Roarke felt a chill.

Lynn walked in a haphazard circle. "Do you believe you can draw things to you?"

"How do you mean?" he asked. But the truth was, he knew precisely what she meant.

"Draw things . . . with wishing . . . or with fear . . ."

"I don't know," he said, and thought of the first time he had seen Cara, a month ago, a lifetime ago, on the street in San Francisco.

Lynn stopped by the black plate of window, looking out as if she had seen something. Roarke tensed . . . but her eyes were unfocused. "All that fear . . . all those years. I knew he'd come." She turned back to look at Roarke. "What if I drew him?"

Time felt suspended between them. Roarke couldn't answer her because she'd just touched on his greatest fear, and he felt a ghost walking over his grave.

"Whatever happened, you knew enough to save your family," he told her.

Her mouth twitched. "But not enough to save the Cavanaughs," she said. The words were like ice daggers in his heart.

"That's not on you," he said.

But now it's on me.

Chapter 36

oarke was far too wired to sleep. Instead he told the deputy to continue down the mountain to the County Scientific Investigations Division in San Bernardino.

All the way down the mountain he could not still his racing thoughts, the sickness he felt that had nothing to do with the vertiginous curves of the road.

Interviewing Tanner had been like looking into a mirror. Tanner, the same age as Roarke's own brother when the Reaper had first been killing. There had always been an abyss of terror under everything about the case, that Roarke had never acknowledged to himself until this night, looking into Tanner's resolute and starkly vulnerable face. The terror that men could do these things to boys, too, that he was not safe, that his brother was not safe, that there was no such thing as safe . . .

The motion of the vehicle abruptly stopped and he realized he'd dozed off in the passenger seat. The deputy was pulling in to the sheriff's department complex, a looming edifice against the night sky, with two horizontal rows of lit windows in continuous bands wrapped around the building. The complex was surrounded by high fencing and the landscaping consisted of a few scraggly banana palms.

Roarke followed the deputy into a glass lobby with an enormous gold sheriff's badge decorating the door.

He stopped in his tracks as a familiar figure walked out the office door behind the front counter. For a moment he was sure he was seeing things.

"Singh?" he said.

His agent pushed back her dark fall of hair and smiled at him. "I am delivering the horse hair evidence from the original Reaper massacres. SAC Reynolds authorized the helicopter."

He could read how he looked in the brief, searching glance she gave him.

"That bad, huh?" he said wryly.

"Pretty bad," she replied. "Can I get you something?"

"Not unless you're carrying around a spare brain. I can't tell you how glad I am to see you. I need the rundown on where we are."

"The sheriffs have given us an office. Come."

In an upstairs office, she laid three separate files out open on a desk before him. She touched the first, topped by a familiar, disheveled photo. "First, I have heard from DAPO. Santos is back in custody. He alibis out for the Cavanaugh murders."

No surprise there, but it was good to have it off the table. Roarke nodded, and Singh closed the first file, gold arm bands gleaming on her wrists.

"Second, I have been calling all equine transport companies that operate in California and Nevada to find any that have routes which include the cities of Reno and Lake Arrowhead. There is a National Horse Carriers Association that considers itself to serve what they call the horse carriers industry. Some have weekly coast-to-coast routes, and there is a west coast route that encompasses Washington

State to Southern California. Of course there are specialized trips as well. It is a vast network. But there are dozens of companies that are not registered with this association."

Not good, Roarke thought, with a sinking feeling.

"I have also been calling all horse transport companies that were operating in California in 1986 and 1987, checking for companies which serviced all three towns where the Reaper massacres took place: Arcata, Bishop, and Blythe, focusing on companies based in or near Arcata. Operating on our assumption that the Reaper went missing or underground after or shortly before the last murders, I asked each company about male employees who left the company shortly before or after twenty-nine October, 1987, the date of the Lindstrom massacre. Also, this theory of decompensation that Agent Snyder writes about interests me. If it is true that serial killers tend to mentally unravel after a certain point in their activities, then I thought perhaps this behavior was noticed by employers and/or other employees, so I also asked each company about employees who were fired for odd or offensive behavior."

Roarke was impressed, and also sensed this was leading toward something. "How many?"

"Out of sixty-five companies, an initial list of thirteen men who disappeared or were let go around the target date. I have tracked down six; of those I have eliminated four. The two remaining are interesting possibilities. In and out of prison and psychiatric facilities. The proper age range. One in Kern Valley, one in Sacramento."

Both close to state prisons, Roarke realized.

"Unfortunately both are transient, no known addresses. But I have alerted local authorities that finding them is a priority. On the others, I will continue the investigation."

"We have a sketch artist working with the Fairchild boy now," Roarke told her. "It's not going to be the most detailed image but it will narrow the field."

"Good news," Singh said.

"Superb work, Singh, thank you," Roarke said. At the same time, he knew it wasn't enough. They had to work faster.

"We need to go see Lam."

The two of them walked out across the parking lot to the adjacent building that housed the crime lab, and took the elevator to the second floor.

Lam sat at a long black lab table, hunched over a dual comparison microscope with dozens of glass specimen jars and evidence bags lined up in front of him. Another table behind him held scraps of cloth, cut-out pieces of carpet, samples of dirt and leaves, all taken from the crime scene. "Hola," he greeted them, as cheerful and tireless as ever. Roarke had never seen him dragging; he seemed to have an inexhaustible flow of energy.

"Give me good news," Roarke told him.

"Well—here's pretty good news. There are mixed horse hairs that could be from different animals from the Leland scene and the Cavanaugh scene, but I've also found several hairs from both scenes that are externally consistent in length and color, quite possibly from the same animal. I've also found very slight traces of fecal matter in the carpet, not just at the Cavanaugh scene, but also in the stored evidence from the Merrill massacre in 1987. Also equine. That particular combination isn't something you see at every crime scene. The evidence is piling up that we are looking at the same killer doing all five massacres, twenty-five years apart. I've already rushed samples of all the hair and feces to Quantico for DNA analysis as a top priority. We could have results in two to three days."

Not soon enough, Roarke thought. *Damn it.* "But bottom line is, we're still hoping that the horse happens to be registered and we can match the DNA to a specific animal," he said aloud.

"True that," Lam said.

Roarke turned to Singh. "And these horse transport companies, they move a lot of animals that aren't thoroughbreds, I assume?"

"Oh yes. Many more that are not registered," Singh agreed with a frown. She understood his point.

She could get a hit on the truck routes or the fired workers, they could get lucky. But Roarke wasn't going to count on it. Sunday was the full moon.

"We can't wait," he said.

Chapter 37

The drive back up into the mountains was like ascending into a dream. A thick mist had materialized, folding itself into the clefts of the hills, blanketing light and sound. The overnight snowfall had left fields of white along the road and ice in slick dark patches on the road, which along with the snaking mist made the journey up the mountain even more precarious. As the deputy drove, Roarke fell into a fitful sleep in the passenger seat, and woke with a feminine voice in his head.

"It's me It wants."

He stared out the windshield, regaining his bearings. They were stopped in the mist-shrouded parking lot of the lodge.

Epps had set one of the larger cabins up as a task force room, with several white boards, crime scene photos, and of course, the police sketch of Cara. Files were piled in various mesh baskets and a couple of deputies worked the phones, now faxing around the image of the Reaper that the sketch artist had come up with, thanks to Tanner.

Epps turned from a white board as Roarke walked in.

"New plan," Roarke said.

Snyder, Jones, and Epps sat in the inner room at a table. Roarke faced them.

"There was horse hair at two of the Reaper's old crime scenes," he told them. "It's him."

But as Roarke reported briefly on the horse company leads, he could see Epps shifting impatiently, obviously aware that all this was leading to something.

"So you're saying, we've got a fistful of dead ends," he summed up flatly.

"Not dead ends necessarily," Roarke qualified. "But our time is running out. We're not going to wait for this guy to strike. We need to be proactive, bring him to us. So what's most likely to bring him out?"

Epps stared at him. "Besides a thirteen-year-old boy? Because I hope to hell that's not what you're thinking."

"I'm talking about the victim who survived him," Roarke said.

He had been turning it over in some part of his mind ever since Snyder recounted what Cara had said to him. Roarke had the strong sense she was right. Out of curiosity or perversity, whatever it was that made the Reaper tick, if they put her out there, he would come after her. If for whatever reason he'd found Lynn Fairchild all these years later, he would find Cara. Instead of waiting for a few horse hairs to ring the right combination of bells, or worse: waiting for the Reaper to butcher another family and praying that they could find enough evidence to track him off that fresh crime scene, they could use Cara.

"What, *work* with her?" Epps said. Roarke imagined his agent's blood starting to boil under his skin.

"Obviously not," Roarke answered, and felt like the liar he was.

They couldn't put Cara out as bait. They couldn't work with her. They couldn't cut a deal. She was the one person who could help them, and they could never, ever use her.

But they could pretend to.

He turned and went to the door and opened it . . . to let a woman walk in. Slim, blond, dressed in black jeans . . . and a black cashmere turtleneck.

Epps and Jones stared. Snyder simply sat back in his chair, nodding.

"This is Special Agent Danielle Soames," Roarke said, and gestured to the men at the table. "Agent Epps, Agent Jones, Agent Snyder . . . meet our Cara Lindstrom."

Agent Soames nodded to the men, and they looked her over.

Singh had pulled her out of the Los Angeles field office. She'd been on the streets in half a dozen stings, she knew the drill. She was a natural blonde, which wouldn't necessarily have mattered, but it helped; and an athlete, with a firm, taut body and a California cheerleader prettiness. In everything but size and coloring she was unlike Cara in every way she could be. But they were creating an illusion.

Roarke had a hard time looking at her.

He addressed the men. "We're going to use the media to create a story about the only living victim of the never-caught serial killer, the Reaper: Cara Lindstrom, the miracle girl, who is assisting the Bureau in catching the killer of her family."

He looked around the room. "No one knows what Lindstrom looks like as an adult. We post photos of Agent Soames on the Internet, in the media. We draw this fucker to her and we nail him." He stopped for breath, feeling exhausted with the import of his speech. There was utter silence in the cramped room. He could feel and see his team processing it.

Epps was the first to speak, reluctantly. "It's good. I don't like it, but it's good."

Roarke nodded to Soames; she took a seat across from the rest of the team. Epps reached a big hand across the table. "Damien Epps. Welcome aboard." Soames returned his grip, and then Jones' and Snyder's. Roarke noticed Snyder studying her thoughtfully, and thought he knew what the profiler was thinking. *Physically perfect . . . in aspect, not even close.* But it didn't matter. She was a stalking horse.

"Where do we do it?" Jones asked.

"Right here," Roarke said. "We can have Agent Soames on site at the crime scene, the Cavanaugh house. That way it looks to him like she's really helping with the investigation."

"So we're going to let it out that the Reaper's back," Epps said uneasily.

It was Roarke's great fear, too. Getting the media involved with anything was a logistical nightmare. Getting the media involved in a twenty-five-year-old legendary, unsolved series of massacres multiplied the nightmare by a hundred. But he didn't see any way around it anymore.

"At this point I think we're going to have to," he answered Epps. "Both for our investigation and for the sake of warning families. We don't know where he's going to strike next. People will panic, but at least they'll be watching out, taking extra care."

He saw that thought pass through the assembled agents like a ripple on water. Lynn Fairchild's vigilance had likely saved her family's lives. He could only pray no innocent people would be shot by panicked gun owners.

Epps turned to Snyder. "You think this guy will be paying attention?"

The profiler nodded abstractedly. "It stands to reason. Serial killers notoriously follow their own press. Though disorganized killers sometimes prove the exception to that rule."

In his own mind, Roarke was still not convinced about how disorganized the Reaper actually was.

Epps was thinking on it. "Do we talk about Lindstrom's recent . . . activities?"

Roarke answered perhaps too quickly. "Nothing about the killings. It would complicate what we're trying to do. We set her up as a surviving victim, that's it. For now."

He turned to the one empty white board and stepped up to tape a map of the town center onto it. "The village center is a perfect contained area to stage a sting. It's surrounded by the lake on three sides so there's only one large entrance we have to cover." He indicated the area on the map. "We do a stakeout, bring the local detectives and deputies in on it, put agents in the stores. Late night, closing time, to keep civilians out of it."

Epps' eyes were distant, visualizing, and he was nodding. "Yeah. Yeah."

"We start by getting the news out to the media immediately to get his attention; we need to get him focused on our Cara Lindstrom instead of anything else he's got planned. We set up the sting for day after tomorrow. The night of the full moon.

"Epps, you're going to coordinate local law enforcement. As many as we can get, to dress the area with fake shopkeepers. We parade Soames around at the crime scene and around town for the next two days, then that night we have her take a stroll in the village down by the lake, around ten, when the last stores are closing. But the only 'shopkeepers' will be our own people. And she'll walk a route that we'll have completely covered, including snipers here, here, and here." He indicated the clock tower and two balconies on opposite sides of the plaza.

All the while Agent Soames was alert, focused, listening to every word, the complete professional. Roarke turned to her.

"Soames, any questions so far?"

"Just one. I've read the entire dossier on Cara Lindstrom and I have to ask." She hesitated. "She really is seeking out and killing predators?"

When Roarke didn't respond Epps glanced at him, then answered neutrally. "Bad guys, yes."

She looked at Roarke, then back to Epps. "Have you ever seen anything like this before?" she said to both of them, but to Roarke more.

The same question everyone asked.

"No," Roarke said.

The response hung in the silence.

"Let's get to work."

Chapter 38

I
t would go down Sunday night. They needed to clear the use of the Village Center with the city officials, meet with the local agencies, coordinate the sting. And wait for the full moon, for whatever twisted reason the most likely day for the Reaper to strike.

The hotel became their command center. A passel of journalists was summoned for a press conference at the lodge so the team could feed them the story.

Before the conference Roarke briefed Soames on what she would say to the media.

"You don't tell them anything beyond the talking points. Refuse to answer questions about your present-day occupation and whereabouts. Keep it brief. You want to keep your life private, but you feel an obligation to assist the FBI in any way that you can, so that no family will ever again have to experience what you have."

She was focused, nodding. "I understand."

In the meeting room of the lodge, Roarke began the conference with a statement about the reopened manhunt for the Reaper. Every journalist and news station got a packet that included the history of the case and the police sketch of the suspect, whom Roarke said was "wanted for questioning." He introduced "Cara Lindstrom" with a strict admonition that questions about her life since her own family's massacre would not be tolerated.

The excitement the whole proceedings generated was almost frightening, the collection of journalists hyped up and shifting constantly in their seats.

Soames performed efficiently and adequately, sticking to the script, affecting a wariness that played as haunted. Roarke could feel the sympathy for her in the room, and a feverish interest under the camera flashes and whirring of equipment. A survivor of one of the bloodiest tragedies imaginable, the Miracle Girl suddenly come back to life, a real-life heroine . . . it was a media wet dream.

This could work, he thought, from beside the podium where Soames stood speaking. Epps glanced at him, and he read the same thought in his agent's face.

Then he heard his own name being called. "Agent Roarke, you're confident the murders of the Cavanaugh family are linked to the Reaper massacres?"

Roarke kept his breath steady as he faced the middle-aged male journalist who had asked the question. "We have evidence to suggest it."

A murmur went through the assembled crowd: mixed horror and excitement. Then a flurry of questions. "How can you be sure?" "Why would the Reaper suddenly begin killing again after twenty-five years?"

He raised his voice to speak over the furor. "We believe this man has been in prison for a crime unrelated to the massacres and was recently released."

A younger female journalist popped up from her seat. "How do you think Cara is going to help you with this case?"

Roarke stepped forward. "Ms. Lindstrom is a material witness to the killing of her family. She remembers many details from that night that are helping us develop a profile of the killer, and after his arrest she will be able to provide direct testimony."

Of course, despite all warnings, one sharp-suited reporter had to push the envelope. "Ms. Lindstrom, you've led a difficult life since your survival. Institutionalization, incarceration—"

Roarke stepped forward. "No personal questions. I'm going to have to ask you to leave—"

"It's all right, Agent Roarke," Soames said softly, and looked at the reporter. "Yes, I was scarred by what happened. It took me some time to find my way. That's exactly why I want to make sure the man who killed my family will never be able to do this kind of damage to anyone, ever again."

Roarke could feel the respect in the stillness of the room.

The last question had been carefully planted with a cooperative journalist. "Ms. Lindstrom, you believe you can identify the man who killed your family?"

Soames looked straight into the cameras. "I'd know him anywhere."

Roarke stepped forward to end the conference there, and he and Epps escorted Soames out, ignoring the continuing frantic queries from the news people.

Saturday was the same, massive coordination of forces. They would be taking Soames over to the Cavanaugh house the next day, after the media had cycled through the story, hopefully reaching the Reaper and drawing him out. Meanwhile, Singh and Snyder had joined forces to go through Singh's files of potential Reapers, using the police sketch and profile factors to evaluate the candidates.

By the time night fell and the news stories hit the local stations, Roarke had been on the phone most of the day, greasing whatever wheels needed greasing to get the permissions and manpower they needed, culminating in a briefing in the business offices at the village center. There was one hundred percent cooperation. The small town had been devastated by the news of the massacre of the Cavanaugh family, and all of the town officials were willing to work with law enforcement in any way that might catch the killer.

It was 9:00 p.m. before Roarke shook hands all around with the village mall officials and walked across the plaza for dinner. The wind off the lake was frigid and penetrating. Beyond the circle of trees he could see the dark expanse of choppy water, and the moon, of course, the moon, shining a trail across the surface.

In the village center beside the lake there was a popular and long-established Mexican restaurant that Epps had already scouted out.

The warmth and the smells of the restaurant hit Roarke as he stepped through the front doors of the restaurant: onion and jalapeño, tomato sauce and cilantro. His stomach rumbled and he realized he hadn't eaten all day.

He walked through the fiesta-lit bar that was the entrance to the restaurant, and into the high-ceilinged dining room with its large plate glass windows. Candles in red glass holders on the tables provided most of the warm, dim light. It all made him think of church, and then something that didn't belong in church: Santa Muerte.

Epps was at a table by one of the arched windows. The walkway they intended to have Soames walk, as bait, was right below them, an asphalt ribbon winding beside the black and icy water. Roarke wanted to be close to it, wanted to be as familiar with it as he could.

Epps frowned and put away his phone as Roarke sat. "You look like shit."

"Happy to see you, too." Roarke reached for a menu.

"Carne asada fajitas," Epps instructed. "Look no further."

"Great," Roarke said, and put the menu aside without opening it. Epps nodded for the waitress and Roarke ordered the fajitas and a Corona. Epps held up two fingers, then as the waitress nodded and moved off, he glowered across the table.

"Serious, when was the last time you slept?"

"Define sleep."

Epps shook his head. "You eat, then you go catch some. Can't have you passing out in the middle of everything."

The beers arrived and both men squeezed lime into the bottles and drank deeply. Roarke felt a wave of tiredness crash over him, seductive and lethal. Epps was right, he had to sleep or he'd become a liability.

Epps put his bottle down. "I never got to hear. How was the witness?"

Roarke had to take a beat to understand that he was asking about Jade. With all of their focus on the new massacre they'd had no time to talk about his trip to juvenile hall.

"Interesting," Roarke said. His voice was bleak. "She was in that tunnel. She saw the whole thing."

Epps tensed. "It was Lindstrom?"

Roarke nodded. "The girl was lying about something, but not about that."

"Will she testify?"

Roarke paused. "It's going to be hard to keep track of her."

"Maybe Elliott can help with that."

Roarke felt a stab of guilt at the mention of Rachel's name. "She said she'd try."

Epps looked at him, frowning, but Roarke was saved from further interrogation on the subject by the waitress bringing the spicy steak, each order sizzling on its own burner, and both agents dug in, spearing meat and peppers to wrap in steaming tortillas.

"That was good work with the Fairchild kid," Epps said between bites. "The sketch gives us something to go on. We caught a break there, him seeing the guy. I hope to God it was the guy," he added as he reached for another tortilla, speared another piece of steak.

"It was," Roarke said. Epps looked up from his plate. Roarke had so far been careful not to speak in absolutes about the sketch, using words like "suspected" and "potential."

"How do you know?" Epps demanded.

"Because *he* knew. Tanner. He saw the guy because he could feel he was in jeopardy. And Lynn maybe knew they were all in jeopardy because she picked it up from the kid. Or he knew because she sensed something about the cat."

Epps shook his head. "You're talking ooga booga."

"Maybe. Or it's just self-preservation. Natural selection. There was something out there, and that family saved itself."

"Evil," Epps said flatly, and there was a note of hostility in his voice.

Roarke didn't answer for a moment. "Isn't it?" They had talked of it before. Epps didn't answer, and Roarke lowered his voice. "I know you believe—"

"*Don't* tell me what I believe," Epps said sharply. He looked away toward the lake and drained the last of his beer. "I don't even know anymore."

They sat in the candlelit dark, and Roarke finally asked the question he'd been holding back all evening. "So she hasn't turned up."

Epps looked across the table at him, and Roarke had one paralyzed moment as he started to speak. "Oh, right. We arrested her and they've got her in county lockup on suicide watch. With everything else going down it just slipped my mind."

Roarke felt heat in his face, knew he'd been had, knew he'd deserved it.

Epps shook his head. "Fool." He concentrated on dressing his food, not looking at Roarke.

"She's here, though," Roarke said, unable to help himself.

"Course she's here. Where would she go?"

Roarke wanted to ask him what he thought Cara was likely to do when she realized that they were putting up an agent in her place to draw out the Reaper. But in his state the beer had hit him hard enough that he was having trouble finding words, and it was an impossible question to begin with. He watched Epps pick over what remained in his fajita pan, though it seemed he'd lost his appetite. He spoke, apparently to the dregs of the pan.

"Full moon. Wild card. All kinds of craziness could go down." And finally he looked up at Roarke. "So get some sleep, because we're all going to need it."

Chapter 39

He is walking down the hallway and every detail is as it always is, the tiled floor, the white stucco walls, cold moonlight through the tall arched windows. He can feel the presence of madness . . . hear the harsh breath of the unimaginable thing that is waiting for him at the end of the hallway.

The terror has turned every cell in his body to ice; his feet barely move him forward. On the floor around him is a pool of dark, he is up to his ankles in it, and there are crumpled shapes on the floor around him, sleeping mounds . . . but not sleeping, no, the eyes are open, staring . . . an entire family, slashed, stabbed . . . slaughtered—

He shuddered awake, and lay still, breathing through the residual images from his nightmare.

He'd been asleep no more than an hour, but the cabin felt unbearably small and he was completely alert and wired, so he got up and dressed, shrugged on a parka.

The cold outside was dry and seductive. His breath steamed in the air as he walked the path toward the main lodge, between slight drifts of snow. The moon shone stark white between clouds, and the frozen ground crunched under his feet.

A shadow loomed up in front of him and he started back, heart leaping . . . before he recognized it as the chainsaw-carved bear.

He exhaled and kept moving.

The heat of the lodge hit him as he opened the door, instantly inducing a hypnotic numbness.

He found a corner table beside one of the tall windows, and ordered Scotch. He sat back watching the light on the snow as a jazz combo played across the room, the sound smoky and longing. The notes of the piano rippled like water.

He looked up as a blond woman walked into the bar and hovered inside the doorway. He froze, the beating of his heart suspended . . . and then he recognized Agent Soames.

She saw him and a complicated look crossed her face. Then she came toward his table.

"May I?" she asked.

He gestured to the chair across from him. She peeled off her parka and sat.

"Couldn't sleep," she said, and he wondered what he must be putting out that women kept looking at him like this. He fought a tidal wave of weariness.

"That's natural," he said.

The waitress came by again and Soames ordered a tonic and lime. *Very professional*, he thought. *Ambitious.*

"I guess I'm a little jumpy," she said, and he thought there was something under her tone, a subtle invitation.

He made his voice harsh. "You should be. I want you on your toes."

"Can we talk a little, then?" she asked, looking at him directly.

"Of course," he said, and braced himself.

The waitress came with her tonic. Soames took a sip of her drink and waited until the waitress was gone before she spoke.

"I'm sorry I went off script today, when—"

He cut her off. "It worked. It was a good call."

She nodded, and looked toward the darkness out the window beside them, and he could see that wasn't the real issue at all.

"The killer . . . he's only killed families so far. Why do you think he'll come after Lindstrom? Or me, as Lindstrom?"

It was a fair question, he had to admit. And he couldn't very well tell her the real answer: that he didn't understand why it would work, he just knew in his bones that it would. Aloud he said, "It's a theory. That he won't be able to stay away. And we've put it out that you are able to identify him, which may spur him to come after you."

"You don't think that will just drive him underground?"

Sure, if logic had anything to do with anything here. "It's a possibility. But we think his compulsion is too strong for him to let this go."

Soames nodded and sipped her tonic, but she wasn't done. "You've met her?"

In spite of himself, he flinched. "Met" was an absurd word. "I've been in a room with her," he said warily.

"What is she like?"

He felt rage rising from somewhere inside him, barely tamped it down. "Agent Soames, this isn't a casting call. You don't have to *play* her."

She colored slightly. "Sorry, sir."

He held back a sigh. "Our unsub doesn't even know what she looks like now. It's all context. He'll think you're her because we're saying you're her."

"I understand." She hesitated, but was bold enough to speak. "I'm just curious."

Fascinated, she meant. *Who wouldn't be?* He made his face and voice hard.

"I want you to stay focused on your surroundings. Now that the news is out, we have to act as if he is right there, wherever we go. Anything that feels off to you, any twinge you have, I don't care how small, you talk to me immediately."

She looked appropriately chastened. "Understood."

She had the police sketch, and Snyder had given her the rundown of what the Reaper might look and act like, the general dishevelment and odd affect of schizophrenia. But Roarke stressed again now: "You need to treat everyone you meet as potentially lethal. We just don't know."

"Yes, sir." There was no more invitation in her voice, only deference to a superior officer.

"Now you should get back up to your room. Try to sleep."

She stood, and reached for her parka . . . then she looked back at him. "One more question."

He looked up at her.

"I was told that Cara Lindstrom is somewhere in the area."

He looked at her steadily. "She was. She may still be. And?"

She faltered. "I . . . just wondered if that had any bearing on anything."

He wanted to say no, to cut her off, but in good conscience he couldn't. "You need to treat everyone you meet as potentially lethal," he repeated, and it occurred to him that he needed to be doing the same thing.

Chapter 40

I n the morning the show began.

Soames was outfitted with a radio mike and given the strict instruction that she was to wear it at all times. She moved out of her room in the main lodge into a cabin of her own, close to the others so as not to draw too much suspicion, but a unit chosen for its blind spots, so that the Reaper would find approaching a possibility. Of course she was armed and would be constantly guarded. There was already a deputy planted in her room who would not leave it until the operation was concluded.

They all gathered in the war room they'd set up as headquarters. Every move they made, inside or outside, was accompanied by telegraphing of purported intentions: stopping on bridges and in open spaces to provide maximum visibility for anyone watching, lengthy greetings and conversations outside before retreating into the room. Then there was an equally telegraphed procession to the cars to drive to the Cavanaugh house.

The day was cold and shrouded in white mist; their breath clouded in the air. Roarke had been obsessively checking the weather sites and reports. The prediction was daytime snow flurries, cold and windy that night.

The agents and detectives took Soames on a full walk-through of the Cavanaugh house again. It was all for show, but it couldn't hurt to go over all of it again. The bodies of the family were gone, but the house still felt like a tomb. Roarke could see Soames bracing herself against every description of the scene.

Snowflakes were swirling in the air by the time the reporters showed up, a few carefully chosen photographers and video teams to create the media show. They staged scenes outside the house, cameramen shooting footage and photographers snapping photos of Soames talking to the agents, circling the house, stopping to point out the side door that was the point of entry, the suspected angle of observation of the house.

They would not, of course, be going anywhere near the Fairchild house. The Reaper didn't need to know that the agents knew that much about him.

Roarke kept looking up at the sky. Sometimes he thought he could feel the moon under the banks of clouds, gathering its fullness.

Chapter 41

The snow had been falling on and off all day. Not a lot, but enough to keep families out of the village center that night, which was a boon. It meant fewer people that the agents would have to steer away. Night now, and the temperature was dropping steadily.

Under the coordination of Epps and Jones, Lieutenant Tyson, and Detectives Aceves and Lambert, they had assembled a team of local deputies and Los Angeles agents, three dozen in all, and seeded them throughout the village at strategic spots. There were two ambulances with full staffs of EMTs positioned at either side of the village, ready to go into action if needed. Most of the businesses had closed at Sunday hours, five o'clock. The ones that remained open were key locations now "staffed" by agents and deputies in civilian clothes.

Despite the icy cold, Roarke was close to overheated, wearing a Kevlar vest under a down jacket with a big hood which concealed his face. He was also wearing a beard to disguise his profile, now that he'd flashed it around for the media for two days. Epps was similarly vested but dressed as a maintenance man, moving in and out of back doors and restricted entrances. It was jarring to see his elegant frame in blue-collar clothes. Jones was in a security uniform, driving the tram that ran along the periphery of the village.

All of the agent/ringers had been in place most of the day, working alongside the regular clerks and storeowners to learn enough of the routine to carry off the illusion of normalcy. Roarke himself had been walking the circles of the Village for hours now, getting familiar with the layout, the possible escape routes, the hazardous areas where they might lose sight of Soames, lose track of her. The village center was a far more extensive complex than it seemed on first look. He was impressed at how perfect a stalking ground it was turning out to be, the parking lot beside the lake and the walkways that went straight down by the water, curving around buildings, with lots of secluded areas along the way.

The shops themselves were already fully decorated for Christmas, with white twinkle lights draping the awnings, windows full of spun white fiberglass clouds and golden angels. Christmas music played inside the stores and out, the fragrance of spiced cider and gingerbread and vanilla candles drifted in the cold air. All an incongruously tranquil stage set for their grim business.

As the evening came, painting the sky in deep purples and blues, the real clerks and owners went home as if their shifts were over. The agents remained, dealing with the few early Christmas shoppers who had braved the snowy roads. Families with children were quietly approached and steered back to their cars.

The agents and detectives had divided the Village into four quadrants, with Roarke, Epps, Jones, and Detective Aceves each commanding a squad of deputies assigned to each quadrant. They had blocked out a path for Soames to walk. The pantomime she was going to play was restlessness: being cooped up in her cabin and now needing to get out. The village center was just a three-minute walk from the lodge, so she would leave her cabin and walk the back road down to the village center, under the watching eyes of deputies posted in other cabins along the way.

Once she got to the village center she would browse in a few of the open shops: two art galleries, the candy shop, the café where she would sit in the front window having coffee, then the wine shop, where she would buy a bottle of wine. Then she would head down the path to walk beside the lake, a darker, circular path that was heavily staked out by agents. It was a long and secluded stretch to walk, with plenty of opportunity for anyone following to attack.

Just before Roarke had left his own cabin Snyder had knocked on the door to look in on him. He would be staked out, too, at the restaurant Roarke and Epps had eaten in the night before, watching the path through binoculars.

Roarke had just been strapping on the body armor they all were wearing, and the two men looked at each other for a moment without speaking.

"What are you going to do, warn me about forces we don't understand?" Roarke said finally.

Snyder's smile flickered. "Be careful," he said.

"You, too."

"I'm not the one who—" Snyder began. And then Jones had breezed in with something or other and they had never finished the conversation.

The one who—what? Roarke wondered now, as he walked the plaza under sparkling strings of Christmas lights. He looked around him at the shops, now only one window lit out of every three.

He drifted into an art gallery and pretended to study the displays. A few moody paintings of village residents, some abstract sculpture of distressed wood and burl swirls, a few large crosses bound in barbed wire. Edgier than the average mountain fare, which often ran toward calico-garbed teddy bears.

He moved on to the next aisle and found himself in front of a wall hung with sculptures, a theme of hearts: two blackened hearts bound together with rusted chain link, another pair of hearts twisted in barbed wire.

He felt something in his own chest twist at the sight.

Then his phone buzzed in his pocket. He fished it out to see Singh's name on the screen.

As he held the phone to his ear, he could hear the tension in her voice. "Chief, I'm sorry to call so close to zero hour, but it's urgent."

"Wait just a minute." He exited the shop into the frosty air and found a bench with no one nearby. "Go ahead."

"I believe I have found him."

Roarke felt an electric thrill.

"Nathaniel Marcus Hughes. He grew up in Arcata, was living there in 1986 and 1987. He drove for an equine transport company based there, which had routes that included all the relevant towns. He was fired for odd behavior some time after the first massacre and before the second, and was arrested four months after the Lindstrom massacre."

"For?" Roarke asked sharply.

"Mutilating horses," Singh said.

Her words were a chill and a rush. *Of course*, he thought. *Of course.*

"He was diagnosed schizophrenic and put on meds in prison. His initial sentence was just two years but he stabbed another prisoner while he was inside, which added the extra time. I asked local law enforcement to go by to speak with him, and they have informed me he has disappeared. His parole officer has not seen him since before the Reno massacre. I have sent through a mug shot."

Roarke clicked over to the message and looked down at a man who looked not unlike Santos, the same dishevelment, the same black void in his eyes. Tanner Fairchild had described him well; the gaunt police sketch was a fair image.

"The photo is out to every agent and deputy involved in our sting," Singh told him. "I am sorry it could not have come sooner."

"It gives us someone to look for. That may make all the difference."

"I hope so," she said, then: "Be careful, Chief."

He stood in the chill, looking down at the photo on his phone, of a man whose face seemed caved in on itself, collapsing from some emptiness within. The piped Christmas music floated in the air, a choir singing.

He spoke into his collar mike. "Do we all have the mug shot of suspect Hughes?"

Affirmatives came from the three other quadrants, and he could hear the tenseness in the men's voices.

Then his earpiece crackled to life and he heard Jones' voice. "Soames is en route."

Roarke felt a chill and a sizzle of adrenaline simultaneously. He forced himself to stay for another minute in front of the gallery, looking through the window at art he didn't see and listening to Jones' muted report of Soames' walk past the cabins manned by deputies. Then he strolled back in the direction of the parking lot, past souvenir shops, clothing outlet stores. The wind gusted through the plaza, swirling dead leaves.

He circled the clock tower, where he knew there was a sniper concealed, as well as other L.A. Bureau agents with binoculars surveying the entire plaza. Then he found a bench under a circle of trees and sat, looking across the plaza.

He saw her instantly as she stepped into the circular space. She wore a down parka to conceal the Kevlar armor he knew she was wearing. Her coat hood was down, the light from the street lamps glinted off her pale hair. He had to admire that she walked with not one hint of the extra weight she was carrying.

She took her time crossing the plaza, stopping at a billboard to read a posted list of events, pausing at a railing to look out over the view of the lake. The full moon was rising over the dark ridge, heavy and huge, and the sight made Roarke colder. Then Soames turned in to the café. He waited edgily as she sat and had her coffee inside the front of the shop, lit up in the window like a precious object on display.

And he felt a chill that had nothing to do with the frigid air: that he was setting this very vulnerable human being out as bait for something unimaginable.

No, not unimaginable, he reminded himself. *A twisted man. Just a man.*

Soames finished her coffee and walked outside again, now moving past the two-story high Christmas tree in the center of a landscape island, toward the wine shop. Inside, she stood near the front store window talking to the "proprietor," who went about selecting a bottle for her, bagging it, ringing her up.

She emerged from the shop with bottle in hand; a good prop, but a better weapon, should the need arise. And finally, she moved toward the stairs leading down to the lake walk.

Moving quickly but without rushing, Roarke took an alternate staircase down to the upper path to follow her, descending past a terrace filled with concrete tables with built-in umbrellas, a restroom hut.

Down by the lake, the wind was icy and merciless, swelling the black water, pushing at the boats. Above the moon climbed higher, icy and round in the sky. Its whiteness made everything colder.

Soames walked the path, moonlight shining on her golden hair. Roarke followed on the upper path, the walkway in front of the dark shops, watching as she drifted, stopping often to look out over the lake.

She reached the corner of the row of shops, and he sped up to make the wider curve around. Now he could see the buildings and tents of the small midway: the arcade, the kid-sized bumper cars. He ducked behind the shadow of a post and looked down over the path to find Soames again. Above him, a cloud passed over the moon . . .

And then he caught sight of something that stopped his heart.

A family had emerged on the path that curved past the fun house. Father, mother, and four children. It was the littlest girl who caught Roarke's eye: five or six and blond, clinging to her mother's hand.

Cara . . .

When he registered the rest of the family, the dread intensified. The family was an echo of Cara's: the tiny girl, a boy in his mid-teens, an eight- or nine-year-old girl . . . and a boy the same size as Tanner

Fairchild. For a moment he could only stare, as if confronted with a ghostly apparition. But the family before him was all too real.

He backed into the shadows between bushes and spoke into his collar mike, his lips stiff with tension. "There's a family on the path, near the fun house. Mother, father, four kids. Get those people out of there *now*. Take them back to their vehicle and drive them out of here. Do not leave them alone."

He tried to keep one eye on the family as he turned back to the path to get a visual on Soames.

She was gone.

The trees towered, dark and needled; the icy lake stretched out, vast and black, with the moon shimmering a wide swath across the center. Shadows arced across the empty path.

"I've lost visual on Soames," Roarke muttered into his collar mike. "Jones, Epps, Aceves?"

For a moment there was silence.

Roarke vaulted over the railing and dropped into the dirt between the bushes below him. He stood concealed in the dark and stared out through the branches. There was no sign of the family or of Soames; the path was empty. He heard only the thin whistling of the wind, the creaking of the tied-up boats, the splashing of water against the docks.

Then he froze, staring out of the bushes at the path. Something glittered on the path . . . shattered glass in a pool of black. The bottle of wine Soames had been carrying, smashed on the concrete.

"Christ . . ." he breathed.

"I see her," Jones' voice came back on his earpiece.

Roarke spoke with sharp relief. "Where?"

"Southeast of the clock tower. By the pizza place."

Roarke frowned, trying to register. The location was on the other side of the Village. "That can't be right." He'd only lost sight of her for a minute. Even at a full run she couldn't have gotten clear across the Village.

"Blond, slender, parka . . ."

Cara, his mind registered. *She's here.*

Chapter 42

He crashed out of the bushes and half-ran along the lake walk, under white lights strung from poles. The dark expanse of lake stretched beyond, pure black and fathomless. Every few feet gates and stairs led down to docks. Soames could be behind any of the fences. Below him boats creaked and splashed, bobbing wildly in the swells.

There was a sharp curve at the end of the path and two forks to take, one that headed up into a small park at the edge of a spit, rimmed with trees, with a swing set and picnic tables, benches looking out on the lake.

The other path curved around to the little children's amusement fairway, with its miniature golf course and autopia. The rides were closed, but he could hear music: at the far end of the park a small carousel, deserted in the cold, was still eerily piping a calliope soundtrack. The notes prickled on his skin.

He turned away from it, back toward the park, and bolted up the short span of steps, scanning the park. The wind tossed empty swings in the air and whistled through the trees . . . the water lapped at the shore. He strode a wide circle around the periphery of the park, searching the shadows. Past a split rail fence a path curved down to the sand.

On the pale drifts lay a dark heap: a crumpled body. He caught a glimpse of gold hair in the moonlight under the trees. He lurched forward, ran for it, pounding down the dune.

He dropped to his knees in the sand beside the body.

"Cara," he said, and turned her over.

It was Soames.

Her limbs were limp, her skin pale as snow. As Roarke reached to turn her head toward him, he saw black blood oozing from a vicious scalp wound.

He shouted into his collar mike: "Officer down. I need EMT *now*. The beach below the park behind the funhouse." He grabbed for her wrist, digging his fingers in for a pulse. It was there, faint.

She was breathing.

The EMTs were on scene in a minute, the ambulance speeding through the Village and onto the path. The EMTs bore Soames up from the beach on a stretcher as Roarke hustled along beside.

"Her breathing is stable," an EMT told him, and Roarke felt the news as a hot wave of relief.

At the ambulance, he hovered over the stretcher while the EMTs opened the back doors. His heart lurched as Soames' eyes suddenly opened, staring straight up at him.

"Soames?"

She murmured something he couldn't hear. "Just rest," he told her. "You're okay . . ."

"Peace," she said thickly . . . then her eyes closed.

Roarke froze. "Soames!" he shouted. But then he saw her lips part, her chest rise in a breath.

The EMT was beside him, reaching for the stretcher. "We've got her."

Roarke stepped back to let her go.

As soon as the van's doors had closed on her, he was shouting orders into his collar mike. "Epps, Jones, Aceves, meet me in the arcade." It was their designated rendezvous for that side of the Village; Roarke had a key card to get in.

He used his key and left the door cracked open. He stood in the dark of the small arcade, with funhouse mirrors on the walls around him. He stared into his own reflection, distorted, rippling images. Inside his thoughts were screaming.

He turned as the door was pulled open and Epps and Jones strode inside, followed a beat later by Detective Aceves.

"What the hell happened?" Epps demanded.

Roarke moved to meet them. "Someone attacked Soames. Head wound. She's alive."

The other men relaxed almost simultaneously, a palpable relief. They stood with their reflections cast in grotesque shapes in the mirrors.

"Did you see him?" Jones demanded.

"I didn't see anything. There was a family—" Roarke stopped, and felt a sudden stab of dread. "Aceves, did your men get to them?"

"We couldn't find them," the detective said grimly.

Roarke stared at him. "What do you mean, you couldn't find them?"

"We never saw them at all. They must have been parked somewhere besides the main parking lot. We stopped every car leaving the Village entrance but there was no sign of them. I got a man on the fairway entrance right away and we went up and down every aisle. No family of that description."

Roarke's blood went cold. "Jesus. We have to find that family. *Now.*"

Epps asked it first. "You want to call off the stakeout?"

Roarke forced himself to be still, to consider. They were in a dangerous place. The case had expanded to three tracks, their manpower now searching in three different directions: Cara, the Reaper, and the unknown, unnamed family.

What is the Reaper thinking?

Why did he attack Soames and not kill her? Why not finish off the job?

At the same time he was thinking it, Epps was shaking his head, saying aloud, "Why didn't he finish Soames off? Why not kill her?"

And it hit Roarke.

Because he had a more important task.

"He didn't have time," Roarke said, his voice hollow. "The family. He left her to go after that family."

He twisted around to face his agent. "Jones, you keep your team here in the Village, looking out for the Reaper or anyone who might have seen the family. Question everyone. Someone must have seen them. Go now, spread out and search."

"Yes, boss." Jones disappeared through the door.

Roarke turned now to the detective. "Aceves, how do we find these people?"

Aceves punched a number on his phone and handed it to Roarke. "Give the dispatcher the description."

Roarke concentrated, called up in his mind the image of the family on the path in the wind. "Parents in their early forties, father five-nine, average build, fit, brown hair, eye color unknown. Mother five-five, medium build, blond, eye color unknown. Two boys, about fifteen and thirteen, brown and blond. Two girls, about eight and five, brown and blond . . ."

Aceves took the phone back. "Put a radio message out to all officers, and one on the website and Village mail loop," he ordered. "Get a team on the phone to all the hotels and motels, find out if anyone remembers them checking in or eating at any of the attached restaurants."

He turned back to Roarke and Epps. "We have to hope they lived in town. The truth is, they could be from anywhere."

"Or that they're not from out of town and they're headed down the mountain already," Epps said.

Aceves spoke into the phone. "I need roadblocks set up at the 189 and Highway 18 junctions, checking every car for that family, is that clear?"

Roarke tried to breathe through his dread. He turned to Aceves. "We need to put together a list of locals and renters that might fit the description of the family and divide it among your men as the possibles are coming in. Have them work in groups of two so one can be phoning down the list while the other is driving them to each location. The ones the team can't reach by phone, they're to go directly to the address and *make sure* each family is safe."

Aceves nodded, planning. "Roger that." He was already headed for the door.

Epps lingered behind. "You didn't see who attacked Soames?" he asked, low. Roarke looked at him. "Are you sure it was the Reaper?"

"Who else—" Roarke started, and then stopped.

Epps nodded meaningfully. "We know she's here. We know she's been watching. News coverage, fake investigation, all of it. What if she didn't like the idea of someone walking around pretending to be her?"

Roarke's mind followed the thought frantically, back to the chilly paths beside the lake, the smashed bottle of wine, Soames' crumpled body on the sand . . .

"No," he said tightly.

"Had to say it," Epps said, equally taut.

"It doesn't make sense that—" Roarke stopped mid-sentence, as it struck him what he had forgot.

"What?" Epps asked, already alarmed.

Roarke grabbed for his phone, speed dialed the sheriff's dispatch. "Agent Roarke speaking. I need to talk to the guard on duty at the Crestline cabin."

"Holy Mother, the Fairchilds," Epps muttered.

Roarke waited in agony as the call was put through, and then a brusque voice came on. "Deputy Shaber."

Just the voice answering was a relief. "This is Agent Roarke checking in. Anything suspicious happening tonight? Anything unusual?"

"Negative. Been quiet all day. The father got here a couple of hours ago. Everyone's upstairs."

Roarke thanked the gods he'd been wrong. "Glad to hear it. Stay alert tonight."

"Will do."

Roarke punched off the phone, turned to Epps. "They're fine."

"Oh, man." Epps looked as if he'd just aged ten years in half a minute.

Through the adrenaline buzz of relief, Roarke knew it had been a mad thought, pure paranoia. There was no way the Reaper, or Hughes, could know where the Fairchilds were holed up.

And yet no more mad than the rest of the case.

"We need to get out there," he told Epps. "Patrol the Village. Look for that family, look for the Reaper. Someone saw something."

Chapter 43

Roarke walked the path by the arcade, past the carousel, the calliope music. He could hear the addresses of potential families to check out coming in over his earpiece. He felt nearly insane with tension, and worse, unsure what to do next.

Think. What does the Reaper want? What would he do?

He found himself at the top of the parking lot. The Jeep the agents had been driving was still parked there.

And the full moon was high in the night sky now.

What would the Reaper do?

And suddenly he was striding toward the Jeep.

Inside the car he was turning on the lights and speaking into his collar mike at the same time. "Epps, I'm taking the Jeep and going down to Crestline."

"What happened?" Epps asked sharply.

"Nothing," Roarke admitted. "I just . . . want to be there. I'll be in touch."

He punched up the address on the GPS and started off, under the arched span of the welcoming sign above the parking lot.

Out of the Village and out on the road, he took the snowy curves of highway faster than was probably safe. He was glad that someone had equipped the Jeep with snow chains. Inside the vehicle the heat was blasting but he could feel the chill of the night leaking through the window beside his face.

In just minutes he was turning off the highway, following the signs toward Crestline.

He sped on the road circling the lake, past the darkened, sprawling family homes set back from the road.

The quality of darkness was thicker here, the full moon high in the sky, seeming bright as the sun, and yet not illuminating the forest below.

His headlights caught the collection of mailboxes, and he made a wild turn down the dirt road toward the lake.

The trees loomed beside the road, slanting shadows in the moonlight, but he drove and drove and there was no sign of the house. The road ahead was so dark he thought he had taken a wrong turn. He leaned forward, stared harder through the glass.

Then he realized with a sickening twist of his stomach that the house was there. There were just no lights anywhere. No porch light, no security light, no inside lights.

He slammed on the brakes and jolted back in the seat, then leaned forward and stared out the windshield, in turmoil. The house was outlined in pure black.

This is wrong, so wrong. Where are the lights? Where are the guards?

He grabbed for his phone and speed-dialed the number for the Crestline guard. His heart sank as the phone rang and rang.

He punched off and dialed the dispatcher. "Agent Roarke requesting immediate back up to the safe house in Crestline. The lights are blacked out. No sign of guards. Send everyone in the area. Now."

He shut out the car lights, shut off the car, and stared through the windshield at the darkness, scanning the front of the house: the trees, the swing set, the porch. The trees obscured everything. The blackness seemed a live thing.

He drew his Glock and vaulted out of the SUV, into the frozen dark. A thin, icy wind buffeted him. The faint smell of pine bit his nostrils.

He approached the house by circling the edge of the clearing, weapon drawn, scanning to all sides of him, cold air sharp in his lungs. To the right a pale figure crouched . . . he spun toward it . . .

And recognized the shape of the concrete birdbath.

He exhaled, turned back to the house, and nearly tripped over a crumpled body. His heart was pounding out of his chest as he crouched beside the form, saw the slashed throat, the black blood leaking. He felt the badge, the buttons of the uniform. A deputy.

He stood, wiping blood from his hands, and hustled for the front door. At the slab of porch he pressed his back against the side wall, Glock aimed into the yard, forcing his breath to slow as he scanned the circle of trees. No motion, no sound but the rustling of the wind in the pine needles . . .

He reached beside him for the doorknob, tried it. Locked, of course. He pressed his back against the wall, gun at the ready in one hand, covering the outside and the door while he felt for the doorbell with the other hand, pressed it hard, multiple times. Not a sound.

Lines cut, he registered. *Lights, power . . .*

The Reaper. How did he find them? How could he know?

And then it came to him with a sick jolt. *Piece*, Soames had said. *Not peace. Her radio earpiece. She wasn't wearing it. The Reaper took it off her.*

He did another scan of the front yard behind him as he pounded on the door with his free hand, shouting, "FBI! Open the door!"

No sound from the house. Nothing.

He knew the door was deceptively sturdy, reinforced. There was no way to kick it in.

He sidestepped off the porch, swiveling, and found the nearest window. Probably reinforced as well. He remembered the birdbath, turned to locate it in the dark. He strode for it, and stood, loath to put his weapon away even for a second. But he shoved the Glock into a pocket, knocked the dish off the top of the birdbath and hefted the concrete base.

He turned and strode toward the front of the house, hurled the concrete pillar through the window. Glass exploded inward.

He drew the Glock again, knocked out the jagged edges of glass and hauled himself through the window, dropped to his feet in a crouch in the middle of the shattered glass, swiveling his weapon in the living room. He slowed his breath, letting his eyes adjust and focus. He saw no one moving.

He swallowed through a dry mouth as his mind raced through his memory of the layout: entry, living room, kitchen to the left, den down several steps to the right.

He sidestepped to the den, peered into the darkness before him . . . and flinched back to see images from his own nightmares: crumpled bodies of the family on the floor . . .

No!

He took a step, stared harder at the shapes . . . and felt sick relief. Not people. Just couch cushions piled on the floor.

He turned in the doorway and looked back into the living room.

There was a thud on the balcony above. Roarke spun to see a human figure looming up on the staircase above him. A blond man hefting a baseball bat, dressed in sweatpants and sweatshirt and looking nothing like the mug shot of the wild-eyed suspect. The father, Paul Fairchild.

For a frozen moment the men stared at each other.

"FBI," Roarke said. He yanked out his credentials wallet with his free hand and held it up, open. "Special Agent Roarke."

"Thank God," the man said. He lowered the bat, but only halfway. His face was ashen. "The lights went out ten minutes ago. We can't reach our guards—"

Suddenly Lynn Fairchild was behind her husband, her face as white as paper. Roarke looked up at her. "Where are the children?"

"Here. Upstairs in our room," she said through lips stiff with adrenaline.

"Have you seen anyone?" he asked her.

"No. We can't get hold of the guards. We called 9-1-1." Her terror was live in the room.

"Backup is on its way," Roarke told them tightly. "I need you to get back upstairs. Keep all of the family into one room with you. Lock the door. Stay there." He stooped to draw his backup piece out of his ankle holster. "Can you use this?" he demanded of Paul Fairchild.

"Hell, yeah," the father said, striding down toward him.

Roarke handed the weapon up to Fairchild, hoping to God the man would not need it.

Lynn gave him a last stricken look before she turned with her husband to go back upstairs.

Roarke turned to survey the room. The broken window was a problem now. It left wide-open access to the house.

Where the hell is everyone? He thought of the long dirt road, the confusion of the darkness.

His mind raced through his options. *Go upstairs, guard the family from the balcony?*

But the Reaper is out there.

Thoughts flew past him at the speed of light. There was another guard he hadn't located, probably dead, but possibly hurt . . .

And the Reaper. I can't let him get away.

He froze as he heard a sound from the kitchen. *Sliding? A drawer? The Reaper finding a knife? Or just the heat going on?*

Back pressed against the wall, he slid around the doorway into the kitchen. His nostrils were hit by a strong animal smell. The back door was open, spilling moonlight into the dark room. Two entrances open now, the window in the living room and the back door. He strode across the room, shut and locked the kitchen door, pulled open the door to the laundry room to check it. The scent of detergent and fabric softener was overwhelming, momentarily blotting out the other smell. But the utility room was empty.

He closed that door and yanked open the back door, pressed himself against the wall. Shielded by the doorframe, he scanned the yard, the empty spaces beneath trees, the swing set off to the side of the house . . .

One of the swings was swaying.

The wind? Or had someone touched it?

"FBI!" he shouted into the night. "Drop your weapon and come out with your hands on top of your head!"

Silence. He scanned what there was of the yard: dead rosebushes, the wooden trash enclosure . . .

He heard a *whuuff* . . . the deep snuffle of a horse . . . but he knew with a sudden gut-twisting certainty that it was not a horse that had made the sound. He spun toward the trees, staring . . . and heard an eerie, high-pitched giggling. It froze his blood. He shouted toward the trees.

"FBI, don't move."

Silence.

"Come out *now* or I'll shoot."

Roarke eased sideways, looking for a better vantage point between trees. The snaking mist and the dead underbrush obscured his view. He tensed at a rustle . . .

The stalker seemed to be about twenty feet away, inside the trees, just far enough back to be invisible.

There was an animal-like snuffling, then a scrabbling sound that was nothing like human. He twisted toward it, saw flying hair, wild eyes rolling back like a horse's in the night . . .

Roarke only had time to think, *What*—before he heard a thunderous boom. Pain exploded in his chest, and he was falling, hitting the ground.

Shot . . .

The blast had slammed into Kevlar, the kinetic force of being hit by a baseball bat. He gasped for breath through cracked ribs, pushed down against the earth with his hands to try to roll. A shadow loomed over him, a gaunt man with stringy, longish hair, and Roarke smelled that animal smell, heavy, equine. The man seized him by the neck. Pain blazed through his chest. And then there was brush of cold metal against his forehead, as the man leaned over to put the barrel of the gun against his cheek . . . and the horse smell surrounded him . . .

And then . . . blood. Blood everywhere. It exploded over Roarke. He could smell it, feel it, hot and thick and gushing. New pain shattered his chest as the Reaper fell on top of him, crushing the wind out of him. The man clutched at his throat and spasmed . . . The hot blood drenched them both as his heart pumped it from his ruined throat.

Roarke pushed out his arms with all his might . . . and the body rolled off him. He gasped out, choking through blood. And looked up.

Cara stood above him, a lithe shadow against the light of the moon. She moved forward, and the light glinted off her hair, and her eyes were locked on his—

And then she was jerked back, as two uniformed deputies grabbed her. As Roarke tried to struggle to his feet he heard the jangle and rasp of handcuffs racheting home.

The deputies held her between them, and there was blood all over her, black against her pale skin, and her hair shone in the moonlight, her image burned into Roarke's mind . . . as all went dark.

Chapter 44

The Reaper was dead. He had bled out in under a minute after Cara had slashed him, was dead by the time the EMTs had reached him.

The deputies brought Cara in to the station, where Epps and Jones arrested her on suspicion of the murder of the pimp Danny Ramirez. She was transported to the San Francisco Sheriff's Department County Jail #2, a pre-trial holding facility on the sixth floor of the curved building next door to the Hall of Justice, little more than a mile away from Roarke's office.

She was being held without bail, as an extreme flight risk, and on suicide watch.

Roarke spent half a day in the Mountains Community Hospital being treated for broken ribs and concussion, then walked out of the hospital without discharge and caught a flight back up to San Francisco.

In one part of his mind he knew that Epps was handling everything that needed handling. Snyder would be digging into Nathaniel Martin Hughes' criminal and psychiatric history to try to unravel the complex web of factors that had created the monster. Singh would be compiling the forensic evidence Lam and Stotlemyre lined up from the cold cases and the present-day cases to definitively establish Hughes as the killer of all five families. Finally the legend of the Reaper would be laid to rest.

In another part of his mind Roarke didn't give a damn. He landed at the airport and went straight to the jail.

Inside the stifling building he passed through security mechanically, turned over his weapon, signed in at the desk, rode the elevators up to the women's wing.

The visiting booth was a narrow cubicle with an equivalent square on the other side of a metal-threaded glass partition, with a counter on each side.

His heart was pounding out of his chest as he sat on the low stool in the claustrophobic room and waited.

The door opened on the other side, ten feet away from him, and the guard let her in. She wore an olive uniform; her feet were shackled, her hands cuffed in front of her. But she sat with grace, folding herself down into the chair.

The phone cord was too short, forcing him to learn forward toward the glass. On the other side, Cara picked up her phone and bent her head toward the glass, toward him, her hair falling around her face.

"Are you all right?" he asked. His voice sounded hoarse, not like his own.

She lifted her cuffed hands and met his gaze through the glass. He saw for the first time that her eyes were green.

"Do you have a lawyer?" he tried.

"They're lining up," she said. "High profile case. Career-making."

It occurred to him that she could afford any number of attorneys, if she still had even a fraction of the insurance money she received from her family's death.

He lowered his voice, and gave her what he could. "It's him. We haven't proved it yet, but it's the Reaper."

Her head was down. She didn't look at him, and he felt a prickling of fear. "It is, isn't it?" he asked. His mouth was dry as dust. "He's dead . . ."

"He's dead. *It* isn't. *It* never dies."

He knew what she meant now. *It.* The monster that made people do the things they do. The monster that in her mind she was killing, over and over.

He swallowed. "I want you to tell me more. I'll be back. If that's all right."

She lifted her head to look at him. Their eyes were locked, and he couldn't breathe.

Behind him, there was a sharp rap on the door, and a voice called, "One minute." Roarke leaned forward, closer to the glass.

"You saved my life." He looked through the barrier, holding her gaze. "It will make a difference."

She shook her head slightly, and he didn't know what she meant by that. He wanted to reach through the glass. "I wish—"

And then the door opened behind her, and the guard stepped in.

"If there's anything you need . . ."

She kept shaking her head, blond hair rippling like silk on her shoulders.

"*Anything.* You have to tell me."

She put her hand on the glass, and his was there to meet it, instantly. They sat that way, not moving, not breathing, eyes locked through the glass.

Cara slid back her chair, stood looking down at Roarke, then turned and walked to the door.

Roarke stayed still, with his hand on the glass. She stopped in the doorway for one second, but did not turn.

And the door closed behind her.

• • • • •

Keep reading for a preview of
Cold Moon
Book III of the Huntress/FBI Thrillers
by Alexandra Sokoloff

CHAPTER 1

The walls breathe.

She lies listening to the thick concrete slabs around her inhaling and exhaling, a rasping breath. From the cells next to hers come the muffled cries of others It had swallowed. The stench of blood and offal. The belly of the Beast.

And outside in the maze of halls, there is the shrieking scratch of talons on metal bars, coming closer . . .

Trapped. Trapped . . .

Her eyes fly open. Her breath comes quick and hard in her chest as she orients. Thin jailhouse mattress beneath her. Stained concrete walls around her in the dark. And a presence.

Her eyes scan, searching the dark.

Through the metal bars, she sees the glow of rabid eyes. Jaws dripping with foam. A man. A beast. *It.*

Watching her. Waiting.

She is trapped in this cage with the monster, and they both know it. *It* will toy with her until she is spent and then It will sink *Its* teeth in. She stares back through the dark and knows that she will use her nails, her teeth, her jaws, every muscle in her body, whatever it takes to fight. Or she will use her teeth on her own wrists, die in blood, before she will let *It* take her.

Its lips curl back from Its teeth, a feral promise . . . and the guard turns away from her cell.

For now.

• • • • •

The fog was icy, drifting sluggishly in the streets. The neon signs still blazed in the pre-dawn dark, lighting the entrances of the sex clubs with their theater-style displays: glassed-in posters of contorted female bodies in G-strings and spike heels, signs advertising Massage, Sauna, Incall/Outcall.

The Tenderloin was San Francisco's infamous sex district, fifty square blocks on the southern slope of Nob Hill, sandwiched between the high-end shopping of Union Square and the scruffier Civic Center. Otherwise known as The Loin, The TL, the Trendyloin, and Little Saigon.

Madam Tessie Wall had opened her first brothel here in 1898 and no one ever looked back. By the 1920s the TL was infamous for its billiard halls, burlesque houses, theaters and speakeasies. It was the birthplace of the porn movie industry in the 1960's, and in the seventies it pushed the envelope even further with live sex acts on stage.

While the rest of San Francisco real estate had skyrocketed in value after the dot com boom, the TL had resisted gentrification. Its streets teemed with junkies looking for a cheap fix, homeless looking for a cheap hotel, men looking for a cheap fuck.

The address Mills had given was an alley between two lurid sex clubs: Barely Legal and Wildcats. As Roarke parked, he saw Epps' tall silhouette striding up the sidewalk in the drifting fog. Roarke got out of the car to meet him.

"Hell is this now?" Epps started.

"I don't know," Roarke answered. He was too tense to speak further.

The agents flashed credentials at the uniform guarding the yellow crime scene tape at the front of the long, narrow uphill alley, and headed for the collection of cops, crime scene techs, and police photographers milling at the far end of the enclosed strip.

The sense of déjà vu was strong. The alley was narrow and dim in the fog, reminiscent of the tunnel where Jade's pimp, Danny Ramirez, had been murdered. Like Ramirez, this dead pimp was also collapsed in a pool of his own blood, at the foot of a short set of concrete steps leading down from a back door of the Wildcats club. Roarke could see the blood was thick and congealing around the edges of the spill, but still deep and liquid in places around the body. He hadn't been dead long.

Mills lumbered over to meet them. "Rear assault incised neck wound," he began without preamble. "No defensive wounds on hands or arms." He looked up toward the steps, the small landing outside the door. "I figure the doer was above him on the stairs. Grabbed his hair from behind, slashed his neck. Same kind of cut we got with Danny Ramirez. No hesitation marks, a clean slice left to right."

Roarke felt lightheaded, and he didn't know if it was lack of sleep or a hangover or the complete sense of unreality.

It was exactly how Cara killed.

Only . . . Cara was locked away.

• • • • •

Acknowledgments

This series would not exist without:

The initial inspiration for the Huntress from Val McDermid, Denise Mina, and Lee Child, at the San Francisco Bouchercon.

My mega-talented critique partners, Zoë Sharp and JD Rhoades.

My incomparable writing group, the Weymouth Seven: Margaret Maron, Mary Kay Andrews, Diane Chamberlain, Sarah Shaber, Brenda Witchger, and Katy Munger.

Joe Konrath, Blake Crouch, Scott Nicholson, Elle Lothlorien, CJ Lyons, LJ Sellers, Robert Gregory Browne, Brett Battles, and JD Rhoades, who showed me the indie publishing ropes.

Lee Lofland and his amazing Writers Police Academy trainers/instructors: Dave Pauly, Katherine Ramsland, Corporal Dee Jackson, Andy Russell, Marco Conelli, Lieutenant Randy Shepard, and Robert Skiff.

And most especially: the best early readers on the planet: Diane Coates Peoples, Joan Tregarthen Huston, Billie Hinton, and Ellen Margolis.

About the Author

Alexandra Sokoloff is the Thriller Award–winning and Bram Stoker, Anthony, and Black Quill Award–nominated author of the supernatural thrillers *The Harrowing*, *The Price*, *The Unseen*, *Book of Shadows*, *The Shifters*, and *The Space Between*, and the Thriller Award–nominated Huntress/FBI crime series (*Huntress Moon*, *Blood Moon*, *Cold Moon*). The *New York Times Book Review* has called her a "daughter of Mary Shelley," and her books "Some of the most original and freshly unnerving work in the genre."

As a screenwriter she has sold original horror and thriller scripts and adapted novels for numerous Hollywood studios. She has also written two nonfiction workbooks: *Screenwriting Tricks for Authors* and *Writing Love*, based on her internationally acclaimed workshops and blog (www.ScreenwritingTricks.com). She writes erotic paranormal on the side, including *The Shifters*, Book 2 of *The Keepers* trilogy, and *Keeper of the Shadows*, from *The Keepers L.A.*

She lives in Los Angeles and in Scotland with the crime author Craig Robertson.